Before We Fall

Also by Courtney Cole

The Beautifully Broken series

Book 1: If You Stay

Book 2: If You Leave

About the author

Courtney Cole is a novelist who lives near Lake Michigan, USA, with her family and her pet iPad. Her favorite place in the world is on the shore with her toes in the water. If she's not there, you can find her wearing cashmere socks and staring dreamily out of her office window.

To learn more about her, visit her website:
www.courtneycolewrites.com.

Before We Fall

The Beautifully Broken Series: Book 3

COURTNEY COLE

HODDER

Originally published as an ebook
First published in the USA in 2014 by Forever
An imprint of Grand Central Publishing
A division of Hachette Books USA
First published in Great Britain in 2014 by Hodder & Stoughton
An Hachette UK Company

1

A CIP catalogue record for this title is available from the British Library.

Paperback ISBN 978 1 444 78589 0
Ebook ISBN 978 1 444 78590 6

Printed and bound by Clays Ltd, St Ives plc

Hodder & Stoughton policy is to use papers that are natural, renewable
and recyclable products and made from wood grown in sustainable forests.
The logging and manufacturing processes are expected to conform
to the environmental regulations of the country of origin.

Hodder & Stoughton Ltd
338 Euston Road
London NW1 3BH

www.hodder.co.uk

Life is scary and dreams get broken.
This book is for anyone brave enough to put
the pieces back together again.

Acknowledgments

I always have so many people to thank. That's because I've come to find out, over the years, that it takes more than just one person to write a good book. It takes a team. I have to humbly say that I have the best team in the world.

First, my family. They are the best teammates anyone could ever ask for. My daughter, my littlest writing assistant, carries around a pen and paper just in case I have a great idea. My teenage sons let me pick their brains—to see how boys *really* think. And my husband is very patient with me when I clickety-clack on my laptop in bed next to him at two A.M. when I get a great idea that just won't wait until morning. They also eat out a lot when I just can't stop to make dinner. I'm forever grateful to them and I love them more than they'll ever know.

My BFF and partner in crime, M. Leighton. You probably know her from books like *The Wild Ones* or *Down to You*. She's the best critique partner and friend that a girl could ever ask for. She's always on call and always a font of good advice. She talks me down from ledges and keeps me from pulling my hair out. I love her to infinity and beyond.

My editor, Amy Pierpont, from Forever. Her insight is more than I ever hoped for in an editor. She can take a look at a scene and see three different things that I'd never thought to look for. Her knowledge and experience are blessings to me, as is her ability to cut right to the important things. I'm lucky to have her.

I'm lucky to have Madeleine Colavita from Forever, as well. She's always so quick to help me, no matter what I ask of her. She's cheerful and friendly no matter what. Her enthusiasm over my character Brand always makes me smile. I love her to bits.

My agent, Catherine Drayton. She's amazing and smart, experienced and awesome. I can't say enough about her other than I'm so freaking lucky to have her. She knows what she's doing and she goes about doing it in such a classy way. She's the best agent out there, hands down.

My beta readers…Autumn from *The Autumn Review*, Natasha from *Natasha is a Book Junkie*, Momo from *Books Over Boys*. You guys are amazing. Your insight and opinions helped make this book what it is today. You helped me polish it until it shone. Thank you!!!

I have to say a special thank you to Autumn for being my sex guru for this book. When I was researching the…er…*darker* side to the sexual nature, Autumn's input was invaluable. The girl knows sex. Thanks for sharing your wisdom with me! Hehe.

My publicity team: Kelly Simmon from Inkslinger PR and Jodi, Marissa, Morgan, and Jane from Forever. You guys rock at what you do and I'm lucky to have you on my side.

My assistant, Avery. Thank you for making my life easier, one task at a time. You're awesome and you know it.

And…YOU. My awesome, amazing readers. Without you, these books wouldn't happen. I get to do what I do because of you. I'm grateful for you every single day of my life. Thank you for being so awesomely amazing.

Before We Fall

Prologue

Then

The slap can be heard all the way down the beach.

The sound of flesh meeting flesh, sharp and loud, is unmistakable, and my head snaps up to find a skinny girl in a red swimsuit standing in front of the biggest bully of the beach, a sixth grader named Heather.

The summer sun is blistering hot, but my cheeks flush even hotter when I see the ugly expression on Heather's face as she towers over the smaller girl. A girl who can't be more than nine or ten and who is even now cradling her cheek with her hand.

I look around, but there are no adults in the vicinity, and Heather knows it. Her leer gets even wider as she leans down into the younger girl's face, intent on doing even more damage than a handprint on a cheek.

That's all it takes to send me rocketing up from my towel and down the beach toward them, my heels flipping sand in the air as I run. I reach them just in time to see Heather snatch some money from the girl's small hand.

A tear slips down the girl's cheek, which causes Heather to grin.

"Go cry to your mommy, little girl," she sneers, in the ugly way only a middle-school bully can.

The sheer sight of it makes me see red and I forget all logic as I rush toward the pair. I forget that Heather has tormented me every day of every summer and I forget that I can't be any older than the skinny girl in the red swimsuit.

In this moment, it doesn't matter.

"What the hell, Heather?" I demand as I skid to a stop in front of them. The other girl, the skinny one, sucks in her breath at my bad language. It's a groundable offense, but my gran is all the way down the beach, sitting in the shade. "Give her the money back."

Heather stares down at me and sweat glistens on her plump chin. "Or what, shrimp? What will you do if I don't?"

I lift my chin and look her in the eye.

"I'll tell everyone, including your friends, what you were doing with Jamie Rawlins under the pier a while back. I saw you. I saw what you did. And if you don't give her the money back, I'll tell *everyone*."

Heather's eyes widen, then narrow. "You wouldn't."

I nod, calmer now than I probably should be. "I would."

Heather looks out over the lake and thinks about it for a minute before she tosses the crumpled-up bills at my feet.

"I hope it was worth it," she tells me hotly. "Because I'm going to make your life hell."

"Whatever." I sniff, trying to appear unconcerned. "It's not like you don't try already."

Heather glares at me and walks off, and I bend to pick up the money, handing it to the skinny girl. I smile at her.

"Here you go. I'm sorry she's so mean. I think someone pees in her cornflakes every day."

The girl seems speechless and she stares at me for a minute with wide blue eyes before shyly handing me a white shell.

"Thank you for getting my ice cream money back," she says so softly that I have to strain to hear her. "I collect these. The big nice ones are hard to find in the lake."

I smile again. "You're right, it's hard to find them. Thank you! I'm going to swim out to the buoy line. Wanna come?"

The girl stares out at the battered line of buoys that bob up and down in the current a hundred yards out. She looks a little uncertain, a little scared.

"I can't," she finally answers. "My mom would kill me. The current's too bad."

I nod as if I understand what it's like to have a mother that cares. My own doesn't even know that I can swim.

"Okay," I tell the girl. "I'll see you around."

She watches me as I jog back and drop the shell on my towel before I dive into the current, swimming over and under the frigid waves like a seal. When I finally reach the buoys, I grab on to one, clinging tightly as it bobs, while I push my hair out of my face with cold fingers.

Glancing back toward the beach, I hunt for the girl in the red swimsuit, but I don't see her anywhere. She's gone, and I realize something.

I didn't even ask her name.

Chapter One

Dominic

Now

I like to watch.

I know that I shouldn't, but I don't really give a shit. I like the flash of skin, the sweaty limbs, the sex smells, the *fucking*...

Watching makes me feel something. It's one of the only things that does.

"Some things never change, Dominic," Kira murmurs as her hand splays across my open shirt, her long brown hair moving in the breeze, tickling my chest as she watches with me. "You're just the same...a freak. I love that."

I don't answer because she's right. I'm a fucking freak. She knows it and I know it, and neither of us cares. If anything, Kira likes it. She must, because she's stuck by me for a long time. She knows me better than anyone...and she definitely knows what I like.

Even though she's beautiful and familiar, I ignore her fingers as they trace across my skin, graze the tips of my nipples, and trail down to my crotch. My dick is resistant to her touch tonight and remains soft inside my pants. Not because she's not hot or sexy, because she is.

But because familiar and normal don't stir my blood. I've seen pretty much everything once and have done it twice. Normal doesn't do it for me anymore.

Forbidden things are what lift my dick. Dark things, bad things.

I stare down from the balcony, looking past the shimmering pool below, past the rippling water that sheds blue light on everything around it, at the images that waver in the night. The images of two people fucking.

Knowing that I *shouldn't* watch is what excites me about it, and so I don't take my eyes from the couple having sex next to my brother's pool.

I take another drink of whiskey, letting the fiery liquid sit in my mouth before I swallow it, letting it curl its fingers around my stomach, warming my gut.

Watching the couple, I lean against the railing, half-hidden by the shadows, enveloped by the night. It's just how I like it.

In front of me, the scene turns rough.

And my dick turns hard.

The girl's teeth sink into the guy's neck, then she whispers something unintelligible into his ear, words that hiss as she drags her teeth across his skin. Hard, aggressive, rough. I can see the red trail of pain she leaves behind from here.

"Did she just bite him?" Kira asks in amusement, her hand frozen at my waistband.

I nod. She did. And it made me hard as a rock. I love watching pain. It distracts me from my own.

The guy smiles, liking it, too. He lifts her legs onto his shoulders as he thrusts into her. Hard. Then he frees one hand to grab her neck. Hard. His fingers dig into the delicate skin there, cutting into the flesh, leaving red marks that just might turn purple by morning.

But she likes it.

I can tell by the way she scratches his back and moans for more. I can tell by the way she draws him even farther into herself, bucking her hips to take him even deeper. I can tell by the way she doesn't even try to take his hand away from her throat.

It always fascinates me when I see women that like getting debased, the ones who like it rough, the ones who want to be dominated or humiliated.

It doesn't make any sense, but I see it all the time, more and more, especially here at my brother's place at one of his endless parties. Around his pool, in his hot tub, on his lawn. People seem to lose their inhibitions when they pass through these gates, which doesn't make any sense, either. Most of them don't know him, not really. But it doesn't stop them from making themselves *very* at home here.

Suffice it to say I'm always entertained when I come to visit.

"Do you think they know we're watching?" Kira leans up on her tiptoes, murmuring with hot breath into my ear as she strokes my balls.

I glance back down at the couple, watching the guy's face contort and twist, and watching the girl moan and writhe beneath him. They have no clue we're here, but I have a feeling they wouldn't care even if they did.

"I think that girl served me champagne earlier!" Kira exclaims, leaning closer to look.

"You're probably right," I answer, staring at the girl's skimpy server's uniform. I briefly wonder where her boss thinks she is. Surely he has no idea that she's fucking a party guest next to the pool.

But that's not my problem.

The bulge between my legs is my problem now. It's grown thicker and heavier and I shift, easing the pressure of my jeans away from my dick. I brush my hand against the denim covering my crotch, stroking myself. Just a little. Quickly and efficiently.

I'm not going to get off right out here in the open. Because of how I make my living, I've learned not to do *anything* out in the open. The press would have a fucking field day if pictures of me jacking off leaked out.

Kira takes care of the situation for me, just as she always does when I'm in town. She pushes me backward into the shadows, where she steps out of her shorts in front of me. She's not wearing underwear.

She's right. Some things never change.

"Fuck me with your hand while you watch them," she instructs me softly, her green eyes gleaming. "Do it, Dom. And then I'll let you come on my face, the way you like to."

I reach for her. She stands limply in front of me, her head resting on my shoulder as I slide two of my fingers in and out of her. I know exactly where to touch her. She sucks in a breath and I have to smile. I know every inch of her. There are some things to be said for familiarity.

She's soaking wet, as though she's been waiting for this since I'd seen her last. She hasn't, of course. Kira and I have an arrangement of convenience. It's convenient because we know each other, we trust each other. And there are no feelings involved. She and I are the same in that way.

I can hear the girl by the pool moaning loudly and it makes my fingers move faster, working Kira harder, in time to the guy's sweaty thrusts. Kira moans with the girl by the pool and I close my eyes, listening to the fucking sounds. With my hand buried in Kira's crotch, the sounds are all I need now.

If I were decent, I'd back away from the balcony and give the couple some privacy and I'd give Kira more coverage from the shadows…just in case someone happens upon us.

But fuck that. I'm not decent. Not anymore.

After a few more minutes of rough fucking, the guy pulls out of the waitress and grasps her hard, yanking her off the chaise and forcing her down in front of him, onto her knees. I can see her skin graze the bricks, just as I can read his lips.

Suck me.

I pause as the girl shakes her head, trying to scramble away, but he holds her fast by her hair, making her take him into her mouth. Making her suck her own taste off of him.

She's definitely not into it now. She swings her arms at him frantically, but he holds her hair tightly, wrapping it around his hands, refusing to let her go.

I watch the fear wash over her face and my gut tightens in reaction.

Fuck.

Kira lifts her head as my hand stills. "What?"

Her eyes are glazed as she stares at me. I nod toward the pool, at the struggle going on down there, at the girl trying desperately to get away from the asshole's grip.

"Hell." Kira sighs. "Ignore it, Dom. It's not your problem. We're not done here."

I sigh, too, because I know I can't ignore it.

This has been happening way too much. People come here and get wasted and out of control. It's not worth the trouble, but Sin keeps having the parties anyway. He says it keeps him relevant, whatever the fuck that means. I don't seem to have a problem with being *relevant*, and I don't host a single party.

I shake Kira's grip off of my wrist, gulp down the rest of my drink, and head down the stairs, ignoring her calls of protest.

It takes a minute to weave discreetly through the masses of people scattered through the house and to make my way across the lawn and onto the stones leading to the pool. But I reach the couple within two minutes, and without even pausing I grab the guy from behind, ripping him backward. He hisses as the girl's teeth scrape his dick.

It serves him right. The fucker interrupted me.

He yelps and I toss him on the ground, watching in satisfaction as he scrapes his face on the stone bricks before he rolls into the lawn.

"Get the fuck out," I snap at him. "No one gets forced against their will here."

"That bitch wanted it," he protests as he climbs to his feet. "She was asking for it."

I shake my head. "The last time I checked, no means no. It's not a new way of *asking for it*. Get the fuck out of here."

The guy looks at me again, recognizes who I am, and then stalks away without another word. I grab a pool towel and wrap it around the girl's shoulders.

Her skimpy uniform, which was barely there in the first place, is hanging around her waist now, apparently ripped in their scuffle. She seems self-conscious, but honestly, I barely notice. She's young and has perky tits, but so do thousands of other women. She doesn't do much for me. Mostly because I know she'd offer herself on a platter if I wanted her to. I briefly consider inviting her to join Kira and me, but don't. She's drunk, and even if she's too drunk to remember it, she's just been almost violated.

"You okay?" I ask gruffly. She nods, sniveling, just as another girl, a gorgeous blonde in a matching uniform, rushes up.

"Holy shit, Kaylie. What the hell happened?"

The blonde is obviously alarmed, concerned, and while Kaylie explains about the asshole, I turn to disappear back into the shadows. Regardless of my profession, I try to stay out of the spotlight when the cameras aren't rolling. Unfortunately, I only make it partway before Kaylie grabs my arm, then wraps herself around my waist.

"Thank you," she tells me shakily, her arms like thin bands, not giving me room to even squirm. I stare down at her, looking past her tear-smeared eyeliner and into her panicky eyes.

"It's not a problem. But you need to stay out of situations like that. There won't always be someone to step in and save you."

From her shocked expression, I decide that I might've been a little too hard on her. But shit. Women have to be more careful. She can't parade around in barely any clothes, have rough sex with a stranger, and just expect him to be a gentleman. Men, by and large, aren't gentlemen. We're assholes.

Kaylie stares at me, too drunk or high to even respond. But her friend isn't so silent.

Big brown eyes snap at me angrily. "Why are you lecturing her? She was just assaulted, in case you didn't notice."

I roll my eyes.

"Is that what you call it? She was having rough sex with that asshole right out in the open. When she was supposed to be working, I might add. It looked to me like it was an incident that just got out of control. I stopped it for her. You're welcome."

Gorgeous Blonde stares at me dumbfounded. "Are you trying to insinuate that she's not a victim, that it was her fault this happened?"

I sigh. "Of course not. I'm saying that she shouldn't have been encouraging a drunk stranger to be rough with her in the first place. Good night."

I start to walk away, but apparently she's not done.

"Who the fuck do you think you are?" she demands. "You might not have heard, but you really shouldn't blame the victim."

"I'm not blaming—" I begin, but I'm interrupted by her gasp as I step fully into the light and she sees my face.

"Holy shit." She breathes. "You're Dominic fucking Kinkaide."

I can't help but smile, just a little, just enough to pull the corners of my mouth up. "Dominic will do. I tend to drop the 'fucking.' Unless of course, I'm *actually* fucking."

She smiles a breathtaking smile that should affect me. The girl is stacked, has legs that go on for miles, and she's wearing next to nothing. She should affect me. But she doesn't. Because nothing affects me anymore. I'm jaded as fuck.

"I've heard you're trouble," she announces matter-of-factly, eyeing me up and down with a slow gaze and fire in her eyes. "That's lucky, because I happen to like trouble."

"I bet you do," I answer back, trying to ignore the way she's acting now that she knows who I am. They all act like this. Every one of them. It gets monotonous. Just once, can't someone surprise me? "Nice to meet you."

I turn around and walk back toward the house, but she takes two steps and grabs my arm. I pause.

"But you didn't," she says hesitantly, a bit unsure now. "You didn't meet me. My name's Jacey."

I sigh. "Your name doesn't matter."

I keep walking, ignoring the way she sucks her breath in, the way she calls after me in agitation, the way she gives up and stops in defeat.

I might be an asshole, but I don't lie.

Her name doesn't matter.

Not to me.

I leave the entire situation behind, out of my sight and out of my mind. Within a few minutes, I'm standing in front of Kira again.

"All taken care of?" she purrs, reaching for me. I nod, burying my face between her heavy, naked tits as she unbuckles my belt. "Bind my hands with this, and come on my face."

She doesn't have to ask me twice.

"You're such a dirty girl," I whisper in her ear as I push her onto the couch and bind her hands above her head, just tight enough for the leather to bite into her flesh. Just the way she likes it.

And then I grasp my dick in my hand and fuck my fist, just the way *I* like it.

For just a second, for some strange reason, the blond chick's face pops into my mind, her eyes wide and brown. I have no idea why, but I shake my head to clear it. I focus instead on the matter at hand.

Within another two minutes, I come on Kira's face, spurting in a cream-colored arc that spatters onto her tanned skin. She licks a drop from her lips and grins at me.

"Welcome home, lover."

"Don't call me that." I shake my head as I pull my jeans back on and collapse next to her. She rolls her eyes.

"Why? It's what we are. You always come back to me, Dom. You know that."

I unbind the belt wordlessly, tossing it onto the floor. I might always come back to her whenever I come home, but I don't fuck her. Not really. I haven't actually fucked someone in years.

"*Lover* would indicate that I bury my dick in your sweet pussy." I glance at her, then reach out to run my finger over the swell of one of her tits, then trail it downward to her crotch. She arches toward my touch. "And you know I won't do that."

I pull my hand away abruptly and Kira scowls. "Yeah, I know that. What I *don't* know is why. Dominic, you've got needs, too. Watching other people fuck or jacking off and coming on my face can't be enough. Sex isn't just sex, Dom. You need all the good stuff that comes along with it."

"Oh, I do, do I?" I ask, amused now. "Like what? Like having women get attached and hoping that I'll marry them? Or worrying that I'll get some fucking disease or…"

"Just stop." Kira interrupts me with a glare. "*I know you*, Dom. I know why you do what you do. You don't want to get close to some-one again. You don't want to give anyone that kind of power over you. But, Dom…it's time. It's time for you to finally get over her and come back to life."

"One, don't talk about her," I instruct Kira icily, staring at her hard. "You know better than that. And two, are you insinuating that I'm not living?"

Kira sighs as she pulls her shirt on, forgoing her bra. She stuffs it into her purse and glances up at me.

"You know damn well what I'm insinuating. You've been a shell for six years, Dom. Six fucking years. That's a long time. I've been patient. I've done everything you needed. But there comes a time when a girl needs to be fucked. I've got needs, Dominic."

I have to chuckle now at the idea that I'm the only one Kira's depending on for her "needs." "Oh, yeah. Because you don't have anyone else to fulfill your needs when I'm not here?"

She glares at me. "You're a dick sometimes. I've got to work early in the morning, so I've gotta go. Call me tomorrow, okay?"

I nod even though I know I won't. I bury my face into the couch cushions, realizing I'm suddenly exhausted and just want to sleep. I don't even hear Kira leave. But I do hear when someone else comes in a few minutes later, right when I'm ready to slip into sleep.

"Dom, what the fuck? You were supposed to pull me out of the game so that I didn't lose my shirt."

I reluctantly open one eye to stare at my brother and find that he *actually* lost his shirt. He's standing in front of me bare-chested. My eyes dip down and I cringe.

He lost his pants, too.

"What the hell, Sin? Put some fucking clothes on."

My brother grins—that cocky, rakish grin that his fans love so much—as he plops himself down onto the sofa next to me, buck-ass naked, crossing his feet at the ankle on the coffee table.

"You wouldn't have to worry about it if you'd pulled me out of the poker game like I asked you to." He shrugs, picking up my glass of whiskey and drinking it all. "Those drunk chicks know how to play poker. Or I just wanted to take my clothes off. One or the other."

I glare at him. "I couldn't bail you out because I was taking care of a situation for you. Fuck, man. You've got to stop having these parties. Someone's gonna get raped or killed and they're going to sue the shit out of you."

Sin only grins, unconcerned. "If they're dead, they can't sue me."

I can't argue with that logic. Instead, I tell him what he missed, not that it bothers him much. He sees it all the time.

"Thanks for fixing it," he tells me casually, as though near-rapes are normal. I roll my eyes.

"Anytime. Now can you get some fucking clothes on?"

He waggles his dark eyebrows. "Sure. If it makes you insecure to look at my package. Not only am I older, but I'm also bigger, and that's what counts."

He's also ridiculous. He's not a centimeter bigger than I am, but I don't waste my breath telling him that.

He yanks one of my shirts out of my suitcase and pulls it over his head. Then a pair of my pants. He decides to forgo underwear, which means I'll have to burn those jeans.

"I forgot to ask how long you're staying," he says as he settles back into the seat, unconcerned that he just ruined my favorite jeans. "Long enough to catch a show, I hope. It's all I've heard about for months from Duncan...how you don't even come watch your poor little brothers play."

I roll my eyes. "Poor little brothers? I think both of you are doing just fine."

Sin snorts. "Only as well as you, big bro. But whatever. We have a show coming up in Chicago next month. If you want to fly back in, we'll get you backstage passes."

I shake my head. "I'll try. Filming starts in a couple of weeks. But I'll see what I can do. I don't want to upset baby Duncan."

"What about me?"

My youngest brother saunters into my room, dropping onto the sofa next to Sin. Neither of them have any personal space issues, that's for sure, because now we're all three crammed onto the one sofa. And we're too big for that shit.

"Nothing," I assure Duncan. "I just said I didn't want to offend your ovaries by not coming to your next show. I'll try like hell to be there."

"That's the furthest thing from my mind right now," Duncan announces, cracking open the can of beer in his hand. "You can see me bang on the drums any time. What I'd like to bang tonight are the half-naked women beyond these very doors. I fucking love your house, man," he tells Sin. "Oh, and there's a chick asking for you.

Said she wants to make sure you know that your brother rescued her. Or some shit."

Sin rolls his eyes, but I elbow him. "It's probably the girl from the pool. You'd better talk to her and autograph her tits or something. You need to keep her happy so that she doesn't think to call the police. You don't want that kind of press, dude. Not after Amsterdam."

The mere mention of how the tabloids had ripped Sin's band up over a wild party in Amsterdam a month ago is enough to sober the two of them up. There had been some underage girls there, groupies who had lied about their age, and if it weren't for the more lax laws in Europe, my brothers would've been screwed.

Sin nods now.

"Fine. Take me to her," he tells Duncan. To me, he hands the bottle of whiskey and says, "Do you ever get tired of being right? Jesus Christ."

"Not yet," I tell him as I gulp down a few swigs, then slide down into the sofa again, closing my eyes. "It's a burden though."

My brothers chuckle as they walk out and I relax, enjoying the way the whiskey has loosened my muscles, the way the warmth has spread to every bit of me. It helps me stay numb...and numbness is a welcome fucking thing.

When I'm numb, I feel safe enough to slip my hand into my pocket. Not for my dick, although that's normal for me, too. No, I wrap my fingers around the cool stone of the pendant that is always there, encased in a white shell and resting against my leg.

The last thing that fills my mind before I sleep is a color.

Aquamarine.

Chapter Two

Dominic

When I open my eyes, almost two hours have passed. I know this by the fuzzy green light of the clock. I'm a little disoriented as I sit up and look around at furnishings that aren't mine, until I remember that I'm not home. I'm at my brother's house for the weekend.

"Morning, sunshine." A soft voice startles me.

Snapping my head around, I find the gorgeous blonde with the strange name from the pool.

She's sitting in the darkness now, scrolling through her phone. *Has she been watching me sleep? Or was she just too polite to wake me up?*

Either way, I fight back a growl that my privacy has been invaded.

"What are you doing in here?"

She's perched on the side of the bed, watching me. She's even hotter than I remember her being: long legs, full tits, tiny waist. I usually prefer taller women, but this girl is perfectly proportioned . . . and there's something excruciatingly sexy about her. Something about her just screams *fuck me*.

She shrugs now, unconcerned with my agitation, her long blond hair falling over the side of her shoulder.

"Your brother sent me up. My friend Kaylie is going to be staying the night here, apparently. With him."

"And?" I raise an eyebrow.

Is this supposed to shock me? This shit happens all the time with Sin. He doesn't give a shit about sloppy seconds. He says that's what condoms were made for. Fucking rock stars. They'll fuck anything that isn't nailed down.

Jacey stares at me, unabashed and definitely not intimidated, her eyes flashing in the dark.

"And she was my ride. Your brother said you'd be happy to drive me home."

"Oh, he did, did he?" Annoyance wells up in me and I glance at the clock. Two fucking A.M.

She nods. "Yeah. He said that he lets you take up garage space here to store your car, so the least you could do is drive it for him once or twice."

"He told you to say that, right?"

She nods again. "Yeah. He said he would rather you take me than call me a cab. He doesn't want some random cabbie tweeting about the party."

As much as I hate to admit it, that's pretty smart. Everyone around here loves to hear news about Sin Kinkaide, and he tries hard to keep his parties secret. Or, at least, the nature of his parties. I sigh. *Fuck.*

"Okay," I tell her tiredly. "I'll take you. Give me a minute."

"Take your time," she tells me graciously, leaning back against the silk bed cushions. I can't help but appreciate her tiny uniform.

It's barely more than a swimsuit, and her tits peek out of the top. I look away, not letting her see that I appreciate her tight body.

Girls like her...they can sense the slightest bit of interest and they latch on like piranhas. I've seen it a hundred times before. Never mind the fact that she's trying to act uninterested now, unimpressed with who I am. She's just pissed that I shut her down earlier.

I walk into the bathroom, splashing my face with cold water before I head back out and grab my keys from the nightstand.

"Okay. Let's go."

She follows me down through the thumping music and the people, the ones dancing and the ones fucking in dark corners. Seriously. Sin's parties get out of control. I'm eternally glad that I don't live his life, with people flooding my house day and night.

The entire world might know my face, but I'm actually a very private person. Every time I come here, I'm always ready to go home by the end of the weekend. It might be entertaining, but trying to avoid all the people who want to interact with me is exhausting.

I lead her past the seven stalls in his garage, to where my charcoal-gray 911 takes up one of the slots. It's my Chicago car. I keep it here so that I have something to drive whenever I come home, something I can take out on the track and race when I get bored. I have one just like it at my house in California, because what's better than one Porsche? Two.

Jacey takes in the car, her dark eyes widening in appreciation, but she doesn't say a word. She simply slides inside, and as she does, I notice that she's definitely wearing panties. I see a glimpse of red satin through the cuff of her short shorts as she crosses her legs. I smirk, because she doesn't know it, but I fucking love red satin on a woman.

She fastens her seatbelt, curling up in the seat like she was born there, oblivious to my approval of her underwear choice.

"Where do you live?" I ask instead as the boxer engine roars to life in the way only a Porsche's can.

"Down by Eighty-Seventh Street," she answers, staring out the window as we roll down my brother's driveway past the manicured lawns.

"Calumet Heights?" I ask, picturing the older Chicago neighborhood in my head. She nods.

"Wow, you still remember your hometown. Impressive."

I roll my eyes, not sure if she's being sarcastic or not. "I'll never forget where I came from."

The car's engine purrs as we make our way toward the gates, and casually I glance to the side, expecting to see the green lawns, trees, and shadows of my brother's estate. But something else is there, and I freeze, my hands tightening on the wheel as I slam on the brakes.

"What the fuck?" Jacey sputters in confusion as her body jerks forward. But I'm already out of the car and striding toward the two people sitting on the bench to our left.

My sister Fiona and my onetime best friend, Cris fucking Evans, look up at me in surprise from the dark. Her arms are wrapped around his neck. His tongue was down her throat thirty seconds ago.

"What the—" Cris manages to say before I yank him off the bench and throw him to the ground. "What the fuck, Dominic?" he barks out, scrambling to get to his feet and balance on his lanky-ass legs, poised to lunge at me if he has to.

I smile grimly and glance at Fiona. "What the hell is going on, Fi? Tell me it's not what it looks like."

My sister sighs and calmly stands up, approaching me carefully.

"It's probably what it looks like. Cris and I are dating, Dom. I wanted to tell you, but with things the way they are between you... well, I was scared about how you would react."

I ignore the ice water that seems to pump through my heart.

"Naturally," I answer calmly. "Of course you are. Because obviously you wanted to find the biggest douche on the planet and date him. If that's the case, you did a stellar job."

"Dom." Fiona sighs again. "I don't know what he did to you, but six years is a long fucking time to carry a grudge. You need to get over it and move on. I love him, and you're going to have to live with that."

"You...what?" The words feel like wood on my tongue, dry and heavy. I can't even believe what I just heard.

Fiona stares at me, her green eyes assessing me carefully. "I love him."

I hear Cris breathing in front of me and see Jacey standing on the perimeter, but everything fades instantly away but this: Cris and Fiona. Together.

The idea that my baby sister would stab me in the heart like this is unfathomable.

"How could you do this?" I demand of her. "You know how I feel about him, Fiona. Does the phrase 'blood is thicker than water' mean anything to you? You're way better than he is, and he doesn't deserve you. He's too fucking old for you anyway. Jesus."

There's a brief pause while Fiona slides her hands to her hips, then she erupts.

"Jesus Christ," my baby sister snaps. "You've got to get over yourself. He was your best friend, Dom. Someone who I grew up with, too. And for all these years, you've expected all of us to just take your word for it that he's some sort of monster without telling us why. If you want us to have your back, you have to trust us with a good reason. If what he did to you was so fucking bad, then you need to tell me what the fuck he did."

I swallow hard, because the only way I can effectively warn her away from Cris is to tell her the truth. And I can't do that. The wound is that fucking deep, open, and raw. It's years old and it still stings as much as it ever did. I can barely even think about it, much less talk about it.

I take a deep breath, then another. As I do, I notice that Jacey has walked up and is hovering in the shadows, watching us uncertainly. I look away from her and back to my sister.

"Can't you just trust me?" I finally ask slowly. "As your big brother, can't you just fucking trust me?"

Cris starts to say something, but I snarl at him. My sister holds out a hand toward him in caution before she looks back to me. She knows me well enough to realize that talking to Cris is only going to set me off.

"Dominic, I love you even though you're bullheaded. I do trust you. But we grew up with Cris, and I trust him, too. I know this somehow must involve Emma. But Dom, she's gone. Whatever happened, it's not relevant anymore."

Fuck. The mere mention of Emma's name is a sucker punch to my gut and I want to bend over so that I can breathe. I also want to toss my sister over my shoulder and carry her away . . . far, far away from Cris.

Not relevant? Untrue. It will be relevant until the day I die.

Fiona stares at me, waiting for me to say something. But the words won't come.

I can't tell her all of the things that she ought to know. I can't force the ugly words out of my chest where they've been hidden for so long. It's best to leave them buried. That's definitely one thing I've learned in life.

"Why don't you ask Cris what he did?" I ask bluntly, staring a hole into my ex–best friend's fucking forehead. "Just ask. See if he'll tell you the truth."

Cris opens his mouth, but Fiona shakes her head.

"We're not doing this here, Dominic. We'll discuss it when we're calmer. And don't you think I've asked before? He said if you want to talk about it, you will."

What a fucker.

Cris clears his throat and I stare at him, looking at him closely. He's been gone for years, away at college and then building up a business. But he looks the same as he ever did. Longish blond hair, blue eyes, lanky form. The years haven't hardened him like they've hardened me, something else that pisses me off about him. He speaks now, hesitantly.

"Dom, we've got to stop this. It's been years, years of blaming me for something that wasn't my fault. It's time to let it go." He drops his big, lanky-ass hands and stares at me, waiting for a reaction, and all I can do is stare at him incredulously.

For a minute, I don't see the man in front of me, I don't even see the boy I grew up with... the boy I played little league with, made forts with, caught frogs with. I see a name.

His name.

Spoken from my dying girlfriend's lips. I wince as I remember how pale she was, how she was shaking and cold, how she could barely speak, but she still managed to say his name.

I glare at him, trying like hell to not wrap my hands around his pathetic neck and squeeze.

"Not your fault? Really? Because the last thing she said was your name. Your. Name. Not mine. Not her mom's or her dad's. Yours. We both know why your name was the last thing on her lips. And you honestly have the balls to stand there and tell me that I have no right to be mad at you?"

Cris looks at me, his expression pained, his eyes guarded. I hear Fiona gasp, but her hand clamps over her mouth and she doesn't make another sound. I'm sure this is the first she's heard of any of this...of Emma's last words.

Cris steps toward me.

"That's not what I said. I said it wasn't my fault. I didn't say you didn't have a right to be mad. You do. You have the right to be pissed at the whole fucking situation. But it was a long time ago. And you don't know everything that happened. You wouldn't talk to me before I left, and you've never picked up the phone so I can explain—"

"And I'm not going to start now," I interrupt. "I don't give a shit about anything you have to say. And I don't give a fuck that it was a long time ago. It happened and I'll never forget it."

"I'm dating Fiona," Cris says bluntly. "So you've got to try."

I shake my head. "Fuck you. That's Fiona's choice, not mine. If there's one thing you should know about me, it's that I don't do anything that I don't want to do."

I turn to leave, and he says, "And you wonder why Emma did what she did?"

That's when I see red.

It billows in from the corners of my eyes like red fog filling my vision, and I lunge at Cris with a roar. I can't hear, I can't think. All I can do is move. Everything is just a blur of fists, swearing, and grunts.

I feel his hair in my fist and then my knuckles connect with his face, over and over; his jaw, his cheekbone, his eye. The next thing

I'm aware of is Jacey thrusting herself in the middle of us, catching me mid-punch. The side of my fist grazes her cheek and her hand flies to her face, cupping it. But she still struggles to get us apart.

Fiona rushes up to Cris, her fingers dabbing at his bleeding lip, her arms hugging him close.

"What the fuck, Dom?" she shrieks, her arm wrapped around Cris's shoulder as if she's shielding him from me. "You're a fucking lunatic. Get the fuck out of here."

I try to ignore the pain of the . . . the idea that not only would my sister date my worst enemy, but that she had the balls to bring him here, where she had to know I'd be.

It's definitely a betrayal and it's something I would never do to her. I take a breath, ragged and raw, and stare at her, not wanting to say anything that I'll regret.

"I'm staying here while I'm in town, Fiona. *You* get the fuck out of here. And take that waste of space with you."

Fiona stares at me in hurt and rage and disbelief as she leads Cris away. Before we can get back to our car, red and blue lights burst to life around us. They flash against our faces, lighting us up against the night.

"Holy shit, someone called the cops."

Jacey inhales sharply and stares at me, one hand limp on my arm, the other holding her cheek. She's covered in blood now, and I'm not sure if it's mine or Cris's. Or maybe even her own. But I don't have time to find out.

Two cops are approaching us, and what comes next happens in a blur, both because of all the whiskey I've been drinking and the fact that Cris clocked me hard in the temple.

How much have you been drinking?

Who started this fight?

Can I search your car?

Son, are these your drugs?

I glance up blearily now, to see one of them holding up a bag of weed. He blurs into three cops, then back into one as my vision comes in and out of focus.

"I'm not your son," I mumble. Jacey gasps and I hear her swearing that the drugs aren't hers, either, and that I'm probably not thinking clearly right now, that I'm not myself. I want to glare at her for making excuses for me, but I can't seem to control my facial muscles. I see her swat at a policeman when he grabs at her wrists, but it's the last thing I see. My chin drops to my chest and my gaze fixes on the ground.

Dew is forming on the grass. That's something I notice as they handcuff me and stuff me into the back of a cop car. I hear my sister's voice, frantic and pissed, but I can't understand her words. It's a bit too hard to stay conscious now, and I let my head fall back onto the seat of the cop car.

Flashes and bits of what just happened run through my head. Jacey's startled eyes, the way she jumped into the fray and tried to help...the way I clocked her in the face and she didn't back away.

He's not himself, she told the cop. I almost smile. Is that what she thinks?

I feel the blood from my knuckles drip onto the handcuffs and down my back and I think about Cris's words.

And you wonder why Emma did what she did?

Jesus. My stomach balls up into a knot, and I will my throat to stay open and my fucking lungs to keep working.

Emma.

The mere thought of her brings a million emotions—that I can't name and can't process—to the surface of my skin, where they crawl along and then dig their claws into my heart. They stab it over and over until I can't feel anything at all.

This is what happened to me. This is why I'm so empty.

So unable to feel jack shit.

Emma.

I squeeze my eyes shut, trying not to picture her, trying not to see her lips smiling at me back then or imagine what she must look like now… buried in the ground, rotting away into nothing.

Fuuuck. I can feel my airway close, tighter and tighter, and I lean my head back, taking slow breaths.

I don't wonder why Emma did what she did. I *know* why. It involves a whole lot of fucked-up ugliness that I can't think about without breaking out in a cold sweat. It's fucked up, but it's just the way I am.

Whether I like it or not, I am the way I am because of her. Because I loved her and because she did what she did.

Chapter Three

Jacey

Oh. My. God.

I close my eyes against the catcalls and lewd comments, although what the hell did I expect? I'm sitting in a freaking jail cell dressed in nothing but a bowtie, a bustier, and boy-shorts. My ass cheeks are hanging out, for god's sake. And I'm sitting right smack in the middle of a group of prostitutes.

Fun fact: they're all wearing more clothing than me.

Another fun fact: I'm the only one here whose face is swollen and whose clothes are covered in blood. To them, I probably look like my dealer (or my pimp!) beat the shit out of me.

Resting my head against the cool wall behind me, I pretend that I'm anywhere but here. I'm at the beach, I'm shopping on Michigan Avenue, I'm getting a manicure.

But I'm not. The cold concrete bench pressing into my thighs and the musty smell of this cell remind me of exactly where I am.

"Jacey Vincent! Time for your phone call!"

Thank god.

A cop unlocks the door and I rush for it, thankful for a chance to get out of this cell.

He leads me back to the booking desk, where I'd been finger-printed earlier, back when the phone had been in use by someone else.

"You've got two minutes," he tells me brusquely. His eyes skim over me and I can see what he thinks...that I'm just another used-up whore like the girls in the cell.

It makes me want to throw up in my mouth. But I don't. Instead, with shaking fingers, I dial the only number I can think of. The first name that comes to mind when I need help nowadays.

Brand.

My childhood friend. My brother's best friend and business partner.

Since my brother Gabe married my best friend Maddy and they moved to Connecticut a couple of months ago, I don't have anyone else to call. But that's for the best. Both Gabe and Maddy would kick my ass for this anyway, although I'm not a hundred percent sure that Brand won't, either.

Regardless, he's the only one I can trust to come get me out of this godforsaken shit-hole. Just like he was the only one I could trust to come pick me up off the freeway when I'd had a flat tire a couple of weeks ago.

He answers groggily on the third ring. "Yeah?"

"Brand?" my voice quavers. I steel myself and swallow hard. "I need your help."

"Jace?" Brand's at attention now, his voice sharp. "Are you okay?"

I glance around at the police station, at the yellowed walls, the stern cops, the criminals waiting to be booked. I squeeze my eyes shut.

"Yeah. No. Maybe. I was arrested. Can you come get me?"

There's a brief, loaded pause.

"You're at the police station?" Brand finally asks, and I have to give him credit. His voice is calm and even. "What were you arrested for?"

"Possession of marijuana and assaulting a police officer."

Brand's not calm now. He erupts into a storm of profanity.

"What the fuck were you thinking?" he finally demands. But before I can answer, the cop next to me taps my shoulder.

"You've got twenty seconds."

My heart speeds up. What if Brand won't come?

"Brand, I've only got twenty seconds. Can you please come get me? I don't have anyone else to call. They weren't my drugs. I'll explain when you get here."

"Time," the cop says firmly, taking the phone from me and replacing it in the cradle. I stare at it, aghast.

"But I don't know if he's coming," I tell the cop limply.

"Sounds like a personal problem," he answers, gripping my elbow and guiding me back to the cell. Every fiber in my being fights against stepping back through the bars, but I've got no choice.

The cop shoves me in and locks the door behind me.

I stand alone and dejected, and the women all erupt into howls and catcalls, and for a confused moment I think it's because of me, because I got thrown right back in here and they think that's funny.

But then I notice that they're all rushing to the bars, pressing their faces against the metal to get a good look at something.

I take the opportunity to grab a seat on one of the empty benches, but I do strain my neck to see what the hell has them crowing like banshees.

I quickly see that it's a *who*, not a what.

Specifically, it's Dominic fucking Kinkaide.

Dominic will do. I tend to drop the "fucking." Unless of course, I'm actually *fucking*.

The memory of his husky voice causes my breath to speed up a little as I watch him being escorted down the hall through the cells.

Even with his face scraped up, he's sexy. His hands dangle freely at his sides, no handcuffs, so he's been bailed out. He pauses in front of my cell, standing in front of the bars, ignoring the frenzied women who are reaching out to him.

Dominic, will you sign my arm?

Dominic, can I kiss you?

Dominic, touch me, touch me.

"Just a second," Dominic tells the cops. One nods and the other barks at the women, "Get back!"

Dominic steps to the bars, staring at me. Unbidden and unconsciously, I get to my feet.

His gaze is locked with mine, the arrogant green gaze that he's famous for.

He's going to help me. He's going to tell them that it's all a big misunderstanding, that the drugs were his after all, and he's going to get me out of here.

I smile in relief as I approach him.

But he doesn't say anything. He just stares at my face, at the bruise that is forming on my cheek. He reaches through the bars and touches it lightly, his thumb just barely touching my skin.

"Uh-uh," one of the cops says. "No touching."

Dominic pulls his hand back, letting it fall limply to the side.

The look on his face turns my stomach into knots...so vulnerable. So tired. So weary. World-weary.

Everything about him is striking, though. Those cut fucking cheekbones...god, in spite of everything, I want to reach out my finger and trace the edges of them. His chiseled jaw covered with the sexiest of stubble, the dark hair tousled in an I-don't-give-a-shit way.

Unlike other wannabes, it actually seems like Dominic doesn't give a shit. About anything.

But most striking of all are those fucking green eyes, dark, dark, dark, but still somehow rimmed in golden hazel with interesting gold flecks in them. As his gaze stays locked with mine, it's like he's burning me, like I'm on fire. And he's the only thing that can put me out.

I know it's stupid to say. But his gaze is that intense. It's like he can see inside of me, deep into my most private thoughts, into where my secrets lie. But then his shoulders drop and his face turns expressionless.

"I'm sorry," he says simply.

He looks away, like a camera lens shuttering closed. Like I don't even exist to him, like I'm beneath him and not worth a second glance. The fire has been extinguished.

He nods at his escorts and they continue on, walking toward freedom while I'm still stuck in here.

Because of him.

"Wait," I call out after them. "Just a second. I don't belong here!" But they ignore me and keep walking, and I shut the hell up because I'm not going to beg.

Dominic fucking Kinkaide got us both arrested and then he gets bailed out within half an hour, just because he's a freaking celebrity. And he left me here to fucking rot.

I roll my eyes at his arrogance, at this situation, at my horrible luck. Life sucks so hard sometimes, and it gets suckier by the minute.

As I slump against the cement wall again, I ponder my rotten luck. And my poor decisions that lead to my rotten luck. That, of course, brings me to thoughts of something else, my poorest decision of them all.

My ex-boyfriend. Jared.

He'd killed someone because of me and is currently in prison for vehicular manslaughter. I can't help but marvel at the irony that we're both cooped up in jail cells at this very moment.

I swallow hard at the thought. I'm seriously in the same position as that little psychotic fuck. Oh. My. God.

After everything I've done throughout the last couple of months to put him behind me…I've gotten counseling, I make conscious decisions every day to not be reckless or wild (both things are fundamental building blocks of my nature), and yet here I am…in the same situation as he is.

Locked away.

I gulp. Maybe it's poetic justice. After all the trouble that he wreaked on my family and friends, maybe I deserve this. Maybe I'll never get away from it no matter how hard I try. I sigh and watch the clock on the wall outside of the bars ticking down the minutes.

Sixty worst-of-my-life minutes later, I finally hear the words I've been waiting for, called loudly through the cells.

"Jacey Vincent. Your ride's here."

I breathe a sigh of relief, and I realize that I'd honestly been worried that for the first time ever, maybe Brand wasn't going to come to my rescue. That maybe he'd called Gabriel, and my brother had told him to let me stew for a while, to think about what I'd done or some bullshit.

But he didn't.

Thank god.

Once I see his face, though, after I've walked past all the hookers and drunks, down the long tiled corridor flanked by jail cells, I'm not sure that I should be thanking god for Brand's rescue. I should probably be praying for my soul, because Brand's furious, and from the look on his face it's a real possibility that he might kill me.

His enormous frame practically fills up the lobby where he's waiting, and I've never seen him look quite as angry as he does right now. He's got to be at least 6'5" and he's built like a brick house, with not an ounce of fat on him, and that makes him a very intimidating presence, particularly when he's pissed.

He served in the Army Rangers with my brother and he looks like he just stepped out of uniform, even though it's been almost two years now. He's let his blond hair grow, so now it's fashionably shaggy and grazes his collar line. If he didn't seem like a brother to me, I'd say he was hot. The women in the reception area seem to agree. Every female eye in the place is glued on him. But his are glued on me.

His blue eyes are hard and glittering as he watches me approach.

He's pissed.

I gulp.

"It's not what you think," I tell him preemptively when I reach him. "They weren't my drugs."

His gaze is fixed on my cheek.

"Are you okay?" he asks harshly. I nod, my fingers brushing across my cheek self-consciously.

"I'm fine…I tried to break up a fight, but—"

Brand cuts me off by grabbing my arm and dragging me toward the door.

"It's not what I think? So I didn't just get called to the police station at four A.M. to bail your ass out? Then I get here and your face is swollen and you're dressed like a fucking prostitute. At the moment, I almost don't give a fuck what you did or didn't do, Jacey. You were supposed to quit Saffron. Gabriel's going to shit."

"Don't tell him," I plead as he holds the door open. And even though Brand's pissed, I can't help but notice that he's shielding my body with his, hiding me from the people in the lobby. As if that can somehow take away my shame for being here. Even still, it's a sweet gesture, especially since he's so mad.

Brand stares at me icily. "Your brother's gonna know about this," he tells me firmly. "Jesus, Jacey. After everything that happened with Jared, and the therapy that you've gone through already... We were starting to think that you were actually going to get your shit together. But now you're assaulting police officers. *Christ*. If that Kinkaide kid hadn't pulled some sort of strings, you'd still be rotting in jail. They don't let people out who assault cops."

This stops me in my tracks.

"Dominic got the charges dropped?" I ask in shock. Why didn't he say anything when he stood there staring at me? All he said was... *I'm sorry*. And what the fuck was he sorry for? Smacking me in the face? Getting me arrested? Leaving me to rot in jail?

Brand leads me to his truck and opens the door, purposely looking away from my ass as I climb in.

"Yeah. I don't know how he did it, all I know is what they told me when I arrived. You're only facing possession of marijuana charges now. You're lucky. Well, lucky until Gabe hears about this. He's going to kick your ass. You're dressed like a hooker, you make tips by flirting with Saffron customers...you might as well be a stripper, for god's sake. Gabe's done everything he can think of to help you, Jacey. We don't even know what to do with you anymore."

He slams my door and I do feel guilty.

After everything went down in flames with Jared, Gabe paid for therapy for me. He and Maddy let me cry on their shoulders for hours and hours. They held my hand as I was taking baby steps to stand on my own two feet.

And since I lost my job working for Maddy when she sold her

restaurant, they put down the deposit for my rental in Chicago, with the understanding that I would find another part-time job to pay my bills while I finished school. Saffron wasn't exactly what they had in mind.

As Brand swings into the truck, I turn to him.

"It's not my fault that I'm still at Saffron," I snap defensively. "I tried to get a normal waitressing job. But I can't make enough money to pay my bills doing that while I'm in school. Working at Saffron is no different from working at Hooters or someplace. All I have to do is flirt and serve champagne to rich people at private parties."

"You mean, rich *men* at private parties." Brand scowls as he jams his keys into the ignition. "You're only one step above a stripper, Jacey, and you know it."

"I've only got one class left," I tell him quietly. "And I'm taking it online. I'll have my business degree in just a few weeks. I'm working on it, Brand. I'm working on everything. I'm doing the best I can." As I turn to face Brand even more squarely, the smell of his aftershave floods over me. That familiar scent, symbolizing something warm and safe, some*one* warm and safe, makes me realize that I'm okay. I'm no longer in a Chicago jail.

I'm safe.

I'm safe with Brand.

He'd rather die than let anything hurt me.

Then why can't I stop the waterworks that suddenly overwhelm me?

There's no reason to cry now, but no matter how much I try to stop the tears, I can't. My sobs well up into a wail that erupts into a shoulder-shaking crying jag.

As I cry inconsolably, I know that with every sob and every quaking breath I take, I'm Brand's worst nightmare.

Chapter Four

Jacey

Brand stares at me in horror.

"Jesus Christ, Jace. Calm down. You're fine. Everything's fine." He tries to soothe me as he awkwardly pats my back, his large hands thumping too hard on my shoulders. "It's okay. I know you're trying. And you've been doing a good job. Everything's fine."

He keeps repeating himself, because he doesn't know what to say. A woman crying is his kryptonite. He has no idea how to handle it.

I launch myself into his arms, burying my face into his shirt. I know I'm getting snot on him, but I don't care. I'm just so happy to be here right now, in this truck with Brand. But more importantly, I'm so happy to be out of jail. I hadn't realized until this very minute how scared I'd been.

"Thank you for bailing me out." I sniff. "I didn't really assault a police officer. It was a reflex...he went to grab me and I pushed his hand away. I didn't mean to. And the drugs weren't mine. They were in Dominic's car."

Brand looks at me with sympathy as he steers us through the parking lot and out onto the dark street.

"Tell me what happened," he instructs. "Everything."

So I do. I tell him all of it. How Kaylie almost got forced into a blow job, how Dominic Kinkaide, *the fucking actor*, had stopped it, but then he'd turned right around and gotten into a fight that ended in both of us being arrested.

"He fucking flipped out on this guy," I tell Brand. "And the other guy clocked him hard in the temple, so I don't know how he stayed standing up, but he still managed to kick the shit out of the dude. I jumped in to try and break it up and one of them accidentally smacked me."

One of them. It was Dominic. But I don't want to tell Brand that.

"And then the cops came and they found pot in his car. He said it wasn't his and I know it wasn't mine, so they decided to arrest us both. The other guy, Cris, told the cops that he didn't want to press assault charges, so all Dominic had to do was admit the pot was his and they'd probably have let us go. But he was an asshole about it. God."

My head drops into my hands and Brand glances at me. "How do you know for sure it was his? Just because it wasn't yours doesn't mean it was his, you know."

I think about that for a second. I guess I hadn't actually seen Dominic with drugs. The cops had just found it on his back floorboard. But still.

"It was his car," I finally insist. "It had to be his. But whatever. All I know for sure is that it wasn't mine."

"Well, you'll have a chance to speak up about that when you appear for court," Brand tells me with a sigh. "You'll need to find a lawyer."

I nod and lean my head against the window.

We're quiet for a while before Brand speaks again.

"So you were actually in Sin Kinkaide's house?"

Even in the midst of all my drama, I can't help but smile at the reverence in Brand's voice. I happen to know that Devil's Own is one of his favorite bands. He plays them all the time when he's working out.

"Yeah," I tell him. "And Sin Kinkaide is pretty fucking awesome. He was so nice in person . . . way nicer than you'd expect him to be."

Brand raises an eyebrow. "Unlike Dominic?"

I shrug, picturing Dominic's brooding stare and the way he flipped out on his old friend. "I don't know. Celebrities aren't the same as us . . . they play by different rules. But he did save Kaylie's ass, so he can't be all bad."

Mentioning Kaylie reminds Brand of the matter at hand and he gets stern again.

"Neither of you should be working there. I don't care if it's good money. Maybe you could come work for Gabe and me as our assistant. We need another one since our last one quit. Working at Saffron puts you into bad situations. Look at you tonight! Jumping into a fight, Jacey? I can't even kick the shit out of someone for hurting you . . . because you did this to yourself. You know better than to get in the middle of a fight."

I stare at the floor, trying not to cry again. He's probably right. I'm too gullible. I've fallen for the wrong guys a hundred times and I'm surprised by it every time. I'm a horrible judge of character. I get myself into the worst situations because of my bad judgment. But all of these things are issues that I'm working on. Because I think I'm already doing the best I can, I don't even know what to say. Brand just doesn't understand.

"Are you listening to me?" Brand demands grumpily.

I nod wearily. Being up all night, getting arrested, and listening to this endless lecture is taking its toll, and I can feel my shoulders droop more and more by the minute.

"I don't want to work for you and Gabe," I tell him limply. "I need to stand on my own. That's part of what I learned in therapy. Thank you for the offer, but I've got to make my own way."

I steel myself for another lecture, but thankfully, the end is in sight. Brand pulls up to the curb in front of my house and sits there for a second, staring first at his big hands, then at me.

"It scared the fuck out of me, Jacey," he admits quietly. "When you called and said you needed help, I mean. A hundred things went through my mind before you were able to tell me what was going on. Don't do that shit. When Gabe moved to Hartford, I promised him I would watch out for you, but you're making it difficult."

He sighs and I swallow hard, hating that I caused him worry. He levels another gaze at me, his blond eyebrows knitted together in consternation.

"I don't know what to say," he continues. "I know you're trying, but try harder. You've got to make smarter decisions. Please. Your brother, me, Madison…we've all had enough drama to last us for a couple of lifetimes, okay?"

The look on his face, serious and tired, makes my throat close up. He *has* had enough drama to last for two lifetimes. He and Gabe both, back when they were still in the Rangers. They're fucking heroes and they don't deserve to worry even a minute about me.

"I'm sorry," I whisper as I scoot over and kiss him on the cheek. "I'm sorry for not being good enough. I don't know why I can't seem to pull things together. Thank you for coming to get me, Brand. And thank you for always being someone I can count on."

I get choked up now, because honestly, there are very few people I can actually count on. My dad's worthless, and my mom's a flake. Brand is a pillar of strength and he always has been.

I slip from the seat before I cry on his broad shoulder again as I remember how he's always been there for me. When I turn to close the door, Brand is looking at me, his blue eyes soft.

There's something there, something gentle, something different from the way he usually looks at me. It suddenly seems not-so-brotherly, and my stomach wavers. But then he covers it up.

"Jacey, you *are* good enough. That wasn't what I meant. All I meant was that you've got to try harder to make better decisions. And you can always count on me. You know that. Call me when you get your court date. I'll go with you."

I nod and slam the door closed, watching his taillights until they disappear.

The look I'd just seen in Brand's eyes bothers me. A *lot*. It's the same look I see in the eyes of every other man on the planet, but it's something I've never seen in his before. Until now.

My heart sinks a little. I can't have Brand thinking about me in any other way other than sisterly.

I need him.

I need him to be the person that he is to me, the person he's always been, a brotherly figure. Someone I can count on. Because so few people in life have ever been that to me. And if anything changes with Brand and me, everything will change, and I can't deal with that on top of the rest of this mess.

With a sigh, I head up to my little bungalow, kicking off my shoes along the way.

I unlock the door to my tiny one-bedroom place and jump into the shower to wash away the feeling of the jail. I can't help but feel gross, like the jail cell has burned into my skin and there's only one way to get it off. To scrub until my skin is bright pink and almost raw.

When I finally feel clean enough to towel off, I pull some

underwear and a T-shirt on and collapse into bed to get a few hours of sleep.

The problem is, sleep doesn't come.

I was arrested tonight, for god's sake. Not only that, but I was arrested with one of the most famous actors on the planet. Dominic's smoldering green eyes refuse to stay out of my head, his expression taunting me.

It's like he *saw* me. He saw that someone died because of me. He saw that there's something so fundamentally wrong with me that my own parents don't want anything to do with me. That I'm flawed.

He saw all of that. He looked into my eyes and saw it. And then he turned away and left me to rot in the jail cell alone.

He's a fucking asshole.

I might be a horrible judge of character, but even I can see that.

I toss and turn in my Egyptian cotton sheets. I'm horrible with money, and I always seem to spend it on things I shouldn't. One of my splurges is good-quality sheets. But even they don't help me sleep tonight. Or this morning, I mean. I glance at the clock. Five thirty A.M.

I know Gabe's up. He usually gets up and goes for a run at five. Because he's just that into self-torture. I sigh and grab my phone, punching in his number. I might as well tell him and get it over with. It'll be better if he hears it from me instead of Brand.

"What's wrong?" He answers quickly, only slightly out of breath and without bothering to say hello. He knows something's wrong if I'm calling this early.

"Don't kill me, okay?" I ask. I hear him sigh.

"No promises," he mutters.

It all spills out and by the end, there's a long pause.

"Jace, it's a good thing you're there and I'm here," he finally says. "Or I might kill you."

"I know." I sigh. "But seriously, Gabe. The drugs weren't mine."

"That's not the point," he tells me tiredly. "You're still at Saffron, and you always seem to be in the wrong place at the wrong time. You've got to pull your shit together. I don't know what else I can do for you."

"That's what Brand said." I shake my head, even though Gabe can't see it. "I'm *trying*, Gabe. It seems like I take two steps forward and then one step back all the time."

"You're going to have to keep moving forward." He sighs. "It's the only way you're going to get anywhere."

He's quiet for a second. "I can't come out there, not right now. Maddy's due in a couple months, work is insanely busy, and I'm trying to get a lot done so I can take off for a bit when the baby's born. You're going to have to handle this on your own. I'll call around and get you a lawyer, but you're going to have to go see him on your own. Can you do that?"

I try not to get pissed. Of course I can handle it. I'm not an imbecile.

"Yes," I finally answer. "Surely it won't be that big a deal. It's my first offense. I'll get my own lawyer and everything will be fine because I didn't do it. It wasn't mine."

"Tell that to the judge," Gabe mutters as he hangs up.

That's exactly what I do six days later as I stand in front of a judge in a dingy Chicago courtroom for the first time in my life.

As Dominic Kinkaide sits behind me flanked by four lawyers compared to my one, I tell the judge everything, how I'm certainly not guilty and how the pot wasn't mine. How I'm floundering a bit, but I'm definitely trying to pull my life together.

But it doesn't matter. I can see that in the judge's steely eyes as I try to plead my case. Nothing I say is gonna matter.

I'm screwed.

Chapter Five

Dominic

Well, this is new. I've never been in a courtroom before.

That's not exactly true. I did sit in a seat like this when I was in the movie *Annihilated*. I played a sadistic serial killer/rapist, so I've seen the inside of a courtroom. Just never in real life. I've never sat and waited to be judged, waited for my fate to be decided by someone else.

Not for real.

It turns out, real life is fucking frustrating.

I sigh heavily and turn to the lawyer closest to me. Like the three sitting around him, he's buttoned up in a white shirt and dark suit, wearing a shrewd, businesslike expression. My manager hired them, a whole team of legal sharks. If these guys can't get me out of this, no one can.

"How long is this going to take?" I ask the head lawyer. Tom, I think his name is. He glances at me.

"However long the judge wants it to take," he answers wryly. "Just sit back and relax. You're going to be fine. You're lucky that Mr. Evans is refusing to press charges against you, or you'd be here for assault as well as drug charges."

I slump into my chair, impatient, and kill time by watching the blond chick standing in front of me. Jacey.

The girl who may or may not have gotten me arrested for drugs.

I watch her tear-streaked face and the way she so sincerely pleads her case with the judge. I almost think that the drugs really weren't hers. But if they weren't hers, I don't know whose they were. They sure as fuck weren't mine.

She turns away from me once again, and my eyes sweep over her from top to bottom.

She's got a tight ass, I'll give her that, barely concealed in a short skirt. My brother would say that she's got an ass like an onion, hot enough to make him cry. As for me, I can just imagine burying my dick in it, pressing my face to her shoulder blades, reaching around her and...

I stop myself, shaking the random fantasy out of my head.

This isn't the time or the place. I turn back to my lawyer. "Did you get those assault charges dropped for her?"

He stares at me. "Yeah. I pulled a couple of strings. She's only being charged with possession of marijuana now, like you. I don't know why you care though. It's probably her pot to begin with."

I don't know why I care, either. Other than the fact that she didn't even know me, but she jumped in the middle of a brawl and tried to stop it. And afterward, she had stood with her little body in front of mine, almost as if she was shielding me from Cris...even though I'd accidentally clocked her in the face.

Why had she done that?

I don't fucking know. But I feel a little responsible that she was even there. Even if it *was* her pot, she wouldn't have been there in the first place if it hadn't been for me. And I can't help but think back to the look on her face when I walked past her in her jail cell as she sat there covered in my blood.

She looked utterly vulnerable in a jail cell full of hookers. That's when I called my attorney and had him get her assault charges dropped. If I hadn't done that, she'd have been there all night.

Oblivious to my musings about her, she stands in front of the judge now, giving him a sob story about how she's trying to pull her life together or some shit. But the judge doesn't even blink, he just stares down at her sternly from his perch above.

"Young lady, you do need to grow up. And I know that some judges like to give pretty little things like you a break. But I'm not in the business of being an enabler. So, you should learn right here and now that this kind of thing isn't a trivial matter." The judge pauses to stare down at her sternly.

"I'm finding you guilty of possession of marijuana. I'm sentencing you to ninety days' community service at a local youth center and six months of probation. Learn from this, young lady. I don't want to see you here again. If you perform every bit of your community service as ordered, I will think about expunging this from your record. My bailiff will give you the details."

Jacey turns around with tear-streaked cheeks, and I suck in a breath over her sentence. My lawyer shakes his head.

"Don't worry about it. She must've rubbed him wrong. You'll be fine. She's got a second-rate attorney who can't argue shit. You've got me."

Unfortunately, as I stand in front of the judge a few minutes later, I can see that having four attorneys isn't going to do me any good. In fact, it might just have the opposite effect. The judge's eyes glitter as he stares at my legal team.

"So, son. You think you can come to Chicago and do illegal drugs, then just hire a team of lawyers to get away with it?"

"No, sir—" I start to argue, but he doesn't give me the chance. He holds up his hand.

"Uh, uh. I don't want to hear it. I find you guilty of marijuana possession and I sentence you to ninety days of community service and six months of probation. I realize that you live in California, but you will remain here in Chicago until your community service has been served."

Before I can even say a word, my attorney sputters.

"Objection!" he protests. "My client has obligations in California. He has a new film hitting production next week. In order to work and support himself, he must return to California. Can't he serve his community service there?"

The judge looks at us drolly. "Are you telling me that your client is on the verge of destitution if he can't return to California? I find that hard to believe, and if that is the case, I of course would need to see some verification of that."

My attorney backpedals. "Of course that's not what I'm saying. What I'm saying is that this is his first offense and he deserves some leniency. If he's not allowed to return home, it will drastically affect the production schedule of his next film, which will have negative ramifications for my client."

The judge smiles now, a humorless grin. "That, counselor, is not my problem. It should serve to teach your client a lesson. The sentence stands. The crime was committed here, the sentence will be served here. If he serves it out in complete compliance, it will be expunged from his record. The bailiff will have the details."

I'm stunned as I sit staring at my hands. Did that really just happen? I'm stuck in Chicago for three months? *And* I have a criminal record now? Holy shit. I glare at my high-priced lawyer.

"So, apparently, you're a second-rate attorney who can't argue shit, either."

I ignore his protests and push away from the table, following the bailiff to learn the details of my sentence. Before the bailiff ducks into a room, he waves me toward Jacey, who is sitting on a bench in the hall. I join her, and together we sit and wait. She's not crying anymore, but she seems just as distraught.

"Can you believe this?" she moans as she drops her head into her hands. "Oh my god. This is crazy. If you would just tell them the pot was yours, this would all go away. You're the freaking movie star. I'm sure you're quite accustomed to making things disappear."

I stare at her mulishly. "Yeah, things like your assault charges?"

Bright red flashes across Jacey's cheeks and she looks away.

"Thank you," she finally answers reluctantly. "I don't know why you did that, but thank you."

As she speaks, something crosses her face and she turns to me sharply.

"Oh my god. You got those charges dropped because you felt bad about framing me for this, didn't you? You can't have this kind of publicity, so you made it look like the drugs were mine. But you're not totally soulless, so you made my assault charges go away to make up for it. Oh. My. God."

She stares at me with her ridiculous thoughts swimming in her eyes, and I shake my head in annoyance.

"Fuck that," I snap. "The drugs weren't mine. Period. I got your charges dropped because I felt like it."

I look away from her pointedly, dismissing her. Instead, I concentrate on the bustling people in the hall, including a hulking blond guy hovering nearby. Jacey's boyfriend, probably. He's exactly the kind of guy I would picture her with: a meathead who mindlessly follows her around like a puppy. It makes total sense. She definitely seems like the kind of girl who wants someone who will just bow to her wishes. I sniff in disdain, then close my eyes.

I get two minutes of peace until my phone rings and my manager's name pops up. I know he's been anxiously waiting to hear what happened here, probably tapping his expensive Italian leather loafer against his marble office floor.

Yeah, he's just that ostentatious. Ridiculously so. In addition, he drives a Ferrari, bright yellow for maximum impact. I always tell him his dick must be microscopic for him to need that much attention.

I answer the phone now with a sigh, not relishing this conversation. "Hey, Tally."

"What's the verdict?" Tally doesn't even bother with a greeting.

"I'm stuck in Chicago for three months," I tell him. "Community service. Then six months of probation. If I'm a good boy, my record will be wiped clean."

Tally erupts into a string of swear words that would make any sailor or truck driver cringe. I hold the phone away from my ear until he's finished.

Finally, he takes a deep breath, calming himself somewhat.

"Fuck. This is bullshit, Dominic. The studio is going to be furious. Not only is this going to fuck with the schedule, they hired you in part based on your reputation. You aren't a troublemaker. You're a mysterious, sexy star. You keep things private, which keeps people guessing about you. This…this fucks with that. Everyone is going to assume that you're an addict now, and that's not the image that we're trying to convey. I've got your publicists already on it, trying to spin it for you. But be prepared. News of this has already hit the web.

"Also, you've got to see if you can at least come home on the weekends. Maybe they can work in some scenes then. Find out if that's a possibility and then call me back. I'll hold off calling the studio until I hear from you."

I don't bother pointing out that the studio won't be happy about going over budget by working the crew on weekend hours. He knows that. He hangs up without another word, and I let my head fall against the wall behind me as I stare at the ceiling.

I can feel Jacey looking at me.

"Will you get fired?" she asks hesitantly. I sigh.

"Maybe you should've worried about that before you brought pot into my car."

I stare at her, hard, and she doesn't flinch.

"It wasn't mine," she answers coldly, then she turns her face away and doesn't say another word. I almost believe her. To be fair, it's hard to know who might've gotten into my car. With all of the people in and out of Sin's house, it could've been anyone.

The bailiff emerges finally and approaches us with a handful of papers.

"You'll both be serving your community service at Joe's Gladiators, a youth center here in the city. Joe Hudson will be your supervisor. He's the owner of the place. Every week, he has to sign one of these for you."

The bailiff hands us each a bright yellow paper.

"It's like a report card. Joe will fill it out and sign it. If you fail to appear for work, if you do a bad job, if you don't do what is asked of you…in fact, if you sneeze wrong, Joe can refuse to sign it. It's in your best interest to keep him happy. Judge Kumarowski doesn't fool around, and if you have to reappear, he won't be lenient. On the other hand, if you do exceptionally well, he'll reward you for your good behavior by expunging this charge from your permanent record and removing your six months' probation period."

The bailiff stares at us both firmly. "Any questions?"

Jacey shakes her head, but I hold up a finger. "Will it be possible for me to go home on the weekends to work?"

The bailiff scribbles something on his paper. "I'll check with the judge and get back to you. It'll probably be fine. Anything else?"

Jacey and I shake our heads.

"Good. You're free to go. You should both report to Joe's by ten A.M. on Monday."

I feel like I have an instant steel manacle snapped to my ankle. Someone to check in with, report to, and, most important, someone to keep me in Chicago.

Fuck.

The hulking blond guy descends upon Jacey, patting her shoulder, and I push away from the wall and head down the hall. I can feel Jacey's stare beating into my shoulder blades, but I ignore it. She should be paying attention to her boyfriend, not me. But like every other woman out there, she's attracted to me because of who I am.

God, I hate that shit. For a brief moment, I remember the way she'd looked at me from her jail cell . . . so soft and trusting and open. Like she was oblivious to my name and it was just her and me standing there.

But that was a lie. She knows full well who I am, and that's what she's attracted to. She's no different from anyone else.

With a sigh I make my way down the dingy stairs, and as I glance outside I see the reporters waiting. I stand still for a second, dreading this, but there's no way around it.

I pull up the hood of my sweatshirt and duck outside.

They descend like vultures, with their microphones shoved in my face, their flashbulbs popping, and their cameras rolling.

Is it true that you've got a drug problem, Dominic?

Are you going to rehab?

Who's the blond girl, Dominic? Is she your girlfriend?

How will this affect your upcoming film?

I ignore them all, shoving through the crowd, and for a minute I regret not bringing security with me. What the hell was I thinking?

My security detail is back home in Hollywood, but Sin had offered me his... and I'd turned him down. I just wanted to get in and out of here today with as little fuss as possible. It's why I told Sin and Duncan not to come. It's bad enough if one of us goes somewhere. But if we go together, the circus around us is ridiculous.

I duck into the crowded sidewalk and lose myself in the people, jogging down the street until I can no longer hear the snaps of the cameras and the chattering reporters. It takes a while, but finally I find myself alone in the quiet solitude of a Chicago alleyway.

I slump against the grimy wall, staring around at the trash, the graffiti, the grayness of the city. Even in the midst of spring, downtown Chicago seems dismal and gray. It might be home, but quite honestly, I would rather be anywhere but here.

I take a deep breath of city smells and then release it.

I'm here now. I'll be here for the next three months. I can't control that so there's only one thing to do.

Suck it up.

❧

As I lay sprawled in a chair in Sin's theater room, I make a gun out of my fingers and point it at my head as my mother lectures into my ear. It had taken exactly two hours for her to see the courthouse footage online. *Why didn't you wear a tie? Why must you wear those horrible hoodies?*

From across the room, Sin laughs as he flips through channels on the behemoth TV hanging in front of us. He's dressed only in a pair of tattered jeans that look like he slept in them. Once again, he's not wearing a shirt.

"Dominic James Kinkaide." My mother sighs into my ear. "I can't believe you have a criminal record. I honestly can't. Your father is going to be so upset."

"Oh, Dad is going to be upset?" I ask, my lip twitching. "Not you at all, right? It's all Dad?"

It's a joke in our family. My mother always blames everything on my father. Things worry him sick, he loses sleep over us, etc. It's all him, not her. It's funny, because he's the most laid-back person I know. Dad has been a producer in the music industry since before I was born. He's got nerves of steel. To blame all the worry on him is asinine, but none of us kids ever call her on it.

Mom sighs. "What are you going to do? You can't stay with Sin. The two of you will just get into even more trouble. You'd better come home. I'll get your room ready for you here."

I think of my childhood home, Castle Kinkaide, a large replica of a Scottish castle perched in the middle of ten acres right outside of Chicago. It's quirky and original, just like my family. And while I love my childhood home and my family, having my mom in my business or listening to Fiona lecture me about Cris for the next ninety days isn't gonna happen.

"Thanks for the offer, Mom. But I'm good here. I might even rent my own condo if Sin doesn't start wearing clothes. We'll see. But everything will be fine. Don't worry. And tell Dad not to worry."

Sin snorts. "Is Dad worried sick?" He cracks up and my mom sighs.

"Sinclair Alec Kinkaide," she snaps, even though my brother can't hear her. "That's enough out of you."

I waggle my eyebrows at Sin before I return my attention to Mom.

"I love you, Mom. I'll come out and see you soon."

I hang up and sink glumly into the leather cushions of the chair.

"Cheer up," Sin chirps. "I'll put one of your movies on to make you feel better."

I roll my eyes because he knows I hate to watch my own movies. "You're way too happy about my current set of circumstances."

He grins. "I'm just happy to not be the only Kinkaide with a record. Thanks for that. Mom can split her lectures between the two of us now."

"Glad to be of help," I mutter. "And at least I kept my crime spree on US soil. I'm pretty sure you're banned from the Netherlands."

Sin rolls his eyes, but then his expression suddenly changes.

"Did you talk to Fiona?" he asks, somewhat hesitantly. "Or just Mom?"

I clench my jaw. "No, I didn't fucking talk to Fiona. It's bullshit that she's dating Cris. And I can't believe you didn't tell me about it. You let me fucking find out on my own."

Sin shakes his head. "I'm sorry, Dom. I didn't realize that they were coming to the party or I would've told you. They didn't know you were in town. But dude, Cris has changed. I don't know what he did to piss you off so fucking much, but the guy's changed a lot since you graduated high school. You should at least talk to him. Six years is a long time, bro. A lot can happen."

"Yeah?" I arch an eyebrow. "People don't change. Not really. They can pretend, they can move on, they can do lots of shit, but to actually reach down into their soul and change the person they are? That's impossible. And Cris has a black fucking soul. Fiona shouldn't be with him."

I tap my phone against my leg in agitation, staring at Sin. He stares back.

"I don't know what to tell you, dude. You can't control her, she's as stubborn as you are. But that trait comes in handy now that she's working for the band. She'll be the best manager we ever had."

I scowl. "Which doesn't do me one bit of good. Unless, as her boss, you can send her to LA or something while I'm here?"

Sin shakes his head with a grin. "Sorry, dude. I need her here. She's working with Tally to put together our next tour. Besides, with her here and you here, maybe you can hash all of this out once and for all. Plus, as an added bonus, you'll get to hear all of the details from Duncan's love life. Trust me, it's not boring."

"Jesus." I roll my eyes. "This is why I don't come back all that often. It's always like a fucking soap opera in this family."

Sin shakes his head, turning back to the television.

"Welcome home, bro."

Chapter Six

Dominic

I stick my hand out from under the covers and flip off the sun. Actually, I'm flipping off the entire day. Nothing good ever comes from a Monday.

With a groan, I roll over and stare bleary-eyed at the clock. Eight A.M. I open my mouth to yawn, only to find my dry tongue stuck to the top of my even drier mouth.

Jesus. Last night is a blur of too much whiskey, padded handcuffs, and Kira's sex-starved moans.

Come on, Dominic. Just fuck me. You know you want to.

She had pleaded, like always. But like always, my answer was the same. Although that didn't stop us from doing several other things that were probably illegal in twenty states. My ass still stings from the belt Kira used, and I briefly wonder if it left marks before I decide that I don't give a shit.

The sheets still smell like Kira's perfume, even though she left hours ago, and I feel the sudden urge to wash it off of me. Something about the light of day and all that. What happens in the dark should stay in the dark.

If two consenting adults do deviant things to each other in the dark, did the deviant things actually happen? There's a question for the ages.

Rolling out of bed, I take a quick shower and head down to Sin's kitchen to scrounge up some caffeine. Not remembering the last time I took the time to eat, I grab a cup of coffee and a slice of cold pizza from the fridge and head out to a lounger by the pool.

I wolf the pizza down in four bites, lick my fingers, then close my eyes. The light is just too damned bright. And four hours of sleep isn't enough.

Before long though, giggling invades my solitude and I can feel eyes on my skin. Why the hell is someone always around this place? It's impossible to ever be alone. Reluctantly, I open my eyes to see who's watching me.

Across the pool, in one of the two large cabanas, two girls are doing a not very good job of pretending not to stare at me.

They're scantily dressed in tiny shorts and halter tops, probably eighteen or nineteen, and they have the smeared makeup of women who have been awake all night. Awake and *used* all night. I can see the sex-glazed looks in their eyes from here.

Sin, the guy who put that look in their eyes, is nowhere to be found, so it's hard to tell what they're up to now. Either way, they're not my guests and not my problem. I don't close my eyes fast enough though, and accidentally make eye contact with one of them.

Fuck. They know I'm awake.

They make a beeline for my side, sitting on the lounger beside me, still giggling with their smeared makeup and last night's clothes. I fight the urge to roll my eyes.

"You're Dominic Kinkaide, right?" the tall brunette asks, purposely sitting in a way that pushes her tits together.

I nod. "Usually."

They giggle again while the little blonde edges forward. "Sin told us that you were staying here for a while," she says proudly, excited to be "in the know."

I do roll my eyes now. I can't help it. Jesus. These girls are always the fucking same. It's mind-boggling. They're perfectly willing to hang around and be used, simply so they can say that they were with Sin Kinkaide. Or me. Or even Duncan, and he's just a fucking drummer.

"He told you that, did he?" I ask. "And where is my brother?"

Brunette gestures toward the house. "He's still in bed. We're supposed to be finding him coffee. He has practice this morning."

I cock an eyebrow. "You mean 'rehearsal'?"

She blushes prettily. "Yeah."

I close my eyes again. "Well, the coffee isn't usually by the pool. It's in the kitchen. If you head that way, someone can help you."

More giggles, then silence, although I can still feel their presence. I hear a whisper, then a hand sliding on my arm.

"Hey, if you haven't had breakfast yet, why don't you join us?"

I open my eyes at Blondie's suggestive tone to find her face sultry and expectant. It's blatantly clear that she's not talking about food.

Oddly enough, the face that I found to be tired and smeared a moment ago suddenly seems almost tempting, or at least doable. My sexual proclivities are rearing their ugly heads. Two girls willing to do anything to please me? The opportunities are endless.

"What do you have in mind?" I ask, my interest piqued.

The brunette pipes up. "*We* could be your breakfast. If you want," she adds, almost shyly.

Her friend nods in agreement. "I hope you have a big appetite."

I smile wolfishly, definitely interested now.

"Well, have you ever heard the phrase 'my eyes are bigger than my stomach'?"

One girl smiles and the other nods. I nod back and lean forward, speaking quietly as if sharing a secret.

"I like to watch," I tell them.

Brunette immediately stands up, gently pushing my shoulders backward until I'm reclining again.

"Then watch this," she tells me confidently. She grabs Blondie and pulls her onto the lounger next to me. "I'm Erika," she announces, as she pushes Blondie onto her back. "And this is Meghan."

"It doesn't matter," I mumble.

But they don't hear me. Brunette is sliding Blondie's shorts off, pulling them down over her hips and then licking each place that her fingers touched. As she moves to the girl's tits, taking off her shirt and then pulling one of those lush little nipples into her mouth, my dick gets hard and I pull it out of my pants.

There is something wrong with me.

I get off on watching other people's pleasure. Or I get off when pain is involved. Or I get off when something is far, far over the line of normal. I don't get off by my own participation. That's fucked up in a million different ways, but I'm not going to analyze it now.

For now, I'm going to watch the girls' tight little bodies sliding together, because that does it for me.

Watching their tongues tangle, their tits press together...that does it for me, too.

And when Brunette's mouth burrows between Blondie's legs and then Blondie comes into Brunette's mouth...I'm a goner. I stroke myself, not caring that any number of the staff inside the house could glance out and see me getting off on the lounge chair.

Before long, Brunette shoves my hand away, replacing it with her mouth. Blondie kneels over my balls, licking them like an ice cream cone.

"Pull on my balls," I instruct Blondie. She grins devilishly and does as I ask. "Harder," I say firmly. "Harder."

Pain shoots through me as she complies, and she pulls ever harder on my ball sack. I like the pain. It blocks out reality.

I smile and take a sip of coffee, as they bob and dip and pull and suck in front of me.

Turns out, this Monday isn't so bad after all.

Jacey

I glance at the clock in the dingy, hot office. Ten thirty-seven A.M. We were supposed to be here at Joe's Gladiators thirty-seven minutes ago.

I actually showed up early, not wanting to get on Joe's bad side right off the bat. The bailiff had said that any little thing could give Joe grounds to not sign my card. Dominic Kinkaide, however, apparently doesn't worry about such things. He's late.

Very late.

To distract myself, I pick up my phone and call my best friend. Who better to commiserate with, right?

Maddy answers on the second ring.

"Hey girl," she chirps cheerfully. "What's up?"

I scowl. "Don't pretend you don't know," I tell her grumpily. "I know that Gabe told you everything. I suck. It's common knowledge."

Maddy pauses. "You sometimes suck," she agrees. "But not most of the time. You messed up. Big deal. You're fixing it now."

"You've got that right," I agree, staring around Joe's cluttered office. "I'm at the gym waiting to start my community service. It's disgusting here. And those boys out there. Oh my god. They're so intimidating. They look like they might shiv someone in the shower."

Maddy chuckles. "You're not intimidated by anyone. That's one of the things I love about you. Suck it up and do your time, Jace. Then you can get your ass out here for a visit. I miss you."

"I miss you, too," I reply. "And I've got to come out while you're still pregnant. It'll be the only time that I get to see you fat."

Maddy laughs at that, and I laugh, too, because I'm sure that even now, my best friend isn't fat. She's gorgeous, like always. But before we can say more, Joe lumbers back into the office, having only been gone for ten minutes.

"Gotta go, Mad," I mutter quickly. "I'll call you later."

I hang up quickly and stare at my new boss. He's a huge man, gray hair, gray whiskers, square jaw, wide shoulders. He actually looks like he could be found on a fisherman's wharf or something. He's maybe sixty or so and he has no tact. As in, none.

"Who the hell does that kid think he is?" he grumbles to me. Or maybe to himself, because he doesn't even look up at me as he drops heavily into his office chair. "I don't give a flying rat's ass if he's famous. I'm only going through your orientation one time. If he's not here in five minutes, we'll start without him and he can just go someplace else to do his time."

Joe looks at me sternly now, his steely blue eyes firm. "I don't put up with laziness or tardiness, Ms. Vincent. You should know that right now."

"Yes, sir," I stammer. For some reason, he just seems like a person I should address as *sir*. He smiles though, for the first time since

I met him. It crinkles the corners of his eyes and spreads to the rest
of his face, lighting up his wrinkles.

"Sir. Ha! That's a good one. Sir was my father. Or my drill
sergeant back when I was in the Army. I'm just Joe, young lady."

Finally. Something to break the ice with him. Relief washes
over me.

"You were in the Army?" I grab at that straw quickly, before he
changes the subject and the topic gets away from me. I don't want to
go back to staring at the clock, waiting for Dominic in uncomfortable silence. "My brother was, too. He was a Ranger. He just got a
Medal of Honor, as a matter of fact."

Joe stares at me now, sufficiently impressed and curious.

"You don't say? That's impressive. It takes a lot to get one of
those. What did he do?"

"His Humvee got bombed in Afghanistan, and according to the
president, he acted with extreme valor in the face of peril, above and
beyond the call of duty. Basically, he risked his own ass to save someone else's."

"You don't get more salt of the earth than that, missy," Joe
drawls sincerely, nodding. "You should take some pointers from your
brother. What does he think about you being here?"

My shoulders slump at the mere thought of what Gabe thinks
about it, and Joe laughs.

"That bad, huh?"

I smile and he smiles back. Thank god. The ice has definitely
been broken.

"Don't worry," he tells me, his tone softening just a bit. "My
bark is worse than my bite, as long as you stay on the straight and
narrow and do your job. These kids here..."

He pauses, staring out the window of his door at the teenagers punching at bags out in the sweaty gym.

"They don't have much, see? If they don't come here, they would get into trouble on the streets. And I don't want that. It's our job to keep them on the straight and narrow. To do that, you've got to be there, too. *Capisce?*"

I nod quickly. "Joe, seriously, this is the first time I've ever been in trouble. That pot wasn't even mine..." But Joe holds up his hand.

"That's not my business," he tells me. "My business is just making sure that you don't get into trouble again. You hear?"

He's stern again, and I know I'm back at an arm's length with him. He's going to be a tough nut to crack, and I'm going to have to earn his respect, but I just get the feeling that deep down he's a good guy. A nice guy. I saw a glimpse of warmth in those eyes a minute ago. Plus, he dedicates his life to helping troubled teens. That's got to mean something.

"I'm sorry I'm late."

The voice comes from behind me, freezing me in my chair.

Dominic.

I would know that voice anywhere now. Husky and low. Arrogant and dark. I don't know why I think a voice can be dark, all I know is his just is. His voice hints at dark things.

I turn in my chair to find him lingering in the door, looking like he just stepped from the big screen into this tiny office. He's bigger than life, even here. He doesn't look at me; instead his gaze is fixed on Joe.

He's got an arrogant, sexy attitude that completely fills up whatever room he's in. And even though he's saying he's sorry, he doesn't look one bit apologetic. He doesn't offer even one tiny explanation for his tardiness, either.

Joe stares at him.

"The next time you're late, don't bother coming in at all," Joe tells him gruffly. "Have as much respect for me and my boys here as you do for yourself and we'll all get along nicely. If you can't do that, get the hell out the same way you came in."

Dominic looks at him calmly. "Noted."

Joe stares at him, his blue eyes meeting Dominic's green. Neither looks away for a minute, until Joe breaks the gaze and looks at me.

"This one's got balls," he tells me, nodding. "Just wait till I break 'em."

I giggle and Dominic stares at me in disdain.

His gaze doesn't stray to my cheek where I have a bruise, and it doesn't meet my eyes. He also doesn't bother himself to comment. That's one thing that's clear about Dominic Kinkaide. He isn't going to go out of his way for much.

"Listen up," Joe tells us, snapping me out of thinking about Dominic. "I don't have much to say, other than what happens here with the kids stays here. These kids have rough home lives, and they don't need you spreading talk about them outside of this gym. You're here to help them in any way you can. Be a mentor. Show them that there is life outside of trouble. Think you can do that?"

I nod.

"It's pretty simple here. Don't be late. Don't mess up. Don't make their lives harder than they already are. Do some good. What you put out into the world, it comes back to you. Got it?"

I nod again, but Dominic sits silent and still.

Joe turns to him. "All right, since you were late, your job today will be to empty all the spit cans from around the boxing rings. Take them into the locker room, dump them out, rinse the cans, and put them back."

Dominic stares at him. "You can't be serious."

Oh, but he's serious. There's not a hint of a smile on Joe's face now.

"Yeah, I'm fucking serious. Don't be late again, or—"

"Or don't bother showing up," Dominic interrupts as he heads for the door. "Yeah, I got it." He walks out without another word and Joe looks at me.

"Your friend might not last long here."

I stare after Dominic, at his wide shoulders striding away from us. He's tall and lean, drop-dead gorgeous and proud as hell. "He's not my friend," I finally answer softly. "I barely know him."

But I have the feeling that's about to change. What I don't know is...how I feel about that.

Chapter Seven

Dominic

After I dump the disgusting cans of old spit down the even more disgusting bathroom sinks, I take them back out to the gym, pausing for a minute as I stare at Jacey. As much as I hate to give her attention, it's hard not to notice her here, especially when she's thrust herself in the middle of a group of at-risk kids and her face is pressed into a punching bag as one of the boys punches at it.

Especially when I walk past her and she smells like apples, crisp and clean.

She's as out of place in this dirty sweatbox as anyone I've ever seen.

She's got that girl-next-door quality that is so underrated among women. They all want to be glamorous bombshells, overly made-up and too sexed out. But even though Jacey is wearing makeup and short workout shorts, she's the classic girl next door, even if that's not her goal.

I bend and replace a spit can next to one of her toned legs, and she glances down at me, her eyes warm and sparkling.

For a minute, there's something in her expression, something mischievous, but she doesn't say anything. Instead, she just braces for another punch from the gigantic kid pummeling the bag she's holding. It's taking all of her weight to hold it still, but she's doing it. I can't help but be impressed.

Mainly because not only is she holding it, but she's not intimidated by him, either. She's half his size, but she just marched right out here and jumped in, just like she jumped in between Cris and me. Completely unafraid.

The kid she's with looks like he could eat her for breakfast, and every time he punches, it practically knocks her into the wall. But she still holds on.

She's stubborn, I'll give her that much. And fearless.

Why I'm thinking about her at all, though, I don't fucking know. Annoyed with myself, I turn around and head to the other side of the room.

That's when I hear the commotion.

Snapping around, I turn just in time to see the kid grab at Jacey's chest, his tape-wrapped fingers twisting her T-shirt and yanking her toward him. For a split second, my heart hammers as I watch the juvenile delinquent manhandling her. The kid is giant, and Jacey is extremely small.

But there's no time for me or anyone else to react before Jacey spins out of his grasp in one deft move, swinging her leg around in a surprisingly powerful roundhouse kick to his chest, knocking him onto his back.

I'm utterly stunned and so is she. I can see it on her face as she stands over him, her hands clenched and shaking at her sides as she balances one tennis shoe lightly on his neck.

"Don't touch me like that again!" she snaps at him. "I'm here to help you, but that doesn't give you the right to grope me."

By now, activity in the gym has halted, and every eye is on Jacey and the kid on the floor. You can hear a pin drop in this place.

The kid is still and silent as he looks up at her, and unconsciously I start to move toward Jacey. Even though I don't want to be involved with her or anything else, I can't leave her there by herself. I'm not completely heartless.

But then the kid smiles, even though Jacey's foot is still on his neck.

"If you let me up, I'll behave," he promises. Jacey stares down at him uncertainly, but after a second, she lifts her foot. The kid climbs to his feet, holding his hand out to Jacey.

She eyes him hesitantly.

"I'm sorry," the kid tells her, smiling again. "My name's Jake. There's no hard feelings, right? I was just messin' with you."

Jacey stares at him and I stop a few steps away.

"I guess not," she finally answers. "No hard feelings. Just don't do that again. I can take care of myself."

"Fuck, yeah, you can," the kid agrees. "Where did you learn to do that?"

Jacey shrugs, relaxing slightly even though she still keeps an eye on the boy.

"My brother's an Army Ranger. He taught me a lot of things. One of those things is how to shoot, and I have a 9mm in my bed stand. It might be pink, but it shoots just as straight as a regular one."

I can't help but chuckle now, at both the thought of this tiny chick with a pink gun by her bed and at the look on Jake's face.

"No worries," he tells her quickly. "I don't have any plans to break into your house. No need to threaten me with your pink gun."

I hear chuckling around me from the kids, and Jacey relaxes.

"Good. I just thought I'd let you know."

"Jake!" Joe's voice booms through the gym, and I glance over to find him standing in his office doorway, a pissed look on his face. "Get in here."

Jake turns slowly and Joe looks at Jacey.

"You okay?" he calls to her.

She nods and so does he. "Good. And nice rotation on that kick, young lady."

Jacey smiles now, a real smile that spreads to her eyes. "Thanks."

Jake disappears reluctantly into Joe's office, his shoulders slumped, and the door closes behind them. Jacey stands limply for a minute, probably trying to decide what to do now…now that she's shown the entire gym that she's an unlikely badass. Noise resumes around us as everyone goes back to their business.

I look at her.

"That was impressive," I admit quietly, because it's the truth. "You looked like a stuntwoman. Or a ninja."

Jacey laughs a warm laugh, real and husky, as she walks toward me, closing the three-foot gap between us.

"Thanks," she tells me. "I guess those endless self-defense classes with my brother paid off. I used to think that he just wanted to inflict pain on me, but maybe there was rhyme to his reason."

She's unflustered now, once again sure of herself. She tucks a stray lock of her blond hair behind her ear, and I can't help but notice her plump lips. They're just the right size to nip at. The tip of her tongue pokes out, licking her lips, and I swallow.

Must distract myself.

"Your brother's really a Ranger?" I ask, refocusing myself. "Because that's badass shit. If he trained you, it's no wonder you can take down a guy twice your size."

Jacey smiles, hovering near my elbow. Close enough to touch, but I don't. Close enough to inhale, so I do, filling my lungs with the scent of apples.

She's a breath of fresh air, whether I want to admit it or not.

"Yeah, he is. Or he was until a year or so ago. He *is* pretty badass."

I'm getting ready to reply when a group of guys headed for the locker room stop off beside us.

"Dude, are you really Dominic Kinkaide?" one of them asks, his face dubious. I smile what I hope is a patient smile.

"Yeah, that's me," I answer. I can feel Jacey watching the exchange with interest, but she remains silent. The kid grins.

"Dude. I loved *Annihilated*. That was some crazy shit! Did you do your own stunts?"

I nod, and the kids start chattering eagerly, asking me questions about leaping from a helicopter and how I'd managed to flip my jet ski over backward. One of them runs to Joe's office to get paper for autographs, and the group grows from three guys to fifteen.

The kid runs back and hands me a stack of scratch paper, and I start scrawling my name, handing an autograph to each boy surrounding me. As I do, I see Jacey slip away from the ruckus. A part of me is disappointed by that. I'm fascinated by the Jacey that just laid Jake out flat on his back.

I want to know more about her, because she seems different from the Jacey who works at Saffron.

After five minutes or so, Joe sticks his head out of his office and barks at the boys.

"Hey! You're not here to get autographs. Let the man do his job and you guys get back to work!"

The kids sheepishly disperse, going back to their punching bags or to the locker room, and I head to the weight room to wipe down the seats. When I get there, I find Jacey already crouched by a machine, cleaning it. When I walk in, she glances up at me and smiles.

"So that's your life?"

I shrug. "Most of the time. It's why I don't go out much. It's just part of it."

I grab a rag and help her, cleaning the other side of the machine she's working on.

"Well, I think it's awesome," she answers. "Everyone loves you. That must be an amazing feeling."

I snort. "Yeah. Everyone loves me. Jacey, no one knows me. Not really. They know my face. They know the roles that I play. But they don't know me. That's okay, though. It's how I like it."

Jacey shakes her head. "That's depressingly lonely, Dominic."

"Not really," I mutter, bending next to her to grab the bottle of sanitizer. As I do, she wrinkles up her nose.

"Jesus. You smell like sex. Did you come straight from a whorehouse?"

I feel myself flush, just a bit, because she caught me dead to rights.

Visions of the girl-on-girl action I was a part of just before I came here flash through my head. I hadn't taken the time for a second shower because I was late enough already.

Busted.

Jacey shakes her head in ... what? Disappointment? Disgust?

Before I can figure out her reaction, she walks away, breaking whatever moment we'd been having and leaving me staring after her in astonishment as she exits the room. No one ever walks away from me like that.

But she just did.

Not only that, but she's not looking back, either. She's not so impressed with who I am that she'll overlook any fault that I might have. Interesting…and unusual.

As I stare at her shoulder blades, I realize it's possible that there might be more to this girl than I thought.

∾

Yeah…no, there's probably not.

I decide this a few hours later as I walk into the parking lot at the end of my shift, after scrubbing toilets, refilling ice packs, and wiping graffiti off the wall.

It's clear that she's exactly like I thought she was.

Kaylie, the girl from the party the other night, is dressed in her tiny server's uniform, and she tosses a bag at Jacey as Jacey piles into Kaylie's little convertible.

Then, right in the parking lot, Jacey hunches down in the seat and changes her clothes.

Seriously?

I can't see anything, but I know what she's doing. And so would the boys in the gym, if any of them happened to look outside. What the fuck is she thinking? One leg extends high into the air, her toes pointed to the sky, as Jacey slips her workout shorts off and her tiny uniform shorts on. The flimsy material sliding over her long legs leaves little to the imagination.

Does she *want* to invite trouble? A boy's imagination is as good as the real thing, oftentimes better. So to give them a glimpse like this is only going to make them want to see more.

But maybe that's what she wants. And maybe that's why she's exactly the kind of girl I thought she was. An attention-whore and a tease, which makes total sense given her job.

I stop for a second and watch.

Because that's what I like to do.

Her shirt comes off, and I get a hint of a slender shoulder, the top of her bra, the curve of her arm. Then she's busy fastening the hooks of her skimpy corset, which pushes her tits upward and together, before she adjusts her yellow bowtie.

Something about the situation... the fact that Jacey is undressing in a very public place, the fact that I like to watch... and the fact that Jacey has a smoking-hot body incites a reaction from my dick and it hardens against my leg.

I hate that I react at all, physical or otherwise, because I wouldn't touch this girl with *Sin's* dick, let alone mine. There's trouble in the way she so clearly needs so much attention. I mean, she works a job where she is half-dressed for the pleasure of men, for god's sake. I want nothing to do with her, or anyone like her. Yet here I am with a stiff dick.

It's at this moment that she turns and tosses her bag into the tiny backseat and her eyes meet mine. She pauses, and I can almost hear the breath as it rushes over her lips with surprise. I can almost see the question in her dark eyes as they widen. *Did he just see me undress?*

But just as quickly as her eyes widen at seeing me, they narrow into a slant and fill with one thing as the car speeds out of the parking lot, the radio blasting.

Disdain.

I don't know whether to laugh or be annoyed. She's the one undressing in the parking lot of a youth center in front of testosterone-fueled boys and heading off to a job where she gets paid to flirt with men... not me. Her disdain should be for herself.

I feel like an old man as I tiredly crawl into my Porsche, letting my head rest against the seat for a second, absorbing the spring sun and the fresh breeze before I fire up the engine. As I do, my phone rings and Sin's name flashes on my screen.

"Yes?" I answer as I back out of my parking spot.

"Dude, I just found out that Amy Ashby is coming to my party tonight. Aren't you costarring with her in your next gig?"

"Seriously?" I have to admit, I'm surprised. Amy Ashby, super-starlet, hardly ever ventures out of California. She doesn't see the need. To her, all intelligent life ends at the California–Nevada border.

"Yeah," Sin answers. "She's dating a Blackhawk now, appar-ently, which is a shame because I'd like to motorboat those tits of hers. Are they real? I know you know. You had a sex scene with her in *Visceral Need*. I know you tapped that ass. You must've."

For just a second, I think about that film, the one that shot both me and Amy to superstardom. And of course, I think about that sex scene. It was my first on-screen sex scene and hers, too. We joked that we were popping each other's cherry. Her tits aren't real, but I don't tell Sin.

"You're ridiculous," I tell him instead. "And fuck, man. How many parties do you need to have a week?"

Sin chuckles. "Don't hate. But hey, I just thought of something. Is this going to cause a problem? Because Kira is coming tonight, too. I know that Amy likes to have your undivided attention—whether she has a boyfriend or not."

I sigh. "Amy is definitely high maintenance. But that shouldn't cause a problem with Kira, because she knows where she and I stand. We're convenient. That's it. But knowing it and *knowing* it are two different things, and she'll probably get jealous and throw some sort of fit. Why'd you invite her, anyway? I don't want to babysit."

"Because she wanted me to call her for my next party," Sin

replies, and I can almost hear him shrugging. It's not his problem, so he's not concerned. "And when the fuck did having a fuck-buddy turn into babysitting? Whatever, dude. We'll make it work."

An idea occurs to me and I grin.

"Oh, it'll work. I'll go home tonight for dinner. Mom's been wanting to feed me, anyway. Have fun at the party."

Sin starts to protest, but I hang up on him and turn the car around, heading the opposite direction toward Palos Park, the Chicago suburb that I grew up in.

The Chicago streets turn into the highway, which eventually runs through Palos Park. The quiet streets that I ran on when I was a kid surround me and I take in the quiet scenery as I drive through town to the country. Castle Kinkaide sits on ten acres outside of town and I can see the spire of the tower a mile away.

Honestly, I can't help but smile. For the most part, I had an awesome childhood and I have great memories of growing up out here in the middle of nowhere, in a house that everyone around considers a gigantic novelty.

As I pull onto the long drive, surrounded on both sides by flowering trees, I take a deep breath of country air and exhale it. I always forget how good it smells here, but returning brings back instant memories. Summer nights chasing lightning bugs, camping out with my dad and brothers, and swinging from a rope swing out by the stream.

It was a surprisingly rural upbringing in a town only a few miles from Chicago. As I climb out of my car, I hear Fiona and my mother . . . their voices drift toward me on the breeze, and I turn to find them walking from the garage into the house. *Fuck.*

How had I forgotten that Fiona is staying with my parents while her new condo downtown is being renovated? *Mother fuck.*

Fiona looks up and sees me first, and for the briefest of moments her eyes light up the way they usually do when she sees me. I've always been her favorite.

But not now. Now her expression immediately hardens and she pointedly looks in the other direction, a not-so-subtle way of reminding me that I'm on her shit list.

Whatever.

She's on *my* shit list. She can ignore me as long as she wants. I can guarantee that I've got more patience than she does.

As they walk up the steps into the house, Mom turns her head and drops the sack she's carrying as soon as she sees me. She runs toward me like she hasn't seen me in a year. It's only been a few months, but you'd think it was an eternity by the way she barrels into me and clutches me tight. Her head barely reaches my sternum, but she buries it there, her hands clasped behind me.

"Dominic James Kinkaide," she scolds. "You've been away too long this time. You're getting too thin. You're not eating."

She looks up at me, her blue eyes snapping. "You get yourself inside and wash up. Dinner's in thirty minutes, and you're going to eat everything I put on your plate."

She marches ahead of me, trying to pretend that she's angry and not happy to see me. But her eyes betray her, because when she stops to let me open the door for her, they're warm.

"It's about time you came home," she tells me as she walks past. "Go see your father. He's in the library."

Fiona ignores me so I ignore her, walking past her into the long hall that leads to the library that serves as my dad's study. When I round the doorway, I find him staring out the window, a glass of scotch in his hand.

"Hey, Dad," I greet him quietly. "Can I get one of those?"

My father turns his head and smiles at me, his temples a little grayer than the last time I was home.

"Hey, Dom. Sure, help yourself. It'll put hair on your chest."

I chuckle because it's the same thing he always says and help myself to a glass. The fiery liquid burns a trail down into my gut and I down the entire thing, then pour another.

"What happened the other night?" Dad asks without preamble. "You can't go around assaulting people. I don't care how pissed you are."

I shrug. "I just found out that Fiona's dating Cris. I don't appreciate it and I told her so."

Dad raises an eyebrow. "And then you showed Cris with your fists? I always told you, Dom . . . I don't want you to start things. You can always finish them, but don't start them."

I shake my head and set my glass down. "Cris started this long ago, Dad. And there's going to come a point where I need to finish it. For real."

My father levels his green gaze at me. "You ever going to tell us what the hell happened with you two? He spent almost as much time here growing up as you did. If there's something I need to know, I'd appreciate you telling me."

My gut tightens.

It's not that I don't want to tell them. It's that I can't. I can't fucking talk about it. Every time I try, the words freeze in my chest and they won't pass my tongue. They're just too fucking ugly to say.

My father raises an eyebrow. "Well?"

I shake my head. "It's between him and me. If Fiona doesn't want to listen, that's her problem."

Dad rolls his eyes and downs his whiskey. "I thought you'd say that. I'm sure you'll be happy to know that he's coming tonight. We didn't know *you* were or we wouldn't have invited him."

I stare at him dumbly. I shouldn't be surprised. I didn't even call to tell them I was coming. But still. It's my fucking home and I shouldn't have to tiptoe around wondering when and if Cris fucking Evans will be here.

Shit.

"Great," I mumble. "It's been good seeing you." I stand up and turn to walk out.

"Don't start that shit," my dad warns. "You should've called to tell us you were coming."

I know he's right, so I don't say anything. Instead, I excuse myself to call Tally.

"Any news?" I ask him. He sighs into the phone.

"They're not happy, but there's not much to be done about it. They'll delay filming and they'll film as much as they can without you. They're wanting you to come home on the weekends though, to film. You're gonna have to make that work."

"I'll get my lawyers on it," I answer. "I can't see that would be a problem. I don't have to be at Joe's on the weekends."

"What's it like, anyway?" Tally asks curiously. "Community service?"

I think about the dingy gym and roll my eyes.

"It's awesome," I answer sarcastically. "You should come and help."

"Nah, I think I'll just see you when you get your ass back here. Hurry it up. I'll tell the studio to expect you soon. I know Amy Ashby is pissed. This is going to throw off her schedule for her next film, too. You're going to have to smooth things over."

"She's actually at my brother's tonight," I tell him grudgingly. "I could've seen her, but I'll do it another time. I'm not in the mood."

"You're never in the mood," Tally grumbles. "That's why she's pissed at you."

That's also true. If Amy had her way, we'd rehearse our sex scenes in my trailer, down to licking each other's nipples and getting each other off. But I don't feel the need. And I just don't fucking want to. She's another one of those high-maintenance party girls who needs attention all the time. I just can't deal with that.

I hang up and head back down the hall, glancing at the framed family pictures as I pass. Pics of me, Sin, Duncan, Kira, Fiona, Cris... and Emma.

I stop for a second, the air whooshing from my lungs as I stare at Emma's sparkling blue eyes staring back at me from one particularly painful picture.

She's tanned and healthy, and she's wrapped her arm around my neck a second before my mom snapped the picture of us in our graduation caps. It was the last picture we'd taken together.

It was the last picture she'd ever take.

A knot forms in my throat as I stare at the necklace she's wearing, a gift I had given her. A happy-graduation/I-love-you/can't-wait-to-go-to-college-with-you gift. A teardrop-shaped aquamarine that perfectly matches the color of her eyes is encased in a white shell that she'd plucked from Lake Michigan. I'd had it made especially for her, and she'd worn it until the day she died.

I reach into my pocket and wrap my fingers around it, feeling the cool stone.

Her parents gave it to me afterward, and I've carried it in my pocket every day since... because it reminds me.

Of everything.

I gulp and yank my hand away from it, like it's a hot coal that will burn me. My problem is that I'm stuck in limbo...I don't want to remember and I don't want to forget. If I remember, it hurts like hell. But if I forget, it might happen again.

And that's one thing I know for sure.

I'll never let myself get fucked over like that again.

Chapter Eight

Dominic

As I head down the main hall to find my mom, I'm startled when Cris steps out of the kitchen doorway. I stop in my tracks for a moment, staring at him.

"Care to come outside? I'd like to talk to you," he says gruffly, his voice hesitant and filled with a thousand things I can't name.

His eye is swollen, which gives me some satisfaction.

"I have nothing to say to you," I answer finally. "So, no thanks."

I start to brush past him, but he grabs my arm in an effort to get me to stay. I look at him sharply, straight in the eye, a *get-your-fucking-hand-off-me* look, and he loosens his grip. I guess he learned his lesson the other night.

Fiona pops ups behind him, her face cautious and sullen.

"Please," Cris adds. "You need to hear this, but I don't think we should talk about it in here."

"Fuck you," I tell him abruptly, pushing past him to the dining room. "Fuck you."

"You're such a dick," Fiona snaps after me. But I ignore her. I just keep walking until I find my mom and I pause to kiss her on the forehead.

"I love you, but I won't come here when he's here."

She protests and grabs at me, but I walk past her, out into the yard and to my car. I ignore the way Fiona yells after me angrily, the way Cris stares at me as I leave, and the disappointed expression on my father's face. I ignore it all.

Because I'm Dominic fucking Kinkaide and nothing bothers me. Nothing touches me, because I won't let it.

Against my will, my eyes sting and I know they're red. I rub at them and then fire up the engine. Even though it's only nine P.M. and Sin's party will be going full force soon, I head back there... because I don't have anywhere else to go.

There's about a million cars lined up on Sin's property when I get there, and I almost want to turn around and drive back out. But I don't. Instead, I park in the garage and make my way into the house, picking my way through the dark.

I wind through the crowded rooms, making my way around the perimeter toward the staircase. As I reach the bottom step, I feel someone watching and I glance to the side.

Jacey is standing still in the middle of the room, dressed in her uniform, letting a party guest lick salt off of her forearm for a tequila shot. She's heavily made up tonight: thick mascara, red lipstick. She smiles up at him with those red lips, a fake smile, and as she does, she catches sight of me.

She freezes in shock, although, what the fuck? I'm the one living here temporarily. I belong here, she doesn't.

Suddenly, a guy comes rushing up to me, someone I don't know. A very drunk someone.

"Dude, can you sign my shirt for my girlfriend? If I take home your autograph, I'll get laid for a month."

He grabs at my arm and I shake him off in annoyance.

"*Dude.* If you were lucky enough to get invited here, then you should know not to approach anyone for autographs."

I'm not usually so rude to fans. But my mood gets the better of me. The guy stares at me, stunned, and I continue on my way. As I do, I feel Jacey's gaze.

She pulls her arm away from the guy, sets down her tray of shots, and makes a beeline for me.

I turn my back on her, intent on continuing up the stairs without acknowledging her, but she won't have it. She grabs my arm, forcing me to look at her.

"Are you all right?" she demands. "That was pretty harsh."

I glance down at her, into her brown eyes, and find her to be sincerely concerned. I must look seriously rattled if she noticed that something is wrong. She barely knows me. Her fingers are warm on my arm, and for a minute I waver.

She's warm and soft and concerned. I know what that might turn into.

A wild night that will make me feel better.

Women are all the same: they want to fix what is broken and they're willing to do anything to accomplish that. I never talk about my past or anything at all about me, but women can still sense that I'm fucked up. What they don't understand … is that I'm unfixable.

I stare down at her again, shaking my head.

"I'm fine. Don't worry about it."

But she looks at me again, really looks at me, her brown eyes probing mine. "I don't think you are. What happened?"

"Why does it matter to you?" I ask before I can stop myself.

Because something about her makes me think that it *does* somehow matter to her, and not just because I'm Dominic Kinkaide. Everything I've seen of Jacey is wild and untamed … she works for

Saffron, pushes cops around, gets dressed in parking lots, and lets men lick salt off her body for tequila shots.

Yet at the same time, she seems warm and real. I haven't forgotten how she shoved her way in between Cris and me and shielded my body with her own. She's a puzzle.

Jacey looks confused by my question.

"It matters because you're not some stranger off the street. You look seriously upset. Of course I'm going to ask you if you're all right. Who wouldn't?"

Most of the people I know in Hollywood, I think.

But I don't say it. Instead, I turn my back and start up the stairs again. I don't fucking answer to her or anyone else.

"Do you need anything?" Jacey's voice is hesitant behind me. "An ice pack or anything? That bruise on your cheek looks like it still hurts."

I pause, not looking at her. Instead I remember her bare leg, stretching toward the sky while her tiny uniform shorts slide over it. The mere memory of the way she'd undressed right out in the open sets my pulse to racing.

Yeah, there's a bunch of things I need, but only one thing that will take my mind off the reason that I need them.

"Yeah, I need something."

There is a moment of silence between us, then another.

Finally she asks, "And that is?"

I turn back around slowly, looking her up and down until my eyes freeze upon hers and stay there. Hers are dark and sincere, waiting for me to say something. She has no idea what kind of person I am. She has no idea that I'm just a shell, completely empty inside.

If she did, she would run far, far away.

I stare into her eyes as I move closer, and she doesn't look away.

I step back down until we're on the same step and her back is against the wall. I press against her, close enough that my rigid dick digs into her hip.

With my mouth mere centimeters from her ear, I say, "You. Spread-eagled and tied up on my bed. That would do for a start."

The mere thought of that, of how I'd shove my dick in her mouth and let her suck me off while her hands were bound, makes me hard.

Jacey sucks in a breath, but remains frozen. Her breath comes quickly, and mine is hot against her neck. I know it because I can feel it on my own lips. What I don't know is why I'm doing this.

Or why she hasn't said no yet.

Disgusted with myself *and* her, I turn away.

"Forget it. Go home. You don't want to play with me tonight, little girl. Trust me."

Jacey

Oh my god. What an asshole.

I don't watch Dominic walk away. Instead, I make my way back through the main hall, my cheeks flushed scarlet. I'm better than this. After Jared made me look like a weak-ass needy wench, I swore to myself I would have more self-respect.

I don't get used. Not anymore.

That Jacey is long gone, buried in a pile of therapist bills.

Then why didn't I say no to Dominic's ridiculous request?

Because for a brief second, I envisioned what being tied up on his bed would be like and warmth flooded my panties. Holy shit, I'm only human. And I'm a hot-blooded female.

And Dominic is *Dominic*.

I've seen him in enough movies, in enough love scenes, to know that his hands are magic. Even though he was acting, there was always such sensuality in his movement, in his eyes.

His eyes.

That darkness in Dominic's eyes...it does things to me. It makes me wonder what he's capable of. Or what *I* would be capable of with him. I can practically feel his whispers on my neck in the dark, his hands scraping my back, his fingertips scratching into me.

Oh my god. My cheeks flush even more. I don't know what's come over me, but it needs to stop.

Dominic is trouble. And I don't need any more trouble in my life. I'm turning over a new leaf and I'm making good choices. Dominic Kinkaide is a bad, bad choice.

Because Dominic Kinkaide does bad, bad things. I can see it in his eyes.

On a whim, I turn and glance behind me, searching for him in the crowd. He isn't hard to find.

He's standing at the top of the stairs overlooking the main floor like it's his kingdom, his arm wrapped around a slender brunette. In the ten seconds since I left him on the stairs, he's already found another woman to fuck with.

Dominic's eyes meet mine and the green in his seems to smolder as he very slowly, very purposefully grabs the girl's ass and grips it hard, pulling her into him, grinding her hips into his crotch.

The girl wraps her arms around his neck, burying her face there, inhaling him, and for a minute I wonder what that must be like. To be so close to someone so...dark. Someone who commands a room so totally and completely.

Dominic still hasn't taken his eyes off mine, and I know that he's doing this for my benefit. He's showing me what I could've had tonight, if I'd just said yes.

His eyes burn me.

So I do the only thing I can do to retain any little bit of self-respect.

I walk away.

Chapter Nine

Jacey

The sunshine is bright as I collapse into the seat of my car with my coffee and my purse. How the hell did morning come so fast? God. Is there anything worse than mornings?

I turn the key and realize that, yes, something is worse.

A morning when your car doesn't start and you're supposed to be on time for Joe's Gladiators or "you can forget about coming back in" is worse.

Fuck.

"You're a piece of shit." I berate my car as I turn the key again and again. But there's nothing. Only a depressing click that announces in its mechanical way that my engine is not only dead, it's really fucking dead.

Poor Brand. Because I do the only thing I ever know to do nowadays. I reach for my phone and call him.

"Yes?" he groans sleepily, forgoing a hello.

I quickly explain my predicament, and true to form, like a knight in a big-ass shining F-150, he rides to my rescue with a droll expression and bed-head.

I smile sheepishly as I climb into the truck.

"I'm so sorry to bother you," I tell him truthfully. "I just didn't know what to do. I have no idea what's wrong with my car and I could take the El, but I'm not sure where the closest stop is to the gym, and if I'm late, I'm done. Joe doesn't put up with that."

Brand shakes his head as he pulls back out into traffic. "Don't worry about it. I'd rather you not get into trouble again. Who needs sleep anyway?" His voice is husky and rough and if I had any doubts that I'd woken him up, I'd be over them now as I listen to his sleepy voice.

"I'm sorry," I tell him again. "I'll pay for your coffee this morning. How's that?"

Brand grins at me good-naturedly. "Deal."

I stare out the window, watching the Chicago bustle as it passes by. So far, there's no sign of the odd look that I'd seen in Brand's eyes the other night, and for that I'm thankful. I really, really just need for us to be normal. Unfortunately for Brand, *normal* always entails saving me from something.

"Do you ever get tired of bailing me out?" I muse aloud. "I know Gabe used to lecture me all the time. You never do."

"That's because I'm a saint," Brand announces as he turns onto a side street and heads his big truck toward the gym. "You can ask anyone."

I giggle. "I don't have to ask anyone. You put up with me, so you should definitely be canonized. I'm gonna have to talk to the pope about that."

"You're not Catholic," Brand points out as he turns into Joe's parking lot.

"I know," I answer. "I'm gonna have to turn on my charm."

"Good Lord." Brand shakes his head. "No need to give the man a heart attack. I'll be back to pick you up tonight. Call a tow truck to come get your car."

I'm kissing his cheek when I hear the roar of a car pull up next to us. The sound of that engine, powerful and loud, is unmistakable, and I know before I even look that it's Dom.

I murmur good-bye to Brand and glance at Dom as I climb from the truck. I can feel Brand staring after me, but I ignore it. I can't think about Brand at all, because frankly, whenever Dominic is near, he owns the vicinity.

He's dressed in black today: dark washed jeans and a tight black T-shirt that skims his chest just right. His green eyes somehow even look black as he stares at me, waiting for me to walk past. He takes in everything…the way I kissed Brand, the way I move from the truck, the way I try not to look at him.

His lip twitches, and once again I get the feeling that he *knows* me. Everything about me. It's disconcerting.

I walk past him and he follows. I can feel every step he takes, his presence behind me a tangible thing, like a force field of sexiness and arrogance. I do my best to ignore it.

When we reach the door, I pause, and he reaches around to grab it, opening it for me. As he does, I catch a whiff of his scent, something unique to him. Musky yet spicy, totally male. I inhale deeply as I walk in, never once looking back at him, even when I mutter thank you for holding the door.

I'm not falling for his sexier-than-thou attitude. Spread-eagled on his bed, my ass. He can kiss my ass right now.

I think I hear him chuckle as I lift my nose in the air, but I'm not sure. And I don't care. I make a beeline for Joe's office to find out what he wants me to do. Dominic follows me at a respectable distance, and together we get our marching orders from Joe, who seems especially crusty today.

"I want you to clean out the locker room," he tells Dominic tiredly before he looks at me. "And Jacey, you can help weigh the boys. We've got to get their weights logged so that they're official for the week. The clipboard is over there and the scale is in the locker room."

"Are you okay?" I ask Joe hesitantly as I reach for the clipboard. "You seem . . . tired."

He stares at me, his steely eyes cloudy. "Do I also seem like I have ovaries? If I want to chat like a girl, I'll let you know."

Burn.

My cheeks explode at the put-down, and I can practically feel Dominic smirking at me. I know Joe's bark is worse than his bite . . . but god. His bark is pretty bad.

"Noted," I answer quietly as I head for the locker room.

Dominic follows me silently.

He doesn't mention Joe's bad mood and I don't, either. I'm grateful for his silence because I feel a little humiliated at the moment. There's nothing worse than putting yourself out there, only to get stomped on.

We set to work, Dominic cleaning the walls and metal lockers, and me weighing giant, sweaty boys.

The entire time, I know exactly where Dominic is in the locker room, even if I'm not looking at him. I feel him. I feel his presence in relation to mine. I hear his breath, his movements. I smell his cologne. *I'm aware of him.* Regardless of how determined I am to ignore him, there's electricity between us, and I can't pretend it's not there.

I know he feels it, too, because every time I do glance at him, he seems to be looking at me, his dark, dark eyes holding something in them that I can't describe.

I gulp and scribble down a weight, then motion the next boy to step up.

Jake grins at me as he pretends to shield himself, his big boyish hands splayed in front of his chest.

"You're not gonna kick me today, are ya?" He laughs as he steps onto the scale. I move the counterbalance to get his accurate weight and roll my eyes.

"Two-eighteen. And no, not unless you try to grope me again."

He laughs and steps off. "I wasn't trying to grope you. That was just me saying hello."

"Huh." I sniff as I log his weight. "Try saying it with your mouth next time, instead of your hands."

He chuckles again. "You're all right, Jacey. For a chick."

I sniff again, but I smile at him this time. Joe did say that I just needed to show them who's boss. The other boys seemed to have learned from Jake's mistake, because they're all friendly to me now, and maybe even a little nervous. I smile at that thought and motion another boy up.

Time passes quickly, and before I know it, Joe comes in.

"You two." He motions toward Dom and me. "Come with me."

We glance at each other but follow Joe's lumbering steps as he leads us into the gym's kitchen. It's a large, older room with crudded-up corners and yellowed countertops.

"The kids out there, they don't usually have enough to eat," he tells us. "I try to make sure that they get something here, an after-school snack, I call it. But really, it's a meal. The walk-in needs to be cleaned up and the food needs to be organized. Throw anything bad out, but only if it's bad. I'm not made of money, and we need to be judicious with supplies. Got it?"

We both nod, and I'm impressed once again with Joe's heart, even if he did snap my head off.

He leaves us and Dom and I look around.

"Well, fuck." Dom sighs, glancing at the dented-in cooler door. "This is going to take a while."

I shrug. "Oh, well. I'd rather be busy than sitting around counting down the minutes till we go home."

"Well, okay then. After you, Princess." Dom gestures with a shrug, holding open the heavy metal door, allowing me to go first. "Don't trip on the rust. Jesus. I think these appliances were made in 1940."

He's right. The cooler is a relic, old and creaky. I don't even like to be near it, much less *in* it.

As we step inside, I automatically shiver, running my hands over my goose bump–covered arms as I look around at the haphazardly stacked shelves of food. It smells like stale food, standing water, and armpits in here.

"God. I don't think this place has been cleaned since 1940, either."

I poke at the food, some of it outdated and some of it fresh, and Dom sighs. "Well, this is gonna take a while. I can see that. We forgot the bucket and sponges. I'll be right back."

He turns back toward the dented door, but when he pushes down the handle, nothing happens.

"What the hell?" he mutters. He wiggles it harder, then puts his weight into it. I stare at him, dumbfounded, watching him struggle to open the door. Finally, he turns around and stares at me.

"We're locked in here."

I try not to freak out as I shrug and stare at the locked door.

"Don't worry. Joe will come hunting for us before he leaves. It'll be okay."

But Joe doesn't.

And it's not okay.

It's freaking cold. It's small. It smells like a swamp. And we're trapped.

We straighten the food on the shelves in an effort to move around so that we don't get too cold as we wait, but eventually we run out of things to do. And I've got goose bumps on every plane of my body, and still Joe doesn't come.

I bang on the door, the cold metal stinging my hands, but no one hears. I shout. But no one hears. I even kick the door. No one hears and no one comes. Finally, I slide to the floor dejectedly.

"Can we freeze to death in here?" I look up at Dominic, who is leaning against the wall, apparently calm.

He shakes his head. "Nah. It's a cooler, not a freezer. It won't be comfortable, but we won't die."

"When do you think someone will find us?" My voice is small and Dominic glances at me.

"It's hard to say. I don't know if Joe walks around and does a final check before he goes home at night, or not."

"Fuck." I sigh, letting my head fall backward against the wall.

"You can say that again," Dominic tells me as he slides down to sit next to me, letting his head rest against the wall, too.

"Fuuuck." I draw the word out for maximum impact. But it doesn't make me feel any better. For a second, the walls close in around me until something occurs to me.

"My cell phone!" I blurt, suddenly remembering that we're in the twenty-first century. I pull it out of my pocket, but am dejected yet again to find that I don't have a signal.

I look over to find Dominic shaking his head. "I don't have a signal, either. These walls on this cooler are thick and metal. Nothing's getting through it."

"I think the universe might be throwing us together," I finally answer, putting my cell back in my pocket.

I'm kidding, but Dominic smirks again, his trademark smirk... the one that made him famous. Even now he seems cool and calm, which is exactly the opposite of how I feel.

"Like fate?" he asks. "I don't believe in it. And if there *is* a Fate, she's a cruel bitch."

I stare at him because there's something in his face now, something vulnerable, just for a second. Something hurt. But then he covers it up and once again, he's a closed book. I can't help but be intrigued by these glimpses. There's so much more to Dominic Kinkaide than anyone knows. I can feel it.

"Well, we're stuck in here together. We might as well get to know each other," I tell him, in large part because of that look in his eye. "Because god only knows how long we'll be here, and the silence is killing me."

Dominic is already shaking his head. "No, thanks. I don't care to see the details of my life splashed across the tabloids tomorrow. But thanks anyway."

He crosses his arms over his chest and settles down, closing his eyes.

I shake my head, feeling a little sad at his outlook on life. "It must suck to be you," I tell him. "To always think the worst of people. You should know, not everyone is out to use you. Or exploit you. Just FYI."

He opens his eyes, raising an eyebrow. "Really? It's been my experience that generally, someone wants something from me. I'm a big one to learn from past experiences."

"I bet you are," I answer wryly. "Too bad it seems like not many of them were good."

Dominic scowls as he tries to get more comfortable on the floor next to me, his long legs crossing at the ankles.

"You don't know anything about me. You only know what my publicist manufactures for the public. Everything you know about me is engineered, perfectly placed, perfectly timed. It's all a game, Princess. The masses just don't know that."

The masses. As if the rest of the world is completely separate from him. Apparently, I'm part of the masses, along with everyone else, while Dominic is alone. In his mind, it's Dominic against the world.

Suddenly, I really do feel sorry for him. He might be rich, and he might be gorgeous, but he wears the utter weariness of his life on his face. It's clearly way too much for someone his age. It's like he's a hundred years old and he's just tired of it all.

"You know, if you don't like your life, you can change it," I tell him, my lip shivering with the cold. "You've got the world on a string. You can do anything you want. You realize that, right?"

Dominic stares at me, his green eyes gleaming in a dangerous way. "We work together for a couple days and you think you know me now?"

I ignore his sharp tone. "No. Of course not. But I know *of* you. And I can see a lot on your face. More than you'd probably like for me to."

He stares at me, his gaze unreadable. "Such as?"

I stare at him, appraising him. "You're jaded. And dark. And something has hurt you badly, something in your past. You think you're all alone and you're tired of everything."

Dominic breathes sharply, not taking his eyes off of mine. "You think you can see all that?"

I nod slowly, not breaking our gaze. "I know that I can. Want to talk about it?"

Dominic chuckles now, a humorless laugh. "Hell, no. Like I said, I don't need to see shit about myself in the tabloids. They publish enough lies about me. I don't need to give them truths to work with. Nice try, though."

I can feel heat from his body emanating from him and I scoot a bit closer.

"Sorry," I tell him when he glances at me. "I'm freaking cold. And you're warm."

"Fine," he answers, lifting his arm to wrap it around my shoulders. "But no pictures. I don't want this on any form of social media. Trust me, you don't, either. They'll hound you for weeks."

I roll my eyes. "I know that might be what you're used to, but taking a picture with you is the last thing on my mind at this point. All I can care about is not losing my fingers and toes to hypothermia."

"Has anyone ever told you that you're a bit melodramatic?" Dominic asks dryly, although his arm does tighten a bit around my shoulders.

I chuckle, but don't reply. I enjoy sitting with him for several minutes before the silence starts to gnaw at me.

"Okay. This quiet is killing me. You might not want to talk," I tell him. "But I'm going to distract myself. Let's play Twenty Questions."

Dominic rolls his eyes, then closes them. "Go for it."

"Did you have a good childhood?"

He doesn't open his eyes. "No comment."

I chew on my lip. "Okay. Have you ever had a crush on a costar?"

I look at him, but he still doesn't open his eyes. "No comment," he answers again.

I hesitate, dying to ask him something, but terrified to do it. But in typical Jacey Vincent fashion, I barge ahead and do it anyway. "That girl you were with at the party . . . was that Emma?"

He completely tenses up, I can see every muscle freeze as he opens his eyes and stares at me. "How do you know about Emma?"

The look on his face is almost frightening in its intensity. "Your sister mentioned her the night we met," I answer slowly. "You were smacked in the head, so you probably don't remember."

I watch a myriad of things cross his face—confusion, sadness, pain, and something else dark that I can't identify—before he finally shakes his head. "No. And I have no other fucking comment."

The mood around us has turned as dark as Dominic's expression, and I'm not sure what to do about it. His reaction is fascinating, but I'm sure not going to press him for more, not if the mere mention of the girl turns his mood so black. So instead I change the subject.

"What's it like being Sin Kinkaide's brother?"

He stares at me drolly now, the ugliness gone from his eyes. "You should ask *him* what it's like to be *my* brother."

I shake my head, amused by his arrogance. "I would, but I'm trapped in here with you, not him. And you're not cooperating in this game."

Dominic smiles slowly. "You're very astute, Princess. That's because I don't want to play. Unless I get to ask you the questions. That would be more fun."

I shrug. "Fine. Shoot. You ask me, I'll answer."

He stares at me. "Are you high maintenance?"

I smile. "That's an easy one. No."

"Do you dream in color?"

I roll my eyes. "You're not even trying now. I think everyone dreams in color. I've never heard of anyone dreaming in black and white. In fact, I had the weirdest dream the other night, and it was in full color. I dreamed that it was raining, but that the raindrops turned into pink rose petals. And then when I looked at the ground, it was covered in a foot of petals, just like snow."

Dominic raises an eyebrow. "So, you romanticize precipitation. Interesting."

I smile. "I romanticize everything. That's just me."

Dominic shakes his head. "That'll probably get you into trouble."

I stare at him. "I think I already told you. It's my nature to like trouble. I'm trying not to, but it goes against my grain. Next question."

"Why did you get between me and Cris? You could've been seriously hurt... even more than you were. "

Dominic is staring at me now with interest, genuine curiosity in his eyes. I shake my head.

"Because I'm a human being," I answer. "I think anyone would step in and try to keep two people from killing each other. It's the decent thing to do."

"Are you decent?" Dominic's lip twitches.

I smile. "Sometimes."

"Why did you and your last boyfriend break up? Was he trouble?"

Holy shit. His abrupt change of direction sends a knife through my gut, because the answer to that question is ugly.

Jared was definitely trouble and he killed someone I love.

But I don't say that. Instead, I murmur, "No comment."

Dominic rolls his eyes. "Then this game isn't so fun. Why don't you just tell me about your childhood or some shit?"

So I do. *Anything to get what Jared did out of my head...To not think of those images. The crumpled truck, the blood spatters, the screams when Maddy came to the accident scene.*

I talk myself blue in the face to get that shit out of my head.

I tell Dom about my childhood and what it was like growing up with Gabe and my suck-ass parents. I tell him about Brand and how he's always been like my brother. I tell him how I used to work in the summers for my best friend, Maddy, but then she married my brother and moved to Connecticut. When I pause to take a breath, Dom has his eyes open again, staring at me.

"That big blond guy is like your brother?" he asks doubtfully. "That's a strange sibling relationship."

His tone is weird and I narrow my eyes. "What are you implying?"

He shrugs. "Nothing. I just sense some incest there, is all."

I literally shudder. "That's fucking gross. Brand taught me to ride a bike."

Dom just looks at me. "All I know is that the way that guy looks at you is far from brotherly. I know what I know."

A weird feeling passes through me, because I *have* been ignoring that new look in Brand's eye. I keep hoping that I'll never see it again, but deep down, I know that I will. And deep down, I know that Dom is right.

"Well, it's nice of you to notice," I tell him snippily. "But you *don't* know what you don't know. And you're wrong."

"I'm rarely wrong," he answers arrogantly. I can see that he really believes that.

"Does everyone around you always tell you what you want to hear?" I demand. "Do they tell you that you're a genius, that you're perfect, and that you're never wrong?"

"They don't have to tell me." He smirks.

Because he already knows. I gag a little and roll my eyes.

"Have they ever told you that you're arrogant?"

He nods, the corner of his mouth twitching a bit. "That might have been mentioned," he admits. I can tell that he doesn't care.

I settle more fully into the crook of his arm, enjoying the way his woodsy scent envelops me, even in the cold air.

"What's it like to film a movie?" I ask conversationally, changing the subject.

I have to talk about something or I'll go out of my mind. I could swear the cooler has gotten smaller since we've been trapped in here. Dominic closes his eyes again and his fingers rest against my side. I don't think he even notices, but I certainly do.

"It's fine," he tells me. "I'm not much of a people person, but even though millions of people see me on-screen, it doesn't seem like that when we're filming."

"So you're an introvert?" I ask with interest.

He nods without opening his eyes. "Most definitely. My brothers got the extrovert genes."

"Ah, yes. The badass rockers. They definitely seem to love the limelight. Is that it . . . two brothers and one sister?"

"Yeah." He nods. "That's it."

"You're lucky," I tell him. "All I have is Gabe."

"And he's the only one who counts because your parents are worthless?" Dominic asks with interest, repeating my words from earlier. It's the first time he actually seems interested.

"So you *were* listening!" I nudge him. And he smiles. A real smile, the first time I've seen it on him. I decide that it's well worth the wait. His smile almost warms the room up all by itself, like the heavens opened up and the light shone down on us through the clouds.

"I couldn't help but listen," he tells me, his eyes almost warm. "You weren't going to shut up and I can't go anywhere."

I giggle and he smiles, and for a second we seem like friends.

"Why exactly are your parents worthless?" he asks after a minute. I'm surprised that he would go out of his way to ask, so even though it makes me uncomfortable, I answer.

"My mom never really wanted to be a mom and she's not good at it. When she and my dad got divorced, she took it as an opportunity to do whatever she wants to do. She has a new boyfriend every week. I rarely hear from my dad. He always thought it was enough to just send my mom a child-support check."

A stab of pain slices through me as I admit it out loud. It's like announcing to the world, *Hey, there's something so wrong with me that my parents don't care if I'm alive.* But Dominic doesn't seem to see it that way.

"Their loss." He shrugs. "That's what I tell myself whenever I hear a bad review or someone totally disses me. It's their loss. Not yours."

"If you really believe that, then I admire you," I tell him. "I guess I've got thinner skin than that."

"Well, there's your first mistake," he answers. "You've got to grow some thick skin. Or some balls."

"I've got balls," I announce. "They're made of steel."

Dominic laughs. "Really? This I've got to see."

In a flurry of sudden movement, his arm snakes around my waist, finding its way to my crotch. With one hand on my back holding me in place, he strokes me with the other, just for a second. The heat from his palm melds with the heat between my legs, and a million needles shoot down into my legs, weakening my knees.

I gasp and my eyes meet his, and I'm frozen as my heart pounds and my fingers shake.

"It appears that you don't, in fact, have balls," he tells me quietly, without removing his hand from my crotch.

"It was a figure of speech," I croak needlessly, although of course he knows that. "You can move your hand now."

"Oh, can I?" His voice is velvet, smooth as butter.

Instead of moving it away, his fingers move against me and my nerve endings burst into flame, spreading a fire from my crotch to my thighs to my chest.

Why aren't I moving away from him?

The simple answer is: I don't want to. I should want to… Dominic Kinkaide is an asshole most of the time. But holy shit, he's a sexy asshole. And to be quite honest, I don't think I could move to save my life. It's like I'm suspended here, dangling from the tips of his fingers.

He lowers his head and his lips graze my ear.

"Still want me to move? Because I know an excellent way to keep warm."

My breath hitches again, at the intimacy in his tone, at the warmth of his lips, at the way my heart has taken off in my chest. I open my mouth to say something and nothing comes out.

Dominic moves his fingers again, rubbing me on the outside of my pants, urging me toward a precipice that I'm not sure I want to climb toward. Not with him. Yet I can't move away. I gulp.

"You want to," he says knowingly. "You're wet. I can feel it through your clothes."

Very purposefully, just like he does everything else, he holds his fingers up like a trophy, his eyes glued to mine. As I watch in astonishment, he raises them to his nose and inhales them.

"Are you feeling warm yet?"

I watch his lips as he speaks the words, husky and low. His lips are full yet manly, and suddenly I ache to lean over and press mine to his, to touch them in any way that I can.

But I don't.

Because I'm not a girl who gets used. Not anymore.

"No, not at all."

But Dominic takes that as a challenge. He's not used to hearing the word *no* and he's not about to start now. I see that in his dark eyes a scant moment before he dips his head and consumes my mouth.

I say *consume* instead of *kiss*, because that's what he does.

He consumes me.

His lips are fiery and hot and he kisses me with a fierceness that touches a secret part of me, moist, hot, firm, sexy. I want to inhale him, to suck him down. I vaguely feel his hands on my back, his warmth emanating through my clothes, his hardness pushing into my softness.

I'm breathless when he pulls away.

"What about now?"

For the life of me, I'm afraid to answer that. Instead I pull away, just a bit, just enough that there is some space between us, but I can still absorb his warmth. As my teeth chatter, both from the cold and from the sudden absence of his lips, I answer.

"I'm good."

He laughs, a husky, low, *naughty* sound.

"Oh, I'm sure of that."

And just like that, I'm drawn back in…in toward his sexy smile, his arrogant gaze, and his knowing smirk. He's bad for me. Very bad for me. I've got to remember that.

He will decimate you, I tell myself.

But my problem is, every time I look into his dark eyes and see the mysterious things that lurk there, I forget that. I forget everything that is supposed to matter.

Chapter Ten

Dominic

Burying my hand in Jacey's crotch makes my balls swell and my dick harden.

It's true.

The idea that she's *good* turns my thoughts to a place I shouldn't be thinking about. It makes me want to find out how good she actually is.

Jacey stares at me in fascination, and for some reason I want to bask in that look, to lay in it for hours, to soak it in. Mainly because she's not looking at me that way because of who I am; she's looking at me because of *how I'm making her feel*. Her eyes are wide and innocent and soft.

I like that.

"Let's get warm, Jacey," I suggest, my meaning very clear as my hand slides to her thigh, where my fingers dig into her leg, kneading it.

"No," she stammers. "I can't. I—"

Suddenly the cooler door opens, bringing with it a rush of warm air. The humidity of it hits me in the face and I raise my head (and my hand) in surprise.

"What the hell?" Joe barks, his harsh voice a sharp interruption as he sticks his gray head in and glares at us, as if we chose to be stuck in here. "Get out of there. We've been hunting for you."

Jacey's startled brown eyes meet mine, then she looks at Joe.

"Sorry, Joe," she tells him as she scrambles to her feet. "We got locked in. Thank you for rescuing us."

He stares at her, then at me. "There better not be any funny business going on under this roof," he finally says. "There's a time and a place for that—and it's not here and now."

Jacey's cheeks flush bright red, and for a split second I think about what would have happened if Joe had shown up a few minutes earlier and found me with my hand buried between Jacey's legs.

I'm pretty sure he would've considered that "funny business," although it was far from funny. *Far* from funny. Somehow, being locked in that tiny room with her made me lower my guard. I forgot, for a minute, who she is and who I am. Who we are in relation to each other—and the answer to that is nothing. We're *nothing* to each other.

We follow Joe out and I keep my eyes glued to his plaid-covered back, my resolve returning. I can feel Jacey staring at me, but I don't return the look. She almost sucked me in back there, with her soft eyes and her laugh that seems genuine.

That's not gonna happen, though. Fuck that. I steel myself against it, against her, pissed at myself for my moment of weakness. *I don't get involved with people.* Jesus.

"Your ride's here," Joe tells Jacey, turning a bit to look at her. "If it weren't for that big dude coming in to look for you, you'd have been stuck in here all night. You're lucky."

Lucky. As we follow him through the gym and then say good-bye and head out to the parking lot, I don't know if lucky is what I feel, even if I am pissed with myself for momentarily lowering my guard.

As I watch Jacey approach that big-ass truck of her "almost-brother's," I can't help but marvel at how different she is from everyone else I know.

Yet at the same time, she's the same. Because she greets the blond hulk with a kiss on the cheek, and as she turns her head and I look into her eyes, I see that I was right. The guy is seriously into her, and she knows it.

And still she lets him haul her around, using him for what he can give her.

Typical woman.

I sigh and open my car door, and for the briefest of seconds I know that something isn't right. There's a shadow in my car, something in the dark that shouldn't be … but I don't have time to really register that before Kira materializes in front of me as the streetlight overhead shines on her face.

Startled, I take a quick step back, my heart pounding. Kira's perched in my driver's seat, her legs curled under her as she grins widely up at me.

"What the fuck?" I manage to get out as I stare down at her in the dark, calming myself and pretending that she didn't just startle the shit out of me. "What are you doing here?"

She's wearing a thigh-length trench coat, cinched at the middle. Her cleavage is spilling from the top. From the mischievous look in her eyes, I have a feeling the coat might be the only thing she's wearing. As she unfolds herself from the car, the belt comes loose, and I get a glimpse of tan skin and nothing else.

I was right.

She leaps from the seat and presses herself against me, wrapping her arms around my neck, her skin smelling like coconut and perfume.

"What took you so long?" she whines. "I was dying of boredom out here. I wanted to surprise you, but damn. I was running out of patience. You know I don't have much in the first place."

Her curvy body folds into me and my body reacts, hardening again. The girl is wearing almost nothing, after all, and I'm only human. Skin is skin and tits are tits, no matter who is wearing them. But as I look over Kira's shoulder, I find Jacey staring at us through her passenger window, and her expression is indefinable.

Hurt? Anger? Disgust? Annoyance?

I don't know. I also don't know why I care.

But I must, in some way or form, because my dick softens and I'm staring after the truck as it drives away with Jacey inside.

"What's wrong?" Kira asks suddenly, pulling away, noticing the change down below. She grabs at me, cupping my balls, kneading them, but I'm not into it and my dick stays limp.

I shake my head. "I don't know. I'm just tired. Not in the mood, I guess."

She raises a perfectly waxed eyebrow. "Since when are you not in the mood to be groped in a public parking lot? I'm naked under this jacket, you know. This is all for you, Dominic."

I know. For a minute, that knowledge, the knowledge that I can have Kira any time I want, weighs on me. It takes the excitement out of what might've been a fun situation. Now, if it'd been Jacey here in my car . . . I quickly put that out of my mind and shrug.

"I'm sorry, Kira. I'm tired and not in the mood. I'll take a rain check."

And with that, I get into my car, leaving Kira standing alone. I roll my window down.

"You'd better get going," I advise her, ignoring her surprised (and pissed) expression. "This isn't a good neighborhood."

I roll the window back up, stifling her sputtering indignation. I watch her climb into her car and wait for her to start it up before I drive from the parking lot, immune to her irritation. There's one thing about me. I don't lie and I don't pussyfoot around. I'm not in the mood for Kira and I'm not going to lie about it.

I rev the engine, enjoying the way it vibrates my foot through the accelerator pedal. The vibration hums in my leg and the Porsche makes short work of the roads leading to Sin's house. For once, his massive house is quiet. I'm relieved as I slip through the halls, thinking that for the first time ever, I'm the only one here aside from the staff. However, as I walk past the main living room, I hear giggling and I pause in the darkened doorway.

Of course I'm not alone. What was I thinking?

Sin raises his head from where he's lounging with two women in a mess of tangled arms and legs and bare skin. One is somehow dangling around his shoulders, and the other has her head in his lap. The room smells like sex, but for some reason he's still got his pants on. For that, I'm thankful.

"Hey, bro," he greets me, his hair standing up in spikes. "Look. Two girls—one for each of us." He waves his hand as if he's bestowing the greatest gift on me, then examines the two girls. He nods at the brunette draped over his shoulders. "You can go with him."

Her face brightens at the prospect, but before she can answer, I shake my head quickly. "No, I'm good. I'm tired. But thanks anyway."

Before I walk away, I see Sin's index finger, the one with the thick silver ring on it, the one with the horns, disappear into the depths of the brunette's pussy. She throws her head back and moans and I can see that she has already forgotten about the idea of being with me.

Good. I turn my back on the whole thing without a backward

glance. Normally, I enjoy watching. But not while my fucking brother is involved.

Jesus.

I seriously might have to get my place. I don't know if I can take ninety days here.

I pad upstairs and down the hall, where I collapse onto my bed and stare at the ceiling. Try as I might to clear my mind, all I can do is think about one thing.

Jacey.

I'm not sure what it is about her that fascinates me so much, whether it's the fact that she doesn't give a shit who I am or whether it's the fact that she doesn't try to hide who *she* is. She's an open book.

You ask, I'll answer, she'd said. Yet I know that there's a lot to her that I don't even know to ask about. Plus, she's not so self-involved that she demands that you listen to her talk about herself. And she doesn't care if you take her or leave her.

I flip on the stereo and turn it up to drown out my thoughts. Hard rock screams at me, thumping and loud. But it doesn't really help.

Instead, I just picture Jacey's tight ass wrapping itself around a stripper's pole to the music. No, she would probably never do such a thing in real life. But this is why a man's fantasies are so good. In my head, she'll do whatever I want her to do. And my imagination is vivid.

After a minute, there's loud banging on my door. "Turn that fucking shit off! You know I hate Jagged Edge. You know they fucked with me last year at Lollapalooza."

I roll my eyes. "Go fuck something, Sin," I call back.

He bangs one more time on my door, then he's gone, and all there is the bass thumping the walls, leaving me free to think about Jacey again.

I slip my hand into my pants as I think about the way her pussy smelled, the way she folded around me, warm and soft, as I fingered her through her clothes. I picture the astonished and embarrassed look on her face when Joe barged in and I can't help but laugh.

Maybe one of the things I like about her is that she seems innocent at the same time as she seems wild and unrestrained. She has an almost childlike gullibility that seems so different from the people I'm used to.

But one thing is for sure. If she is distracting me this much, I've got to stop thinking about her, because I'm never going to get close to anyone again. Fuck that. I'll never give anyone that kind of power over me.

Never.

Again.

I pull my hand out of my pants and roll over, closing my eyes, letting the music surround me as I get lost in the raging beat.

I think one last conscious thought before I slip away into the oblivion of sleep.

Fuck you, Emma.

❧

Days pass at the gym and I slip into a routine, one day running into the next as I try to serve out my fucking sentence and get the hell out of this place.

Each day, I stay a respectable distance from Jacey. I'm civil, but not friendly. I'm detached, but I still watch her from a distance. I never acknowledge what happened in the cooler…our conversation or the intimate way I'd touched her…and the way she'd let me.

She fascinates the hell out of me because I can't help but want to figure her out. She's contradictory, and something about that pulls me to her. But I can't let her know that.

She seems hurt at first when I ignore her, but then she cools toward me. She makes a point of not looking at me, and whenever she can help it she avoids being in the same room with me. That's the way it ought to be.

Today, I head toward Joe's office and stop outside the door when I hear him on the phone.

"Yeah, I know what I owe. It's my accountant's fault. He told me what to pay and I paid it. I don't do my own taxes. What kind of fool does that?" There's a pause and a sigh. "Yeah, I understand. One way or the other, you'll have it by the first."

The phone slams onto his desk and I'm still for a moment.

No wonder Joe has been crabby lately. He's having tax trouble. I file that away in my head and round the corner, entering his office like I didn't just hear his conversation.

"What?" he demands, swirling in his chair to stare at me.

"I just needed to get the clipboard for the weights," I tell him, grabbing it from its hook and heading toward the door.

"Kinkaide!" he barks, and I pause. "You going back to California over the weekend?" he demands.

I nod. "Just for the weekend. My lawyers finally got it arranged. I've got to get some filming in so the studio doesn't fire me."

"Not my problem," Joe answers. "Just make sure you're not late to work on Monday."

So much for being nice. I nod wordlessly and head back toward the locker-room scales.

Jacey looks up from where she's talking to a couple of the boys, Jake and Tig. It's the first time she's made eye contact with me in a couple of days, and even though at first her expression is cool, her brow furrows as she stares at me.

"You okay?" she asks. "You look pissed."

I nod.

"I'm fine," I answer, just as cool.

Jacey stares at me for a minute longer before she returns her attention to the boys, turning her body away from me.

As she moves, I can't help but notice her slender shoulders and her tight-ass top, stretched tautly across her tits. It's impossible not to notice, and Tig can't restrain himself. I notice him continually glancing down before he yanks his gaze back up to her face. His cheeks flush red, even though no one but me notices.

When Jacey walks away a few minutes later, I follow her.

"You might not want to wear that shit here," I mention to her. I know my tone isn't friendly, but I can't help it. She's being ridiculous dressing like that in a gym for troubled teen boys.

She raises an eyebrow. "What shit?"

I motion toward her with my hand. "Tight tops, short shorts. Look around you and remember where you're at. You're surrounded by teenage boys who get a hard-on in a stiff breeze. Surely you don't need attention so badly that you need to use these kids to get it."

Heat flares into her cheeks and they turn bright red as she glares at me.

"What the *fuck* is wrong with you?" she demands. "You're so hot and cold. You haven't bothered to talk to me for days, and now, even though I haven't done shit to you, you don't hesitate to snap my head off for no reason. Why the hell do you care what I wear?"

I feel a small twinge of guilt. She's right. It's not my business. But somewhere, in a deep down place that I don't want to acknowledge, I hate the fact that these kids are ogling her. I know what they're doing in their beds at night while they're thinking about her.

I hate that thought. I hate that in my head, she's mine to play with, mine to discard, mine to balance in the palm of my hand...

just like I did in the cooler last week. In my head, she's an option...
an option I can choose at any moment, but an option I'd be smart
to ignore.

"Well?" Jacey stares at me. "Why do you care?"

"I *don't*." I shrug. "I just don't want any of them to say something inappropriate to you and then get into trouble. You're inviting
the wrong kind of attention, Jacey. It's not fair to them."

She narrows her eyes. "Oh, it's all about them for you now,
right? I can tell that by the way you never talk to any of them. You
think they're beneath you—just like your view on the rest of the
world. You need to get over yourself."

She stomps off and I stare at her tight ass as she does.

"She's got a temper," Jake observes from where he's changing his
shirt nearby. "I like it."

I stare at him, a hard and level gaze. "Don't even think about it.
You're jailbait for her."

The kid rolls his eyes. "You've gotta lighten up, man. I was just
making an observation. Jacey's badass."

He grabs his bag and ducks out of the room, and I notice something. Jacey's cell phone is lying on the bench where she was sitting
as she was talking to Jake. I know it's hers by the pink flowered case.

I walk over and grab it, sliding it into my pocket. Something
about it makes me smile. Pink flowers. Like her pink gun. Jake was
right. Jacey's pretty badass. Yet she has a softer side. And she's all
woman, sexy as hell.

She's a puzzle...and one I get more fascinated with every day.
The more I think about it, the more I know what I have to do.

I just need to get to know her. If I give her a chance, she'll disappoint me, like everyone else. And then my fascination will be over
and I can go about life as normal, as the jaded asshole that I am.

But a little while later, after I've finished weighing the rest of the boys and set off to find her, I discover that she's already gone.

"Her boyfriend already picked her up," Joe tells me when I ask. "You're outta luck."

Her boyfriend/surrogate brother. I roll my eyes and feel oddly disappointed.

"I have her phone," I explain to Joe. "She left it in the locker room. I don't suppose you have her address, do you? I know she lives in Calumet Heights somewhere. I could drop it by her house on my way home. I doubt she'll want to be without it."

"Yeah, I can get it for you. You should let her worry about it, in my opinion. Then she'd be more careful with her stuff. But if you want to…"

His voice trails off as he hunts for her file, then scribbles the address on a sticky note.

"Don't share that with the boys," he says needlessly.

As if I would. I nod and leave, and within a few minutes the nose of my car is turned in the direction of Calumet Heights.

It's time to exercise my option.

Chapter Eleven

Dominic

I pull up in front of a tiny little house, encased on either side by identical tiny houses.

The handkerchief-sized front lawn is encircled by a short metal fence, and daffodils line the front sidewalk. There's a pair of beat-up running shoes beside the door, well used and dirty, and a black-and-white decorative sign is hanging next to the door topped with a pink bow.

No Soliciting! My soul doesn't need saving, I hate magazines, and I already have a vacuum (I just don't use it much). Unless you're selling Thin Mints, I'm not interested.

It makes me smile because it's so Jacey, blunt and to the point.

I rap on the door and she appears, her face in total shock at seeing me on her porch. She's dressed in her tiny Saffron outfit already, although I know there's no way she's been home for long.

"I don't have any Thin Mints, but I thought you might be interested anyway." I smile my most charming grin, but she stares back at me straight-faced, not cracking a smile.

"What do you need, Dominic?" She sighs. She doesn't even bother asking me how I got her address.

"I was in the neighborhood. And thought I'd bring you back your phone."

I slide it out of my pocket and offer it to her. She's clearly puzzled as she takes it, her fingers colliding with mine for a minute before she yanks them away.

"Thanks," she says uncertainly. "But this isn't in your neighborhood. Not by a long shot."

"Whatever," I answer casually. "I thought you might want it."

"I can't believe I left it," she admits. "It hardly ever leaves my side, because I can't afford to lose my stuff. Thank you for bringing it. I'm running late for work, or I would invite you in."

She looks at me pointedly now, and I glance at her up and down, at the sexy bustier that positions her tits just right, to her barely-there boy shorts, to the yellow bowtie. She stares at me expectantly, waiting for me to leave, but I don't.

It's been a long time since I do what I do next.

"Call in sick," I suggest. "I'm bored. Let's go do something."

As soon as the words are out, I regret them. I'm shocked by them. I want to rush to take them back, but I'm too collected for that. Instead, I want her to turn me down, yet at the same time, I'm eager for her answer.

Deep down, I want to spend more time with her.

Even though I don't *want* to want to.

She narrows her eyes again. "What about your girlfriend? I think she'd have something to say about us doing something together."

My girlfriend? I'm confused, but then I remember Kira. Jacey's seen me with her a couple of times...in fact, she thought Kira was Emma. I swallow hard.

"I don't have a girlfriend," I answer, although I don't offer an explanation about who Kira is to me. That's my business.

Jacey stares at me wordlessly, probably trying to decide if she believes me or not.

"Come on," I urge her. "Let's blow this place."

Jacey sighs. "Why should I? You're an asshole, Dominic. I never know what's going to set you off or when you're going to snap my head off. It's not a game I like playing. In case you haven't noticed, being around you isn't really a treat. I thought we were getting along, and then all of a sudden, you act like I don't exist. I don't get you. I really don't."

I feel guilty again, just a little, because I know she's right. I am an asshole. And most of the time, I don't care.

But there's hurt in her eyes, real hurt, and that's something I haven't seen in a while. Most people I'm around have thicker skin and they're almost as jaded as I am. Sometimes I forget that Hollywood is practically in a different dimension from the rest of the world...and those of us who live there are pretty much alien creatures.

"I'm sorry," I tell her. "Sometimes, I'm an asshole without meaning to be. Sometimes, I do mean to be. It's true. But I'm sorry that I was an asshole to you. I could explain, but it would bore you. Let me make it up to you. Let's go do something fun and touristy. I promise to be nice."

She pauses and I smile, flashing her my trademark grin, the one that chicks eat up. It's not her fault that I'm an asshole. And even though she's all swagger and talk, I can see that she's easily wounded. She just hides it. Like the rest of us, she puts on a front.

She wears a mask.

With another grin, and before I can think the better of it, I decide to take that mask off of her. To see what lies behind it. To see if she's really as different as she seems to be.

It will be an experiment of sorts. I'm not getting sucked in, I'm not getting involved. It's just an experiment for scientific purposes… to see if there can possibly be one decent human being left in the world. And I'm guessing my dick is going to enjoy this experiment.

Jacey rolls her eyes at my expression.

"Don't even try it," she warns. "I can see through you. Don't try to charm me."

I grin again and I can see her give in.

"Fine." She sighs. "But only because I'm tired and I really don't want to work anyway. I was going in today to cover for someone else. I've been picking up too many extra shifts. It's wearing me out. I need a break."

That's not the reason though. I can see it on her face. She's as intrigued by me as I am by her. The difference is… she's not as good at hiding it or keeping her distance.

"Come in," she gestures. "I'll call and then change my clothes. Where do you want to go?"

I think for a minute, trying to decide on somewhere I can get lost, somewhere I won't stand out. "How about Navy Pier? We can find pretty much anything to do there. And we can get something to eat."

"'K," she answers, showing me to her tiny but neat living room while she punches a number into her phone. "Make yourself comfortable."

As she talks to her boss, I look around. The space, like many Chicago houses and condos, is small. It's neat, though, and she's got it furnished with chic, eclectic furnishings. I'm guessing she saved up her paychecks for them because they're quality pieces.

She hangs up the phone, staring at me cautiously. "Okay. I don't know why I'm doing this, but I've called off. I'll be ready in a minute."

She disappears into her bedroom and I wait for exactly one minute, then follow.

Why? I don't know. But I walk quietly into her doorway and stand there, watching as she bends in front of me.

Her slender back is bare as she bends to slide off her work shorts. Even though she isn't very tall, she's got the grace of a ballerina. Her thighs are long and slim, her calves perfectly shaped. Her skin is golden and smooth, and all of a sudden I just want to run my hands up the length of them, grip her ass hard enough to leave marks and…

"What the hell?" Jacey's voice snaps me out of my fantasy.

I grin as she turns around, at her outraged expression as her hands cover her tits. I can still see them though, full and lush, as they spill around her hands, her pink nipples poking through her fingers.

"I told you I'd be ready in a minute. And by that, I meant to wait in the living room."

She's standing in front of me now, confident and sassy, her bare chest pushed out and her eyes snapping.

"Settle down," I tell her. "I was just taking a tour of your house." I scan the little bedroom with its black-and-white décor, then focus again on her. "I like your bedroom. It's got nice scenery."

And by *nice scenery*, I, of course, mean her tits.

She grits her teeth. "Get out of here. I'll be out in a minute."

I laugh and she glares at me, tucking her hands even more firmly around her chest, and I duck back out, dropping onto her sofa to wait. I entertain myself with my memory of her bare body until she comes out a few minutes later, dressed in short cutoffs and a tight white T-shirt.

"One question," I request with a smirk.

She raises her eyebrow.

"Are you wearing panties now?"

Because she wasn't before. An image of her bare ass bent over in front of me flashes through my head and sends the blood rushing to my dick.

Her cheeks explode into color, effectively answering my question, and she glares at me again.

"What prompted this?" she demands, ignoring my very valid question as she sits to strap on some weird strappy sandals that lace around her calves. "Why are you really here? This doesn't seem like you. Except for the invading my bedroom part. That totally seems like you. But I'm sure you didn't come all the way over here just to catch a glimpse of my ass."

I stare at her thoughtfully.

"I don't know. You've got a pretty nice ass."

She stares at me, unfazed, and I grin.

"I don't know, if you want the truth. I'm bored. I don't want to hang out with Sin or Duncan and I like talking to you. You treat me like a normal person. And unlike my brother, you usually wear clothes. Although, if you feel like taking your clothes off, I won't complain."

She ignores that part. "You *are* a normal person. My grandpa told me once that no one is better than me, that everyone is the same—some just have more important jobs. That's why you don't intimidate me...because you're not better than me. And for the record, I kind of like talking to you, too. When you're not snapping my head off, anyway. I like that you don't bother blowing smoke up my ass about anything. You just tell me like it is."

I nod. "That's kind of how I am."

"I like it," she answers approvingly. "It's refreshing."

Which is ironic, since that's exactly how I think of her.

Refreshing.

We walk outside and I open the passenger door of the Porsche for her and she slides in, her legs spreading before she tucks them into the car. I get a shot of her crotch up the leg of one of her shorts. That's how short her shorts are, and it answers my earlier question.

She's not wearing panties.

It sends my pulse racing, which annoys me.

This girl doesn't affect me. It's just that I'm bored and have nothing better to do. I'm killing time while I'm stuck in Chicago. Nothing more, nothing less.

As I grip the steering wheel and stare at the road, I decide that it's a bad fucking thing when you have to try to convince yourself of something.

We find a parking spot in one of the garages and I pull a ball cap on, just as a precaution. I'm not as likely to get spotted here as I am in California, because no one is expecting to see me here. People are on celebrity high alert in Hollywood. But it doesn't hurt to be careful.

We quickly lose ourselves in the crush of people on the pier, and as I push through them, I realize that I've lost Jacey. Looking back, I find that she's just a few steps behind me.

The breeze from the lake, brisk and cool, has blown her hair away from her face, and to be honest, she looks like a runway model.

"What do you want to do first?" I ask politely. "When was the last time you were here?"

She shakes her head. "Forever ago. I was a teenager. I hate fighting the crowds."

I stare around us. "Let's do a boat ride. What do you think?"

"Speedboat or cruise tour?" she asks, wrinkling up her nose.

"Definitely speedboat," I answer, staring at the sign that advertises "Thrill Ride Speedboat" tours. "The faster, the better. Just like I like my women."

Jacey rolls her eyes.

"Speedboat it is," she agrees, ignoring what I said about fast women. I laugh as I head to the ticket booth.

"I'll take all the tickets for your next boat ride," I tell the girl quickly. She stares at me dumbly.

"All of them?" she repeats slowly. Then she looks at me more closely, and I can see the recognition on her face. "Holy cow. Are you—"

"Yes," I interrupt her. "But that's our secret, all right?"

She nods, wonderstruck, and I sigh.

"Can I buy out the tour?" I prompt her. She shakes her head, bringing herself back to the matter at hand, then clicks on a computer. "I've already sold a few, but I can rearrange them to a later tour," she tells me shyly.

I wink at her. "Thank you. I really appreciate it."

She blushes. "Can I have your autograph?"

I hear Jacey tittering behind me, because clearly she doesn't feel my autograph is a valuable commodity. I ignore her and sign the paper that the cashier shoves toward me, then I hand her my credit card and purchase the tickets. When I'm done, I turn to Jacey.

"Can I have your autograph?" she asks mockingly, grinning from ear to ear. I stare at her.

"Well, I don't see any paper . . . so I'd happily sign your tits."

Once again, her cheeks burst into flame, and I decide that I like making her blush. "Do you have a marker?" I add mischievously. "I can sign them right now, if you want. I know you're not shy."

"How about we just go get a drink while we wait for our tour,"

Jacey suggests, her cheeks still pink. "I could use a drink to deal with you, and we've got half an hour to kill."

I shrug. "That's not as fun as autographing your body parts, but as you wish."

We grab a drink at a nearby bar, sitting in a dark corner, out of the fray. As I hand Jacey her frozen margarita, she stares at me.

"Do you always do things like buy out tours?" she asks politely, taking a sip of her drink. I watch her lips form a vacuum around the straw before I answer.

"If I can. I prefer not to have to interact with the public much. And yeah, before you lecture me, I know I am where I am because of them. But you don't understand. Women actually faint sometimes when they meet me. *You* don't, but I'm not lying. Some do. I'd rather not deal with that."

Jacey fiddles with her straw. "Well, in their defense, I'll just tell you that you're an intimidating person. It's easy to get overwhelmed by who you are and forget that you're a real person, not just a name. But if you don't like what you do, with all the attention and everything, then why do you do it?" she asks curiously. "It doesn't seem like something you should've gotten into if you don't like attention."

She has a valid point, and, of course, it's one I've thought of many times over the last few years. But honestly, I do what I do because it's fantastic money. So I tell her that.

"Money isn't everything," she announces sagely.

"Says the waitress." I sigh. "No offense, but it's easy to say that money isn't everything if you don't have it. Unfortunately, my tastes have evolved over the years and I need money to support them."

Jacey crosses her legs and I stare at her ankle, then her calf, then her thigh. I follow the slender length of it all the way up to where it junctures into her crotch. That's when I look away, before I start thinking about the fact that she's not wearing panties.

When I look up, Jacey's staring at me, watching me check her out.

"And what are your tastes now?" she asks hesitantly, her eyes probing mine. I smile what I imagine to be a wolfish smile.

Leaning toward her, I answer.

"Would you like to find out?"

I think back to the cooler incident, when my hand was buried between her legs, and I can see on her face that she's thinking of it, too. She sputters, leans back, then grabs her drink. Sucking on the straw, she regains her composure.

"How did you even get into acting?" she asks conversationally, ignoring my previous question and my wandering eyes.

"I went to the University of Chicago," I tell her as I settle back into my seat. "While I was there, a talent scout liked my look, and he was searching for an unknown to work on *Visceral Need*. The rest is history."

She raises her eyebrow. "So you weren't even trying to be an actor?" she asks incredulously. "Do you know how many starving waiters are out there, just trying to get a break in the acting world?"

Yes, I do. But that's not my problem.

I push my chair back.

"We've gotta go," I tell her instead. "We're gonna be late."

"Yeah," she agrees, standing up. "We don't want to inconvenience the other passengers."

She snorts and I lead the way, and once we're out in the sun again, Jacey turns to me.

"For the record," she says sassily, "I might have let you sign my boobs back then... back before you became cocky... when you were an 'unknown' normal person. It's okay to be 'normal,' you know."

And with that, she flounces down the gangway and onto the bright yellow boat. I stare after her and she looks back over her shoulder with a grin.

"Coming?"

"Babe, when I come, you'll know," I spout back. She grins and I grin back, like we're both normal people with dirty senses of humor, and I follow her onto the boat.

When we sit down, she slips her hand into mine, her fingers small and slender. I startle for a minute at the familiar and intimate gesture, but then the boat engine starts up and we rip across the bay with the wind in our faces. All of a sudden, it feels perfectly normal to sit with her like this, with her hand in my lap.

It's a thought that scares the shit out of me, like literally *scares* me. My pulse beats faster, it's hard to swallow, and my palms get clammy.

When I can, I pull my hand away and tuck it into my pocket instead.

I'm not normal, so there's no way in hell I should pretend to be.

Chapter Twelve

Jacey

I fight not to roll my eyes at Dominic as we glide over the top of the lake in the speedboat. He yanks his hand away from mine so fast you'd have thought my palm was burning him. I was just being friendly. Jesus. And seriously. He's the one who showed up at my house out of the blue. I didn't ask him to come, and I certainly didn't ask him to invite me here on this... date? Is this a date?

I don't know what the hell this is, to be honest.

The tour guide speaks into his mic excitedly, probably just happy to have Dominic on his boat. He stands at the front while we lounge in the back. Since there are at least twenty empty seats in front of us, I feel kind of silly.

The driver of the boat races through the bay and out onto open water, spinning in huge circles and causing a spray of water to drench me.

"Did I mention that I'm glad you wore that T-shirt?" Dominic asks with a grin. My T-shirt is white. And wet. And perfectly transparent at this point. I sigh.

"You're sort of a dog, you know that?" I ask him.

I'm just getting ready to ask about the girl he was with in the parking lot the other night, when suddenly the tour guide points toward another tour boat. Dominic and I turn to look and find it speeding up to get closer to us. All of the passengers are standing, craning their necks to see in our boat, cameras in hand.

"I think you've been spotted," our tour guide says apologetically.

I look immediately at Dominic and his face has tightened. He looks pissed as he nods curtly.

"Can you take us back to the pier? If we don't head back, they'll chase us around the lake. We can get off this boat a lot faster than they can all get off theirs."

The captain nods and whips the boat around, speeding once again toward the shore. I look over my shoulder to find the other boat chasing us. My stomach does a somersault. To me, it's a little exhilarating because this isn't something that happens to me all the time. They're right on our tail and excitement snaps in the air around us.

I mean, *someone is chasing us.* Oh my god.

But as I look at Dominic, I can see that excitement is the very last thing he's feeling. His chiseled features are twisted into a scowl and he just looks…tired. Beautiful, sexy…and tired. I swallow and feel guilty for being excited because this must be frustrating for him. It must happen everywhere he goes.

"When we dock, we're going to have to run, okay?" Dominic tells me quietly, his dark eyes stormy and focused on my face. "Seriously. Just follow me."

I nod, fascinated by this entire situation…by the novelty of it, by the annoyance Dominic feels, by the rush of wind over my face as our boats race toward the shore. We're going so fast that we slam into the water as we crest each wave, jarring my teeth. But we're back at the pier within a minute.

The large boat nudges the bumpers against the dock, and almost before it stops moving, Dom has leapt from the boat, grabbing my hand and helping me climb out. And then we run.

Ducking through the crowds, we weave in and out of people until we've made our way to the iconic Ferris wheel that stands proudly against the Navy Pier horizon. Dom glances at it, then heads straight for it. Throwing some money at the guy manning the line, Dominic utters, "Tell them we went the other direction."

The guy stares at Dominic in surprise, but then recognition and understanding quickly flood his face and he nods, ushering us through the little gate, and we drop onto the seat of a gondola.

As the large covered gondola lifts into the air, I peer over the edge, my face pressed against the glass. I can see a couple of passengers from the tour boat running around, looking about, but the gondola operator comes through for us. He points in the other direction and the fans take off, hunting for any sign of Dominic.

It seems that we made our escape. I settle into the seat and stare at Dominic.

"And I really wanted to take that tour, too." I smirk, but he grimaces.

"I'm sorry," he tells me seriously. "And I'm sorry that you had to run in those shoes."

I glance down at my feet. Honestly, it hadn't bothered me. I'm a chick who wears five-inch heels all of the time. I can run in flat sandals.

"Not a problem," I tell him. "And I'm fine with ditching the boat. No biggie. I'm sorry for you—I know you were looking forward to your fast boat ride."

He shrugs, then grins. "That's all right. I've still got a shot with a fast woman."

I roll my eyes, shaking my head. "I don't know what you think about me, but I'm pretty sure you've got it wrong. I'm not a slut. Do I like sex? Yeah. Of course I do. Do I fuck everyone I come into contact with? Of course not."

He slides around the seats of the gondola until he's sitting next to me. Even though the gondola is large, having all of our weight balanced on one side tips the car a little and I grab the edge, panicked.

Dominic laughs. "Afraid of heights?"

I shake my head, staring over the edge again. "No. I'm afraid of falling to an early death."

"Oh, I won't let anything hurt you," he says smoothly, and slides his arm around my shoulders. For a minute, the mood changes and I believe him. I can feel the muscle of his arm pulled taut against my back, and I know that if he wanted, he could protect me from all harm.

But it's hard to say what Dominic wants...his mood changes with the wind.

"Why did you come to my house?" I ask him curiously, staring up at him, still nestled in the crook of his arm. He's mere inches away, which makes it hard to concentrate. His thigh is pressed firmly against mine, sexiness exuding from every pore. I try seriously hard not to be impressed with him, but shit. He's Dominic fucking Kinkaide. And he's here with me.

Right now.

If I think about it, it's daunting. So I try not to think about it.

He stares at me, laughter in his green eyes. "Why? Can't I be spontaneous every once in a while?"

"Of course you can." I sniff. "But you don't even like me. You think that I got you into trouble with that pot and I'm the whole reason that you're stuck in Chicago. I didn't, by the way."

"It doesn't really matter anymore what happened," he answers easily. "It could've been Sin, for all I know. All that matters is that

I'm stuck here. And since I am, I felt like making the most of it this afternoon. I was in the mood to have a little fun."

"And has your mood changed?" I ask curiously. Getting chased by a boatful of rabid fans could understandably do that to a person.

He levels a gaze at me, one full of dark and naughty things, and I take a quick breath.

"No."

With that, he reaches his other arm around me, his fingers playing with the hem of my frayed denim shorts, his skin on mine. "I've been wanting to do this since you bent over in front of me in your bedroom," he whispers. "Your ass was bare and tight and I just wanted to plunge my dick into it."

The world freezes and I inhale sharply as I stare into his eyes. Did he really just say that?

"Into my ass?" I ask breathlessly.

He nods. "You'd like it," he answers knowingly, reaching around to slide his fingers under my leg, cupping my ass as he pulls me closer to him.

His fingers are strong, and long and for a minute I think about the naughtiness of what he's suggesting. Why I'm not moving away from him, I don't know. But I'm planted firmly in this seat and I don't want to go anywhere.

I swallow hard. "I've . . . um, never done that."

He laughs, a velvety sound. "Babe, I could show you a bunch of things you've never done. And I guarantee you'd like every one of them."

For some reason, I have no doubt of that. It's an exciting thought.

He bends his head and nips at my neck, then soothes the bite with a soft suck. His lips, so soft and smooth, ease the pain of the bite away. His nearness is intoxicating, and everything about him screams that he is capable of so many things...things that would please me...things that would embarrass me in the light of day.

But still, I don't move. I stay right with him, my gaze frozen on his.

Keeping his eyes on mine, he slowly dips his head and plunges his tongue into my mouth, completely plundering it, consuming me yet again. It's like he can't kiss me without devastating all of my senses at once, annihilating my thoughts and causing my blood to throb as it all races toward one destination...the V between my legs.

Right where I ache for him.

He's like a drug...and one taste just isn't enough.

I open up my mouth and breathe around his lips, sucking in air, grasping at his back and pulling him closer. He reaches back and grabs my hands, holding them together at my wrists and pinning them over my head against the Plexiglas gondola cage. I'm trapped here with him, yet there's no place I'd rather be.

The energy around us now is primal and raw...and it's exhilarating, too, because we're out in public. Every time the gondola swoops along the ground before it begins its upward ascent, anyone could look in and see what we're doing. They could see Dominic pinning me against the wall, and his other hand buried in my crotch, if only they looked closely.

Honestly, I think he might like that idea.

"What are you doing?" I finally manage to whisper, pulling away just ever so slightly.

His eyes are a little unfocused, his pupils dilated. "What would you like for me to do, Jacey?"

He knows. Oh, god, he knows. He knows exactly what I'd like for him to do. I can see it in his eyes. I can feel it in his hands as he releases my wrists and slides both of his hands down, over every curve and plane of my body.

He takes his time, sliding his palms down, down, down… everywhere at once, slow and leisurely. He palms my curves, savoring them. He's firm, slow, and purposeful…someone who knows what he's doing and what he wants.

I twitch when he passes over my nipples. They're hypersensitive in my cold, wet shirt. He barely brushes them before he trails farther down, down my sides, over the swell of my hips. I want to buck against him when his hands cup my breasts as he pulls me toward him.

I don't need to, though. He slips his fingers under my shorts because he knows I'm not wearing underwear. He slips those long fingers in, all the way in, into me.

Into where I'm waiting for him.

I moan long and low. He's feeding the fire he slowly built inside of me and I don't ever want him to stop.

I glance up and everything around is a blur. We swoop past the ride operator on the ground, past the crowds, past the food smells and the sunshine, past the sidewalks and the shops. All of it is a blur and none of it matters.

The only thing that matters is what shouldn't.

Him.

He shoves up my shirt and pulls one cup of my bra down, licking at my nipple, teasing it until it's standing up at full attention, as erect as his dick is. I can feel him, hard and rigid, pushing into my leg. But he doesn't rub against me. He doesn't act feverish, like me; he acts calm and controlled, slow and easy. He's not asking for anything in return, he just plays with me with his mouth.

His tongue is wet against my skin, against my nipple, against me. It's hot and moist, and just when I'm ready to beg him to fuck me in this very public place—suspended 150 feet in the air—he stops.

Just like that.

"We should go," he says quietly, his arms collapsing casually back into his lap. Like we're just sitting here, taking a normal ride on the Ferris wheel.

I yank my head up and realize that we're coming to a stop on the ground. The ride is over. I pull my shirt down and stare at him, trying to focus my blurry eyes.

Seriously?

He's unaffected as he climbs from the gondola and holds his hand out to me, waiting for me to let him help me from the car. I pointedly ignore his hand, choosing to dismount all on my own with my rubbery legs that feel like jelly.

Oh my god, I've never felt so humiliated, because I'm so affected and he's so . . . not. It's so easy for him to turn it on and off, to stay so fucking detached. My cheeks burn as I follow him down the sidewalks of the pier, as I focus on his broad shoulders swaying through the crowd, at the back of his neck, at his hips.

Everything about him is unfazed.

And I'm an idiot.

I totally just let him play with me. In public. And for what purpose? So that he'd have a fun distraction from the people that were chasing us in the streets?

Fuck that. I'm no one's distraction and I should've known better.

We get into the car without speaking and we drive silently down the streets of Chicago. Several minutes pass before he even glances at me.

"What's wrong?" he asks innocently, as if he doesn't know.

I glare at him.

"What the fuck was that about?" I demand, although I'm

madder at myself than him. I let him do that. I let him fuck with me. After all of the lectures I've given myself over the past few months about having more self-respect, I let him finger-fuck me on a Ferris wheel. I'm pathetic.

"What was what?" he asks, staring sideways at me. "It was just…having a good time. You seemed to enjoy yourself."

I glance at his crotch, remembering the way his hardness had strained into me just moments before.

"You seemed to, as well," I remind him. "But why? I don't understand you at all. The entire world isn't your plaything, Dominic. *I'm* not your plaything."

"I never said you were," he answers easily as he turns onto my street. "You didn't say no. If you didn't want to participate, all you had to do was say the word."

And that's what pisses me off. I didn't say the word. I didn't say the word because I wanted him.

I want him still.

That's why I'm so pissed. I want a man who couldn't care less if he's with me or not. He couldn't care less how I react, how I feel. It's exactly the kind of thing that I always do, and it always gets me into trouble.

I've. Got. To. Stop.

I grit my teeth and open my car door.

"Want me to come in?" Dominic asks, raising an eyebrow. He looks so relaxed behind the wheel, stretched out and casual. Not hot and bothered like me. I don't affect him in the same way, and that pisses me off.

And crushes me.

"No." I answer curtly. Leaning into the car, I pause for just a minute. "Thank you for an interesting day."

I slam the car door and take joy out of his startled expression.

Apparently, no one slams doors into Dominic's face, because he looks absolutely stunned.

This makes me smile as I unlock my door and head into the house. I toss my purse down and head into the kitchen, where I immediately pop the cork on a bottle of red and drink several gulps straight from the bottle.

When my fingers have stopped shaking, I pour myself a glass and head to the bathroom, where I run a bubble bath and soak away my agitation.

The smells of lavender and vanilla assail my senses, soothing away my stress. Or so I hope. But try as I might, I can't get Dominic's face out of my head. I can't forget the way his hands felt, the way his fingers slipped so easily inside of me. The astonished expression on his face when I stalked away from his car.

There's something to be said for surprising someone and putting them in their place. And Dominic needed to be taken down a few notches. He's too arrogant by half.

I'm toweling off, still smiling about that, when the doorbell rings. Puzzled, I pull on my robe and pad down the hall to answer it.

Dominic stands in front of me, casual and sexy and bigger than life, a bottle of wine dangling from his hand.

"I don't take no for an answer very well," he says with a slow grin. His trademark sexy grin. The one that drops panties. The one that turns my knees weak even though I'm pissed at him, even though I want to tell him that my *no* means no. That I don't want him here.

But that isn't true. I *do* want him here. And when it comes to him, my *no* doesn't mean anything at all.

Chapter Thirteen

Dominic

I'm a hostage of my hormones. Or of my fucking fascination with this girl. And why? She's just a girl. Blond, big-busted chicks are a dime a dozen in Hollywood. What's so fucking special about this one?

But as I stare at her...I don't see a blond, big-busted chick. I don't see a Hollywood chick. I see a girl, naïve and feisty, who is standing in her doorway in a pink fuzzy robe with an innocent expression, her pink lips slightly parted. Her brown eyes are wide, and there's something in them that says, *I want to trust you. Don't make me regret it.*

And I want to tell her not to fucking trust me, not ever, because I *will* fucking hurt her. After everything she's revealed to me about herself, I know that I'm the last thing she needs. She needs someone who is everything I'm not.

But of course I don't say that. I can't...because something in me pulls me to her, and I'm too selfish to resist it. So instead, I hold out the bottle of wine.

"Just a glass of wine. That's it. I promise to keep my hands to myself, unless you ask me not to."

She looks at me. "Hmm. I don't think I should."

I roll my eyes with a sigh. "Trust me. I'm not going to do anything you don't want."

"Maybe that's what I'm afraid of," she answers softly. I'm startled, staring at her, but she opens the door wide and gestures me in.

She leads me to the kitchen where I see an open bottle of wine already on the counter, but she ignores it. Instead, she grabs a corkscrew, and when she turns back around she finds that I have trapped her in the corner. We're both in the small space, so close I can practically hear her heart beat. I can definitely feel the heat emanating from her body. She takes a breath, and I take a step back, holding up my hands.

"See? I come in peace."

She grins and grabs the bottle from me, popping the cork and pouring a couple of glasses. I watch the red liquid sloshing against the sides of the crystal glass as I carry mine to the living room. We both drop onto the sofa, and Jacey turns toward me, curling her legs beneath her.

"So. Is this your M.O. with all the girls? You pretend to hate them, then you seduce them into the sack?" She smiles and takes a sip of her wine, but I can see in her eyes that it wasn't completely a joke. She's as confused by my behavior as I am.

I laugh it off. "Yeah, it usually works like a charm. How's it working for you?"

She shakes her head, not gracing that with an answer, instead giving me a direct look and following the look with a very direct question.

"Who was that girl, Dominic? The one at the party. She was the same one in the parking lot. She means something to you and you definitely mean something to her." She pauses and swallows, then looks back at me. "I like spending time with you—when you're not biting my head off—but not if you belong to someone else."

I scoff at that. I can't help it.

"I don't belong to anyone," I answer wryly. "And trust me, few people 'mean something to me.' That girl…her name's Kira, and I grew up with her. She's been a friend for a really long time."

"Do you make out with all your friends?" Jacey answers dubiously. She stretches her leg out, and I can't help but watch as her robe falls slightly open and I can see even more of her thigh.

"No," I tell her, reluctantly pulling my eyes up to her face. "Not generally."

I feel a twinge at the thought of Kira. Not because I'm cheating on anyone, because I'm not. But because Kira has called about ten times this week and I haven't returned her calls. Whenever I'm in town, she puts her life on hold, always making sure that she makes herself available to me.

My thoughts are dangerously close to guilt, which annoys me, so I shove them aside. I don't deserve to feel guilty. Booty calls with me are a choice Kira makes. I don't force her, by any means.

"So you're not dating her?" Jacey confirms slowly, her eyes still doubtful.

"I'm not dating her," I promise. Because I'm not. Fucking her up the ass, yes. Tying her up and coming on her face? Yes. Whipping her? Teasing her? Sucking on her? Biting her? Yes to all. But dating her? No. And I'm not above using semantics to get around a question.

"Did you mean what you said…few people mean anything to you?" Jacey asks hesitantly, her hand wrapped tightly around her glass. "Because that's really sad, Dominic."

I stare at her harshly. "Don't judge me, Jacey. You have no idea what it's like to be me. You don't know what's happened in my life, you don't know how people try to use me. Trust me, it's just easier to not give people the chance."

She sniffs. "Whatever. I get that you're on a different plane from the rest of us mortals, but still. People are people. And everyone needs other people. And everyone gets hurt in life and everyone gets used. We have to get over it and move on. If you let people who have hurt you or used you or pissed you off influence your actions, you're letting them win, Dominic."

I stare at her, at the way her jaw is set and her face is determined. "Says a person with experience," I answer with interest. "What happened to you, Jacey?"

She blushes now, something that only makes me want to know more. With a quick flip of her hand, she downs the rest of her wine, then pours herself another glass. I notice that her hand is shaking and I raise my eyebrow.

"What happened to you?" I ask again, softly this time.

She shakes her head. "Nothing. I'm just a dumbass who always picks the wrong guy. Over and over. It's a pattern."

Yet her hand is still shaking as she takes a large gulp of her drink. I shake my head.

"Uh-uh, that's not bad enough to put that look on your face. Something else happened."

I'm not sure that I care so much as I'm curious. But either way, I want to know. Jacey sighs and stares out the window, not looking at me.

"It's *bad enough* because it's a pattern, Dominic. I've got some issues. I'll just tell you that right now. And because of those issues, I usually fall for the wrong guys."

I'm intrigued as I stare at her. "But that time it was worse somehow. What happened to make it worse?"

Jacey sighs, looking away from me.

"I fell for the devil himself. My friends, my brother...they all tried to help me keep away from him, but eventually, like the dumbass I am, I went back to him because I fell for his line of shit. And one day, he did something terrible. Really, really terrible, and it fucked up everyone around me. Is that bad enough for you?"

I'm not sure what he did, but clearly it wasn't pretty. Jacey's face is pale and grave and sad and I don't push her anymore. Instead, I simply nod.

"That's bad enough."

A tear runs down Jacey's cheek and she wipes it away quickly, burying her face into her wineglass, refusing to look at me.

"And that's why I made a pact with myself. No more choosing the wrong guy. I'm working on myself and I'm not going to settle for anyone less than the perfect person for me. Someone who values me and won't push me around. That includes you."

I reach out and turn her chin toward me, forcing her to look at me.

"I don't remember offering to be with you," I remind her gently. "Jacey, I'm not a good person for you. Not in the long run, not for real. What I'm interested in is someone to hang out with while I'm here, someone to have fun with and someone to keep me company. What I'm *really* interested in is seeing if you're as decent of a person as you seem . . . because I'm at the point where I doubt that anyone actually is. That's it. I'm very, very capable of hurting you . . . but not if you don't let me."

She looks at me with watery eyes. "I'm not decent, Dominic. I can tell you that right now. A decent person wouldn't have let Jared get anywhere near me or my family, much less dated him. But you can bet your ass that I won't let you hurt me. I won't get attached to you. I've already promised myself that."

I nod. "So let's see if you can keep that promise. You want to see if you can hang out with me and not get attached to the wrong kind of guy yet again, and I want to see if there is one decent person in the world. It's a win-win situation. I can make you feel good and you can do the same for me. It sounds like we both need it." I pause, staring at her.

She stares back.

"So it's a no strings attached, you like me, I like you, win-win situation. I won't fall for you, Dominic." Her voice is calm and even.

"I don't want you to," I tell her just as evenly. "That's the whole point. Come on. Take the challenge. Let's see if you can do this."

"And let's show you that there really are decent people in the world," she answers stubbornly. "Because there are."

"Whatever." I shake my head. "I'll believe it when I see it. You'll just have to show me."

"Deal." She nods. "I will."

I lean forward a little, staring into Jacey's dark eyes.

"So . . . now that that's settled, do you want me to make you feel good?"

My words are loaded, my meaning quite clear. I emphasize it by gripping her thigh, hard, with my fingers. When I take away my hand, there is a white mark on her leg.

She's fascinated by that. She looks at the mark, then looks at me.

"Yes," she murmurs.

"That's all I need to hear," I tell her quietly. "It's my favorite word."

Her back arches as I pull her into me and she molds into my body. Hers is soft and small, her arms thin bands that close around my back. I flip her around so that she's back on the couch, her spine pushed into the cushions. With my eyes locked on hers, I part her legs with my knee.

She opens them hesitantly.

"Are you wet for me, Jacey? Could you possibly be wet for me already?" I ask, raising an eyebrow as I trail one finger down her chest, opening her robe with it.

She's displayed now, in the sunlight, her tits pointing to the ceiling, her hips bucked upward. I trail my finger downward and around her nipple and she moans. But I don't stop there. I continue down, over her hip, across her flat belly, and down to her pussy.

I trail that one finger over the tiny nub of her clit.

She twitches into me, but I still just keep that one finger there, rubbing that little swollen bump.

"You *are* wet," I point out. "For me. What would you like to do about that?"

"Surprise me," she breathes.

I chuckle lightly, slipping that one finger into the folds of her pussy, into her body where I move it… in, out, slow. She throws her head back and I add a finger.

"Wrong answer," I tell her softly, leaning over to kiss and suck her neck. I'm being gentle with her now, easy. The hard stuff will come later. "You've got to tell me what you want."

Her eyes glaze over as I rub her, as I stroke her, as she grows even wetter. She swallows hard, I can hear it.

"Fuck me," she says simply. "Make me feel good."

I chuckle again, even though my groin tightens at her words.

"You have to wait for that, Princess."

She opens her eyes. "Why?"

She pauses her movement, her hips suspended against me.

"Because that's the way I work. I don't jump into the sack with just anyone."

I don't jump into the sack with anyone. At all. But of course I don't say that. She'll soon learn that 'fucking' me has a very different definition from what she probably assumes.

"But I'll still make you feel good," I add.

I get to my feet and pick her up, scooping her easily into my arms. She wraps her arms around my neck, but we don't go far. I carry her into her bedroom and drop her onto the bed, where she bounces, then rolls over.

"How do you want me?" she purrs. "Spread-eagled?"

I smile, remembering when I'd told her that earlier, a couple weeks ago. "Yes. On your back. Do you have any scarves?"

She looks puzzled but gestures to her top dresser drawer, where I find a heap of silk scarves. She looks hesitant when I climb over her on the bed and straddle her, lifting her arms above her head.

"Do you trust me?"

She looks unsure. "I barely know you."

I stare into her eyes. "But do you think I'd physically harm you?"

She doesn't hesitate, she just shakes her head.

"Good. Because I would never. Not unless you ask me to. If you ever say the word no, it's all over. I'll immediately stop what I'm doing. Got it?"

She nods.

"I'm going to tie your hands and feet to your bed frame. And you're going to like it. Yes or no?"

She stares at me in confusion. "How do I know if I'll like it?"

I stare back and repeat myself slowly. "I'm going to tie you. And you're going to like it. Yes or no?"

I ask it with more emphasis this time, more force.

"Yes," she finally whispers. And I can see on her face that she believes it. I smile as I peel off her robe, then bind her hands, then her feet.

She's totally immobile now, spread out on the bed like a gorgeous offering. Her full tits point toward the ceiling, amazingly perky for being natural. Coming from Hollywood, it's rare for me to find real tits nowadays.

I crawl up over her, her curves rubbing against my dick, hardening it. I nip at her neck and whisper into her ear. "I'm going to blindfold you. And you're going to like it. Yes or no?"

Her lips almost tremble as she replies, "Yes."

I smile again, then bend and tie a black scarf around her head, covering her eyes.

"You trust me not to hurt you, because I would never physically harm you. Not unless you ask for it. Yes or no?"

I'm trailing my fingers along her torso now, over her ribs, along her sides. I watch the goose bumps form as she whispers softly.

"Yes."

I smile, then kiss her hard. I feel my teeth against her lips, her tongue automatically plunging into my mouth. Her lips open for me, sucking me down. She wants more. She shows it with every movement.

I bend my head, trailing my lips along the silkiness of her skin, sliding it along her nipple before I pull that pink tip into my mouth, sucking it soft, then harder. She pushes up toward me as far as her restraints will allow.

"You like that. Yes or no?"

"Yes," she moans. In answer, I suck harder.

She moans louder.

I kiss every inch of her belly now, taking care to trace the hollow that her hipbone makes. It's my favorite part of the female body, although I don't know why. There's something very feminine about it. I stand for a quick minute, peeling off my clothes so that I can feel her warm skin pressed to mine.

I press my rigid cock against her hip, enjoying the way her hipbone cuts into it, crushes it. It's a good pain.

"Sometimes, pain is good. I'm going to fuck you with my mouth today, not my cock. You're going to ache for me to fuck you, so much that it might hurt, but you're going to have to wait. I'm going to make you come with my mouth though—right now. Yes or no?"

"Please," she begs me softly, bucking her hips against my fingers. "Please."

"Yes or no?" I repeat insistently.

"Yes," she answers breathlessly.

That's all I needed to hear. I drop onto my hands and knees and bury my head between her legs. The smell of her, clean and musky, invades my senses and makes me crazy. I slip my tongue in, licking her slowly, then burying it in her. I rub her with my fingers, with my tongue, with my lips, until she is thrashing beneath me.

"You love this. Yes or no?" I ask raggedly. Because watching her powerless beneath me, blindfolded and restrained and unable to do anything but orgasm, turns me on. I'm rock hard now and I stroke myself with my left hand, even as I finger her with my right.

"Yes," she ekes out. "Fuck me, Dominic."

"No," I answer firmly. "Not yet. Some pain is good, Princess."

"But I want to feel you fuck me," she murmurs, arching upward, trying to touch me as best as she can. In answer, I turn both of my hands on her, fucking her with several fingers with one hand and rubbing her clit with the other until finally, she screams my name, then falls limply against the sheets.

She breathes quickly and shallowly, her delicate body curved into the bed. I stand, pull my clothes on, then untie her hands and feet. I leave her blindfold on.

"You loved that. Yes or no?"

"Yes," she says quickly, remaining motionless on the bed, even though she's no longer restrained. With one hand, she reaches over and finds my rock hard cock. "You loved it, too. Yes or no?"

"Yes," I say with a smile, before I stand up again. "I'll see you soon." And I walk from the room and I don't look back.

This is what I do.

I don't get attached.

I don't get involved.

But I think about the look on her face when she was coming, the open and innocent expression, and I smile.

I don't realize it until I'm in my car and I glance into my rear-view mirror and find that my lips are curved up ever so slightly. It's such a foreign expression that it startles me.

And then it shames me.

I shouldn't be happy about anything concerning Jacey. Because once I'm through with her, there won't be anything left to smile about.

There never is.

Chapter Fourteen

Jacey

My phone buzzes in my pocket, and from the way Dominic is looking at me from across the gym, I know it's a text from him. My stomach flutters, and I take a break from stacking clean towels so I can pull out my phone.

You want to fuck me. Yes or no?

A thrill runs through me and I smile. I can't help it. I glance up at him and find him staring at me with that look, the dark look that makes my heart pound. The one that makes me want him even when I've sworn to myself that I don't.

I shake my head at him, even though it's a lie. And he knows it's a lie because he laughs, sliding his phone back into his pocket as he turns back to holding a bag for Tig.

I sigh, picking back up the towels.

It's been two days since Dominic tied me to my bed.

When he walked out, I'd been astounded for two minutes, then all I could do was laugh. His penchant for being detached is becoming a pattern, and it's something I have to get used to if I want to continue with this . . . *whatever* this is.

But definitely whatever this is, it's fascinating.

It's exciting.

Dominic fucking Kinkaide was in my bed. We didn't exactly have sex, but it was just as intimate, at least to me.

Out of curiosity, I did a search for him online, to find out if he does this often...if he leaves behind a string of crushed hearts. Unfortunately, I couldn't find much.

He doesn't date a lot, although he's been linked to a couple of starlets, including Amy Ashby. He doesn't have any scandal around him...he's kept his nose clean. And there's not one thing mentioned about Emma, whoever she is.

His publicity team must be very good.

Or he's actually as detached and distant as he pretends to be.

After these last two days of flirting and texting, two days of not progressing into anything else, I'm starting to think that's the case. He's actually that detached. He does things that pleasure him, but he doesn't get involved.

It's like...he flips a switch when he starts thinking that he's getting too personal, and then he shuts down. I don't get why he does it, but it seems more and more to be the case. And if I want to continue our "relationship," I've got to accept it.

Because honestly, even though he's got some drawbacks, he's got a lot of pluses too...

I like his intensity.

I like his sexiness.

I like *him*. I can't help it. There's more to him than he wants me to know...than he wants anyone to know. It fascinates me. Every once in a while, there's something in his eyes...something that says he's vulnerable. He covers it up, but it makes me want to get close to him. To know him.

But I know he doesn't want that. He doesn't want to get close to anyone. *There's very few people I actually care about.*

There's a pang in my heart as I stack another row of towels and remember his words.

I know myself well enough to know that if I were in this for real, for a real relationship, someone like Dominic would never be good for me. Because of my own issues, I need more than he can offer. I need someone who would be an active participant in my life, someone who would make me feel important, like a priority.

But I'm not in this to get close to him, I remind myself. This isn't a real relationship. I'm in this because it's fun. I'm not getting used. I'm just entertaining myself. Soon, he'll go back to Hollywood and I won't see him again... unless it's on the movie screen. But it'll be fun for now. It'll be a cool story someday.

I turn back around and meet Dominic's gaze. He's got his phone in his hand again and a dark look in his eye. He's tall, slim, and cool in the middle of all of the surrounding sweat and heat and grime.

My phone buzzes.

Don't you need to put those extra towels somewhere?

My eyes meet his again. He knows that I do. And he knows where.

Buzz.

Go.

He stands watching me, confident that I'll run to the supply closet and wait for him. But I don't. Maintaining eye contact, I slowly and purposefully stack the leftover towels on the floor next to the rack. I look back up at him and his lip twitches.

Buzz.

I glance at my phone.

You get three chances. This is your second. Go.

I square my shoulders and stare at him. Who the hell does he think he is? He thinks he can just tell me to go and I'll run? Whatever. I'm only controlled when I want to be, like when I let him tie my hands in the bedroom. That was different.

I saunter away, pointedly ignoring him as I wind my way around the gym and into the locker room to toss dirty towels into the washer.

I'm not there for two minutes before my hips are pressed against the cool metal of the machine. There is warm breath against my ear and a warm body pressed against my back.

"You know you want to," Dominic whispers, his hand gripping my ass. Hard. "Just go. That's all you have to do."

I glance to the side, to make sure no one else is here with us before I slip from his grip and flip around, staring into his eyes.

"You know *you* want me to," I answer. As I do, I reach out my hand and cup his crotch, the first time I've actually done so. I stroke the denim for a second before I grip him through it. He swallows hard. "Don't you?"

He looks at me dangerously, his eyes darkening as his crotch hardens. He doesn't say anything, so I grip him harder.

"Yes or no?"

He doesn't flinch, even though my grip must hurt now. He stays hard, but that shouldn't be surprising. He *did* say that a little pain is good.

"Yes," he finally answers, shocking me. I didn't think he'd admit it.

I smile, a slow smile that spreads across my face. "So go," I instruct him.

The dangerous light glints in his eyes and I can see that he likes my commanding tone. He turns on his heel and walks away. I watch his broad shoulders disappear from the room, excitement building in my stomach. I wait just a minute before I follow him, making my way to the supply closet.

I open the door, but am surprised to find it empty. He's not here.

"What the..."

But then he's in the doorway, filling up the room, closing the door behind him.

"You thought you'd get to tell me what to do?" he asks softly, walking me backward until my back is pressed to the wall. "That's not how this works, Princess. Although I admire your balls."

"I thought we already established that I don't have balls?" I raise an eyebrow. He laughs, a husky, low sound.

"Maybe I should double check."

I was expecting his hand.

But his hand isn't what I get.

Dominic drops to his knees, and as he does, he pulls my shorts down. Since they have an elastic band, they're easy to peel off, and he takes full advantage of that. He slides them down until they drop around my ankles.

Without preamble, he thrusts his tongue into me, wet and hot. The room is immediately filled with his energy, with his dark, dark energy. It's a primal thing...like Dominic is taking full control of the situation. It's delicious. My head immediately falls back on its own accord and I grip the shelves behind me.

"Anyone could come in here," I manage to gasp as I struggle to inhale deeply, trying like hell to catch my breath. Dominic pulls away.

"True," he acknowledges, pausing. "But they won't. Only you and I come in here. And you are going to come *right now*."

He thrusts his tongue into me again, over and over, until I am panting and clinging limply to his back.

And then I do come.

Just like that.

I come and come, the muscles of my uterus contracting, my thighs trembling.

Dominic immediately stands up, grinning like a Cheshire cat. He bends, pulls my shorts up, and then dips his head to my ear.

"I love the taste of you."

And then he walks out. Like this never happened. Like he always does.

I grip the wall behind me, catching my breath and waiting until my knees stop shaking. It happened. I was just licked to orgasm in a supply closet... by Dominic Kinkaide. Holy shit.

When I can manage, I slip back out into the gym nonchalantly, as casually as I can. Dominic is holding a bag for a boy I haven't met yet, and he catches my eye as I walk past.

"Everything okay, Jacey?" he asks innocently, as if he doesn't know that my legs are jelly. Or *why*.

"I'm good," I answer back, every bit as innocently as he does. He winks, then runs his tongue across his lips.

"I know," he replies.

And just like that, my heart takes off like helicopter blades again. The man can barely look at me and I'm a goner. Like, I seriously just want him to carry me off to bed, where we can hole up for a weekend and not do anything but stare into each other's eyes.

Fuck. That can't be good. Because he doesn't want to stare into my eyes. He wants to render me helpless with his sexcapades. I square my shoulders and turn away.

I try to ignore Dominic for the rest of our shift, and instead of talking to him, I focus on other things. The moistness in my underwear reminds me from time to time, though, as does his mischievous grin whenever I accidentally meet his gaze. But I stubbornly avoid him anyway.

Why?

Because he's dangerous to me.

Because even though this is supposed to be fun, temporary, and lighthearted, I can feel myself getting pulled in. I feel myself getting attached and I can't do that. That wasn't supposed to be part of this.

I don't remember offering to be with you. That's what he said. He doesn't want me like that, not for something real. He runs cold and hot and he's always, always detached. If I make the mistake of wanting something real from him, then I'm going to be crushed, just like always, because I'm making yet another bad decision.

My heart twinges as I remind myself of that. But it's the truth. I don't shirk from the truth.

I do hide from it sometimes, though. Like when Dominic turns to me in the parking lot after work and says, "Hey, I have to go to California on Friday night so I can shoot this weekend. Would you like to come?"

One word instantly comes from my mouth before I can even think about it, before I can remind myself yet again that I'm not going to get sucked in.

"Yes."

❧

Dominic

I slide my hands up Jacey's dress, pulling her to me, her hips grinding into mine.

"Fuck me," she whispers into my ear, her fingernails cutting a trail down my back. The pain of it turns me on, but her scent turns me on even more. I lift her up and bite her lip, thrusting my tongue into her mouth before I unbuckle my belt and pull off my pants.

I hover over her for just a minute before I plunge deep inside of her. She moans and writhes beneath me, her fingers twisting into the sheets.

"Dominic," she whispers. "Get up."

I pause and look at her in confusion, because I'm rock hard right now. "I *am* up, babe," I answer. "And it's for you." I thrust into her again and she smiles.

"Get up," she answers again, chuckling. But her voice is deeper now, manly. Not her normal sexy voice.

I'm confused for just a minute more until I realize that I'm dreaming. But now I'm awake and I'm not with Jacey at all. In fact, Sin is standing next to my bed, cackling like a rooster.

"What the fuck, Dom?" He laughs. "What the hell are you dreaming about? Or I guess I should say, *who*. You were moaning like a son of a bitch."

I grab a pillow and thrust it onto my face, breathing in the goose-down smell, trying like hell to get rid of my boner. *Margaret Thatcher. Naked. On a cold day.*

"Get out," I growl at him. "What the hell, Sin?"

He cackles some more before he thrusts my phone into my hand. "You left this in the kitchen, and Tally has called four times already. You might want to call him back."

"What time is it?" I ask groggily, but it's too late. I can hear the door closing as Sin leaves. I lie still for a few minutes longer and then I throw the pillow against the wall.

What the hell? I'm pissed at myself for a bunch of things, but most importantly, for dreaming about *fucking* Jacey. What. The. Fuck? I've turned myself into a fucking celibate monk (or my version of one) for good reasons. And there's no good reason that I should be dreaming of fucking anyone, Jacey included.

I glance at the clock. Nine fucking thirty. I guess it's a good thing Sin woke me up, or I'd have been late for the gym...and I believe what Joe says. If I'm late one more time, I shouldn't bother coming back. Jesus.

I pull some clothes on, spray on cologne, and head out the door, calling Tally from the car.

"What?" I ask when he answers. "What was so important you needed to call four times?"

Tally sighs into the phone. "I just want to make sure you're going to be on the plane tonight. I've got it arranged...And I told Amy Ashby that she could share the flight. She's in Chicago visiting her boyfriend. She'll ride back with you."

"I'm going to have someone with me," I tell him as I turn out into traffic. "I need you to add her to the passenger list. Jacey Vincent."

Tally sighs again. "Oh, that's gonna make Amy happy."

"I don't fucking care," I tell him honestly. "It's my plane. She's coming back from visiting her boyfriend, anyway. She shouldn't care, either."

But he and I both know that she will. Because Amy Ashby is bitchy like that. She thinks that everything and everyone is hers. Jacey is feisty, though, and I know she can handle it. A quick memory of her roundhouse kick to Jake's chest flits through my head and I smile. Yeah, she can handle herself in any situation, whether it is with a Hollywood mean girl or a juvenile delinquent.

"Since when are you hauling around a woman?" Tally demands after he has me spell her name for the flight manifest. I roll my eyes.

Since a woman has wormed her way into my head and I started having erotic dreams of fucking her. But of course I don't say that. I growl and hang up instead.

I spend the rest of the drive to the gym in silence, staring at the road. I stare at my hands, at the sky, at the traffic. But it doesn't distract me from what Tally said. *When did I start hauling a woman around?*

It's a good fucking question.

And the only answer I can come up with is: since I became fascinated with one. It's the first time in a long, long time, and even though it's not smart, I'm not ready to pull the plug on it yet. I don't know why.

That's puzzling to me, as well. I'm just as curious about my own feelings regarding her as I am about Jacey herself. I *do not* like getting close to people. I *do not* like giving them the opportunity to hurt me, use me, or exploit me.

But *she hasn't given me a reason to believe that she'd do any of those things,* I remind myself. That's the point of this whole thing. I'm giving someone a chance, for the first time in a long time, to prove to me that she's not like everyone else. But the second she does…it's over.

The *second* that I think she's not the genuine and open person that she seems to be, we're done.

When I get to the gym, Jacey's friend Brand is dropping her off yet again, and I have to fight back a scowl. I don't like the familiar way he handles her. I don't like the way she *lets* him.

She says that he's like a brother to her. That there's no way he thinks of her as anything but a brother. But there's no way she can't see the same things I do.

I stare at the guy as he watches Jacey walk to the door. He's most definitely not watching her as a brother would. His eyes sweep from her ass to her shoulders, back to her hips. It's a gaze of appreciation.

And then, abruptly, he looks at me as I hold the gym door open for her.

I see a million things in his eyes, a myriad of emotions. Jealousy, resentment, frustration. But most importantly, a threat.

Stay away from her. It's unspoken, but the meaning is clear. I return the gaze calmly, not backing away, and he finally breaks the stare and drives away.

"What the hell?" I snap at Jacey. "Aren't you ever going to get your car fixed?"

She looks at me sharply, surprised by my annoyance. I'm surprised by it, too, but I can't help it. There's no fucking way she can't see how into her Brand is. And because there's no way she's that oblivious, it means that she's not as decent as I'd so like to believe, because she's still leading him on.

Which means she's let me down. Even though I expected it, I'm surprised by how disappointed I am.

"Not all of us are made of money," she snaps, bringing me back to the matter at hand. "I'll fix my car when I can."

I shake my head and follow her inside. Could it be that she really just needs his help and she's not purposely using him? It's a notion I'd love to believe, but I'm having a really hard time swallowing.

"We're leaving straight from here," I tell her just as sharply. "Did you bring a bag?"

She nods. "Yeah. If you're in a better mood this afternoon, then I'll actually go with you."

With that, she flounces off. I watch her go...her nose in the air, her shoulders back and her ass tight in her short shorts. I have to smile at her attitude. I think it's one of the things I like best about her. She's spunky. That's for sure.

But I freeze as I realize what I just did.

I just admitted that I like Jacey.

Fuck. That can't be good.

That means it's time to end it. Now. That, in combination with this whole Brand thing, is enough to just pull the fucking plug and get it over with.

I yank my phone out of my pocket with full intention of acting like I just got a call from Tally to tell me that shooting had been canceled when I glance over at Jacey.

She's kneeling on the ground, looking up at Jake as she tries like hell to unknot his shoes for him. His laces are muddy and gross, but she doesn't seem to mind as she tries to help. Her smile is genuine as she laughs at him, and when she looks over at me, she smiles, too.

With a deep sigh, I slide my phone back in my pocket. I can't do it yet... not because I'm scared of my own feelings for her or because of my suspicions about Brand. Those aren't good enough reasons.

The point of this whole thing is to see if I can get past my misgivings about humanity and give her a chance.

And besides, I'm not done with her yet.

Chapter Fifteen

Jacey

I've never been in a chartered plane hangar before, but I try not to act like it. I try to restrain myself from gazing around like an idiot... at the shiny jet, the staff who is waiting to meet us, and the carpet that is rolled out for us to walk on.

Holy crap. Is this seriously how famous people live?

Nonchalantly, I follow Dominic up the steps and onto the plane, trying my best to seem blasé. But as Dominic turns to ask me which leather sofa I'd like to sit on, I can see his eyes twinkling, and he knows. He knows that I'm way over my head. But I still don't give him the satisfaction of admitting it.

"Anywhere." I shrug. "They all look the same." As in, they're all expensive, soft-as-butter Italian leather. Dominic grins.

"Okay." He shrugs back. "We'll take that one. Amy can have the other."

"Amy?" I raise my eyebrow. Dominic looks surprised.

"Did I forget to tell you? Amy Ashby is in Chicago right now. She's sharing this jet with us."

I feel a monster-sized weight form on my chest and I swallow hard.

"Uh, yeah. I guess you did forget to mention that part." I'm going to be riding with one of the biggest actresses on the planet, and not only that, but she's notoriously bitchy. Super.

Dominic stares at me curiously as he sits, pulling me down next to him. "Is that a problem? I'm sorry that I forgot to tell you. I just found out myself last night."

I shake my head. "No, of course it's not a problem. I'm good."

I'm not good. My legs are shaking again, and that pisses me off. *No one is better than you*, I remind myself. She's famous, not better. I'm practically muttering to myself as I settle in beside Dominic, automatically resenting that he's so calm and cool.

But he's used to this. He's used to fancy planes and Hollywood stars and people being at his beck and call. I take a deep breath. I might not be used to it, but I've got this. I can do this. I turn to him.

"So, how much will you have to shoot this weekend? I've heard horror stories about how sometimes shooting can go on all day and night."

Dominic chuckles. "It all depends. But right now, we're doing bits and pieces, the smaller scenes. We won't get into the meat of the movie until I'm back in LA for good. I'm a character actor, so it's hard for me to bury myself in my role when I have to keep flying back and forth between Chicago and LA."

"And your studio is okay with that?" I ask dubiously.

He starts to answer, but is interrupted by a female voice.

"They might be, but I'm not," Amy Ashby snaps as she hauls herself onto the plane with a little yappy dog in her arms. She's spindly skinny with giant boobs that must be fake. "This is bullshit, Dom. Serious bullshit."

Dominic turns to me, rolls his eyes, then turns back to Amy with a sigh. "Hey, Amy. So good to see you."

I want to giggle at his resigned tone and the outraged look on her heavily made-up face, but I don't. Something tells me that wouldn't be the best first impression.

She stares at me with narrowed eyes, extremely interested all of a sudden. "Who's this?"

"My friend Jacey," Dominic answers easily, sitting back in the seat with his arm looped loosely behind me. I enjoy the sense of security that brings me, the warmth from his arm. It's like an anchor in a sea of unfamiliar shit.

"It's nice to meet you," I tell her politely. "I love your work."

She sniffs, looking down her nose at me before she deposits her tiny dog on the seat and turns to the flight attendant. "I need some water for Pichachu. He only drinks Acqua Panna. If you don't have any, you're going to need to find some before we take off." She turns away without waiting for the attendant to reply, and I can't help but chuckle because her dog's name sounds like a sneeze.

"Why are you coming?" she asks me bluntly as she settles the dog on her lap, stroking its puffy hair. "The set will be closed."

"Since when?" Dominic asked her sharply. "I didn't request that."

"I did." Amy stares at him. "Well, I'm going to. I don't need your little girlfriend watching our sex scenes." She levels a brilliant blue gaze at me, and I'm astounded at her hostility when I haven't even done anything to her.

Jesus. What a bitch. She's an even bigger nightmare than I thought she'd be. Dominic chuckles humorlessly as Amy crosses her skinny legs and stares at him.

"It's not like we actually have sex, Amy, on *or* off set. But whatever. Do what you need to do." Amy's cheeks flush and she turns away, lifting her nose in the air.

Dominic turns to me. "You can either hang out in my trailer or you can stay at my house by the pool. Either way, you'll have a good time. I promise."

He puts his hand on my leg now, possessively, and he stares back at Amy. She can't help but stare back at him, and I'm not sure exactly what he's trying to convey, but whatever it is, it's effective. She's noticeably pissed.

"Whatever, Dom. You know that's not true. You and I both know it."

Her words are icy and laced with venom. *Dominic won't show you a good time.* That's what she means.

But Dominic ignores her. He stares at me instead, angling his body so that he's blocking her completely out.

"I've got some things planned," he tells me conversationally. "I think you'll like them." I hear Amy sniff, but she doesn't remark.

"I'm sure I will, too," I answer. I take note that his hand is still on my thigh, his fingers lightly gripping me. "Can I have a hint?"

Dominic smiles, leaning down to whisper into my ear. "What did you pack to wear?"

I stare at him, but before I can answer, he continues, "Because you won't be needing it."

I gulp, then smile. "Maybe." I shrug. "We'll see."

He smiles knowingly. "Oh, we'll see." He chuckles again, and the dangerous glint is back in his eyes. The one that I love. It means I'm going to like whatever comes next.

"I brought you something," he tells me quietly. "It'll help pass the time on the flight."

I stare at him. "Something tells me it's not a crossword puzzle."

Dominic laughs, his teeth gleaming white. "Uh, no. It's a million times better." He reaches into his jacket pocket and pulls out a little nondescript box. Leaning forward, he whispers into my ear again, his breath warm on my cheek. "I like kinky things. Dirty things. Is that a problem?"

I suck my breath in. Kinky things? Regardless of my trepidation, I smile.

"I'll try anything once," I murmur.

He grins the grin of the devil. "Good. Go to the bathroom. Put this in."

In?

I stare at him again, half in shock, half eager to see. I hold out my hand, a thrill shooting through me as he hands it to me.

"Trust me," he whispers with a wink.

Oh, yeah, right. Trust him. For some reason, I can practically see Lucifer himself saying the same thing with the same expression on his face. In all honesty, Lucifer might be safer than Dominic.

Regardless, I make my way to the bathroom in the back of the plane and lock the door behind me so I can open the box in peace.

As I slide the lid off, I suck in a breath. Lying in the white tissue paper, there's a silver bullet–looking thing, shining in the dim light of the bathroom. I pick it up and it's heavy and cool in my fingers. There aren't any instructions, but I instinctively know where it's supposed to go.

Where it's supposed to go *in*.

Good Lord. I feel a moment of panic, but then calm myself. He might be Dominic fucking Kinkaide, but I'm Jacey fucking Vincent and I'm not scared of anything. I've got this. I've so got this.

I like new things, damn it.

With trembling fingers, I pull down my shorts and my panties and insert the silver bullet, nestling it up to where it needs to be. Inside of me. I suck in another breath as the cold metal slides in.

I stand back up and straighten my clothes.

It's not so bad. It's like a metal tampon. I hardly even know it's there. I drop the box into the trash and head back out to Dominic.

"Everything go okay?" he asks innocently, watching as I buckle up next to him.

"Of course," I tell him. "Child's play."

He rolls his eyes now. "*Nooo*," he drawls. "It won't even be close to child's play. I promise."

And there *is* a promise in his voice, a dark and sexy promise. I stare into his eyes and find myself lost there for a minute, inside the glimmering green depths.

I shake my head, shaking away my trembly feelings, and stare out the window as the plane taxies down the runway and takes off. After we've leveled off in the air, I settle into the seat, into Dominic's arm. Flying always unnerves me a little, but I always relax after takeoff.

"Comfortable?" he asks softly. I nod.

"Yeah. I think I might take a nap."

"Oh, I think not," he murmurs. And with his words, the bullet inside of me starts to buzz urgently, enough to snap my head back. As the vibrations spread through my body and threaten to overwhelm me, I notice that Dominic's holding something in his left hand.

A tiny remote control.

My eyes fly to meet his, and that look is there, lurking in his. That dangerous, sexy look.

Fuck.

I want to throw my head back into the sofa cushions, to embrace the vibrations that are cresting me toward an orgasm, but I can't.

Amy is across from me. Her nose is buried in a magazine, but any minute she could look up and notice me writhing in my seat.

So I sit rigidly, my knees clamped together, my jaw clenched.

And Dominic smiles.

As he does, the vibrations stop. His finger falls away from the button and he stares at me with a grin.

"How do you like the ride so far?" he asks innocently. I take a deep breath and gather myself, willing my tongue to form coherent words.

"It's nice," I tell him finally. "I've never been on a private plane before. It's different than I expected."

He chuckles now, a genuine laugh. "Oh, I'm sure," he grins. He moves his hand and I flinch, preparing for another onslaught of vibration, but he reaches for a glass of water instead. He grins at my reaction.

"You're jumpy," he observes. "You should calm down. The ride should be very smooth. Nothing to worry about."

I roll my eyes. "I wasn't worried."

"No?" He raises an eyebrow, and I jump as the vibrations flood my nether regions again, and I find that my palms are actually sweating. "How about now?"

Amy glances at us over her magazine, but as soon as I meet her eye, she looks away. She pointedly doesn't want to interact with me, and at the moment, that's *very* fine with me.

"I'm perfectly fine now," I manage to say in a very normal and casual voice. "Very fine."

Dominic chuckles, and for a moment I cuss him out silently. But at the same time, the pulsing bullet is spreading warmth through me, building orgasmic waves that I want to float on forever. Something about the vibrator itself, combined with the fact that I'm in public—in front of one of the biggest actresses in the world and a team of flight attendants—makes this whole thing exhilarating.

Apparently, I'm a freak.

Just like Dominic. I can see on his face that he's getting off on this. He loves thinking about me coming in front of all of these people while they're all blissfully unaware. I can see it in his eyes.

I grit my teeth as an attendant bends in front of me.

"Would you like a pillow, dear?" She smiles, and sweat breaks out on my forehead.

"N-no," I stutter, then gulp. The vibrations kick up a notch to a faster speed. "No, thank you," I finally manage to say. She looks at me in concern.

"Is everything all right?"

I grit my teeth again. "Yes," I eke out. "It's fine."

She looks at me again with concern, but smiles. "Okay. Just let me know if you need anything."

I nod, unable to speak now, my entire body melting into the sofa. I couldn't stand up right now if the plane was on fire and I needed to run for my life. I'd be totally screwed.

I reach over and grip Dominic's right hand, hard. My fingers curl around his, my fingernails cutting into him as he ramps up the speed of the vibrator even more.

"Holy shit," I breathe. He grins a beatific smile. I close my eyes and breathe deeply again—in, then out. And then I hold my breath, because I know that I'm going to come. Right here in front of god and everyone on this plane, I'm going to fucking come.

It happens and I feel like climbing the inside wall of the plane as the sensations rock my entire body, hard. My leg twitches and I'm pretty sure that my eyes bug out. And still Dominic smiles. I grip his hand even tighter, my fingers damp, until he releases the button and the sensations stop.

I let go of his hand and fall back into the sofa, my head on the seat.

"Feel better now?" Dominic smirks, curling his long arm around my shoulders.

I nod. "Very much. I feel like I need a cigarette."

Dominic raises a brow. "I didn't know you smoked."

I smile, closing my eyes. "I don't."

He chuckles, but I know I'm not going to last long now. I'm completely spent...from the orgasm and from trying to hide the orgasm. It took a lot of energy. I don't know how long it takes, but it's not long before I'm asleep. The last conscious thought I have is of Dominic's scent filling my nose...musky, manly...so uniquely him.

Being on a private plane, *his* private plane, is leaps and bounds better than flying commercially. What's that old airline slogan? "Fly the friendly skies"? Yeah, Dominic should totally make up his own slogan.

Come and fly with me.

As in, fly with me and I'll make you fucking come.

Suddenly though, the thought of Dominic doing this with anyone else sends a hundred-pound weight slamming into my stomach. I'm shaken as I realize that I don't want him to be with anyone else.

Only me.

I gulp, because that's a dangerous thought when we're talking about someone like Dominic.

Someone who, for all intents and purposes, cannot commit, cannot get close, cannot be intimate. I know I'm supposed to be proving that I can casually be with someone without falling for him, but I don't think that's me. I'm not the kind of girl who can do that.

I've got to face the facts, and they're not just about me. They're about Dominic, too.

He isn't the "friend with benefits" kind of guy.

He's the kind of guy who gets fallen for, *hard*.

～

True to Dominic's word, the flight is smooth. I don't open my eyes again until after the wheels have touched down and he shakes my shoulder.

"Do you need to use the restroom or anything?" he asks me. "It's probably nicer on here than it is in the airport."

That's no lie. I nod and climb out of the sofa, only to realize that Amy is following me to the back. When we get there, I pause.

"Do you want to go first?" I ask her hesitantly, because she's looking at me so oddly. She shakes her head.

"No. I just wanted to tell you something."

Oh, great. Here it comes.

"And that is?"

She smirks. "Dominic will never fuck you. So I know you're walking around thinking you're god's gift right now, but just know that he'll never fuck you. He's probably secretly gay or something."

I stare at her. "Or he just didn't want to fuck you," I suggest firmly. "You think just because someone doesn't want to fuck you, it means they're gay? Jesus."

I turn away, but she grabs my arm with talon-like fingers. "Dominic likes to play games. He'll string you along until he's done with you. Don't say I didn't warn you." She smirks again. I roll my eyes.

"Oh, yeah, out of the goodness of your heart, I'm sure."

Amy stares at me, her eyes as hard as glass. "He'll get you to do more perverted things than you ever thought possible," she says icily.

"And you'll do them all because you'll want to please him. Because you think that you're proving yourself to him. But in the end, it won't be worth it. Because he'll never be anything more than a perverted asshole."

I close the bathroom door in her face and sink onto the toilet, trying to collect myself. What the fuck was that? Why would she tell me such a thing? I mean, she's a catty bitch, but seriously. If Dominic didn't want to sleep with her, then he simply didn't want to sleep with her.

The only thing is... the only thing that gives me pause is... that he hasn't slept with *me* yet, either. I've flat-out asked him to and he said *not yet*.

That begs the question: What the hell is going on with him?

He's not gay. I know that. I can feel it in the way he looks at me. There's also nothing physically wrong with him. He can definitely get it up. I've felt his erection pressed against me too many times to count.

Why then doesn't he want to actually use those perfectly good erections?

Or maybe he does. Maybe Amy's right and he just wants to use them to do perverted things. This whole making me come in front of Amy thing was pretty kinky. Finger-fucking me on the Ferris wheel was kinky. Going down on me in the supply closet was kinky.

He *is* perverted.

There's no question about that. The only question is *how* perverted? And why? Something seems to scream out to me that there's something really, really wrong with him.

Which is exactly what Amy is trying to imply.

It's either that, or he just enjoys playing fucked-up games.

She's implying that, too.

I take out the bullet, stick it in my pocket, and wash my hands, and when I go back out Amy's already gone, deplaned with her stupid little yappy dog. I have to admit, that's a relief. I don't want to deal with her again. I know a million fans would love to be around her right now, but that's because they don't know exactly how much of a bitch she really is. It's unfathomable unless you witness it firsthand.

Since we don't have to traipse through the airport like normal people, we are out and into a car within a few minutes, sitting in the back of a limo while it drives us toward Dominic's house.

"This is the first time I've been in California," I mention absently, trying to be casual, trying to hide the unsettled things that I'm thinking about Dominic now as I stare out the tinted windows at the suburban landscape rolling past. It seems to be dry here, with only a few specks of green. Dominic glances up from his phone.

"Really? How is that possible?"

I laugh. "It's very possible. I've never had a reason to come out here before."

Dominic shakes his head but doesn't comment. I stare at the back of the driver's head for a while and ponder telling Dom what Amy had said, but decide not to. What's the point in it? I know him well enough to know that he's not going to give me a straight answer, and he doesn't seem the least bit bothered by her or her implications anyway.

The ride to Hollywood Hills doesn't take long, and I have to admit that driving into the exclusive community sends my tummy rolling. I watch out the window, wondering who I might see stepping out of a mansion. And then reality hits me, and I remember that I'm sitting in a limo with one of the most famous actors on the planet.

Reality check.

I stare at him for a minute, at the way he's so casually graceful in the dark of the limo, his legs sprawled in front of him.

"Cool trick with the vibrator," I tell him. "I didn't see that one coming."

He rolls his eyes. "How is that even possible? You work for Saffron and you don't know what a bullet is?"

I shake my head. "I'm a waitress, not an escort, dickhead." He grins.

"Fair enough. Are you still wearing it?"

I take it out of my pocket and hand it to him. "No. I didn't trust you not to use it again."

Dominic laughs. "Smart." He nods. "Very smart." He slips it into his pocket and stares out the window. "We're almost there," he tells me, gesturing toward a house at the end of the street, nestled onto the side of a huge hill.

I almost gasp when I see the house.

"Holy shit. Your house is even bigger than Sin's," I exclaim, pressing my nose to the window. And it is. It's enormous and sophisticated and modern. Everything I should've known it would be.

Dominic grins, satisfied with my answer. "Regardless of what Sin says, everything about me is bigger than his," he announces. I burst out laughing as I get out of the limo.

"Well," I answer, still giggling, "I'm sure you've had no complaints."

That was me fishing... trying to get him to say something, *anything* about women he might have slept with before. But he doesn't say a word.

With a sigh, I stare upward at the house looming above us.

It's majestic. And overwhelming.

"Do you have staff here, or do you somehow take care of this whole thing by yourself?"

Dom shakes his head. "I have housekeepers that come in once a week or so, but that's it. I like my privacy. I do have a security detail, but they don't live here. They only come with me when I go out. This is a gated community, so I don't need them when I'm at home."

I exhale slowly as we walk in the door, my heels clicking loudly on the stone floor of the foyer.

"I can't believe you have such a huge house all for yourself," I marvel as we wind our way up the curved staircase. He leads me to a bedroom and opens the door.

I pause in the doorway. "I get my own room?" I raise an eyebrow. "I wasn't expecting that." I was expecting to sleep in his bed.

He stares at me, his gaze hiding a million things. "I thought you'd want privacy."

"That's considerate of you," I murmur as I walk past him and into my lush quarters. I can't complain. It's gorgeous...from the sunken marble tub to the fantastic view of the surrounding hills.

"If you need anything, just ask," Dominic tells me graciously. "I'm going to leave you for a bit to freshen up while I take a shower. Want to meet on the veranda in an hour for dinner? The sun will be going down and you'll want to see that."

I nod and he leaves as I drop onto the bed in a heap. All of a sudden, everything here is overwhelming. This mansion, Amy's bitchy attitude and her ugly implications...all of it. Including Dominic and his games.

His games.

Is he playing a game?

If he is, it's clear that I don't know the rules.

Chapter Sixteen

Jacey

"Why are you acting so weird?" I demand as Dominic sticks a bite of cheese in his mouth. He stares at me.

"Am I supposed to swallow without chewing?" He raises an eyebrow and I roll my eyes.

"You know what I'm talking about." I sigh.

I gesture around me with my arm, at the fancy picnic Dominic had delivered from a catering service, at the romantic setup with the candles and the twinkling overhead lights, at the wine... at the way Dominic is all the way across the veranda from me. Earlier, when I had gotten up and sat next to him, he had waited a few minutes, then moved away again.

"What the hell, Dominic?"

He stares at me bemused. "What were you expecting, Jacey?"

The way he says my name annoys me, it's so fluid and smooth and detached. It's like he doesn't care if I'm upset, if I'm annoyed— or actually, it's like he doesn't care about anything at all. It frustrates me, because more and more I know that I need him to.

"You know what I was expecting." I snap. "You're confusing, and I'm starting to think you're doing it on purpose as part of some fucked-up game. You wanted me out here with you, and you even brought a sex toy onto the plane to make me squirm, but now that we're here, in the privacy of your home, you don't want anything to do with me. I'm in a separate room, you're sitting across the veranda from me...I don't understand you."

"That's what you're worried about?" Again, he raises an eyebrow. "You're upset because I've brought you out here and haven't fucked you yet? I don't fuck just anyone, Jacey."

His eyes are hard now, dark.

"Or are you upset because you don't understand me? Because if that's it, trust me, nobody does, so you're not in the minority."

I stare back at him, not sure what to address first. "Do *you* understand you? Do *you* even know what you're doing?"

He shrugs, unconcerned. "Not really. I have no idea what I'm doing here with you, if you want me to be honest."

"Now we're getting somewhere," I tell him. "Amy told me some ugly things on the plane. She said that you're a pervert who likes playing games. Is that true?"

Dominic's green eyes darken. "What do *you* think?"

I shake my head. "No. Don't throw this back on me. Is it true?"

He shrugs now, trying to seem unconcerned, but something tells me that he's more bothered than he cares to admit. "It's all relative, I suppose," he says calmly. "Amy's a bitch. I didn't play fucked-up games with her. She knew from the beginning what I wanted, and she only got pissed when I wouldn't give her what *she* wanted. As far as being a pervert, I'm more perverted than some, less than others."

I stare at him. "Is that why I'm here? Because you want to do kinky things to me?"

He shakes his head, his eyes darkening even more. "Jacey, I've wanted to do kinky things to you from the beginning, but that's not the point. I want you here against my better judgment. But now that you're here, I'm not sure what to do with you."

That instantly annoys me. The way he said it was so condescending. *I'm not sure what to do with you.* Like I'm a thing. Or a toy. Something he has complete control over. "Oh, so you beckoned to me and I came?" I stand up, annoyed, throwing my napkin onto the large ottoman in front of me. "Fuck you. You don't crook your finger at me and I come running. I'm here because I like you. Period. But you don't get to play games with me, Dominic. After what I told you about the kinds of guys I've struggled with, it pisses me off that you would even try. It's not fair."

I stalk away past the shimmering pool, back through the glass doors of his house, but when I reach the doorway, he has caught up to me and he grabs my arm.

"Stay," he urges me quietly. "I'm sorry. I'm not trying to play games. I'm trying to be honest with you. It's a new concept for me, and I'm probably fucking it up. But I do want you to stay."

I look up at him, staring into his eyes, and I find sincerity there. He wasn't trying to upset me or control me.

"I'm sorry," I murmur. "I shouldn't have let Amy get under my skin."

The planes of his face are angled, and the moonlight reflects off of them, and suddenly I just want to run my fingers along his cheekbone. I don't know why.

But I do it anyway.

I trace the outline of his cheek, trailing my fingers along his jaw. I feel his jaw flex as he stares down at me, his eyes thoughtful.

"I don't understand you," I finally whisper.

"Neither do I," he admits. "But does it matter? Do you still want to be here?"

I do. I shouldn't want to, but I do.

I let him lead me back to the veranda, back to the cushioned chaises and ottomans, where he sits down next to me and watches me, thoughtful now. This is the first time I've seen this side of him . . . this introspective side. I tell him that, and he smiles.

"Would you believe me if I told you that I don't hang around with people much?" he asks, picking up a cracker and smearing pâté on it before handing it to me. "I don't like gatherings, unless it's with my family. And now . . . well, with Cris dating Fiona, I won't be going to many of them any time soon."

I take the cracker and settle back into my seat, watching him as I eat.

He's so graceful and sophisticated, even though he's not much older than I am. I know those things, his statistics, because I looked them up online. He's twenty-four. He's 6'2". He's right-handed. Dark hair, green eyes. But those are just things, facts. I don't know what he *thinks*.

"Why are you so upset about your sister dating Cris?" I ask hesitantly. "I know you don't really want to talk about it, but I'd like to know. I hate seeing how much it bothers you. You love your family. It must be something huge to make you stay away from them."

Dominic tenses now, his leg crossed tighter than it was, and he looks away, out over the valley.

"You're right. I really don't want to talk about it," he finally answers slowly. "I'm sorry that you do, but I can't. It's something that happened a long time ago and I honestly just can't talk about it."

His face is filled with pain and vulnerability, a unique combination that I haven't seen there before. I reach up and brush the hair away from his forehead.

"It's okay," I murmur. "You don't have to. I just…it makes me sad to see you upset. I'd like to try and help you figure it out, if I can."

"You can't," he answers sharply. But then he softens his tone and actually picks up my hand. It makes me want to hold my breath, because he's made it obvious he doesn't like intimate contact. Yet here he is, holding my hand.

"I'm sorry," he adds. "It's just…you need to know that if you're going to be around me, there's a bunch of shit about me that you can't fix. So I don't want you to try. Don't get invested in me, all right?"

I suck in my breath at his acidic tone and stare at him as I unconsciously pull my hand away.

"All right," I whisper limply, stunned by his bluntness. "I'm sorry, I couldn't help asking about your family, because it's something that I'm curious about…it's something that I can see hurts you. I like you. I like you more and more each day. And as your friend, I don't like that anything hurts you."

"Are you my friend?" he asks suddenly, turning toward me.

I can't explain why, but the expression on his face hurts my heart. It's open. For the first time since I've known him, his face is completely open to me. I know that he doesn't do this often…he doesn't show his vulnerability.

"Yes," I answer slowly. "I'm your friend."

He nods, and I honestly don't know what's going on here. "And you like me more and more each day?"

I nod in confusion.

"Dominic," I whisper, not sure of what to say. He looks up at me rakishly, the breeze tousling his hair, and he's utterly beautiful.

"Don't love me," he says simply. "Or I'll break you. I won't want to, but it will happen."

I'm stunned at the utter bleakness of his words, of his voice, of the heart-wrenching expression on his face. I don't know what happened to him to put it there. But before I can say a word, before I can react, he reaches for me.

I know that for whatever reason, he needs me right now, and god help me, I want to save him from himself. From whatever pain he's feeling. From whatever it was that hurt him.

I fold into him and inhale his mouth, his tongue sweet and hot against mine. His lips are soft and plunder my own, his hands sliding everywhere. He's got an urgency now that I can't understand. I don't know where it's coming from, or why he's in an even darker mood than usual.

Whatever else he is, I can't deny that he's sexy. Everything about him is sexy and everything in me wants him. Right now.

He kisses me until I'm breathless, leaning me back until my head barely grazes the chaise behind me. He pulls at my shirt until he's able to run his thumbs over my nipples, rubbing them into hard nubs.

"Still like me?" he whispers, his eyes boring into mine. I swallow hard and don't answer. "Yes or no?" he asks, dipping his head and running his tongue in circles around each point.

"Yes," I whisper limply.

He stands up and unfastens his pants, dropping them to the ground. Crawling over me, he rubs his bare penis against my wet opening, the friction of it creating a firestorm in me, causing me to cling to his strong shoulders.

"What about now?" he rasps into my ear. He's as breathless as I am, I realize.

"Yes," I murmur, trying to pull him closer, to pull him inside of me. But he pulls away, standing back up and then pausing in front of me, gripping my legs.

Without another word, he bends down, shoving up my skirt and burying his head between my legs.

As feverish as I am, his tongue brings me to a climax within a minute. The wetness of it rakes over me as his hands ravage the rest of me, sliding, kneading, pulling.

I close my eyes, blocking out the moonlight, the veranda, the lights from the valley. I revel in the feel of being close to him, as close as I've been yet. He might not have exposed much to me, but I could see that he wanted to. He's just afraid. And knowing that makes me feel as though he let me in somehow… just a little.

But now he wants to annihilate me. I can see that in his eyes, as he makes me come over and over again with his mouth. His dark eyes gleam, and they are all I can see of his face as he stares intently at me from between my legs. I try to pull him up, to get him to crawl over me, to kiss me, to plunge into me, but he won't. He stays down… making me come yet again.

I arch into the air, reaching for him, but he won't allow it.

"I want to feel you inside of me," I tell him urgently. Because I do. I want him to fill me up. To give me, for just a minute, what he's not willing to give me otherwise.

Himself.

Completely.

Not bits of him, not pieces of him, but *all* of him.

He pauses, staring at me, and I can literally see it as his eyes shutter closed. He's closed to me now, and whatever progress we made tonight is gone.

He smiles his normal smile, the rakish one, the one that millions of fans have seen and loved.

"Not yet, Princess," he tells me as he climbs to his feet. "Not yet."

Chapter Seventeen

Dominic

What.

The.

Fuck?

I let the cold shower water run over my body, over my head and my shoulders, down my hips and down to where I really need it.

What the fuck was I thinking?

I was *this* close to spilling my guts to Jacey. *This* close to inviting her into my life, telling her my secrets, *letting her in.*

I blame it on the look in her eyes. The sweet, genuine, I'm-so-concerned-about-you look...and I know that she is. She genuinely cares that something has hurt me. But the problem is...she thinks she can fix it and she can't.

No one can.

That's the bitch of it.

I grab a towel and step out of the walk-in shower, before I head to my bed naked.

And alone.

Chapter Eighteen

Jacey

I don't know what to think.

Even though something felt like it changed last night, like our paradigm shifted, Dominic is back to being cool and aloof. He popped his head into my room early this morning to tell me that he was going to the studio, that he'd be back later…and to relax around the pool.

"Make yourself at home!" he'd called over his shoulder in a very polite way as he walked out.

He didn't kiss me good-bye, he didn't touch me at all. He stayed in the doorway where he stood, beautiful and graceful but so very distant.

It's gorgeous here, and the infinity pool that seems to slip right over the edge of the valley is picture perfect. But there's only so much time I can spend lounging by the pool. I'm alone and I'm restless.

So I go exploring.

I spent quite a bit of time in his library, rifling through his shelves and shelves of books. He's got everything from the classics to Tom Clancy. None of the books show any signs of wear, so I have no clue if he actually reads them or if they just line the walls.

His large desk is sleek and modern, made from glass and ebony wood. No pictures adorn it, nothing personal at all. The middle drawer is locked, but I'm guessing it just contains checkbooks and such anyway.

The art on the walls, the many paintings and original photos, fascinate me.

I can tell the masculine abstract paintings are original, but the signatures aren't anyone I recognize. I'm guessing they're local artists… that perhaps Dominic just picked out pieces he liked because he didn't feel the need to buy originals painted by the masters.

The kitchen is nice, but boring. Granite, steel, marble floor. It's sterile because it's never used. I can see that. To me, kitchens should be the hub of the house, the heart, where everyone congregates. But that's not so here.

There are too many guest bedrooms to count, all of them lavishly decorated, just like the one I slept in last night. After he'd left me on the veranda.

I don't know what to think about him. He's a complete mystery, totally hot and cold. It must say something about me that I want to figure him out, that I'm not running in the opposite direction. I probably don't want to know what it says about me, actually.

I'm needy.

I'm fucked up.

I know these things, so I push them out of my mind. I already know *me*. What I want to know now is *him*.

I stand hesitantly outside of his bedroom door. Maybe I can find some answers within, answers that he'd never tell me. Something, anything, that would make his behavior make sense.

If he doesn't want you to know, my conscience argues, *then you should respect that.*

But…fuck you, the devil side of my brain answers. And that's the side I listen to. I turn the doorknob, and before I can even think about it, I'm in his room and it's done. I've officially invaded his privacy.

His room is dark and quiet and decorated in masculine colors… grays and creams and blacks. His bed is enormous, and there isn't anything odd in here, like I think I was expecting. No sex swings or whips or chains. It's uncluttered. In fact, it's incredibly clean. It almost seems as devoid of personal effects as a hotel room.

I feel a little guilty as I open his drawers, but I only find neatly folded clothes. The drawers all smell like cedar, like him. I take a deep breath, inhaling the scent, as I eye his closet, and before I can talk myself out of it, I get to my feet and open the doors.

It's enormous and contains a dressing room inside. A wall of shoes, loafers, and sneakers, and neatly hung slacks, jeans, shirts, and suits. It's a closet worthy of a king. I've never actually seen such a thing before. I sit on a cushioned bench for a minute, just to take it all in.

Like the bedroom, his closet is neat to the point of sterility. There's nothing here to indicate what he's actually like. Not one thing…except for the clear fact that he has a lot of shoes and clothes.

But as I stand up, I notice the bench I'm sitting on has hinges. They're cleverly concealed, but they're there. Hesitantly, I open the lid and I find myself staring at a shallow black velvet box. The rest of the bench is empty.

Breathing quickly, I lift the box out and stare at it. It's very light so it can't contain much. I don't waste time pondering it. I take the top off.

Inside, there's a stack of cards and letters, banded together with a rubber band. There's a little jewelry box, which I quickly discover is empty, and an unopened envelope with Dominic's name on the front. It was clearly written by a woman and says simply, *Dom*.

The ink has begun to fade and there's something hard inside, like cardboard or plastic.

I'm utterly frozen as I stare at it, because I can sense the significance of what must be inside. It was written by someone who knows him well, someone who calls him Dom.

But whatever it is, Dominic doesn't want to hear it. He doesn't want to see it. So he closed it away in this bench, away from the light, away from the world, away from him. But even still, even though he can't force himself to read it, he also can't force himself to throw it away.

I'd been wrong to come in here. Because I know that whatever I'm holding in my hands is so very intimate. It's personal and private. And it's not my business. But also, he's even more of an enigma now than he was before. I don't have any answers... I just have even more questions.

With a sigh, I stare at the stack of cards and letters wrapped with the rubber band. They're all opened. I can see the frayed tops of them, sliced through with an opener. Surely it won't matter if I just take a peek. Right?

I slip the rubber band off, and it's old enough that the rubber is tacky and has lost some of its elasticity. I can tell that Dom hasn't looked at these letters in quite a while, maybe even since he first opened them. But yet, just as the other letter, he can't throw them away. I look at the top card. There's a cross with sunshine pouring onto it.

With Sympathy for Your Loss.

I open it, skimming past the canned Hallmark words, skipping to the handwritten note at the bottom.

Dominic,

I'm so sorry for your loss. The world has lost a light in Emma. I know this is unbearable for you now, but I'll be praying a prayer of peace for you. I know that even without her, you'll be able to go on and do great things.

With love and deepest condolences,
Jada Milnay

My breath freezes in my throat, and a brick seems to settle on my chest as I stare at the words. A realization dawns on me, cold and heavy.

Emma died.

I have to assume that she was Dominic's girlfriend...and she died.

My fingers fly as I shuffle the rest of the cards and skim through them.

My condolences.

Heaven has gotten another angel.

My prayers are with you.

She's in a better place.

Trite words, although what can people really say? There are no words when something tragic like that strikes.

I can hardly breathe as I get to the last card, as I stare at what lies beneath the cards, hidden at the bottom of the stack. Letters.

From Emma.

Girlish, curly handwriting fills notebook papers, with flowers and hearts doodled in the margins. My fingers shake as I read the first one.

Dom,

Thank you so much for taking me to the beach yesterday. It was the perfect day! You laughed at me so much for trying to find the perfect shells, so I enclosed a few for you. I want you to remember the day just like I remember it being: perfect.

Em

This letter makes sense, because beneath the stack of envelopes, a smattering of tiny shells line the bottom of the box. They're clearly old, clearly fragile, and now they make perfect sense. They were a memento of a perfect day.

My breath comes quickly as I read the next one.

I feel like I'm looking in on the lives of two lovers.

Because I am.

Dom,

Last night was amazing. I woke up this morning and you were the first thing I thought of... and you were the last thing I thought of last night before I went to sleep. I always knew you would be my first—and it was amazing. I'm so glad that we shared that together, that we can say that we were each other's first.

I love you,
Em

My heart hurts. He took her virginity and she died.

I fly through the rest of the letters...but nothing in them gives me any clue as to what happened to her. Just random notes about high school, their mutual friends, their dates, and how much she loves Dominic. There are at least twenty of them, and they seem to span most of high school.

I know what she looked like now. Because in the last one, her senior picture is enclosed. She's slender and blond, with shining, friendly blue eyes that smile at the camera. She was a gorgeous girl, and it's clear that she loved life. I can see it in her eyes.

Knowing that she's dead now makes me feel like I'm surrounded by a ghost. It gives me chills, and I quickly gather all of the letters back together, looping them with the cards within the aged rubber band. There's only one letter left...the letter that Dominic hasn't even opened.

As I stare at it, I notice something. The handwriting on the envelope is the same.

Emma had written the unopened letter...the one simply addressed to *Dom*.

And Dominic can't bring himself to read it.

For some reason, because I'm sentimental, because I'm soft-hearted, or maybe just because I'm human, that sends a railroad spike through my heart, and the pain that I sometimes see in his eyes makes sense.

Of course it crushed him. Obviously he and Emma had been together for several years. They lost their virginity together. They loved each other. And then she died.

I'm pretty sure that a piece of Dominic died with her.

I'm sorry, he'd told me. *But I'm fucked up.*

Of course he is. At least that part makes sense now. The *why* of it, anyway. The *how* is still a mystery, but I'm not sure that it matters. Emma is dead and there's no bringing her back. But some other things are still unanswered...like why Dominic blames Cris.

I hear a noise downstairs, a noise like a door closing, and I leap to my feet, making sure that I put everything back exactly as I found it before I rush out the door, closing it quietly behind me. I rush downstairs toward the veranda.

After dying to know more about Dominic, I'm completely conflicted now and I regret snooping through his things. Something about that black velvet box made me intensely sad and melancholy.

Emma died.

She was a huge part of his life and she died. And not only that, but he refuses to talk about her or anything remotely concerning her. I know in my heart that whatever is wrong with Dominic, whatever is broken inside of him, is because of Emma.

But as sure as I know that, I know that the secrets I found today will have to stay hidden until Dominic is ready to talk about them. If that day ever comes.

With each day that passes, I grow more and more afraid that it never will.

Chapter Nineteen

Dominic

I find Jacey exactly where I figured she'd be. Soaking in the sun by the pool.

I stand in the doorway, watching her for a minute before I go out and wake her up. She's got a magnificent body, stretched out like a cat, basking in the warmth. I have to smile about that, and as I do, she opens her eyes and looks at me.

"Hey," she greets me sleepily. "How was your day? I didn't figure you'd be home until late."

I shrug. It fucking sucked. Amy Ashby was being her normal bitchy, entitled self, and I'd counted the minutes until the day was over. I went so far as to call Tally on the way home and tear him a new ass, telling him that I'd never work with Amy again. And he'd calmly reminded me that the public loves seeing us together . . . that it makes me money.

And it does, so I shut up and finished driving home in silence. But I did have a revelation.

As I crested the hill to my drive I realized that I'd been looking forward to seeing Jacey. That the anticipation of seeing her was the reason that my day dragged by so slowly.

It was a startling thought, but now that I'm here, staring down at her, it doesn't seem so startling. Being with her feels *right*.

And *that's* a startling thought.

"It was just a day," I tell her. "How was yours?"

"Oh, it was good. I snooped through all your stuff and swam all day. So it was just a day, too." She stares at me and there is something in her eyes, something I can't name, but then it's gone and she grins.

I shake my head.

"I don't have much for you to snoop through," I tell her, rolling my eyes. "I hate knickknack shit."

"You've got that right," she tells me with a yawn, sitting up to stretch. "This house seems almost like a hotel. There's nothing interesting here, except for the art on the walls. But thank you for having lunch sent over to me."

"No problem," I answer, pulling her to her feet. Her hand is warm and moist in mine, her touch electric. I drop her fingers as soon as she's standing. "I don't want to hang around the house tonight. Are you up for a surprise?"

She nods immediately. "I love surprises. What should I wear?"

"Shorts and a T-shirt are fine," I answer. "And comfortable shoes. We're going to be gone for hours, so I hope you had a nice nap." I smirk, but she doesn't even flinch.

"Awesome." She grins as she dashes inside. "I was bored."

I sit down on the veranda, staring at the water, pleasantly surprised by her reaction. Most women would've wheedled and moaned, wanting to know where we were going. But not Jacey. She likes the thrill of a surprise, I guess. And she must trust me.

The idea of that slams into my gut and I push the guilty feelings away.

She doesn't trust me with real-life stuff. She trusts me in a vague way, like she trusts that I'm not a psychopath who would take her somewhere and rape her or leave her for dead. That's a big difference from trusting me in general.

That's what I tell myself, anyway. But by the time the chartered helicopter lands on the front lawn and we board, Jacey's eyes are excited and amused...and they tell me more about her than I really want to know. She does trust me...with more than I'm comfortable with.

I ignore it because that's the only thing I can do. Instead, I focus on buckling up and signing the flight agreement for the pilot. When I turn back to Jacey, we're taking off, and she is practically bouncing up and down like a child.

"I've never been in a helicopter before," she tells me radiantly. "This is amazing. Where are we going?"

"You'll have to wait and see," I tell her with a grin. "You said you liked surprises."

"And I do." She nods.

The helicopter shudders a bit, then wobbles as the pilot gains control of the weight balance on board. Jacey's eyes light up and she stares downward as we fly higher and higher, lifting up and away from Los Angeles.

She chats for a while, but I can barely hold my eyes open. I'm tired from getting up so early to be on set, and comfortable in the afternoon sun that's shining in on my seat.

Before I know it, Jacey is shaking me and squealing like a kid.

"Oh my god. It's the Grand Canyon. I can't believe you brought me here."

I open my eyes to find that I've been asleep for over two hours and that the Grand Canyon is spread beneath us, majestic and dry and red.

"Have you ever been here?" I ask Jacey as I stretch, but I already know the answer to that. She shakes her head.

"No. I actually haven't been many places."

"I thought the Grand Canyon was a staple on family vacation lists," I mention as I stare out the window. Jacey sighs.

"Probably. But my family wasn't normal. And I didn't go on very many family vacations. I didn't go on *any* after my parents got divorced."

Fuck. Like the asshole I am, I'd forgotten about her shitty childhood.

"I'm sorry," I tell her quickly. "I forgot about that. Well, I'm glad that I get to be the first to show you this place. I know I'm weird… it's dry and desolate, but to me, it's one of the most beautiful things in the world."

Jacey presses her face to the glass, staring down as we fly across the cavernous gap of the canyon.

"Thank you for bringing me," she tells me, and she sounds almost shy. "What the hell?" she exclaims as the helicopter starts its descent. "Are we landing *in* the canyon?"

I chuckle at the wonder in her voice. "I thought you might be hungry," I explain. "The pilot is going to drop us off for a couple of hours so we can have a picnic and explore a bit, then he'll be back to pick us up at sundown. Is that okay?"

"Holy shit." Jacey shakes her head. "I didn't even know that was possible. Of course it's okay. It's amazing."

She reaches over and grabs my hand, holding it as the pilot settles the big bird on a flat plane of the canyon. I'm not sure if she's nervous because of the landing, but just in case, I don't pull away. It shudders, then comes to a stop. The pilot gets out, then helps us out, cautioning us to duck our heads. I let Jacey hold my hand until I have to shake the pilot's.

"We'll see you in a couple of hours," I tell him. He nods, climbs back inside, and Jacey and I are alone with a picnic basket and a blanket.

As he flies away, the wind blows our hair away from our faces, stirring the dust around us. Jacey spins in a circle, trying to see everywhere at once.

"I can't believe how gorgeous this place is," she exclaims. "It's so...desolate, like you said, but it's so vibrant and beautiful. It's like...it's so tough, yet such beautiful things still grow from it. It's like a metaphor for life. There's beauty even in the roughest parts."

"You think?" I raise an eyebrow as I set our stuff down, staring at the few dots of green that grace the red and dusty horizon. "Are you always so deep?"

Jacey looks at me, thoughtful and quiet, with a strange expression. "I don't know. It's just what this place brings to mind. It reminds me almost of the human spirit. We're too tough to be kept down, no matter what."

"Okay, now you're scaring me," I tell her, and I shoot her a dubious look. "You're getting *really* deep."

"No deeper than you were last night," she tosses back as she spreads the blanket and opens the basket. "And this place sort of demands it, you know? It makes me feel so small."

"We *are* small, in the scheme of things," I answer as I settle next to her. She sifts through the basket, pulling out tiny sandwiches, gourmet olives, and wine, and then she looks up at me.

"Now this is a picnic," she announces, pulling out the wine and glasses. "When you do something, you do it right, Dominic."

That's true. I do. But I don't answer. Instead, I pop the cork on the wine, pouring us each a glass.

She hands me a turkey sandwich and takes a drink of wine.

"Why did you arrange this?" she asks curiously as she takes a bite. "It's awesome, but it's so out of the blue. What made you do it?"

I don't fucking know.

I chew my sandwich, swallow, then take another bite.

"I don't know," I actually admit, surprising myself. "I thought you might like it. And we're supposed to be hanging out. We didn't say that all of our 'hanging out' had to be sexual. We just said we want to have fun. And this is fun for me."

Jacey smiles, satisfied with my answer. "It's fun for me, too."

We finish our meal in silence, but words aren't really necessary. We're surrounded by one of the Seven Wonders of the World. A conversation would mar the experience.

As we're putting our trash back into the basket, Jacey's fingers brush mine and she turns to me.

"I see you, you know," she says quietly. "I know you're different than what you want people to think."

I pause, staring into her dark eyes. "Oh, really? And you gathered that from a trip to the Grand Canyon?"

I try to sound sarcastic, to sound flippant, but the sharpness dies on my tongue, because there's something in her eyes that tells me she does see into me.

She shakes her head. "No. Not from this trip. But from a lot of little things that you don't want me to see. You know what Jake told me before I left yesterday? That someone miraculously paid Joe's back taxes. He has no idea who, but the amount was huge... thousands of dollars. And there's only one person I know who has that kind of money and might help Joe out."

I freeze, refusing to look away from her. "Oh, really? That was nice of someone."

Jacey rolls her eyes. "Yeah, it was nice of someone. Why do you pretend to be such an asshole, Dominic? When I know that you aren't, not really. You just like to pretend that you are. You're good at pretending."

I grab her hand, intent on squashing her delusion about me right now . . . and on getting that soft look out of her eyes once and for all. Every time I see it, every time I see how soft she gets when she thinks she sees something good in me, it twists my guts up and spits them out. Because she's wrong.

"Jacey, I'm not good. I'm the opposite of good. Have you ever wondered if people are monsters inside, down where no one can see? Because I don't have to wonder. I know that I am. Did I pay Joe's taxes? Yeah, I did. I've already got a bunch of time invested in community service with him and I don't want to have to go somewhere else. Period. I'm not a good guy, Jacey. I'm not the person that you'd like to believe. Please know that. Don't make the mistake of romanticizing me."

She looks at me doubtfully. "So you paid thousands of dollars of his taxes so that you wouldn't have to get used to another supervisor? Whatever, Dominic. You can say what you want, but I don't believe you. You helped him because you wanted to. Because you can see that he's a decent person and you wanted to help him out. Why can't you admit that? Why do you insist on acting like such an ass?"

I shake my head. "Because I *am* an ass. You need to get used to the idea, Jacey. I'm not going to change."

"Whatever," she says dismissively, getting to her feet. "I don't buy it. But I'm tired of talking about it."

She stomps off and I sit for a second, trying to decide whether to go after her or not, when she comes stomping back.

"And another thing," she says before she stops, her eyes widening. She freezes in place, staring at me.

"What?" I ask in confusion. "Why are you looking at me like that?"

"Don't move," she says quietly, looking at something past my shoulder as she takes a tentative step toward me. "Don't move a muscle, Dom."

That's when I hear it. An unmistakable rustle of something big behind me. The hairs lift up on the back of my neck and I stare calmly at Jacey.

"What is it? Bear?"

She shakes her head and the color drains from her face. "Mountain lion. I think. It's a huge tan cat with really big teeth. It's just sitting there staring at me, about five feet behind you. What do we do?"

I try to think, while at the same time I mentally distance myself from the situation so that I can stay calm. "I don't think we play dead. That's for a bear. I'm pretty sure we're supposed to act intimidating."

"How the hell do we do that?" Jacey hisses, her eyes frozen on the animal behind me. "It's pretty intimidating itself."

"Well, first, we can't run," I tell her as I calmly pivot and slowly look behind me. But when I see the cat, the first thing I want to do is run.

To say it's intimidating is the biggest understatement I've heard in a while.

The massive cat must weigh as much as I do, and its fangs glisten in the dying sunlight. It stares back at me with golden eyes and it looks almost bored. But then it growls, ever so slightly, enough to let me know that it's far from bored, enough to send shivers down my spine. It's very interested in us, even though it remains motionless.

"We can't run, or it will think we're prey," I tell Jacey quietly. I take a slow step back, and it growls louder, its golden eyes watching my every movement, tracking me.

"Fuck," I mutter under my breath. "Jacey, go. Walk away slowly and I'll stay right here. I'll figure something out."

"Like hell," Jacey answers snappishly. She waves her arms. "Get out of here, you fucking animal! Go!" Her shouts only seem to amuse the cat and it stares at her with even more interest, its long tail flicking in the air. It moves one large paw, planting it in the red dirt. I suck in a breath.

"Jacey, I don't think that's helping," I point out. "It thinks you're an appetizer."

My heart is pounding by this point, because honestly, for the first time in as long as I remember, I don't know what to do. All I know is I don't want to meet my end at the end of those pointy teeth.

Jacey shouts louder, and the cat growls menacingly as she bends to pick up a large round rock, a foot in diameter. The cat opens its mouth and roars, a shrill and hoarse sound like a scream. Jacey freezes, and what happens next is so fast it's a blur.

The cat roars again, standing up on its hind legs and batting at the air with its paw before it lunges toward me.

Jacey shrieks and jumps in front of me, hurling the rock at the giant animal, hitting it squarely in the face. But as she throws it, she trips and sprawls in the red dust directly in front of the giant cat.

She's entirely at its mercy.

For a second, my heart stops. I move to shield Jacey from an attack, but the cat turns, shaking its head, as if to clear it from the impact of the rock. It stumbles for a second, then to my surprise, it spins around and retreats, loping off into the distance.

I'm frozen for a moment before I scramble to get to Jacey.

"What the hell?" I demand. "You could've been killed. You don't go rushing at a wild animal like that!"

Jacey stares up at me, her eyes wide and filled with pain. "I didn't mean to. I tripped. But either way, it worked. The fucking thing is gone, isn't it?"

"What's wrong?" I ask her quickly. Her eyes are watering and she's gripping her ankle like she's never letting go.

"My foot," she says through gritted teeth. "I twisted it. How cliché is that?"

Adrenaline is coursing through me and I swallow the acidic taste.

"Jacey, you could've died. The chopper isn't coming back for us for another hour. If that thing would've attacked you, we might not have made it to a hospital in time. Why the fuck did you do that?"

She opens her eyes and shrugs, determined to make it seem like a small deal. "Because it was going to jump on you. It was the only plan I could think of."

"Your plan sucked," I growl as I grab her up and haul her onto my lap, lifting her foot to examine it. As carefully as I can, I pull her sneaker off. Her foot is already swollen, and it's turning purple fast.

"I don't know if it's broken," I tell her quietly. "It might be. Or it could just be bruised. Either way, it's going to hurt."

"Going to?" she grimaces, gritting her teeth. "I don't think I can walk on it."

"I'm sure you can't." I eye it. "There's no way. We'll just stay right here until our ride comes back. You'll have to see the Grand Canyon from here. I'm sorry."

"I'm not worried about it," she answers, nestling back into my arms, molding herself to my chest. "I just hope he doesn't come back.

Oh my god. He sounded like a woman screaming, didn't he? Holy shit. I'll never forget that sound."

"Me, either," I admit, looking around. "I don't see any more lurking around. You scared the shit out of that one. I doubt he'll be back." I glance down at her swollen foot and wince. "I wish I'd thought to bring some ibuprofen or something. I'm sorry. God. This is the second time you've been hurt because of me."

Something akin to guilt wells up in me, but she shrugs, curling up on my lap. It's been awhile since someone has lain there for a reason other than sucking my dick. I try not to think about that as I wrap my arms around her and keep her close.

She just risked her life for me.

I don't know anyone, other than my parents or Sin or maybe Duncan, who would do that for me. It's mind-blowing, actually.

When the helicopter arrives an hour later, I realize something else startling. I've been holding her hand this entire time and I didn't even know it.

Chapter Twenty

Jacey

My foot throbs like bloody hell as I curl up once again on Dominic's veranda and soak in the moonlight. Since I can't move from my seat, I make sure to enjoy the scenery, which consists of Dominic's perfect ass and chiseled abs. I've been staring at both things off and on for the last hour.

"Thank you for having a doctor come by," I tell him once again. "I didn't even know doctors made house calls anymore."

"People will do anything if you pay them enough," Dominic answers tiredly, bringing a tray of food through the glass doors. "He's the doctor we use on set. I'm just glad your ankle isn't broken."

"Nope," I reply as cheerfully as I can. "Just bruised. I'll be good as new in a week or so."

Dominic rolls his eyes. "Are you always this cheerful?"

I shake my head. "Hell no. Try waking me up before nine A.M. and you'll see a whole new level of ugly."

He chuckles, settling back into the cushions. "Do you want to go to bed? You must be tired."

I shake my head. "The pain meds your guy gave me are making

me a little sleepy, but I'm sort of too amped up to rest. Can we just talk for a while?"

Dominic looks pained. "Oh, yeah. My favorite thing to do."

The way he says it makes me laugh and Dominic smiles. "So glad to be a source of amusement to you."

I smile again as the warm breeze lifts the hair away from my face. "Can you help me into the pool? It was so hot and dry out in the canyon that I'd like to get wet."

I left myself wide open for a sexual jab by Dominic, but he ignores it.

"Are you sure?" He raises an eyebrow. "The doctor said you should rest your foot."

I shake my head. "He also said it wasn't broken. Trust me, I've got enough pain meds in me to put out a small horse. I'm feeling no pain." To prove my point, I stand up awkwardly, swaying a bit before I catch my balance. I strip off my shirt, then sit back down to take off my shorts.

Dominic doesn't say anything…he just sits back and watches me, his eyes darkening as I strip off my bra. There's a million things hidden in his eyes right now, but he doesn't voice any of them. Instead, he just stands up and gently grabs my arm.

"Ready?"

I nod, expecting him to help me hobble into the water, but that's not what he does. Instead, he scoops me up and carries me directly into the pool, pausing only for a second to kick his shoes off at the edge.

Other than that, he's fully clothed.

He carries me straight into the water, completely soaking his clothes. I stare at him in shock. "Why didn't you undress?"

He stares down at me, his dark gaze meeting mine. "Jacey, you jumped in front of a cougar for me today. If you say you want to swim, I'm going to drop what I'm doing and carry you into the water."

A weird feeling ripples through me, warm and tingly.

"Seriously? That's all I had to do to impress you? I just had to jump in front of a hungry wild animal? Why didn't you tell me? I would've done it a long time ago."

He throws his head back and laughs, a genuine laugh and his teeth gleam in the dark. He tightens his grip on me for a second, then he lowers me carefully into the water, holding me up as I gingerly set my foot down, then pick it back up and tread water.

"Who says you impressed me?" he asks mockingly, treading water in front of me. "I'm only admitting that I owe you. I pay my debts."

I roll my eyes now. "Whatever. I know you're impressed. And what's more, you like me. You just don't want to admit it. You don't want to admit that I'm a decent person...because you think that the world is only made up of assholes. To admit that I'm not horrible would mess up your deep-seated belief system. I wouldn't want to do that."

Dom cocks his head, studying me in the night. "I thought you said you weren't decent?"

I shrug, my fingers slicing through the cool water. "I don't think I am. But compared to your opinion of humanity, I think I do okay."

"If you're not decent, then who is?" Dominic demands, swimming toward me. "Because I'd like to meet that person."

"My best friend Maddy," I answer immediately. "She's pretty amazing. But she moved to Connecticut, so you probably won't ever meet her. That's good though. She's drop-dead gorgeous, and my brother would kick your ass if he caught you drooling over her, so it's for the best."

"Do you really think I would drool over her if you were in the room?" Dominic asks softly, treading water very close to me. The moonlight makes him look pensive, thoughtful. And I stare at him.

"Probably," I answer finally. "Everyone does."

"Not me," Dominic replies firmly. "I wouldn't have any need to."

"Why are you being so nice to me today?" I demand quickly. "First a picnic in the Grand Canyon, then you ordered a private midnight snack on your veranda, and now you're giving me compliments. You're freaking me out, Dom. Knock it off."

"I haven't even begun to get nice yet," he tells me, his voice growing as dark as his eyes. He pushes me through the water until we reach the side of the pool, where he rests his hands on either side of my hips. "Want me to start right now?"

He doesn't give me a chance to reply. Instead, he kisses me, suddenly and thoroughly. His mouth covers mine, his lips cold and wet. I wrap my arms around his neck and hold on, melting into him, absorbing his heat, enjoying the way his wet body feels against mine.

"Why did you do it?" he whispers into my ear. "Why did you risk yourself like that for me?"

He nips at my ear and trails his lips down the length of my neck until he reaches my collarbone. "Tell me," he demands. "I need to know. I don't see what you gained from it."

I force myself to pull away from him, just for a minute. "I didn't gain anything from it," I answer sharply. "Just the knowledge and satisfaction of knowing that you didn't get eaten. That was enough."

He pulls away, too, just for a minute, and stares into my eyes. In the night, his eyes look almost black. Without saying another word, he kisses me again, and again, and again. Hard, soft, brutal, exquisite.

"Take off your clothes," I urge him. "I want to feel your skin."

To my surprise, he does. He peels off the wet clothes and flings them onto the stone deck, turning again to pull me to him. His chest is hard, his stomach flat, and his dick hard. Very hard. It wedges between my legs and I shiver a bit, at the mere thought that it's all for me.

He's hard for me.

He lifts me up and I wrap my legs around his waist, kissing him yet again. I decide that I could kiss him forever...he's perfect at it. His tongue slides along my lip and he bites at it, just a little.

"Do you want more?" he whispers. "Yes or no?"

"We're back to that?" I answer softly. "You can't tell what I want?"

He looks at me. "I just like hearing the word *yes*."

"I'd think you'd get tired of hearing it all the time," I reply as he holds me up in the water.

"Not from you," he answers. He kisses me again, his lips consuming me. And then he stops, looking at me seriously.

"I'm a very good actor," he tells me matter-of-factly. "I'm good at pretending that I'm someone else. And tonight, I'm going to be someone else. Does that bother you?"

I'm surprised by his sudden turn and by the oh-so-serious expression on his face, but no, I'm not bothered. I tell him that and he smiles.

"But who do you want to be?" I add curiously. He shrugs.

"Anyone but me."

He pushes me against the side of the pool, thrusting his hips against me, rubbing me. His weight is perfect, hard, rigid, amazing.

I take a deep breath when he bends his head and nips at my breast, sucking my nipple into his mouth. I throw my head back as he sucks harder.

"But why?" I manage to persist, even though he's trying his best to distract me. "You're pretty amazing. Why would you want to be someone else? Are you sure that you just don't want *me* to be someone else?"

Dominic stops what he's doing and pulls away, looking at me with a hard expression. His green eyes have a dull light in them now, something that happens when he's annoyed. I stare back, trying to be unabashed.

"What do you mean?" he asks slowly. "Why would I want you to be someone else?"

I shrug, trying to ignore my pounding heart. Why did I choose this moment to bring this up? Why? But I'm not one to back down, so I don't.

"I don't know. I just thought maybe you were pretending that I'm Emma."

As soon as the name falls from my lips, I know it's a mistake.

Dominic's face immediately closes, his eyes turning into hardened marble. He releases me quickly as though touching me is burning his hands. And then he turns his back on me and walks out of the pool.

"What's wrong with you?" I call after him as I follow. "It was just a question. I was just wondering. About her."

Dominic turns, and for a minute his face is filled with pain, but then he conceals it, replacing it with a hardened mask. "You don't have any right to be curious about her," he answers starkly. "Please don't bring her up again."

"But—"

Dominic holds up his hand. "No buts. She isn't significant to you. Just leave it alone. Good night."

He actually turns around and stalks back into the house, leaving me to stand wobbly and naked on his terrace alone.

What the hell was that about? He can't even hear her name? I think I have every right to ask if he's imagining that I'm her. But then again, he has no idea that I saw the letters...and her picture. He doesn't know how much I know of her.

And how much it tells about him.

But as I think of it, I realize, too, that I don't really know all that much at all. What I do know is that if we're going to continue whatever it is that we are doing, I need to know.

I need to know about Emma. I need to know how she broke Dominic.

Chapter Twenty~One

Dominic

I lay in the dark, naked and alone, and try to pull myself together.

Quit being such a pussy.

But Emma's name, coming from Jacey's lips, was such an unexpected shock to the system that it took the wind out of me. Jacey has no idea how much I *don't* pretend that she's Emma. She has no idea how much that name guts me.

And she won't ever know, because there's no way in hell that I'm going to talk about it. Jesus.

I can't believe I'd been so close…so close to simply pretending that I was someone else tonight…and fucking Jacey in my pool.

I almost let my guard down that fucking much.

It won't happen again. I flip over onto my back and shove a pillow onto my head so I can sleep.

∾

The flight home is awkward and quiet. Jacey stares quietly out the window, barely saying anything. I want to say something, but I'm not sure what. I'm not sure what there *is* to say. She wants more of me than I can give. She wants to know me.

Well, she *thinks* she does. If she did get to know me, she'd take back that wish. I can guarantee that.

I drop her off at her house, and she barely looks at me as she kisses my cheek and gets out of the car.

She doesn't talk to me for two days.

It's a long fucking two days.

She ignores me at work, and by the first night, I itch to call her. I go so far as to pull out my phone and start to dial her number before I stare at it and sigh.

Call her and say what?

There's nothing to say. We're at an impasse. She needs more than I can give.

The strange thing is that I wish it were different. For the first time ever, I wish that I could be *that guy*. The guy who can do a relationship. The guy who can do the give-and-take thing. But I know me. And I know that I'm the guy who just takes and takes.

I don't have the ability to give.

I put my phone away.

On the second day, as I round the corner into the locker room, I hear Jacey's voice and I freeze, not wanting her to see me.

"I know, Mad." She sighs, and I know that she's on the phone with her best friend. "I know. But he's not like Jared. I swear to god. He's not like that."

There's a pause while she listens, and I'd give my left nut to be able to hear what Maddy is saying.

"He won't talk about it," she continues. "Trust me, I tried. But—"

Maddy must've interrupted, because Jacey abruptly stops and listens.

"Yeah, I know that. I know I can't control how other people act. I can only control myself. I know."

She sighs.

"I'm falling for him, Mad. I tried not to. But I can't help it. There's something more to him. Something deep and hurt. Deep down, he's a good guy. He's just injured on the inside."

Pause.

And then she protests. "No, it's not like that. Mad, it's like when you met Gabe. You knew he might not be good for you, but your gut told you that there was something really good inside him. And there was, Mad. I think Dom might be the same way."

Another pause, during which my tongue feels like a piece of lead.

She's falling for me?

My heart runs away in my chest and I'm utterly frozen to the ground.

I can't be the person she wants me to be. I'm *not* good deep down, not like she thinks. No matter how much I like her or how much I like being around her, I don't see the sense in continuing this when I know what the end result will be.

I owe her that much. If she can't protect herself from me, I'll do it for her.

I walk around the corner, and Jacey looks up from where she's sitting on a locker room bench. Her eyes widen at the sight of me.

"I've gotta go, Mad. I'll call you later. Love you, too."

She stands up and slips her phone in her pocket. As she turns toward me, her eyes so fucking soft and gentle, I have every intention of firmly ending things.

Very firmly. So firmly that she won't even try to change my mind.

But then she speaks, and what she says takes me by surprise.

"I'm sorry, Dominic," she says simply, staring into my eyes. "About the other night, I mean. I shouldn't have brought up an old girlfriend like that. Whatever happened with you and her…it's not my business. We're just having fun…and that was out of line. I'm sorry."

I'm shocked that she would apologize. I'm shocked she would say that we're just having fun when I'd just heard her tell Maddy that she was falling for me.

It's so drastically different from the conversation that I thought I'd be having right now that all I can do is nod.

I nod, because if she wants to pretend that we're so fucking casual, if she wants to go on with the status quo and not acknowledge the feelings that might change everything, then I'm not going to stop her. Not yet.

I'm too fucking selfish for that.

So, nodding, I answer, "I'm sorry, too. I probably overreacted."

Jacey stares at me in shock, light gleaming in her eyes now. "Did you actually just apologize to me? Was that your first time? Did it hurt?"

I roll my eyes. "I was thinking the same thing about you. But hey, I'm not going to question a girl who punches cougars in the face."

"Whatever." She shoves my arm. "I didn't punch it in the face. I threw a rock into its face."

"Same thing," I tell her wryly, and with that, the tension between us is lifted.

Just like that. We're back to pretending again, our stupid little fantasy where we act like we're got everything under control, that we're nothing more than friends with benefits.

That's okay with me.

I'm an actor. I can fucking act.

The problem is, this isn't a movie. Jacey and I are balancing on a very thin line between a façade and reality. We're treading on very thin ice. In real life, when people walk on ice for too long, they finally break through.

And when that happens, someone drowns.

Chapter Twenty~Two

Dominic

Being the fucking actors that we are, Jacey and I pretend that everything is fine. We talk back and forth for the rest of the day about nonsense things, gossipy things, things that don't fucking matter.

When it's almost time to go home, I'm getting ready to see if she wants to duck out with me and grab dinner when Jake, Tig, and two other boys come walking through the gym with about a million balloons, all of them pink.

All of them say HAPPY BIRTHDAY.

Surprised, I stare at Jacey and find her grinning wildly.

"How did you know?" she squeals as she rushes up to hug them.

"I might've said something," a deep voice rumbles. The balloons part and a guy steps out. Big, dark haired, dark eyed. He's got Jacey's eyes and a tattoo on his bicep: DEATH BEFORE DISHONOR.

"Gabe!" she shrieks, running at him in a dead sprint and leaping into his arms. "How are you...why are you..."

Her voice dies off and he laughs, holding her easily in his heavily muscled arms. He and Brand were certainly cut from the same cloth.

"I finally rendered you speechless?" He grins. "Well, that only took twenty-four years. And you think I'd miss your birthday?

Really? I called Joe and asked if we could surprise you here. He roped the boys in on it, too."

Jacey pulls away and looks at him. "But Maddy's due soon. You shouldn't have left her."

Gabe chuckles and sets his sister on the floor. "I'm only here for the evening, just to be on the safe side. I'll fly back home tonight. But Maddy sends her birthday wishes—she's going to call you tonight."

"She actually called me just now. She couldn't wait. And she didn't let it slip that you were here. Oh my gosh, I miss you guys so much!" Jacey cries, and her eyes actually do well up. Gabe glares at her mockingly.

"Don't cry on your birthday," he instructs her with a grin. "You're so dramatic."

She arches an eyebrow. "Dramatic? I haven't seen you in months."

"Well, I'm here now," he pacifies her. "I'm going to take you to eat, and I want to hear everything that's going on. Brand's picking us up."

They brush past me, and as they do, Jacey pauses, looking at me. "Gabe, this is Dominic Kinkaide."

"The actor," Gabe points out, his eyebrow raised as he stares at me. I can actually see the thoughts in his eyes. The protective big-brother genes have stepped in, and he wants to know what I am to his sister.

"Guilty," I tell him, holding out my hand. Technically, I'm only addressing what he said out loud. But I'm also admitting guilt to the question in his eyes. Yes, I've done inappropriate things with his sister. No, I'm not sorry.

And no, I'm not afraid of him. He probably sees all of that in my eyes, just like I see all of the questions in his.

"Gabe Vincent," he says politely, shaking my hand. "It's nice to meet you. Brand's told me all about you—and how you and Jacey wound up here together."

Fuck.

But I keep my expression calm. "That was a messed-up night, and I'm sorry that Jacey was involved in it at all. Thankfully, we'll be done with our community service soon and we can forget it ever happened."

Jacey stares at me, and there's hurt in her eyes because it sounds like I'm saying that I want to forget about her, too. I feel a twinge of guilt about that, in addition to the fact that I didn't even know it was her birthday. But I'm saying what her brother wants to hear. Gabe nods.

"It's good to meet you."

And they disappear through the door. I follow them so I can get to my own car and step outside just in time to hear Jacey squeal again.

What the hell?

Brand is driving up in a little red Honda Civic. He looks like Grape Ape in the thing with his head grazing the ceiling, but the situation is clear.

Either Brand or Gabe bought Jacey a car for her birthday.

She's jumping around like a lunatic, hugging them both and shrieking like a kid.

"Oh my god! I can't believe you did this!" She's crying and shrieking and Gabe laughs.

"You thought I'd let you drive that piece-of-shit death trap around forever? Whatever. Happy birthday, sis."

She hugs him, then hugs Brand. When she stares up at Brand, with her arms around his neck . . . the way she looks at him, like he's a fucking hero or something, causes my stomach to clench.

Jesus.

His big hands hold her close, and Gabe catches me staring. I can see in his eyes that he sees what I see. Brand's in love with his sister.

Whether Jacey is still denying it is unclear.

"Come on, Jace." Gabe pulls her away from Brand. "Let's get some dinner. I'll buy you cupcakes for dessert."

They pile into Jacey's new car and drive away.

Joe stands behind me, watching them leave. "Those boys got medals for their time in Afghanistan. Jacey comes from good people, son."

I don't bother reminding him that I'm not his son. It doesn't bother me as much this time as it usually does. Not now that Joe actually seems to like me.

"She does," I agree as I start toward my car. Too bad one of them is in love with her.

"Kinkaide, wait!" Joe calls. I pause, turning back toward him. "I know what you did."

"Pardon?" I ask, staring at him in confusion. I'm thinking that he's figured out that Jacey and I are seeing each other, but no.

"I know you paid my taxes," Joe says firmly, staring at me. "Don't bother denying it. It had to be you. You overheard me on the phone with the IRS."

"I'm not denying it," I answer, just as firmly, my hand on my car door. "I didn't want this place to have to close. I don't do enough humanitarian things, so it was just as much for me as you."

"Well, I'm not a charity case," Joe tells me proudly. "And I'll pay you back every cent."

"You don't need to do that," I tell him quickly. "It was something I wanted to do."

"Yeah, I do need to," Joe replies. "And I will. And I don't want you thinking that you get special treatment around here. You're still going to have to get here on time, and you can't miss days. I won't cut you any slack because of this, got it?"

"Of course not," I answer wryly. "I wouldn't have dreamed of that."

And I wouldn't have. Joe doesn't play favorites, and he's only just starting to like me. I climb into my car, but before I can close my door, Joe says my name again.

I look up at him. "Yeah?"

Joe stares at me with faded blue eyes. "Thanks."

I know it was hard for him to say, so I just nod and drive away without making a big deal of it. I'm surprised how good helping him has made me feel, though. I'm buoyed by a sense of moral goodness, and that's something I rarely get the chance to feel. It's a novel fucking feeling.

I drive aimlessly for a while before I pick up a sandwich. I'm restless and I know why. I want to know what's going on with Brand and Jacey.

Is it my business?

Hell no. Because I'm not supposed to care.

But what the hell are they doing right now?

I'm being pathetic, like a jealous teenager. At the same time, I feel like an ass because I hadn't known about her birthday. The girl risked her life for me, for god's sake. The least I can do is know when her birthday is.

But better late than never.

I scroll through my phone for the flower shop nearest to her house and make a call.

After five minutes, I smile as I speak. "Great. That's exactly what I want. Yes, I know it's an unusual request. Yes, I'm sure people usually like the stems, too."

I head to the nearest bar and drink a couple of whiskeys before I drive for Jacey's house. I haven't texted her, so I have no idea when she'll be home. All I know is, when she does come back, I'll be waiting for her.

Well, me and a yard full of flower petals.

I stand at her gate, smiling as I stare at her tiny lawn. It's completely blanketed by several inches of pink rose petals. I can smell the thick rose smell from here. The wind rustles them, spreading them across the sidewalk, carrying their scent on the breeze. It looks like something out of an abstract painting. Or a dream.

Her dream.

I sit on her porch and wait.

I entertain myself by scrolling through my phone, and it's almost dusk when I hear her talking. I pick my head up to find Brand walking Jacey along the sidewalk in front of the house.

"You didn't have to follow me home," Jacey tells him, smiling up at him. My gut clenches yet again over the expression on her face. "I've watched my brother fly away a million other times when you guys were still in the Army. I'm fine."

"Well, I just wanted to make sure," Brand says quietly. "I know it's hard, Jace. I know you feel all alone here, but you're not. I'm still here."

They stop in the middle of the sidewalk, and neither of them have noticed me yet. Jacey stands on her tiptoes and kisses Brand's cheek. "I know," she replies softly. "You always have been. Thank you for an amazing birthday, Brand."

"You're welcome." He stares down at her, and the moment suddenly seems painfully intimate. I can't take it. I clear my throat and they both startle, staring at me in surprise.

"Dominic!" Jacey exclaims, stepping away from Brand and peering into the darkness toward me. "I didn't even see your car. What are you doing here?" And then she notices her yard.

"Holy shit." She breathes, her eyes widening. "Oh my god. Did you do this?"

I nod. "I'm sorry that I didn't know it was your birthday."

She stares at me, her eyes still wide. "And so you made my dream come true? You're responsible for the death of a million roses now, but oh my god. It's so beautiful."

I stare at her, trying to ignore the awe in her eyes. "I came to see if you wanted to hang out for a while. For your birthday. I didn't know you'd still be tied up."

I glance at Brand and back at Jacey. She's shaking her head. "Brand just followed me home. He was afraid I'd be upset over Gabe leaving. He keeps forgetting that I'm a big girl now." She laughs, and Brand looks pained.

I know that he's actually very aware that she's a big girl now, but I don't say that.

Instead, I quickly try to think of something that I can do with Jacey, somewhere to invite her that would seem like a date. I want to drive home to Brand that Jacey isn't his.

I smile as I get an idea. "I thought I'd take my car out to the track to blow off some steam. Would you like to come?"

Jacey looks intrigued. "To a race track? Sure, that might be fun. I'll try anything once. But only if I can drive, too."

I roll my eyes. "As if you could handle it." I'm pretending that Brand isn't even here, but Jacey turns around to kiss him on the cheek again.

"Thank you again, big bro," she tells him. I swear to god I can see him flinch at that. I fight back a smirk. "I'll talk to you later." She turns back to me. "I've just got to run to the restroom and then I'll be ready."

She darts into the house, leaving me with Brand. He stares at me, his gaze sharp and pointed and I sigh.

I knew this was going to happen at some point, and it might as well be now. I turn to him.

"Do you have a problem with me?" I ask him. I might as well just get it out there. Brand stares back at me, and Jesus, the guy is enormous. I don't give a shit though. I'm not intimidated by anyone.

"Why do you ask?" Brand asks, his lip twitching in amusement. I don't find anything funny.

"Because I can tell that you do," I say calmly. "I can't figure out why, since Jacey told me that you guys are just friends, that you're a big brother to her."

I hit a nerve there, but I meant to. Something passes over his face, but he doesn't acknowledge it.

"I've known her for a long time," he says instead. "And I watch her back. Keep that in mind, friend."

"We're not friends," I point out, like the asshole that I am. "We only just met."

Brand nods slowly. "True. But we're not enemies, either. Yet. I'd like to keep it that way. How about you?"

There's not a threat in his voice, more like a promise. If I fuck with Jacey, I'll be his enemy. I feel fairly confident that that isn't a good thing to be.

"Noted." I nod. "Let's keep it that way."

He stares at me for a minute before he walks away. He climbs into his truck and sits there, waiting for us to leave. It occurs to me that he doesn't like the idea of leaving Jacey and me alone together. It's a thought that makes me smirk again.

"What?" Jacey asks innocently as she emerges from her house and catches me grinning.

"Nothing," I answer, as we walk to my car and I open her door. "Are you ready?"

She nods, tosses her purse on the floorboard, and we drive away. Brand's truck follows us for a while, and I can feel his eyes burning into the back of my neck, but the next time I look, he's gone.

"So, how long have you been racing your car?" Jacey asks curiously.

I shrug. "I don't know. Years. I like speed."

"I know." Jacey sighs. "Fast cars and fast women."

I chuckle and rev the engine at the light. When the light turns green, I squeal my tires and take off from the line like a shot. When I glance over at Jacey, she's relaxed in her seat, staring out the window.

"Nothing?" I ask her. "No reaction whatsoever?"

She giggles.

"Did you expect me to be terrified? Not gonna happen. I grew up with Gabe and Brand and they did some dumbass things with cars…usually when I was with them. I'm never scared…not if I trust who's driving."

I glance at her quickly before I look back at the road. "And you trust me? Silly girl."

"I know." She rolls her eyes. "I don't know what I'm thinking."

"Obviously," I answer.

One of Sin's songs comes on the radio, so I turn it up and we ride the rest of the way with Duncan's steady drums thumping in our chests and Sin's voice in our ears. It's one of his slower songs, a dark love song, and when I glance over at Jacey she's got her eyes closed and she's moving her lips with the words.

My soul is black, black as night, but you love it anyway.

Your heart is cold, cold as ice, but it's mine to take.

I'll take it and crush it because that's what I do,
And you'll ask for more, because that's you.

Something about the way the dark words move her tightens my chest. It's like she understands what he's saying because she's been there. Only unlike the rest of us, she came out of it unscathed, still innocent... and to be honest, I envy her that.

As we arrive at the track and get out of the car, I mention the song to her.

"I've asked Sin a few times what this fucking song means. He always just shakes his head and tells me that if I don't get it, I'll never get it. He sees himself as a complex artist and music is his canvas."

I meant it as a joking dig at my brother, but Jacey looks up at me in surprise.

"You don't get that song? It's easy, Dom. It's about a coldhearted guy who uses people for what he wants—women, usually. He can't feel anything. I guess I just thought Sin wrote the song about you."

I stop in my tracks, staring at her. I can't help it. "Do you think I'm coldhearted?"

I don't know why I care, but I don't like the thought.

But Jacey is already shaking her head. "No, I don't. But I think you do. And I think that every day, you try to live up to your own idea of yourself. You're not giving yourself enough credit and you sell yourself short on a daily basis."

I feel my eyes widen and then I get a hold of myself, shaking my head and hiding my thoughts. "Whatever, Dr. Vincent. Maybe you should be a psychiatrist instead of a waitress."

"Maybe I will." She sniffs. "I'm pretty good at reading people. But whatever." She turns around. "What do we do now? I've never been here before."

"You've never been to the Autobahn?" Before my words are even out, Jacey is snorting.

"Dominic, my old car couldn't even make it to work, let alone around a fancy country club racetrack."

"Good point," I mutter. "Thank god you have a new one now. We have to start out by signing in and grabbing a helmet and a tracksuit. Then they'll look at my car really quick for an inspection and we'll hit the track. There won't be anyone else here because I've arranged for them to stay open late for us."

Jacey nods and we set off for the clubhouse. Within fifteen minutes, we're suited up and buckled in, waiting for a green flag.

"You do this a lot?" Jacey asks, her voice muffled a bit by her helmet.

I nod. "Whenever I'm in town. It's a good stress reliever. To just come out here and open up the throttle? I can feel the stress melting away already."

The green flag drops and I floor it.

My engine roars as I double-clutch shift, my foot vibrating with the power beneath it. Jacey is gripping her door, her eyes gleaming with excitement.

"How fast can we go?" she shouts.

"How fast do you want to go?" I answer, shifting into third.

We take off like a shot, weaving in and out of the curves of the road, hugging the asphalt like a second skin. Jacey laughs, her head thrown back against her headrest because of the speed.

"Faster," she urges.

I oblige. There's basically no one else out here, so we've got the track to ourselves. That makes it easier to open it up and just go.

Jacey is utterly unfazed by the speed, by the danger that speed represents...and honestly, that pleases the hell out of me. I don't even know why. I just like that she's so able to toss her cares away, enjoy the freedom speed brings...and trust me not to lose control.

It's at least one area where her trust is not displaced. I very, very rarely lose control. Of anything.

She looks over at me, laughing. "I want to drive. Can I?"

I don't give a moment's thought to the fact that this car costs more than Jacey probably makes in several years as a waitress. I don't even think about the fact that she's never driven something so powerful. All I can think about is the fact that she wants to.

I pull over on the next straightaway. "You don't have enough experience to take a curve, but you can drive this straightaway. You can totally open it up, if you want to. Just start to brake by that yellow sign, okay?"

She nods, we switch seats, and the tires are squealing almost before my seatbelt clicks.

I grin as we fly down the straightaway, because the girl has no fear.

Jacey shifts gears flawlessly, moving fluidly from one gear to the next like she's been driving this way her whole life. As we pass the yellow sign, her speed flashes.

"One eighty!" she crows as we start to slow down.

We stop and she takes her helmet off, then tugs at mine.

She leans over and kisses me hard, the exhilaration of speed turning her on. I kiss her back, hard, because I know how that feels. I feel that way every single time I get behind the wheel here. When she finally pulls away, her eyes are shining.

"That was fucking awesome," she announces. "Now I see what you love about it. Let's do it again."

I chuckle, but open my door. "We can't. The club will be closing soon and we need to head back to the front. I'd better drive now, Andretti." Jacey grumbles, but gives in.

As we drive back toward the club entrance, I glance over at her.

"So...about you and Brand."

Jacey stares at me, her face closing up cautiously. "What about us?"

I steer around a curve fluidly before I continue. "You say that he's like your brother. But it's clear to anyone who watches you that he doesn't feel the same. Not anymore. He probably did once upon a time, but you've grown up. And he's fallen in love with you."

Jacey swallows, then stares at the floor. And it's completely evident that she knows.

"You knew," I say simply, and ice floods my heart. I'd been holding out hope that she wasn't coldhearted. "You knew and you've been using him, anyway."

Her gaze snaps back up to mine, and her eyes are gleaming.

"No. It's not like that. I haven't wanted to believe that it's true. But lately, I haven't been able to ignore it. I know you're right. But I don't know what to do about it. I love him like my brother. He's always been there for me, and I don't want anything to change. And I don't use him."

Relief washes over me, but I try to ignore it.

"So you don't feel the same way about him?" I ask carefully as I pull the car in front of the clubhouse.

Jacey sighs, staring into the night sky. "I wish I did. It would make things a lot easier. Brand would never hurt me. Not ever. He'd rather die. And that's the kind of person that I need. Sometimes I feel like I should just be with him, that maybe I could grow into loving him like that. He's definitely someone worthy of that kind of love. But then again, because he's so worthy, he deserves more than I can give him."

"I know that feeling," I admit, and I'm startled when I say the words. Jacey stares at me, and her voice is hesitant.

"What does that mean?"

"It means that I find myself liking you…more and more each day. I don't want to, because I know what happens when you open yourself up to someone. You get hurt. Or you hurt them. The world is full of people hurting each other, Jacey. And I don't want to do that. Not anymore."

I don't know why I brought our conversation to this dark and serious place. What happened to acting casual and normal? But truthfully, deep down, I think I just can't stand the inevitability of it all.

I can't stand pretending that everything is fine when I know that one day, very soon, everything is going to implode.

Right now, even I can hear the emptiness in my voice, and Jacey hears it, too.

She stares at me. "Who hurt you, Dom?" she asks gently. "Was it Emma?"

Like always, her name forms a vise around my heart. I close my eyes, refusing to answer.

"I know Emma hurt you," Jacey continues, refusing to back down. "I don't know how. But I know she did. You've got to open up about it, Dominic. If you don't, it will eat at you forever."

I open my eyes and stare at her bleakly. "It will eat at me forever anyway."

"So you're just going to keep closed off to be safe, then?" Jacey asks, and she sounds sad and distant. "I know that whatever happened with Emma has defined who you are, from your sex life to your career. It's why you keep to yourself, why you're so distant. You want to protect yourself by never opening yourself up again. You shouldn't do that, Dom. It's not healthy. I know from experience. Do you want to know how I know?"

She stares at me, waiting, so I finally nod.

"Today's my birthday, and neither of my parents bothered to call me. No card, no call, no gift, not even a 'Hey, we brought you into the world on this day twenty-four years ago, so have a good day.' They didn't contact me at all. That's why Gabe came here...because he knew they wouldn't. And just like always, he wanted to protect me from that. But he can't. Because even though he came and it was awesome, it doesn't take away the fact that they didn't even call. But even though they're horrible parents and they hurt me all the time, I know that I can't close myself off. That would only end up hurting *me*, Dom."

I feel bad for her, because honestly, I can't imagine what it must be like to have parents who don't give a shit. And even though Gabe clearly doesn't like me much, I'm glad that he's such a rock for his sister. Even still, I don't know what parallel Jacey is trying to draw.

"What does that have to do with me?" I ask woodenly. "What point are you trying to prove? Are you trying to show me that your parents fucked you up, but you're trying to get past it? Because good for you."

Jacey shakes her head.

"I want you to see what I learned...because you need to learn it, too. It's taken me a while to learn it, and honestly, I'm still trying to deal with it all. But even though our situations are different and we react to our situations in different ways, we're dealing with the same kind of pain."

She pauses, and I stare at her dubiously.

"It's true, Dom. People have hurt us. But the lesson for us both is that people will hurt us in life, and we just have to get over it. We have to keep going and keep opening ourselves up to people. Will we get hurt again? Maybe so. But maybe we won't. Maybe we'll end up with something real."

I don't say anything, so Jacey continues.

"If something doesn't change, you're going to end up sad and alone, Dominic. I don't want that for you. It doesn't have to be this way, you know. There's something between us...and I know you can feel it, too. We have the opportunity for something real, Dom, even though we're pretending that we don't. We really do."

A sharp rap on the window interrupts her, interrupting the moment at the same time. A worker hands me the clipboard to sign out, and I scrawl my name. I fire my engine back up and drive toward Chicago and try to ignore my pounding heart.

There can be no more pretending now. Jacey just confronted things head-on.

We're quiet now. Awkward. Tense.

I can feel Jacey staring at me from time to time, waiting for me to react to what she said, but I don't say anything and she doesn't, either. As I pull up to the curb, I make no motion to get out.

"I'm sorry," I tell her tersely. "I can't do this right now. I'm tired. Good night, Jacey."

I'm once again trying to delay the inevitable.

She starts to get out, but pauses, looking into my face. With a cool hand, she traces my cheekbone, and I fight the urge to close my eyes and lean into her hand. But I don't. I remain rigidly in my own seat.

"Dom, if you ever want to talk about it, I'm here," she says quietly. "I'll never breathe a word to anyone, I'll just listen."

Her face is so sincere, so genuine...it's all I can do to remember to breathe. She doesn't ask for anything, she's just concerned about me.

"Thanks for the offer," I tell her. "But..."

"I know," she interrupts. "But you'll pass. Why don't you come in, Dom? We don't have to talk. We can just watch a movie or something. I don't want you to be alone."

I don't bother telling her that I'm always alone, even when I'm surrounded by people. Instead, I just shake my head.

"Not tonight. I think I'll just go. Happy birthday, Jacey. I'm glad you got to see your brother."

Jacey hesitates, then gets out, closing the car door. She stands there, gorgeous and quiet in the night. As I stare at her, I know what I have to do. I swallow hard. If I don't do it now, it will be too late and I'll have crushed her.

For once in my fucking life, I'm going to do the right thing.

The decent thing.

"Jacey, I can never give you what you want. You want someone who can open up and discuss feelings, someone who will be an active participant in your life. That's not me and it never will be. We need to pull the plug on this thing now, because once again, you're falling for the wrong guy."

Jacey sucks in her breath and she's frozen for a second. But then she leans down, staring in at me, and there's something pained in her eyes.

"What are you afraid of, Dominic? Really? What are you afraid of?"

I stare at her, long and hard, before I answer.

"Everything," I admit.

And then I drive away.

Chapter Twenty-Three

Jacey

How is it that I've fucked up so badly once again?

I've opened myself up to someone who is emotionally unavailable and has more baggage than he can even keep track of. He's detached. Distant. Unable to give me what I need, and, what's worse, has never tried to hide it. He told me all along.

But still, I fell for him.

Still my heart breaks because he's gone from me. Because I honestly thought that he was different. That deep down, he was a good guy and I could save him. Once again, I thought I could save someone who is apparently unsaveable.

I've done this to myself.

I grab a pair of boxing gloves and start swinging at a bag. I catch the attention of Jake and Tig and they come over to observe. Tig watches while Jake holds the bag.

My foot is still sore, so I can't kick, but I can take out my aggression in punches—so that's what I do, until I'm dripping with sweat and I've taken all of my frustration out on the bag. When I'm finally spent, Jake stares at me.

"Anything wrong, Jacey?" He's hesitant, and I have to smile.

"That apparent?"

"Uh, yeah," he answers. "I thought you were going to punch the bag off its hook. I'm just glad it was the bag and not me this time."

I chuckle, but I don't answer as I pull off my gloves. There isn't a women's locker room, so I have to wait to shower and change until I get home. After I grab my bag, I pass Dom and Joe in the hall.

"You heading out to California this weekend?" Joe asks Dom. Dom nods, and my heart breaks again because it's a reminder that we're truly separate now.

Separate lives. Separate people. We're nothing to each other.

"Yeah," Dominic answers. "And I know, don't be late on Monday or don't bother coming back."

Joe chuckles, and part of me is happy that he is finally warming up to Dominic. But the other part of me is crushed because Dom barely looks at me. It's been two days since my birthday, two days since Dominic broke things off. He's been virtually silent ever since.

No texts, no calls, and almost no communication at work.

He's like a wall . . . vast and silent.

Joe continues into his office, but Dom doesn't turn around to talk to me.

Again.

Surprising myself, I decide I have to let it go. One thing I've definitely learned in life is that you can't make someone love you. Or like you. Or want to be with you. It's a lesson I've learned hard and well, but it doesn't take the sting out of the rejection.

When Dominic almost reaches his car, I call out to him.

He turns around. He doesn't say anything, but he looks directly at me, a question in his famous green eyes.

"Fuck you," I tell him stoutly. Because even though I know I have to let it go, it still fucking hurts.

The corner of his mouth twitches, but he doesn't answer. He just drops into his Porsche and drives away, leaving me standing here alone.

It seems fitting. It pisses me off even more that I can't be mad. Dominic told me from the beginning not to get drawn in, not to get attached.

I'll crush you without meaning to, he'd said. How he can't see that Sin wrote that song about him, I'll never know. He must be fucking clueless.

I sigh and head home to get ready for Saffron.

As I drive past a tiny little bar on the way, I glance at it, briefly tempted to stop. Not to get a drink, but to soak in the attention that I know I would receive there.

Seeing the eyes on me, the guys who would inevitably hit on me... it never fails to bolster my self-confidence and make me feel better.

But not this time. My hands grip the steering wheel and I force myself to drive past.

I'm going to break old patterns. I don't need another guy to make me forget Dominic.

I don't.

My heart hurts, but I've got to do the only thing I can, the healthy thing. I've got to keep going and keep putting one foot in front of the other, instead of dive-bombing into the nearest bed.

I can do this. I can stand alone.

Before I know it, all of this will be a distant memory...

❧

Kaylie touches her lipstick up in my mirror and turns to me with her ass cheeks hanging out of her little Saffron shorts. Part of me dies inside, because I know that Gabe and Brand and even Dominic are right. This is no way to make a living. I have to admit that part of the reason I've worked at Saffron is to bolster my confidence.

It's a façade. These guys lust after me, and it makes me feel like they really want me. They don't. They want to fuck me, and there's the difference.

I need to find my self-respect again, which means getting another job ASAP.

Kaylie scrunches up her nose. "So, let me get this straight. You've been hanging out with Dominic Kinkaide for weeks now. And you haven't fucked him—although he took you to his Hollywood Hills house for an entire weekend? And now it's all over and you aren't seeing each other?"

I nod silently, wishing I hadn't chosen to vent to her. I love Kaylie, but she's got a one-track mind, and unfortunately it's always on sex.

"You're insane," she decides, handing me the red lipstick. "You need a touch-up before we go. And hurry up. We're going to be late. Again."

I put the lipstick on as Kaylie stares at me. "If he's anything like his brother in the sack, then you missed out. *Big time,*" she adds, for good measure. "Seriously. In fact, I think I'm going to get a tattoo on my ass. *I fucked Sin Kinkaide.* Ohhh. Or maybe *I've Sinned.*"

"Classy," I mutter. "I get the point. I'm sorry for bringing it up."

"What are friends for?" Kaylie turns to me, grinning widely, and all of a sudden I just really miss Maddy. Kaylie's fine, but she's a superficial friend, someone to have fun with. Maddy's levelheaded and smart and she knows me better than anyone. I make a mental note to call her tonight on one of my breaks.

Kaylie and I pile into my new car and we drive to the Saffron office. Our boss, Big Jim, calls to us from behind the counter.

"Hey girls! Your jobs for tonight have changed. Well, not yours, Kaylie. You're still serving at the Gable bachelor party. But Jacey, your presence has been requested at Sinclair Kinkaide's house yet again—and he's paying me twice your normal wage to make sure you're there. I don't know what you're doing, but it better not be anything illegal."

Big Jim stares at me, but then grins. I shake my head. "I don't want to. I'm sorry. You'll have to send someone else. Send Kaylie."

Big Jim scowls now, his big jowls twisting as he shakes his head. "No. It's gotta be you. And if you value this job, you need to go. My word is my bond and I already promised that you'd be there."

"Can't you call him back and say that I'm sick?" I ask as panicky feelings well up in my lungs. "I can't go there, Big Jim. I just can't."

"You can," he assures me. "And you have to."

"What about me?" Kaylie demands. "Did Sin say anything about me?"

Big Jim shakes his head. "Not a thing, darlin'."

I feel sick to my stomach as I stare at Kaylie. "You might want to hold off on that tattoo."

She scowls at me, but I sit down in the chair by the cash register. I don't think I can do this. I don't want to face Dominic. Not after he dismissed me the way he did. And then I all but told him that I'd fallen for him. Why the fuck did I do that? Don't I have one little speck of self-respect left? God.

Maybe not, but there's only one way to fix that: find it. And find it fast.

"Okay," I say aloud to no one in particular. "I'll go."

Big Jim doesn't even glance at me, because to him it'd already been settled. I slip outside without another word and head my little car in the direction of Sin's mansion. The closer I get, the heavier my heart feels, but I ignore it.

I can do this. I can walk in there with my head up and be totally unaffected by Dominic.

I can do this.

I'm practically chanting that as I walk around the house and go in through the back door, making my way to the kitchen. I already have this routine down pat; I've done it several times already. When I step inside the kitchen though, Henrietta, the shift leader, looks up at me.

"You're supposed to find Mr. Kinkaide the second you get here," she says to me curiously. "I don't know why."

She's looking at me as if I can offer her an explanation. I shrug. "I have no idea."

She doesn't believe me, but I don't care. It's not my problem. I make my way out into the main part of the house, intent on finding Sin but avoiding Dominic.

It proves to be easy. Dominic is nowhere to be seen, and Sin is lounging in his main living room, in jeans and no shirt. For a minute I smile, remembering how Dominic has complained several times about Sin always walking around half-naked, but the smile dies at the thought of Dominic.

"You wanted to see me?" I ask Sin quietly. He's looking through a pile of papers and seems deep in thought. He looks up.

"Oh, hi. Jacey, right?"

He knows my name. And he knows that's exactly who I am.

Sin Kinkaide knows who I am. It's mind-boggling. He grins, and I can see Dominic in that grin. It's cocky, charming, and sexy all at once. "I requested for you to work my party tonight."

"I know," I tell him slowly. "But why?"

"Because my brother's been happier these last few weeks than he's been in a very long time," Sin tells me seriously. He twists a bottle of beer around in his hand as he speaks, and each time he moves, a silver ring with a ram's head on it clicks against the glass. I must look doubtful because he laughs.

"It's true," he assures me. "I know it's difficult to tell when my brother is happy or when he's not, but trust me. He's been happier, which makes my life happier, since he's been staying here. But he came home in a bitch-ass mood last night, and when I asked why, he almost bit my head off. Logically, I know that can only mean one thing. He fucked things up with you."

I start to protest, but Sin holds up a hand.

"Did he or did he not?"

I swallow. "You don't understand. There wasn't anything to fuck up. We were just hanging out to have fun. We were never going to be anything serious, so there wasn't any need to bring me here. Trust me, if Dom was in a bad mood, it wasn't because of me. It was his idea that we stop hanging out."

"And he told you that yesterday?" Sin raises an eyebrow.

I see where he's going with this. "Yes, but that was just a coincidence. Trust me."

Sin shakes his head. "Trust me. I know my brother. But this brings me to my point of having you here. I'd like for you to serve him tonight exclusively. Follow him everywhere. If he goes to his room, you go. Don't take no for an answer."

This annoys me, and I glare at Sin. "What the hell do you think I am? I'm not a personal servant or a sex slave."

Sin stares at me. "I know you're not. But I think you care about my brother. You must, or you wouldn't have put up with his shit for this long. Look, my brother has been buried under a rock for way too long. Years. But he came out from under that rock for you. I'd like to see him stay that way. The key to that is you. Trust me."

"I seem to be doing a lot of 'trusting you,'" I point out. "And I don't even know you."

"Of course you do," Sin pacifies me. "Everyone knows me."

I have to roll my eyes. I can almost hear Dom in his arrogant tone. "Everyone knows *of* you. They don't actually *know* you," I remind him. "Including me."

"Okay, valid point," he concedes, his face a blank slate but for a smile. "Tell me what I can do so you'll trust me. Sing you a song?"

I start to laugh, until something occurs to me. "Tell me about Emma. And why Dominic blames Cris."

Sin sobers up quickly, staring at me. "Hmm. Straight for the jugular. So Dominic won't tell you?"

I shake my head. "No. All I know is that she was his girlfriend and he blames Cris for something really bad. That's all I know."

Sin sighs and takes a swig of his beer as he settles back into his seat.

"I don't know why he blames Cris," he admits. "We all have our suspicions, but no one knows for sure. Dom won't talk about it and Cris won't say. But I can tell you that it fucked him up. Big time. Whatever else happened, Emma died and Dominic blames himself. But that's all I can tell you. It's his story and he should be the one telling it. Maybe he'll get the chance tonight … because you're going to be his shadow. I don't think he's home yet, but I'm pretty sure he'll be back soon. He's going to stay at the party for a while before he flies out to LA."

"What if I don't want to be his shadow?" I ask as cold fingers of dread curl around my stomach. Sin smiles.

"You might think you don't want to, but I think you really do. And from what I've seen of you, you don't do anything that you don't want to do."

I stare at him, not wanting to say anything, because deep down I know he's right...on both counts.

I turn to leave, but hesitate. "Do you really think he's been happier since he met me?" I ask slowly. Sin nods.

"I know he has."

I walk out quietly, lost in thought. Dominic blames himself for Emma's death? That's quite a bit different from just grieving a dead girlfriend. A million different scenarios run through my mind, but I'll never know the truth unless he tells me.

I don't see that happening.

With a sigh, I turn into the main hall and grab a tray of champagne. Until I see Dominic, I might as well hand out drinks.

It doesn't take too long. Twenty minutes later, I feel him walk into the room. I feel his stare, buried between my shoulder blades. Sure enough, when I turn around, Dom's green eyes meet mine, and I can see a strange fire in them.

I set my tray down and walk straight to him. He doesn't move, he just leans against the door frame and waits.

"Jacey," he greets me, nodding. "To what do I owe this pleasure?"

So polite, so civil, so distant.

My throat tightens up. Maybe Sin was wrong.

"Sin brought me here," I explain, fighting the urge to run my fingers through his hair, to push back his rakish bangs. "I'm supposed to exclusively serve you tonight."

This interests Dominic. I can see that strange light in his eyes glow even more, working into a flame now.

"Really?" he asks, his eyes on my lips. Self-consciously, I lick them, and he grins wolfishly. "So you have to only be with me tonight? Exclusively?" He puts emphasis on that last word, and I swallow.

"Yes. My boss made me come, and I need this job for now. So here I am."

"So you're here because your boss made you," Dom says slowly. "It has nothing to do with wanting to see me?"

"Why does what I want matter?" I demand. "You didn't seem to care what I wanted the other night when you ended things. But I'm here now...getting paid to personally serve you drinks."

"And cater to me," Dominic adds. "That's what you do with all the other men...you shove your tits in their faces and laugh at their jokes. I'll want the same treatment. I want to get my money's worth."

His face is dark now, stormy. Dangerous. For a minute, I consider walking out and forgetting about all of this. But I can't. Until I get a new job, I need this one to pay my rent, which happens to be due next week. But silently, I vow to search the classifieds for a new job as soon as I get home tonight.

"Yes," I answer sharply. "I suppose if you want me to hang on your arm, I can do that. And if you really want my tits in your face, I guess I can do that, too."

I can't read Dominic's face. I can't decide if he's disappointed that I gave in so easily, or if he's looking forward to the night. Either way, I'm prepared. He's amusing himself. Nothing more, nothing less. I'll go through the motions tonight and quit this fucking job as soon as I can.

Dominic holds out his arm.

I stare at him hesitantly.

"Come on, Princess," he urges. "I'm not going to hurt you. You should at least know that by now."

"Not where anyone can see, anyway," I mutter as I lightly place my fingers on his arm. Dominic raises an eyebrow, but doesn't say anything.

He leads me out of the hall, out of the house, and down the stone path to the pool. Once we step out onto the patio, he sits on a bench and motions for me to sit next to him.

"Why did you fall for me?" he asks bluntly, staring at me in the dark.

I feel like he might as well have bitch-slapped me with such a blunt question. I'm not used to it from him. He usually takes the avoidance tactic. I pause a second, take a breath, then shake my head. "I didn't."

Lie. I fell fucking hard.

Dominic raises an eyebrow. "No? Are you lying, Princess?"

I stare at him, my breath caught in my throat, and I decide that I don't want to lie.

"Yes," I say simply.

Dominic startles at my honesty, staring at me hard. I'm quick to continue.

"I fell for you because I thought there was more to you. I thought that deep inside, there's something ugly and broken, but that I could fix it. I thought you felt more for me than you did. But I was wrong. I know what you and I are. We're nothing. Once again, I've proven to myself that I can't trust my own judgment. Once tonight is over, I would appreciate it if you told Sin not to request my presence here again."

I don't know how I managed to say the words, not with the way he's looking at me. But I do. I say them and they float between us, hard and ugly.

Dominic nods slowly, and once again I can't read his face.

"Jacey, you try and see the good in everyone. That's your mistake. You think that if you look hard enough, you'll find it, that everyone has something in them that deserves you. But that's so fucking wrong. Very few people deserve you. And that includes me."

My heart clenches at his words, at the way he's trying to validate me, to compliment even my very worst trait. My heart breaks, because I know that not only does Dominic not think he deserves me, he also thinks that he doesn't deserve *anyone*.

"We're so fucked up," I manage to whisper. Dominic nods solemnly.

"Me more than you."

I don't say anything.

Dominic stares at me with those fucking dark eyes, and finally he speaks again.

"After tonight, I don't want you to come around me, Jacey. I don't want to hurt you any more than I have already. Tonight is all we have left."

I nod curtly, his meaning stark.

He smiles a glittering, hard smile.

"So we'll have to make it count. Know this right now. You don't have to do anything that you don't want to. You know me. If you say no, it's over. Got it?"

I nod. But Dominic shakes his head.

"You understand. Yes or no?"

"Yes," I murmur.

"If you say no, you can walk out at any time and I promise you that Sin won't contact Saffron and you won't suffer any consequences with your boss. Tonight will be…a good-bye. A good-bye worthy of you and me. Yes or no?"

I'm a fucking masochist, because I see the gleam in Dom's

eyes...the dark, dark gleam that can only mean dark, dark things...
and I welcome it. I want it. I want him...even if it's only for tonight.

I love him. The knowledge is so, so painful.

"Yes," I whisper.

Dominic smiles. "Good. You wanted to know about me the other night. You wanted me to share with you, to explain why I am the way I am. You wanted to know if Amy Ashby was right, if I'm perverted. I want to answer that for you now. I could tell you in words all day long, but it wouldn't even make sense to you until you see exactly *who* I am. Until you see exactly the kind of things I like. So tonight, I want you to see it. Can we do that?"

I stare at him in confusion. "See it?"

"My brother has a wild life," Dom explains. "You've seen it. And I'm sure you've noticed that at every party, there is always a private, secret party going on in the basement. A party that most aren't invited to. I'm inviting you tonight. Do you want to come with me?"

My heart pounds, both in apprehension and in excitement. I *have* noticed the secret party in the basement. Of course I have. It was always part of the confidentiality agreement that I had to sign in order to work at Sin's house.

Never go into the basement.

But that changes tonight. And with that, I just might get a glimpse of who Dominic really is.

Answers.

Finally.

"Well?" Dominic prompts, staring at me.

"Okay," I start to say. But at his look, I amend that. "Yes."

He smiles.

"Come with me."

He holds out his arm and I take it. As I touch him, he looks down at me and for a moment, my heart flutters. Everything about him pulls me in. His smell, his touch, his stare. His excruciatingly sexy personality. I must definitely be a masochist, because I know beyond any shadow of a doubt that tonight will annihilate me.

Yet I follow him willingly into the house.

Into hell.

Or Eden.

Chapter Twenty~Four

Jacey

Dominic leads me down a back hallway into the exquisitely lavish basement of the house, then through two more hallways until we stop in front of a set of heavy wooden doors. He turns and looks at me.

"You want to do this. Yes or no?"

I'm not sure. I can hear music thumping on the other side, but I can also hear moaning. Sex sounds. Thumping. Lashing? Moaning. More Moaning. Screaming. Shrieking. Moaning.

I look at Dominic and my heart is in my throat.

"Yes."

He smiles, then opens the doors.

The room before me is a myriad of panting and fucking bodies.

The first thing I focus on are the women in cages.

On all four corners in a huge dimly lit room, there are round cages with bars. There's a woman in each cage, each wearing a collar. Their collars are attached to the chains in the cages. They're naked but for strange leather straps that crisscross around their breasts, then crisscross again above and below their hips. I'm confused for a second, until a man opens the cage door of the girl closest to me and steps inside.

It's only then that I see that the leather straps are attached to the roof of the cage. The girl can suspend herself in the air by pulling on the straps. And when she does, they tighten around her breasts and her crotch, so much so that her flesh turns white.

But she seems to like it. She moans as the man dips his head and sucks on her nipples, suckling at the taut flesh. My gaze flies to Dominic, and he's staring at me, his expression intense.

"They like it," he assures me. "Trust me, they're here on their own free will. They like to be tied up, whipped, sucked. They enjoy the pain and I enjoy watching it."

My heart pounds and warmth spreads to my crotch, moistening my panties. I can't believe it, but watching it turns me on. All of it. The smells, the sounds, the idea that all of this shit should be happening in the privacy of bedrooms, but instead it's out here in the open for other consenting adults to watch. It makes my heart pound.

I stand in the doorway and scan the room.

It's like nothing I've ever seen.

The walls are covered in stone tile and there are round columns here and there, and fountains. It reminds me of ancient Greece. The ceiling is painted like the night sky, with swirling clouds and brilliant stars, and above us, in a circle on a ledge around the ceiling, statues of the Greek gods stare down at us in approval. Of course they approve. They were all fucked-up freaks, too.

There are huge round silk ottomans everywhere, big enough for groups of people to sit on. And groups of people *do* sit on them, all of them involved in orgies.

This is an orgy of epic proportions.

The realization slams into me, and I feel my knees grow weak because I'm even here.

Everywhere around me, people are fucking, sucking, licking,

whipping…I can't wrap my mind around it. I didn't know that things like this even existed.

"Is this even legal?" I ask Dominic stupidly. He leads me into the room and closes the doors behind us, then shrugs.

"I don't know. Everyone is here on their own free will. And this is secret. It isn't spoken of beyond these walls."

I nod. I definitely won't be admitting that I was here. Jesus. My brother would fucking kill me.

I take a deep breath, inhaling the sex-laden air, and turn to Dominic. "What are we doing here?"

He smiles, ever so slightly. "We're watching. It's what I like to do."

Pulling me to the side, we sit on a large sofa hidden in the shadows. He pulls me down onto his lap and turns his attention to the room in front of us.

"Do you come here a lot?" I ask him suddenly. For some reason, even though I'm frustrated with him, and pissed at him, it makes me sad to think that he was spending his time in this room when he and I were still together. He shakes his head.

"Only sometimes," he tells me. "Why? Does that bother you?"

"It's your life," I tell him flippantly.

He stares at me dubiously, but I look away, over to a couple that's fucking against the wall. They're both completely naked and glistening with sweat. The man has the woman pinned, slowly fucking her with a red and swollen cock as her legs wrap around his waist. His cock is red from her slapping it every time he pulls out. But he loves it. He moans in ecstasy every time she strikes him.

"Why do you like this?" I ask softly, unable to take my eyes away. Dom smiles, a sardonic smile.

"I'm not sure. Probably because I can linger in the shadows. I don't have to interact with anyone, I can just watch. And if I do interact, it's not on a deep level. It's superficial, a mutual pleasuring of two people. Nothing more, nothing less."

"So it's empty, then," I say, lifting my eyes finally and looking at him. He shrugs.

"If you want to see it that way."

I look at the people around me, at the whipping and the lashing and the red marks.

"Do you like the pain, too?"

He shrugs again. "Perhaps."

Something twinges inside of me, a realization of sorts.

"Because you feel like you deserve it," I observe. It's not a question now. I know it in my heart and he doesn't deny it.

"Are there famous people here?" I ask quietly, changing the subject. Dom smiles.

"Always. Sin's parties are famous. People fly in from all over."

This isn't a "party." This is an orgy.

Dom falls silent now, watching a girl in a cage. A second man has joined the first, and while the first man sucks hard on her breasts, the second lashes her with a velvet whip from behind. She moans, "Fuck me, fuck me, please."

She's got lash marks on her back from those velvet tassels, and still she moans. Still she enjoys it. Still she arches her back and comes and comes and comes. As she comes, a second woman steps into the cage and sucks on her other breast. The woman screams even more...because she loves it.

I feel wetness gush into my panties and I feel like a freak.

"Why do I like watching this?" I wonder aloud to Dominic. "I've never watched anything like this before."

"That's probably why you like it," he whispers to me, his lips close to my ear. "It's naughty, it's forbidden. Forbidden things are exciting, no matter who you are."

He wraps his hand around my thigh, squeezing at the soft flesh there. Kneading, pulling, squeezing…causing just the slightest bit amount of pain. And I want more. All of a sudden, I want more. I want him to make me hurt…in a good way.

He looks at me. "This room turns you on. Yes or no?"

I'm embarrassed to admit that it does.

"Yes," I admit limply.

"Are you wet?" Dominic asks, his voice husky.

"Yes," I whisper.

"Can I check?"

I'm surprised he asked. But suddenly, I want nothing more.

"Yes," I answer.

His fingers find me, cool and slender. And then they're inside of me, in and out, slow and then fast. My breathing catches and I turn into him, my face pressed against his chest as I grasp at him.

"No," he rasps, turning my shoulders around. "Keep watching."

So I do.

I watch the couples having sex, the couples whipping each other, the lash marks, the bruises, the scratches. I watch fingers slipping into bodies, glistening skin, thick penises, slick folds. I watch all of it.

And then I watch Kira enter the room. Dressed in a strapless gown, she walks in like she owns the room, looking around, searching every corner. I know who she's looking for.

Her gaze finds him, and in an instant she starts in Dominic's direction, but then she sees me on his lap. Her eyes narrow and she freezes in her tracks.

Dominic's fingers have never stopped moving within me, even with Kira watching.

I am both embarrassed and pleased by that.

Dominic watches Kira retreat to a place by the wall, where she stands alone for a few minutes until Duncan comes in. Dominic's younger brother assesses the room, assesses the situation, his gaze sweeping over me and Dominic, then Kira. And then he heads toward Kira, pulling her toward a padded ottoman to her left.

At first she shakes her head, but then she follows him, sitting with him on the silk. She watches Dominic for a reaction, and it's very apparent that she's waiting for him to protest that she's with his brother.

But he doesn't.

Instead, Dominic strokes me, his breath coming harshly. His fingers feel good, incredibly good, but it's even more amazing because of where I am . . . surrounded by sex of every nature.

A naked woman with pale skin and red hair that tumbles to her waist stops in front of us, blocking my view of Kira.

"Do you want me to suck you?" she asks Dominic. He looks down at me.

"Do you want her to?"

For a minute, I consider it. And then I'm amazed that I consider it at all. The idea of anyone touching Dominic in that way, anyone other than me, shreds me, and I shake my head quickly.

"No."

He immediately shakes his head at the girl and, unbothered, she continues on to the next couple. I watch in amazement.

"This place . . ." I murmur, my voice trailing off. I look around yet again. "I've never seen anything like it."

Dominic chuckles, low and dark. "Sin wanted it to be like ancient orgies were rumored to be. In the next room, there's a Roman bath. Do you want to go in there?"

I glance at Kira and Duncan. Duncan is kissing her neck, but Kira's eyes are frozen on Dominic and me.

"I don't think Kira would like that," I point out, trying to ignore the fact that Dom's fingers are still inside of me. "She's watching us."

"She likes watching me," Dominic says easily. "She's been a friend for a long time."

"Apparently, she's a good friend of your brother's, too," I answer wryly. Dominic ducks his head, nipping at my neck, and I arch against him against my will.

"Why am I here?" I ask him suddenly. "Why did you bring me? To further prove your point that I'm like everyone else?"

Dominic stops moving and looks up at me, his gaze dangerous and dark.

"You're not like everyone else," he answers. "I know that you're not. But I needed you to see what I am. Before we go our separate ways and I never see you again, I needed you to see that I'm fucked up. That way, you won't always wonder if we did the right thing by breaking things off. You can rest easily and know that we did. Because you don't deserve someone like me."

His frankness surprises me, and I stare at him. He shrugs. "It's true. And you need to know that."

"How are you fucked up?" I ask, keeping an eye on Kira. She watches me, her eyes narrowed as her legs wrap around Duncan's naked hips.

"Isn't it apparent?" Dominic asks, his eyes gleaming. "I can't get off on normal things. It takes the dark things, the taboo things. If I can get off at all. I'm fucked up, Jacey. Let's just leave it at that."

"But *why* are you fucked up?" I ask bluntly. "Just tell me that much. The Dominic that I know is funny and witty and smart. And he is good, deep down where he tries to hide it. The Dominic that I know isn't fucked up. Not really."

Dominic stares at me, his face a perfect mask. "That's because you don't know the real Dominic. You've sensed him all along. I've seen it in your eyes. I'm showing him to you tonight."

"I don't believe it," I whisper, and the words slip through my lips in a hiss. "This isn't you. This is who you want to be for some reason. You don't think that you deserve real things—good things. So you let yourself believe that this is your life. Your life could be more, if you'd just let it be, Dominic. I know it."

I pull away from him. "Look around you. This is sad. Yes, it's a turn-on to watch . . . but only because it's so naughty and dark. These people must have such sad lives—especially those women in the cages. They don't have anything healthy or real, so they come here to get debased. Look at Kira! She's in love with you, yet she's having sex with your brother right now. What the fuck?"

Dominic grips my arm, hard. "There's nothing wrong with these people," he tells me in a low voice. "This is just what they like. Most of them are like me. They're jaded and they've seen everything, so the normal doesn't do it for them anymore. And Kira . . . she's not in love with me. She likes this. It's who she is. She's fucked up, too, like me."

I look at her again, just in time to see a tear slip down her cheek before she closes her eyes, and I startle.

"She's crying," I snap at Dominic. "It doesn't look like she enjoys it anymore."

The words are no sooner out of my mouth than Kira jumps up and runs from the room, toward what looks to be a bathroom. Before I can even think about it, I pull away from Dominic and follow her.

I find her in a heap on a bench in an ornate bathroom. Tears are streaming down her face and her arms are wrapped around her sides. I approach her carefully.

"Are you okay?"

She doesn't answer. She just continues to cry, staring at the wall.

"I'm sorry," I offer quietly.

She looks up at me. "Are you?" Her words aren't sharp or ugly, just a blunt question. I nod.

"I can see that you're upset. And if I'm at fault, I *am* sorry."

Kira looks away, wiping at her eyes. "It's actually not your fault. I'm pissed because I shouldn't have been with Duncan." She looks away, her eyes watery. "I've always wanted him, you know...Dominic. Always. Even before Emma died. And after she died, I stuck by him. I was everything that he needed, all of these years, but it's never mattered. I've never been enough. Don't fool yourself into thinking that *you* are, because you won't be. What he needs is dead. And she's never coming back."

"Kira, stop," Dominic says coldly, and I spin around to find him at the door. He takes two steps toward us and stops again. His face is deadly calm, his voice like ice. "You need to stop."

I stare at him. "Are you still in love with Emma? Is that what's wrong with you?"

Because I can't compete with a dead woman.

"It's not that simple," he says, turning to me; but Kira laughs, a cold and empty sound.

"It *is* that simple. He's in love with her. He must be. I don't know what's wrong with him or what he needs. I don't know if *he* knows. Don't waste your time with him. Trust me. I've wasted years. He'll suck you down and you'll drown with him."

I stare at her, then him, and my eyes well up with tears at the thought that she might be right. I hadn't even realized that I wanted to save him, but I do. I want to save him from *this*...from all of this.

But maybe Dominic is unsaveable simply because he doesn't want to be saved. Or maybe he just doesn't know what actually would save him. Either way, it seems hopeless.

Dominic looks at Kira and something softens in his gaze. "Kira, I'm sorry. I never knew that you wanted more from me. You never said and I never saw it. You've been such a good friend to me for so long. And you were a good friend to...*her*, too. I didn't mean to hurt you."

"No?" Kira looks up at him, another tear slipping down her cheek.

"No," Dominic answers firmly. "I promise you. I would never hurt you on purpose."

"But you did, anyway," Kira says softly. "Just like you hurt Emma." She turns to me. "And just like he'll hurt you, too."

A tear escapes from my eye...and I'm crying for everything. For the pain in her voice, for the hopelessness of the situation, for the hurt that I see in Dom's eyes. And for my heart.

Because it's broken.

"Now do you see?" Kira asks quietly. She hands me a tissue, and I wipe my eyes. I do see. I see with my own eyes what could happen to me, what Dominic has been trying to tell me all along.

I fell in love with him and all he can do is obliterate me.

But only if I let him.

I shouldn't be here. In this moment, I realize something.

The difference between normal people and me is that I don't make smart decisions for myself. I never know when to say *when*. I never know when to stop fighting for something, when to call it quits in order to protect my own heart.

That ends today.

For the first time in my life, I'm going to make a smart decision, no matter how hard it might be.

I pat Kira on the back, then walk out the door.

Chapter Twenty-Five

Dominic

Jacey slips out of the bathroom before I can stop her.

Quickly, I follow her, winding my way through the crowded room, only to find no sign of her in the long hallway. I almost run through the house, through the people, until I'm standing in the middle of a mass of parked cars. I'm just in time to see Jacey drive away.

I know I should let her go.

But I'm too selfish for that.

I head for my car, and within a minute I'm on the road behind her. My Porsche catches up to her. I motion for her to pull over, but she doesn't. I can see her crying; I can see the black streaks of mascara running down her cheeks. I motion again, but she refuses. She won't even look at me.

Gunning my engine, I pull in front of her, forcing her off the road. We're in a secluded section of Sin's neighborhood. She kills her engine and gets out of her car, glaring at me angrily.

"What the fuck are you doing, Dominic? I would have thought you'd figure out that if I left, then it means I'm done. But just in case, this is me saying *no*. No to you, no to your fucked-up life, no to doing anything else with you tonight. Got it?"

Her words instill panic in me, and I don't know why. All I know is that the thought of her driving away from me, leaving me...I can't take it. Suddenly, the thought of it is crushing.

I grab her arm. "No. I don't accept that answer."

"Why?" Jacey demands. It's raining now. The rain hits her face and gleams under the streetlight. "You've always said that no means no. You don't have many rules, but at least you have that one. You never wanted me, Dominic. You want a dead woman, and since you can't have her, you wanted a game. I played it. And now I'm done with it."

She pulls away and stomps toward her car, but I grab her again, whirling her around and pulling her to me.

"It's not a game. I meant it when I said I'm fucked up. But I mean it when I say that I don't want it to be over, too. Whatever it is...you and I...whatever we're doing. I don't want it to be over, Jacey. I'm not ready."

She stares at me in astonishment, her gorgeous face shocked.

"So you want me to hang around until you're finally ready for it to be over? Until you're done with me? You want me to end up like Kira...a sniveling wreck on the floor of a bathroom? No thanks, Dom. That's not me. Not anymore. I've been a work in progress for quite a while, and I guess I can finally see that I deserve more than that. I'm *worth* more than that."

I swallow hard, a thick lump in my throat, and I'm not sure why it's there.

"Kira isn't my fault," I tell her wildly. "I've told her from the beginning what I can offer her. And she wanted to be with me, anyway. She's always known. She knows me, Jacey. She's always known me."

"Just like *I* know you, Dom," Jacey says in resignation. "This isn't about Kira. This is about *me* and how *I* know that you'll hurt me. I know that even though I don't want to fall for you, I already have. I can't make it worse now. I just can't. I have to be strong enough to walk away. You've told me all along that you aren't good for me. And guess what? You're not."

Her words cause my stomach to tie into a knot. I know I'm not good for her. I'm not good for *anyone*, but for her, for Jacey, I want to be.

If I lose her, I don't know what I'll do.

"Jacey," I continue, trying to make my voice steady, "I don't know what I can offer you. But I'll try to offer you something more than... this. I know you deserve more. Trust me, I know that. You're different from everyone I know. You're a breath of fresh air, and I just want to keep breathing you in. That's a big thing for me, you have no idea."

"You don't know what you can offer me?" she asks slowly, her brown eyes pained as she stares at me. "How about... yourself? Offer me yourself and I'll stay. But I want all of you. I want a real relationship. I want you and your problems and the truth and the ugliness. I need to know all of it. Can you do that?"

Can I?

The idea of telling Jacey everything causes my heart to pound, and I see horrific images in my head. They blur together... Emma's cold hands, her pale face, the blood. The lights from the ambulance. The blood. Her headstone. My guilt. The blood.

I close my eyes for a minute, and behind my lids it's red from the blood that I can't stop seeing. I open them helplessly and I can't say anything. I can't get my tongue to work.

All I can do is grab Jacey and pull her to me, forcing her lips to my own. Hers are soft and yielding, kissing me back for just a second until she pulls away. When she does, there are tears streaking down her face again, falling in black rivulets down her cheeks, mixing with the rain.

"I didn't think so," she says softly when I don't say anything. "Answer me one question, Dominic. And be honest. For once, please, just be completely, brutally honest." She swallows hard, her hands clenched, and looks me in the eye.

"Are you still in love with Emma? Yes or no?"

She might as well have hit me with a Mack Truck. I stare at her, silent, trying to figure out how to explain.

"It's not that simple," I say helplessly. But she shakes her head.

"It's a yes or no answer, Dom. You taught me this game. Are you still in love with Emma? Yes or no?"

She stares at me, waiting. From the look in her eyes I can tell she's wavering between wanting to know and being afraid to know.

"Yes or no?" she whispers.

I draw in a shaky breath. "Yes."

Her breath exhales in a feathery hiss and she shoves her hair out of her eyes with shaking fingers.

"The word *yes* has never hurt so much." Her voice is a whisper, so soft I can barely hear it. I reach for her, but she shrugs away, out of my reach.

She walks away, her shoulders slumped as she gets into her car and drives off.

I stand in the rain for what seems like forever, watching as her taillights disappear into the rain, and the night swallows up her car.

I stand there and let the rain run into my eyes until I can no longer see.

Until I can no longer see that she left me.

When I get into my car, I'm empty inside, more empty and numb than I've been in years. Emptier than I've ever felt before.

There's only one place I can think of to go, one place that

will absorb my pain. As I pass through the gates of Mount Olivet Catholic Cemetery, the darkness surrounds me, and I feel a sense of comfort . . . of familiarity.

I haven't been here in years, but I find Emma's headstone easily. I go straight to it. It's easy to see. Her parents bought an enormous white marble stone encircled by the wings of an angel.

I kneel in front of it and trace her name under my fingers.

Emma Brandt.

She was no angel, but I loved her anyway. Her stone is cold to the touch . . . as cold as ice, as cold as my heart. I think of Sin's song.

Your heart is cold, cold as ice, but it's mine to take.

My heart *is* cold as ice. It will stay that way . . . because of Emma. I curl up in front of her name and lie with my cheek against the stone, staring into the night.

She wrecked me. She might as well have me.

I'm not fit for anyone else.

In a while, it starts to rain again, a light, cold rain that soaks into my clothes and lingers on my skin. I don't even care, and honestly, I barely notice. It can't wash away who I am, what I've done, or who I've been. I fall asleep listening to the rain falling on Emma's stone.

When I open my eyes again, it's morning.

My clothes are wet and my throat is raspy since I breathed damp night air all night long. I sit up and look around, ignoring the odd looks from a cemetery worker. He goes back to weeding a flower bed, but still glances at me every now and then, probably wondering if I'm crazy. I should save him the trouble and just tell him that I am.

I check my phone and find ten messages from Tally. Because, fuck, I missed my flight home. I should be on-set right now. I sigh and climb back into my car.

Everything seems like it's falling apart and I don't know how to stop it. This is the reason I'm carefully detached, always. I'm cool and calm and collected and I do the things I need to do. Always. I do it so that I don't fall apart.

But now there's Jacey.

And nothing is the same as it was before.

Jacey

I can't see through the tears streaming down my cheeks. They're hot and salty and drip onto my clothes.

I pick up the phone and dial Maddy's number, wanting to cry on her shoulder, to get her sage advice, but her voice mail picks up.

I wait, then try again a few minutes later, but still no answer.

I drive aimlessly until I realize where I'm headed.

Brand.

I shake my head. Of course I'm headed for Brand. It's what I always do when I need help or when I need comforting.

I know I shouldn't run to him anymore, because he would like to comfort me in ways that I don't want. He wants to be with me. For real.

But I can't think of anything but Dominic. My heart hurts in such a way that it's almost blinding. It's all I can feel.

I pull up out front of his condo building and almost sprint for his door. When I reach it, I'm out of breath, my makeup is smeared, and I'm a sniveling wreck. He answers the door, shirtless and in workout shorts, and stares at me.

"What the hell, Jacey?" he asks quickly, pulling me inside. "What happened? Are you all right?"

I nod, then shake my head, then drop onto his sofa and cry. He sits next to me awkwardly, patting my back with his giant hands.

"Tell me what to do and I'll do it," he tells me helplessly. "Did he hurt you? I'll fucking kick his teeth in if he did."

I shake my head, then nod.

"But not how you think," I add quickly when Brand immediately starts to get up. With his military background, whenever he hears the word *hurt*, he automatically assumes it's in a physical way. "He didn't lay a finger on me."

Brand pauses, then stares down at me with confusion in his blue eyes.

"Then what did he do?" he asks hesitantly.

I drop my face into my hands, taking a moment to catch my breath.

"He obliterated me," I say limply.

I curl onto my side, burying my face into the sofa cushions, and sob. I cry for all the things I can't say, the things I can't put into words. How Dominic is so haunted and damaged, and how I thought I could help him by showing him that people are good. That not everyone will hurt him. How I can't make him see that. How he makes me feel so alive and so sexy, yet at the same time, he must be so toxic for me…because right now I'm empty and it's because of him.

I cry for all of this.

For all of these things that Brand doesn't know.

Regardless, he stays next to me, patting me, soothing me. And he stays that way, just letting me cry until I can't cry anymore. He does what Brand always does…makes me feel better just by being here for me.

When I finally sit up, my eyes are hot and tired.

"What did he do?" Brand asks calmly, his gaze level and strong. "Tell me."

"He told me from the beginning not to get attached to him," I admit. "But I did anyway. He told me, Brand. It wasn't his fault. I guess, deep down, I thought I could fix him somehow. He's got issues. His girlfriend died and he still loves her and it's just a messed-up ball of shit."

Brand stares at me sympathetically.

"Jace, you should know by now that you can't fix anyone. And if his girlfriend died... well, it's hard to say how that will affect him. Grief does strange things to people."

"But it was six years ago," I tell him. "Dominic blames himself for some fucked-up reason. I don't know why, because he won't say."

Brand stares at me, and something flickers in his eyes. I've seen him look that way before, haunted and sad. But then he hides it and shrugs.

"If he won't say, then maybe he *should* blame himself. Maybe it *is* his fault," he suggests softly.

"I doubt it," I mutter. But then I see Brand's face, and his soft gaze, and I'm reminded once again of the truth.

For him, I'm no longer his little sister. His feelings for me have grown. I can't cry to him anymore about my issues with men. Not when he's in love with me.

God. Why did I come here? My heart squeezes in my chest and I reach for Brand's hands.

"Brand, I'm sorry to unload on you like this. It isn't fair now that I know how you feel..."

My voice trails off like the dumbass I am. But Brand levels a stare at me.

"How do I feel?" he asks quietly. He's hesitant and nervous and appalled. If I tried to lie, it would be an insult to him.

"I can see how you feel about me," I say limply. "I'm sorry, Brand. I wish I felt the same way. You're the best person I know. It's why I always come to you, because you're so fucking *amazing*. I wish that I loved you like you want me to."

He flushes, the first time I've ever seen him flush.

"It's okay," he says quietly. "It's my issue to deal with, not yours. It's not your fault that things changed for me and not for you. I'll get a handle on it. We won't change, Jace."

I stare at him, at the goodness in his eyes and his heart. Brand is just so... good. Through and through. All along, I've been chasing what's bad for me when maybe the very best thing for me has been in front of me all along.

On impulse, I lean over and kiss him. On the mouth.

He kisses me back. For one split second. Then he pulls away. I try to cling to him, but he pushes me away.

"Make me feel better, Brand," I murmur pleadingly. "Please."

Brand glares at me as he takes a deep breath.

"Jesus, Jacey. Give me a second."

He pulls himself under control as I breathe harshly on the opposite end of the sofa. He finally turns and looks at me, and there is pain in his eyes.

"You don't want me," he says pointedly. "Not really. I know that and you know that. You want Dominic Kinkaide, but you can't have him, so you want to use me to fill up the rejection that you feel. It's not fair, Jace. Not to me and not to you."

He's breathing hard as he watches me, as he waits for my reaction. I close my eyes and he continues.

"This is what you always do, Jacey. You've done it since you were a teenager. I've stood by and watched it. Your dad was never home, he never cared, and you sought out that acceptance and approval for years from random guys. And when you're rejected, you run straight to the next guy. But you can't do that anymore."

I choke on my tears because I know he's right. Because I know it and because that's exactly what my therapist told me. It's humiliating and true and horrible.

"I don't know what's wrong with me," I mumble before I start crying again. "I'm a horrible, weak person. I'm sorry if I led you on, Brand. I didn't mean to. I love you. You're like my brother, and I can't stand the thought of being without you."

Brand pulls me into his arms again, pulling me to his chest where I hide my face. I try to ignore the fact that my chest is pushed against him. I'd never have worried about that before, and I hate it that I think of it now.

"First, you'll never be without me. Not ever. Got it?" Brand stares down at me, his eyes stern. I nod.

"And second, you're not horrible. You're beautiful and strong. And what's more, you've pretty much got this shit figured out. You chose to walk away from Dominic because he can't be what you need. That's half the battle, Jacey. Now all you've got to do is figure out how to stop running to a new guy to make you feel better. You don't need their acceptance, Jacey. You're strong enough to deal with things on your own."

I snivel into his shirt, breathing in his familiar cologne.

"I don't think I am." I sigh. "I don't feel strong. Ever since Jared...did what he did, I've tried not to be weak. I've tried to change, but I'm starting to think it's impossible. At least for me. Because against my better judgment, I fell for Dominic, Brand. I knew better, and I did it anyway. And he was the worst possible person for me to fall for."

"But you walked away, Jacey. That's huge."

"Yeah," I mumble. "And I came here and tried to force myself on you instead."

Brand's chest rumbles as he speaks with a voice that has always had the power to soothe me, even now when he's in love with me and I'm crying to him about another guy.

"You want to know what your grandma told me once?" he asks, and I raise my head.

"My gran?"

Brand nods. "Yeah. It was one summer when I was staying at their lake house with you. She and I were down by the lake and I was upset over some girl…she'd broken up with me and I thought that the world was ending. I told her that I was never going to love anyone else again, because falling in love was the dumbest thing in the world because it hurt so much."

I have to smile, because I can practically see teenage Brand saying that. Brand is and always was a one hundred percent in or out kind of guy. "What did Gran say?"

"Your grandma was the wisest person I ever knew." He nods. "She looked at me and she said, 'Branden, the best things in life are worth the greatest risk. Falling in love is one of those things. Can it break our hearts? Yes. Most definitely. But more often than not, before we fall, we fly.'"

"What the heck did that mean?" I ask in confusion. Brand nods again.

"That's exactly what I asked her. It didn't make any sense. But then she explained and it was perfect. She said we're like birds who leap from trees for the first time, terrified that they're going to crash and die on the ground below. The bird will almost always fly before it falls to its death. So, too, will we, and so we shouldn't be afraid to do the things that will bring us the greatest reward…like falling in love."

"But what if we fall in love with the wrong people?" I stammer. "Because I've done that a hundred times, and each time I've gotten hurt or hurt someone else. I'm tired of doing that. How many times do we have to fall before we finally fly?"

Brand shakes his head and grins wryly. "I didn't ask your gran that."

I shake my head, but Brand lifts my chin with his finger. "It might take several failures, but eventually it will happen. I don't know if it will happen with this guy or not, but you'll learn something from each failed attempt. So at least there's that."

I can't help but stare at him. "I'm not sure that's comforting."

Brand chuckles. "I know. And that's actually what I thought back when your gran had this discussion with me in the first place. But just think on it, and after you do, you'll see that what she said is true. Before you fall, you'll fly, Jacey. Whether it's now or later, it'll happen. I promise."

"I just hope it happens before my wings get broken," I mutter, curling up on his chest. He chuckles softly and pats my back. I rest that way for a while longer before I sit up and straighten my clothes.

"I'm sorry, Brand," I tell him, looking him in the eye. "I'm sorry that I always run to you. That you always have to pick me up and put me back together. I'm sorry that it seems like I use you. I don't mean to. It's just that…deep down, I always feel like I'm not good enough. And you always make me feel like I *am*. But I'm going to stop depending on you to remind me of that. I'm going to have to remind myself."

Brand bends forward and presses his lips to my forehead.

"Just be you, Jacey. You are always good enough and then some. You really have come a long way since everything happened with Jared. Just keep it up. Tonight was just a tiny slipup. You came to me because I'm familiar. That's all. You're doing great."

I can't help but smile as I get up and walk out. Pausing in the doorway, I look back.

"Thank you. You'll never know how much I love you."

Brand smiles, but I can see the sadness in it.

"Don't worry," he tells me easily in his Brand-like way. "I know. I love you, too, but I'm going to need some space for a while, Jace. I'm going to pull my head together and sort this out so that I love you the way I should...the way you love me. I'm always here for you if you need me, but try not to need me for a while, okay?"

I nod as my heart swells in my throat at the thought of how I have accidentally hurt one of the people I love most in the world.

"Okay," I agree. "I'll give you space. I'm sorry, Brand."

I feel utterly sad as I walk out to my car, but I have to admit that I feel stronger. Being with Brand *always* makes me feel stronger. He knows me. He's always known me. There's comfort in familiarity like that. I hate that I can't give him what he needs, and in a weird way, that only makes me feel closer to Dom.

Because I know how he feels.

He can't give me what *I* need, either.

Sighing, I blink my tears away and drive into the night.

Chapter Twenty~Six

Dominic

The world is unraveling.

After I arrive a few hours late and receive a firm chastising from the director, I go through the motions on-set, then fly back to Chicago, then go to work at the gym. The entire time, I can't feel anything. I'm utterly numb. But when I walk into the gym, my breath catches, because for the first time in days I feel something.

The desire to see Jacey.

And when I do see her, when I bump into her, she turns away like I'm not there, like I don't even exist, exactly the way I've treated her a hundred times in the past. And that moment is when I know why the world is falling to shit.

I need her.

I need her in my life. I knew I wanted her before, but to know that I *need* her is something entirely different, something terrifying, and the mere thought causes my heart to pound. The problem is, she doesn't need *me*. She barely acknowledges my presence, barely glances at me.

She's definitely learned the art of being detached from its best practitioner.

Me.

Being on the receiving end of such iciness is complete shit. For the first time in years, my heart fucking hurts... because I've opened it up to that. It's an aching reminder of why I've always shut myself off, away from people.

It isn't worth the pain.

I look around as I wipe off the counters in the kitchen, musing about how much has changed in a few weeks' time. I just finished making twenty peanut butter sandwiches and wrapping them in foil. Why?

Because Joe insists on sending sandwiches home with the boys, because so many of them don't have enough to eat. Why does this signify change? Because I just found myself making a mental note to buy some pre-charged debit cards to send home with some of them for groceries. They shouldn't have to worry about eating.

But this isn't something I would even have thought of a month ago.

Just like how a month ago, my heart wouldn't be hurting. It would be safe and sound in its cage of ice. I'm not sure what's better.

Jacey sticks her head into the kitchen, interrupting my thoughts and talking to me for the first time since we arrived this morning.

"Hey, have you seen the ladder?" she asks me quietly, hesitantly. She glances around the kitchen for it at the same time I do.

"No," I tell her needlessly. "It's not here."

She starts to turn away, but I say her name and she looks back at me. She pauses in the doorway hesitatingly, her eyes saying what her lips won't.

I trusted you. But it was a mistake and I won't do it again.

It gives me pause and I close my mouth, swallowing all of the words that I'd wanted to say.

I'm conflicted. I might need her, but that doesn't change the fact that I can't give her what she needs.

She looks impatient, but all I can do is shake my head. "Never mind."

She turns and walks away, but not before I see the disappointment flash across her face.

To distract myself from thinking about her, or about the fact that I might've let the only good person that I know in the world slip through my fingers, I pile the sandwiches in several neat stacks and fold napkins to go with them.

As I fold the last napkin, I hear a commotion coming from the gym. Curious, I head out to see what's going on, only to find a crowd of boys congregated around the ladder in the middle of the room. Some are kneeling, some are standing, but they're all in a circle around something.

My heart starts pounding as I see Jacey's pink tennis shoe poking through the legs.

Shoving through the crowd, I get there just as Joe does.

Jacey is motionless, crumpled on the floor, and my heart stops as I stare down at her limp form. She's utterly still, her face devoid of color, her eyes closed.

Holy fuck. I can't breathe. Because I can't lose her. Because she doesn't deserve this.

Because I can't do this again.

"What the hell happened?" Joe barks as he kneels down beside her. I'm motionless, frozen, as I stare at her still body.

"She was changing the lightbulb like you asked," Tig explains quickly. "But she tripped coming back down the ladder. I think she hit her head on the cement."

"Jesus," Joe mutters as he feels her head. "That's a big lump. Someone call an ambulance." No one moves, so he barks, "Now!"

Jake bolts for the office and I'm finally able to move.

I woodenly shove through the boys and drop to my knees beside her. I grab her hand and her fingers are so cold. The coldness sends panic rippling through me, and I shake her shoulder. Hard.

"Jacey, wake up," I tell her firmly, my heart firmly lodged in my throat. "Wake up."

She doesn't even twitch.

This can't be happening again.

"Jacey." I shake her. "Jacey."

I'm panicked now, overwhelmed by emotion and déjà vu, so much so that I can't think straight. The last time I was in this situation it didn't end well.

It can't happen this time.

This time, all I can think is that I need to make Jacey wake up, no matter what it takes. I squeeze her hand and shake her shoulder, chanting her name.

"Be careful, son," Joe advises. "You shouldn't move her neck."

"I'm not your son," I tell him without even looking up. "She needs to wake up."

"Yes," Joe agrees calmly. "She does. But don't move her."

I ignore him and shake her lightly one more time, and we're both surprised when she opens her eyes. A thrill like a jolt of electricity ripples through me.

"Dominic?" she asks groggily, staring at me with blurry eyes, trying to focus. "What happened?"

The relief that floods me is overwhelming. *Thank Christ.*

"You fell," I tell her softly. "And you hit your head, but you're going to be fine. We're going to take you to the hospital."

"An ambulance is on the way," Jake calls out, jogging over from the office. "Did you trip on your bad foot, Jace?" he asks, kneeling next to me and staring down at Jacey.

She shakes her head in confusion. "I don't know."

Guilt eats at me because I didn't even know her foot was still bothering her. What I do know is she hurt her foot in the first place because of me. *Protecting me.*

I sit with her wordlessly, holding her hand until the paramedics arrive. They load her onto a gurney and roll her into the back of the ambulance, where I insist on riding with her. She's still disoriented, and I can't stand the thought of sending her away alone.

"Are you a family member?" one of them asks, staring at me curiously. I see the realization when it dawns. "Aren't you Dominic Kinkaide?"

"Yeah." I nod. "I'm her brother."

Jacey's eyes are fluttering closed again at this point, and the EMT looks at me, knowing that I'm lying but not questioning my words. "Keep your sister awake," she instructs. "I'm going to start an IV."

I squeeze Jacey's hand.

"Jace, you've got to stay awake. Let's talk about the Ferris wheel at Navy Pier. Or about racing. Do you want to go back out to the track?"

"Not with you," she tells me groggily, her eyelids fluttering. "I'm not going anywhere with you again, Dom. You're fucking toxic."

The EMT glances at me as she pushes a syringe into an IV line. "She's probably confused. It's common with head injuries."

Jacey's not confused. At all. She's never made more sense. But her words have never been more painful.

"It's okay, Jace," I tell her. "We'll talk about this when you feel better. For now, you've got to stay awake. You hit your head hard. You picked one of the only spots that isn't covered with a mat to fall on. You probably should've planned that a little better."

She doesn't crack a smile. Her eyes stay closed, but I know she's awake because she's still squeezing my hand from time to time.

I talk with her the entire ride to the hospital, but when we arrive, they wheel her away on the squeaky gurney and make me stay in the waiting room.

The emergency room waiting area seems like a wasteland for lost souls. People are hunched over and tired, people are sick, people are curled up and sad. It sucks the energy out of me, and I hunker down in my seat, hoping no one recognizes me. I'm definitely not in the mood for that.

I keep my nose buried in tattered magazines until I'm called back an hour later.

"You're her brother?" the doctor asks. I nod. What's another lie in the scheme of things?

"Your sister has a mild concussion. She's actually really lucky, because from what I was told, she fell from rather high up. We can keep her overnight, but she'd be more comfortable in her own bed. The thing is, she shouldn't be alone. Would you or someone else be able to stay with her? Wake her up every couple of hours to make sure that she's lucid? If she acts out of it, or if you can't wake her, call an ambulance. Do you feel comfortable with that?"

I nod. "Of course. I'll stay with her myself."

The doctor smiles tiredly. "Great. I'll get her paperwork ready and she'll be ready to go soon."

More waiting.

The clock ticks slowly on and I sigh. Apparently, it doesn't make it go any faster to watch it.

I get a cup of shitty hospital coffee, arrange for Jacey's bill to be sent to me, and am back in the waiting room by the time a nurse comes wheeling her out. Jacey looks disgruntled and she hasn't even seen me yet.

"I don't need anyone to babysit me," she grumbles to the nurse as I get to my feet. I have to smile at her attitude.

The nurse looks at me in relief, probably anxious to get Jacey off her hands.

"Your brother is here to take you home. He's going to watch you tonight."

Jacey's head snaps up and she looks around.

"Gabe's here?" she asks, and it pains me to hear the excitement in her voice. I hate to be the one to disappoint her.

"No, it's just me," I tell her. "I'm going to sit with you tonight."

She stares at me, her expression falling like a stone, but she doesn't reveal my lie to the nurse. She waits until exactly five minutes later when we're in my car alone to rip into me.

"What the fuck?" she snaps as I drive out of the parking garage and toward her little house. "You think you can take advantage of me when I'm down? Really? That's how you operate? I don't want you to stay with me, Dominic."

"I just want to help," I assure her, glancing at the way she's rubbing her head. "I'm sorry you fell, Jacey. I feel responsible because you hurt your foot in the first place because of me. Just let me take care of you tonight, then I'll leave you alone. I promise."

"No," Jacey says loudly, staring at me, her brown eyes snapping. "Just...no. Stop the car and I'll call someone else."

"Like Brand?" I ask acerbically. "You want him to come riding to your rescue again and you can pretend that you don't know what he feels for you?"

Jacey stares at me, her gaze falling, and for a minute I feel bad for goading her. But shit. She can't keep running to him every time she has a problem.

"I'm too tired to argue," Jacey finally says wearily, leaning her head against the window. "Brand and I had a come-to-Jesus, and you were right, okay? Is that what you want to hear? You were right. Brand's in love with me. I don't feel the same way, and it's driving a wedge in between us, so I can't call him. I'm on my own. Just…take me home and drop me off, if you want to help. I'm so tired that I can't stay awake."

I'm stunned about her and Brand. I'm stunned she would tell me that I was right all along. I'm stunned that she's not going to call him anyway because she leans on him for everything.

A part of me feels intense satisfaction that she's not leaning on him tonight.

I'm here instead.

"I'm sorry about Brand," I tell her. "I know how much you love him."

"Let's not talk about him," she answers firmly. "Let's just…not."

"Okay," I reply, ignoring her icy tone. "Then I'll just tell you that you're not on your own. I'm here. And it's normal to feel sleepy. You can go to sleep when we get to your house, but I have to stay with you and wake you up every two hours. Doctor's orders."

"Oh, fucking great," she mutters, closing her eyes. "I can't wait."

When we get to her house, she changes into a nightgown and then climbs into bed.

"You can sleep on the sofa," she tells me firmly as I pull the blankets up to her chin. I nod.

"Whatever makes you comfortable."

"You leaving would make me comfortable," she grumbles, and rolls onto her side, dismissing me. I settle myself on the sofa.

I don't sleep. Instead I read a book until it's time to wake her up the first time.

As I stare down at her, I can't help but notice how innocent and beautiful she looks while she's asleep. Completely trusting. I gently shake her shoulder and she opens her eyes.

"Jacey, do you feel all right?"

She nods.

"Yes or no?" I clarify.

"Yes." She sighs.

"What's your full name?"

"Jaselyn Elizabeth Vincent."

"I didn't know that," I tell her. "It's pretty."

It suits her. But I don't add that.

"It's after my grandma." She yawns. "When I was born, Gabe couldn't say it very well. He called me Jacey, and eventually everyone else did, too. Can I go back to sleep now?"

"I don't think so," I tell her uncertainly. "I need to make sure you're lucid first."

She stares at me, and I can see when the sleep lifts and clarity sets in. Her expression hardens.

"Why are you here, Dominic?" she asks suddenly. "You could've told the hospital the truth—and they would've asked me for someone else to call. You didn't have to stay there and you don't have to stay here now. What kind of game are you playing?"

A tiny muscle in my jaw ticks. "I don't know," I answer her honestly. "But it's not a game. For once, it's not a game. I want to be here."

She sighs, a tiny sound in the night. "But why? You're only making things worse. You're dragging things out when we need to just end them. It's cleaner that way. Less painful. Trust me, I know all about endings."

"I don't want to end things," I tell her raggedly. I know that her response could crush me, but I can't take it back. "I don't want to end things," I repeat.

As I say the words aloud, it validates what I feel even more. I *don't* want to end things. I don't know what I want, but I don't want that. Somehow, against my best efforts, I've let her in. And now that she's in, I can't let go of her. I can't experience that kind of loss again.

She closes her eyes. "You can't give me what I need, Dominic," she says plainly. "So what's the point? I can't settle for less. Not anymore."

Panic wells up in me, leaving a bitter taste on my tongue, because she might be right. Not because I don't want to give her what she needs, but because I might be incapable.

But I can fucking try.

"What do you need?" I ask, and the words scrape my throat painfully.

"You," she answers simply. "All of you...and you aren't able to give me that."

My breath comes quicker now, in rasps and almost pants. I don't know what a panic attack feels like, but I think I might be getting ready to have one. My ribs are like steel bands constricting my lungs in a vise. I suck a harsh breath in, then let it out slowly.

"How do you know?" I ask finally. "I haven't tried."

"Because I know you," she says simply, her eyes closed and her eyelashes dark against her pale cheeks. "I know you."

"Do you?" I ask, my voice empty. "Do you *really*?"

Jacey opens her eyes again, and I see a million things there. Painful things, confused things.

Hopeful things.

"Fine. Maybe I don't, so why don't you tell me?" she suggests softly. "Tell me who you are. Tell me about Emma. That's a start."

Jesus. I can't breathe.

The vise around my lungs moves to my heart, constricting it, crushing it, grinding it to a pulp while I try to breathe.

I manage to take a breath and stare into the corner of the room, into the dark.

"Why that?" I manage to ask. "Why do I have to talk about Emma? She doesn't affect you and me."

Jacey stares at me, her gaze dark. "Doesn't she?" she asks softly. "You're in love with her, Dominic. And she's there…in every little thing you do."

I squeeze my eyes closed, trying to force out the truth. But I know she's right. Everything I do, everything that is fucked up about me, is because of Emma. And if I ever want to get past it, if I ever want something that is real and good, I have to confront it. I have to confront *her*.

"See?" Jacey asks quietly. "I knew you couldn't do it. Just go, Dom. I'll call Kaylie to sit with me."

My eyes fly open.

"No," I say firmly, fueled by desperation. "Let me try." Jacey stares at me doubtfully, afraid to hope now.

"I'm not *in love* with Emma. She's dead. I know that. But I can't help but love her. She was my first everything. My first kiss, my first love, my first time. I'll always love her. Because of everything that happened with her, I'll never get away from it. From her."

I pause, letting the words soak in for Jacey.

"Emma's dead. She died a horrible death and it was the worst thing I've ever seen. I don't think I can describe that night, I can't even put it into words. I've never been able to talk about it with anyone…not even my family. I think about her face and that last night and I freeze up. The words die in my mouth and I can't say them. But if you need this...if this is what you need...I'll try."

The air is charged between us, and it hangs heavily. But it doesn't matter, because the one thing I need happens...Jacey's face softens at my words and she nods.

"I'm sorry," she whispers softly. "I know it's hard. But I *do* need this. I need to understand what happened, because I think it will explain everything. I need to know you, Dom."

I feel weak with relief, but at the same time I'm tense. I know I have one shot to explain, to make her understand, and I have to get it right. Even though there's no getting anything with Emma's fucked-up situation *right*. It was always all wrong. On every level.

I look out the window at the night sky as I speak. I can't look at Jacey's face...it might kill me to see her reaction. There's no way I want to see her face when she hears what I did. Who I was. How I acted.

"Emma and I grew up together," I begin. "She was always at my house, with Kira, playing with Duncan, Sin, Fiona, and me. We were all like family."

"Until you started dating," Jacey interrupts. I smile, just a little, at the memory of my first date with Emma.

"Yeah. Our first date was an accident...when we were sopho-mores. Her car died on our road. I was on my way out, so I picked her up and took her with me. I was driving my dad's old classic Nova...and it had a cassette tape stuck in the deck. If we wanted to listen to anything, our only choice was "Brown Eyed Girl." We prob-ably listened to that song fifty times that night...but it turned out all right because the night ended with a good-night kiss. All of a sud-den, we realized that we didn't feel like brother and sister anymore."

Jacey stares at me, a knowing look in her eyes. "That's how you knew about Brand. You recognized it because that's what happened with you and Emma."

I nod.

"We dated all through high school. No one said our names separately...we were like one person, Dom-and-Emma. But then, my senior year..."

My voice trails off as pain rips through me. Memories are so vivid, so fucking vivid, and I close my eyes against them.

The blood, the pain in Emma's eyes. The guilt, Jesus Christ, the guilt.

My spine feels like it's being ripped out of my body at the mere memory.

I swallow hard, then swallow again. Jacey waits patiently, but I can feel her watching me, wondering if I'm going to be able to do it.

"Emma killed herself because of me," I finally manage to say thickly, and my tongue feels like a dead thing in my mouth.

All the blood, *her blood*, swims in front of my eyes, and for a moment I only see red. I'm starting to wonder if it's the only color I'm ever going to see.

Jacey gasps a ragged breath and her eyes widen. "Oh my god. Jesus, Dominic." She takes another breath. "What happened?"

I try to make myself numb, like I always do when I think about this, about Emma.

I reach into my pocket, turning the aquamarine pendant over and over in my fingers. Like always, knowing that she used to wear it around her neck when she was still healthy and alive calms me down enough so I can speak.

"Does it matter?" I finally answer. "The important thing is that she did. And it was my fault."

Jacey stares at me, her eyes still horror filled, but now there's something else, too. Curiosity. A need to know. A need to understand. And beneath all that, a hope that I'm wrong—that I'm not to blame.

But I am.

"I can't imagine how it was your fault," she answers slowly. "Suicide is a personal choice. You couldn't have made her do such a thing. But if you think that's true, then we need to talk about it, because it has definitely affected you."

I squeeze my eyes shut hard, trying to blink away the red, then take another breath.

"Emma cheated on me with Cris. She told me about it and she cried. She was *so sorry.* Apparently, they got drunk one night when I was out with other friends. One thing led to another, and they had sex. She was *sorry* and I was devastated."

Jacey freezes now, her eyes glued to mine. "That's why you hate Cris now."

I nod silently.

Jacey stares at me a second, then speaks hesitantly. "Okay. I can see where you would be pissed at him. But to this degree? You were kids, Dom. I mean, you were teenagers. Even adults make that mistake."

"I know." I sigh. "But Emma got pregnant, Jacey. And since we always used condoms, we had a pretty good idea that the baby was Cris's."

I look away. "I remember standing over a pile of pregnancy tests in Emma's bathroom, all of them showing a fuzzy pink plus sign. If I could go back in time to any one moment, it would be to that one. I would handle everything differently."

I wouldn't have annihilated her.

Jacey sucks in her breath, her hands twisted in her lap. "Jesus. I don't know what to say, Dom. What happened?"

I failed her.

"I was so pissed at her," I admit. "I screamed and she cried, but at the end of the day, it boiled down to one thing. I loved her. More than anything. More than a pregnancy, more than her cheating on me."

"So you stayed with her?" Jacey asks hesitantly. I can see that that notion doesn't match the idea of me that lives in her head. That's because that version of me died with Emma.

"She swore to me that it was a one-time thing, an accident. That she'd been lonely because I'd been away so much, visiting colleges. I'd pulled away from her a little and Cris moved in. He took up my slack and hung out with her all the time. I should've seen what he was doing, but I didn't. He was my best friend and I was blind."

"So you think it was your fault that Emma cheated on you?" Jacey asks doubtfully.

I ignore that and take a gulp of some water. "Because I could see that it was true, that Cris had swooped in on her and I'd been neglecting her, I forgave her. He took advantage of her. And they were drunk. But I demanded one thing from her in exchange for my forgiveness."

I pause, staring out the window again as I remember the way Emma's head had dropped when I told her. How I'd stood over her and how I didn't feel sorry about what I was asking. I didn't care that it devastated her. I didn't care about anything but myself and my own pain.

I hadn't even begun to know pain yet. I just didn't realize it at the time.

I don't want to say the ugly words to Jacey. I don't want her to know. But she prompts me.

"What did you demand?" she asks quietly, but there's a certain knowingness to her tone, an aching fragile timbre. *She knows.*

"An abortion. I demanded that she have an abortion. I wasn't man enough to raise his baby. I forgave her, but I couldn't do that."

Jacey's quiet now, still. She watches me, waiting for me to continue. I don't want to, but I know I have to. The bullet is out of the gun now. There's no putting it back.

"We were just eighteen," I say quietly, staring at the wall. "We were getting ready to go away to college together. We were going to have a new start, away from Cris. I made my forgiveness contingent on that one thing. She had to get an abortion. If she wouldn't, then I was done. I made that very clear."

Emma's face is in my head, innocent and young, as she pleads with me.

Dominic, I can't, she'd cried. *My parents would kill me. And it's wrong, Dom. It's wrong.*

"I pressured her hard," I finally continue, even though those words are a gross understatement. "Every day. Every hour. She cried and I raged and I refused to give in. I didn't care that her family was strict Catholic. I didn't care that she thought her soul was in jeopardy and that her parents would never forgive her. In my head, I thought of the baby as an *it*, as Cris's mistake. I didn't think of it as an actual human life. I was too blinded by my anger and my hurt and my hate to care about anything but myself."

I pause and stare at Jacey. "Do you see how selfish I was?"

Jacey is deathly pale as she stares at me, as a million thoughts flash through her eyes. "Anyone would've been upset, Dominic," she finally answers hesitantly. I can see that she doesn't know what to say. I can't fault her for that... because who would?

I turn away, staring into the dark, trying to focus on the night instead of the memories in my head.

"I took her to get the abortion. It was a quiet ride. They wouldn't let me go back with her, so she had to do it alone. On the way home, she huddled into the car door and cried. She wouldn't talk to me for days. But she talked to Cris. Because a few days later, on our graduation day, I went over to her house and got there just as he was leaving. I lost my shit. I told her that I never wanted to see her again, that if she wanted Cris she could have him. So after making her have an abortion for me, I left her anyway."

Jacey utters a weird noise, a guttural sound that I've never heard pass her lips before. Her knuckles graze her teeth as she presses her fist to her mouth.

"Emma skipped the graduation parties. She didn't come and I didn't care. I went to a party with Sin and Duncan that night, determined to get drunk and forget all about her. So that's what I did. I was getting a lap dance from Taylor McKay when Emma called me. It was late and she was babbling and I couldn't make heads or tails out of what she was saying...except that she'd cut her wrists. And that she needed me."

"Did you go?" Jacey whispers, and I can see from her face she's afraid of the answer.

"Of course I went. But it was too late to save her."

Jacey shakes her head in disbelief now, like she's expecting that I'm just spinning a tale, acting out a scene. "Dom...I..."

She doesn't have the words. Because the answer is clear. I'm a horrible person. A monster.

I nod curtly, once, determined to keep my composure.

"Emma was a light. Everyone who met her knew that. She was too good for me. And I failed her. She trusted the wrong person, because I turned away when she needed me the most. I abandoned her. The worst part is that she loved me anyway."

And she did. I'll never forget the look on her face when she saw me come in. It was like everything was right in the world, even though she was dying in a sea of her own blood.

"What happened when you got there?" Jacey whispers.

I'm wooden now as I force the words from my lips. I stare back out the window, away from Jacey's horror, as I see the memories in my head.

"The bed was covered in blood, and Emma was pale and shaking and cold. She'd sliced her arms from wrist to elbow, and I knew that it wasn't a cry for help. She wanted to die. She didn't want to be saved. She was surrounded by poems that she had written, all about death. I don't know how I didn't see that I'd broken her so completely."

I pause, trying to untangle my tongue, trying to swallow the emotion that lingers there, trying to swallow the memories so that I can act calm. I'm a fucking actor, for Christ's sake. I can act calm.

I somehow manage it, because my words come out in a wooden monotone. "There was so much blood. There were bloody footprints everywhere. I've never seen so much blood. She grabbed my shirt and clung to me and her hands were so cold. Her lips were so blue."

She was so pale.

The blood.

The blood.

The blood.

I pause. "There was so much blood. We had towels wrapped around her arms, but they soaked through within minutes. The EMTs came in and she acted like they weren't even there. She just kept apologizing to me. Telling me how sorry she was for killing our baby . . . a baby I'd never wanted in the first place. I begged her to hold on until they got her to the hospital, I begged her to try. But she didn't even make it to the ambulance. I begged, but she died anyway."

The room is quiet now, utterly silent but for the soft sounds of Jacey's breathing. I close my eyes, and behind my eyelids a movie plays out. The movie of my life. The movie of the night that destroyed me.

"There was so much blood," I murmur, seeing it like it was

yesterday. Some emotion has slipped through my voice, but only a little. I'm still in check. For now. "I've never seen so much. Emma's entire bed was covered in it. The towels were soaked, my clothes were soaked. It was all over my hands, my face. Her mom was screaming on the phone with emergency dispatch . . . her dad was crying. Emma and I were on her bed, and she got weaker and weaker so fast, and then she kept trying to tell me something, but she couldn't get the words out. But I finally figured it out."

I turn and look at Jacey. "She was saying Cris's name."

Jacey opens her mouth, but closes it again. There's nothing she can say.

"I ignored it. I pretended I didn't hear. Instead, I just told her that I was so sorry that I'd pressured her. I told her that I loved her and that I would always love her no matter what had happened with Cris. Nothing else mattered in that moment because I knew she was dying. I knew she only had a few minutes left, and I didn't want to spend those minutes being ugly. In the end, all that matters is life. You forget the ugliness, you forget the pain. Just for one moment."

My eyes burn and I look out the window, seeing Emma's face. She was so beautiful, even then, even with her lips blue and her eyes wide and scared and sad. Her body was so slight, so cold as I held her.

"She died in my arms."

Jacey is utterly silent, horror in her eyes. I don't know what else to do but keep talking.

"I was drunk, but I'll never forget how still she was. I didn't even know she was gone at first . . . I was clutching her to me, pleading with her, and then all of a sudden I realized that she wasn't answering. I pulled away from her, just a little, and she was like a rag doll. Her eyes were empty." I pause, taking a deep breath, filling up lungs that don't deserve the oxygen.

"She died while I was holding her, and I didn't even know it. I don't know when she took her last breath. Even at the end, she deserved so much more than me."

"Jesus." Jacey breathes, and horror is in her eyes as she looks at me. She finally sees me for the monster I am, but I don't get any satisfaction from it. "Dominic, what she did wasn't your fault. You were young and scared and you asked her to get an abortion. You didn't ask her to kill herself. She did that on her own."

"I did do it," I argue firmly. "I annihilated her. I pushed her. She loved me so much, and all she wanted was to be with me. I practically pushed her into Cris's arms by neglecting her. It was my fault. And then all she wanted was for me to forgive her, and I made her do an unimaginable thing. She couldn't take it. She couldn't live with the guilt."

Jacey reaches over and grabs my hand again, her fingers small and cold. She holds it and I let her, but my heart is cold and empty. For the first time since it happened, I've told someone. And it doesn't feel good.

"No one knows," I add limply. "Her parents don't even know. She didn't leave a note. All she left were those fucking poems about death. I didn't see the point in telling them all of the ugliness."

"It might've given them some closure," Jacey points out hesitantly. "They've probably been torturing themselves, wondering why she did it."

"That didn't occur to me," I admit shakily. "I was so wrapped up in my own grief. After the funeral, they moved away. Mr. Brandt got a job in New York City and they moved to New Jersey. They couldn't stand to stay in the same house where she died."

Not in a house where one room was covered in their only daughter's blood.

"I don't blame them," Jacey answers quietly.

"Me, either," I agree. "It's one of the reasons I moved to California and rarely come home. Trust me, I totally get it."

"And Cris," Jacey says hesitantly. "You've never talked to Cris about it?"

"Fuck no," I spit angrily. "I forgave Emma for what happened, but I'll never fucking forgive Cris."

"You're carrying so much anger and hatred still," Jacey points out slowly. "You blame Cris, you blame yourself. You're mad at Emma, you love Emma. Those are a lot of unresolved emotions to carry, Dom. You're not being fair to yourself. When we hate someone so much, we think that we're hurting them. But we're not. We're only hurting ourselves, because carrying that much ugliness around is toxic."

A knot forms in my throat, heavy and hard. I can't swallow past it, and my eyes sting. I look up at the ceiling, I look out the window, I look at the floor. Anything to avoid looking at Jacey.

"Dominic," she says softly. "Look at me."

Reluctantly, I look at her.

"It wasn't your fault that Emma died. She died from something she shouldn't have done. If you'd known, you would've tried to stop her."

I nod stiltedly. At least that much is true.

"And you can't keep blaming yourself for such a terrible accident. Because it was an *accident*, Dominic. Emma wasn't in her right mind. She was just a kid herself."

I take a breath, and it's ragged in the dark.

"She couldn't live with the guilt. Before she started asking for Cris, she kept crying incoherently about the guilt. I told her that I'd forgiven her and she just shook her head. She couldn't forgive herself and she couldn't trust me to forgive her, either. So she killed herself. I might not have cut her wrists, but I killed her all the same."

Chapter Twenty~Seven

Jacey

My chest literally hurts at the look on Dominic's face...at how shattered he is...at how shattered he's always been.

"You've carried this for so long," I finally manage to say. "This has been so much to carry, Dominic."

He sits slumped in the chair by my bed, his hands in his lap. I'm holding his hand, but his fingers are limp. He doesn't even think that he deserves comfort. It's heartbreaking and I feel mine shatter into a million tiny pieces.

"Dom," I whisper. "You didn't push her into Cris's arms. This wasn't your fault. She made the choice. Not you."

He doesn't say anything, he just closes his eyes. I see that his hands are shaking, and it breaks my heart. Such a young girl, so much loss...and *Dominic*. God. He was so young, too. Too young to carry such a heavy burden.

My head pounds, but I ignore it as I roll out of bed and kneel in front of Dom.

"Look at me," I tell him softly. He keeps his eyes closed, so I repeat myself more firmly. "Look at me, Dom."

He opens his eyes, and they're so, so dark. Filled with grief, filled with guilt, filled with unimaginable things.

Things that he has actually seen.

"Is this why you won't get close to anyone?" I whisper, gripping his hands hard. "You think that you're not fit to be with anyone because you killed Emma. Is that right? That's what you think?"

He just stares at me.

"Yes or no?" I ask bluntly.

There's a beat, then he nods once.

My heart breaks and I feel a tear slip down my cheek. "And you can't trust anyone to not hurt you like that again, right? She crushed you. She died and left you...she left you with all of that guilt, and you were furious at her for that, right?"

He closes his eyes.

"Yes or no, Dominic?" I know I sound harsh, but he has to face this or he's never going to get past it. I'm no expert, but even I know that.

He nods once more.

"Anger is a normal response when someone dies," I tell him softly. "Trust me, I know. Remember when I told you that my last boyfriend did something terrible? Well, he was a psychopath. And I shouldn't have gone back to him, but I was weak and I did. And when I did, a good friend of mine died because of my actions. He died because he tried to save me. And when he died, I was so pissed. I was pissed at him for trying to help me, but then I was pissed at myself...because if I wasn't so weak, he wouldn't have had to save me in the first place."

"It couldn't have been your fault," Dominic finally speaks. I stare at him.

"No? I tell myself that. But I'm not sure I believe it. Not deep down. That's something you know a lot about, right?"

Dominic nods. "But your situation is different than mine."

I shake my head. "No, it's really not. Someone I love died because of a decision I made. You think someone died because of you. The difference between you and me is that my friend *really* died because of me. Emma died because of a choice she made herself."

"And your friend made that choice himself, too," Dominic tells me, his voice as dark as his eyes. "He chose to try and help you."

"I know," I tell him softly. "It's something I think about every day. Because he was close to me, because he loved me. That guilt is hard to carry. But it's also something I know that I have to let go... and I'm working on it. I've been working on it ever since that horrible day. You have to let this go, Dominic. You have to try. Regardless of why, Emma is gone. You can't bring her back, and it's not going to help anything to carry the blame forever. It won't help."

"I know," he says softly. "You have to believe that I'd do anything to let it go. I feel chained by her... by what happened. I feel trapped by everything. It's around me all of the time. I can never get away from it. Every day, I know what I did to her. I love her and I hate her at the same time. I feel like there's a wall in front of me and I can't move forward. I would give anything to break through it and be able to move on."

"You can do it, Dominic," I tell him urgently, squeezing his hands. "You really can. You just have to go through the motions."

"I don't even know where to start," he answers limply. "When I met you, when I got to know you... for the first time since Emma died, I felt a need to get close to someone, *to you*. But even you can't save me from this. You can't help. No one can. And if you try, Kira was right... you'll drown right along with me."

"You want to get close to me?" I ask quietly, incredulously, because his actions have been so contradictory lately.

"I did," Dominic admits, looking away. "But then I realized that it's not fair to drag you into my toxic life. That's when I ended things. Not because I really wanted to, but because you deserve far, far better than me."

"Why don't you let me decide that?" I suggest gently. But Dom just looks away, his jaw clenched. I can see in his eyes that he's thinking of Emma, and of how he let her in and she decimated him. How he thinks that he killed her. How he thinks he wasn't enough to save her, as if that was ever within his power in the first place.

The look on his face, so sad, so vulnerable, so hopeless... it shatters me. And so I do the only thing I can think of to do.

I kiss him.

I take all of my sadness for him, all of my heartache, and I channel it into a kiss. It's the only thing I know to do. I want to take his sadness away, I want to absorb it in the only way I know how.

At first, Dominic is limp, sitting still as I envelop him in my arms. But after a minute, his hands slide up my back and I feel the warmth of his fingers gripping me. His breathing picks up, ragged and harsh.

"You shouldn't be with me," he tells me again desperately. But I ignore him.

We kiss again and again, and our hands are everywhere, a sudden and feverish frenzy. I want him. I want to take his pain and replace it with something good. He deserves that... if only I can make him see. His heart beats against mine, loud and strong as I run my hands down his chest, down to his belt buckle.

"I don't think I can do this," he rasps against my ear. "I want to. But I don't think I can. I haven't been able to... *be* with anyone since Emma died. I have this debilitating fear of trusting someone again. After Emma died, I didn't handle my grief. I suppressed it. I focused so much on the fear and the guilt that it grew into a monster that I can't get past. There's something inside of me that's broken, Jacey."

I stare into his eyes, into his heartbreak, and I melt.

"Then let's fix you."

I silence his protests with my lips as I crawl onto his lap and suck down his pain. I breathe it in as my hands stroke him everywhere, his face, his chest, his arms. I take his guilt and his sadness and his angst. My chest presses against his, my heart beating with his.

Both of them are racing, pounding, breaking.

"Fix me, Jacey," he whispers, his hands pulling at my night-gown, pushing it up and pulling it over my head. "If you can."

Oh, I can.

I tug at his clothes until there is nothing left between us but skin and heat. Heat and skin. The delicious smell of him, the feel of his fingers and his tongue. There's so much emotion between us now that my body feels so sensitive, electric. Every touch of his fingers sends me arching toward the sky, pulling him onto me.

Because I want more of him.

I'm finally going to get all of him.

We tumble onto my bed together, his hand behind my head. He kisses me again and again and again, and our heat feels like it's going to explode in a firestorm of emotion. I'm not sure I can take this much sensation. It's too much to bear.

Everything is a blur now…a blur of emotion and need and heat. His hands, his face, his eyes…his aching.

His guilt.

All of it wraps around me and I inhale it. I want to free him of it.

In this moment, he wants to change, and I want to help him do it.

"Be with me, Dom." I breathe. "Be with me."

The energy in the room is palpable as he fluidly slips his fingers into me, cool and long. His body hovers over me in the dark, his breath warm on my face.

"I'm not sure I can do this," he says again, uncertainly. "I..."

"We can," I assure him firmly. "You can."

I can.

I slip from under him and flip over on top of him, straddling his hips as I stare down at him. His face is beautiful in the dark, even as it is tortured.

"Do you want me?" I whisper softly, leaning forward to trail my fingers down his cheek. I can feel his erection pressing against me, rigid and hard. "I know you do."

He nods and I raise an eyebrow.

"Yes or no?"

He smiles ever so slightly, but I can see the pain behind it.

"Yes," he murmurs, his hands gripping my hips and pulling me closer. With one movement, I lift and sink onto him, burying him deep within me. He glides into me easily, deeply, completely.

The moment is frozen in time, like the world stops.

Like it's so fucking reverent.

Like the universe knows how significant this is.

We gasp at the same time, then Dominic groans, closing his eyes as my warmth surrounds him, as he sinks into a woman's body for the first time in six years.

"Jesus," he mumbles, his fingers digging into my skin as I rock on top of him. I start out slow, but I can't keep from growing frantic. I want to please him, to pleasure him...to save him.

As a whole, what we're doing is so much more than this simple action. It's more than a simple fuck. And we both know it.

It's significant on a thousand different levels.

Words escape me as I watch his face...at the look of wonder, amazement, and raw pleasure. I realize in this moment that he actually thought he couldn't do it. He had an actual mental block and he thought he'd never get past it. It took me pushing him...taking matters into my own hands to make him do it.

"God, you feel good," he murmurs, opening his eyes and staring into mine. I lean down and kiss him, my tongue tangling with his, my heat pouring into him.

"See?" I ask him, rocking softly atop him once again. He reaches up and cups my breasts, kneading my skin, his thumbs rubbing over my nipples, gentle at first, then harder. "You thought that only the dark and taboo worked for you. You thought you deserved that. You thought you deserved dark corners and hidden rooms. But you deserve this, too, Dom. You deserve to be loved."

Dom stops and looks at me, his eyes widening.

"You love me?"

His voice is quiet and shocked. And he's no more shocked than I am that I said the words out loud.

I stop all movement, shoving my hair away from my face as I stare at him. The idea of putting myself out there like that is terrifying. But I have to do it.

He has to know.

"I love you," I whisper hesitantly. "I do."

Dominic closes his eyes, squeezes them closed as his hands slide lightly down my back, his fingernails grazing my skin. "Don't," he whispers. "Don't love me."

I bend and cup his face in my hands, kissing him on the mouth. "Too late," I whisper against his lips. "It's too late."

A tiny bit of wetness escapes from Dominic's eye, streaking down his cheek. I wipe it away as he opens his eyes.

"Well, god help you then," he says simply.

He groans and flips me over, pinning me against the bed before he plunges into me, hard and fast, deep inside of me, as far inside as he can be. He throws his head back and practically growls. I grip his back, scratching into him as I kiss his arm.

"More," I tell him urgently. "Give me more."

He thrusts harder and faster, moaning into my neck, nipping at my skin. I feel his heart beating, I feel his heat, I feel the moisture from his skin. His scent surrounds me, uniquely him, and I inhale it, pulling it into me along with the rest of him.

"More," I say again, and he thrusts again.

His eyes are glued to mine as he thrusts. His green eyes are almost black and all the hidden things that usually linger there are gone. His intense gaze is open, and it's all for me.

I limply cling to his back until finally he shudders, throwing his head back before he collapses on top of me, pulling me close. He breathes into my neck as his hands caress my back. It's a long time before he speaks.

"I don't know what to say," he finally admits quietly.

"Don't say anything," I answer softly. "You don't need to."

And I mean it. Words aren't necessary right now. I know what he's afraid of. I know what he thinks he is. It's up to me to show him that there's nothing to fear.

Dominic's eyes fly open.

"We didn't use protection," he says shakily. "Jesus. I didn't think about it. I haven't had to worry about that in a long time."

"And don't worry about it now," I tell him calmly. "I'm on the pill and I haven't had unprotected sex in a very long time. I'm healthy. You don't need to worry about me getting pregnant. You won't have to go through that again. I promise."

He closes his eyes and I feel him relax into the bed next to me.

"Okay. I'll just worry about fucking you up with my fucked-uppedness," he mutters as he pulls me into his arms.

"Don't worry about that, either," I tell him softly, pressing a kiss to his damp brow. "I'm fucked up enough on my own."

He smiles, his eyes still closed, and I have to wonder if *I* should worry. Closing my eyes, I decide that I won't. Not tonight.

I can start that shit tomorrow.

For now, I fall asleep in the arms of the man I love.

I love.

I love.

I love.

I love him.

He rejected me, but he came back. I stood my ground and he's willing to try. Maybe there's hope for us both.

I love him.

He's sad and broken and amazing and sexy and haunted. He's all of those things and I love him. It's a wonderment to me and it's the last thing I can think of as I drift into sleep.

Chapter Twenty~Eight

Dominic

I lean up on my elbow and watch Jacey sleep. The sunlight shines across her face and it makes her look almost angelic. I smile at what would be her surprise if I told her that.

I glance at the clock, then pick up the phone to call Joe. There's no way Jacey needs to go into work today, not after I had to wake her up every couple of hours in the night. She's going to be exhausted. Thankfully, Joe understands and even tells me to take the day off to look after her. I hang up and look back at Jacey, and when I do, she's staring at me.

"Good morning," she says lightly, but her gaze is heavy. "So... last night was... something."

I smile, just a little, and shake my head.

"If by 'something' you mean an earth-shattering breakthrough for me, then yeah. It was *something*."

Jacey smiles and reaches for me, pulling me down to her.

"Last night was intense," she rephrases.

My heart feels oddly numb, but beneath the numb layers it feels happy for the first time in years. I feel Jacey's lips curve into a smile against my skin.

"Where do we go from here?" Jacey asks quietly, her face still buried against me.

"I don't know," I answer honestly. "This is all new ground for me."

"We'll figure it out," she says confidently. "Don't worry."

"I'm not," I tell her. And I find that I mean it. It's such a good fucking feeling. "I don't know how I'm going to work through what happened, but I was able to talk about it for the first time last night. You and I are…a step in the right direction. That's got to mean something."

"I know it does. We'll figure it out. And you don't have to stay with me today," she says with her lips against my neck. "I feel fine. I have a headache, but that's it."

"Oh, really," I drawl, running my hands up her back, trying to lighten the situation. "You've been wanting me in your bed for a month, and now I'm here and you want me gone?"

Jacey pulls away and looks at me, her expression serious. "I do want you in my bed," she confirms. "But I want a lot of things. We're going to have to talk about it, Dominic. Last night was amazing, but it's only the beginning. I want *you*, Dom. And we're going to have to talk about how much of you you're willing to give."

I stare at her, at her wide brown eyes, her slender shoulders, her full lips. "You can have all of me," I tell her simply. "I don't know why you want it, but you can have it."

She stares at me, her lip quivering, then she dives into my arms, burying her head next to my chest.

"Then I'll take it," she announces. "But it's going to be work, Dom. It will be a process. You're hurting inside. And you're not going to heal overnight. You know that, right?"

I sigh and nod. "I know. For now, I'll be satisfied with just being with you. Is that fine with you?"

She nods, then hesitates. "Yes. But there's something else. Cris said that there's things you don't know. I really think that in order to really start moving forward, you need to know everything there is to know. Don't you?"

I roll my eyes, unable to contain my disgust.

"I never want to look at Cris again," I tell her truthfully. "I'm not transferring my blame to him, trust me. I blame myself plenty. But he's just as at fault. And he won't admit it. I don't want to talk to him."

"But he knows something you need to know," Jacey points out. "And you need to heal. Please, Dom. I want to be with you. I do. But I need for you to start out with an open mind, ready to be in a relationship with me. To do that, you need to put your relationship with Emma to bed once and for all."

Her words float in the room around us, on the sun, on the air, and I know she's right. But that doesn't mean I can do it.

Because I can't.

I throw back the covers and stand up, pulling on my clothes.

"I can't," I tell her simply. "I'm willing to try with you, but I can't do that. Not yet."

I walk out, leaving her alone in her bedroom as I slide into my car and drive away.

I feel empty and crushed as I drive, oddly disjointed from the situation. But I've always been good at that, at detaching myself when I have to. It's what I've always had to do to survive.

I haven't even reached the end of the street when Jacey texts me.

Don't throw this away, Dom. You deserve to be happy. Don't run from me.

The words stop me in my tracks, right in the middle of the road. I don't care that someone is honking behind me.

Don't run.

That's what I've been doing for years. I've been running from what happened, hoping I could hide from it, hoping to never deal with it.

Running.

Only a fucking pussy does that.

I turn my car around and go back, striding up the walk, not even bothering to knock on her door. I just walk directly into Jacey's house. She freezes in the doorway of her bedroom, standing there in just a T-shirt and panties. She doesn't look surprised to see me.

"Fine," I tell her curtly. "I'll listen to Cris, but I can't promise that I won't punch him in the throat."

Jacey smiles, a wide and beatific smile.

"I can't ask for everything." She sighs. "But this is good, Dom. Seriously. Should we call him and have him here, or should we go to your parents'? Where should we meet with him?"

"Sin's," I say automatically. "I don't want the drama of doing it at my parents. And I don't want him stepping one foot into your house. We'll do it at Sin's. He won't mind."

"Okay," Jacey says quietly. "Thank you for doing this for me, Dominic. I hope you see that we're really doing this for you, too." I nod, and my gut clenches at the look on her face. It's genuine and real and she loves me.

She loves me.

❧

Sin's house is quiet when we arrive, and Jacey turns to me in surprise.

"I've never seen it this empty," she observes as we walk in the front door. "Is there anyone downstairs?"

By "downstairs," I know what she means and I shake my head.

"No. Sin's parties aren't ongoing, although they seem like it. There's usually not anyone down there during the day. Besides, he knows we're coming to talk to Cris. I'm sure he'll want to sit in. He's been curious about what happened for years."

Jacey slips her hand in mine, and for the first time in a long while I feel comfortable leaving it there. I don't know why. All I know is that I want to touch her, and now it seems okay.

We make our way to the living room, where Sin's already waiting. He's even got a shirt on.

"You're up early," I observe. Sin grins.

"Since when is four in the afternoon early?"

"It's early for you," I amend.

"What's going on?" Sin looks at me curiously. "Why the change of heart about Cris?"

I shake my head. "I didn't say I had a change of heart. I said I want to talk to him. Jacey talked me into it. It's a good idea to know everything so that I can put everything surrounding Emma to bed."

Sin nods in surprised approval. "It's time, Dom. It really is."

"I know," I answer simply. "And Sin, if you're going to be here today, there's going to be some stuff you didn't know...I should probably just go ahead and tell you. Emma got pregnant back in high school. And it wasn't mine."

"What?" Sin asks stiltedly, his face suddenly deathly pale. But I don't have time to answer, because Cris clears his throat in the doorway.

"I'm here," he announces. Jacey squeezes my hand in encouragement, to calm me down, to prevent me from punching Cris's face in right off the bat. I glance down at her, and she stares at me in support.

"You can do this," she tells me quietly.

I nod. I know I can. I have a brief moment of clarity. This whole mess originated with Cris, with what Cris did with my girlfriend. The pressure should be on *him*, not me.

I motion for Cris to come in, and Sin, of course, pours him a drink, shoving it into his hands.

"I'm guessing you'll need that," Sin tells him. "Sit anywhere you'd like."

Cris chooses a chair across from me and sits, wildly banging his foot against the chair leg. When he sees me looking at it, he stops moving.

"Fiona didn't come?" I ask curiously. "That doesn't seem like her."

Cris shrugs. "She felt that this was between you and me. She didn't want to choose a side."

Oh, really? Now she decides that? She didn't feel that way the last time she was here at Sin's, screaming at me about what a lunatic I am. Interesting.

"Okay." I draw in a deep breath. "Thank you for coming. I... felt like it was time for me to talk to you about what happened with Emma. About what you know that I don't."

Cris nods hesitantly, staring me in the eye. For a minute I see the kid he was, back when we were best friends. He's nervous. And because of that, I know whatever he's going to tell me is going to be bad. His eyes hold something ominous.

"Just tell me," I say quickly. "Just get it out in the open. I can tell it's not going to be pretty."

Cris looks away. "I actually don't even know where to start. It's been so long. I've thought about it a million different times, tried to figure out what I'd say if you ever gave me the chance, or if I even *should*. But let me just start out with... I'm sorry. I'm sorry that this has split us apart. I'm sorry for any part I had in making you so... damaged."

He says *damaged*, although I know he's really thinking *fucked up*. I can't fault him for that. The rest of my family feels the same way, because it's true. I stare at him wordlessly.

He stares back.

"There's always been something…something I wanted to protect you from. Something bad, Dominic."

I'm unresponsive as I prepare myself, as I sit waiting.

Cris looks at me.

"Should I just lay it out there?" he finally asks. "Or do you want me to sugarcoat it?"

"Do I look like I want you to sugarcoat it?" I answer stiffly. "Just say it."

Cris looks away.

"I've watched you over the years," he admits. "I've kept an eye on you. I knew when you graduated school, even after you had to pull out to go film *Visceral Need*. I watched you give interviews after your first movie was a hit. I watched you retreat from public life as much as they would let you. I watched the way your face grew tired and haunted. And I knew, I could see it on your face, that you were as haunted by Emma as I was."

He pauses, and Jacey squeezes my hand.

You can do this.

I can practically hear her saying the words. I squeeze her hand back.

"I was haunted, am haunted, by a different reason than you, of course," Cris continues. "I'm haunted because I failed her. She trusted me with knowledge that I carried around in secret, just like she'd asked, because we thought it was for the best. As a kid, I didn't realize that some secrets should be exposed, some promises should be broken. So I kept her secret. I should've tried harder to tell you, because she changed her mind at the end. She wanted you to know. I failed her because I couldn't get you to listen to me."

My impatience swells up in me like a sudden cresting wave. "I'm listening now," I snap. "Just fucking tell me."

Cris levels a gaze at me. "Do you remember the day of Emma's funeral...I tried to talk to you and you wouldn't listen? I only managed to get a few words out before you shoved me into the wall. Do you remember what I said?"

I think back to that day, to the day that was filled with black... black dresses, black suits, black emotions. There was so much blackness that I couldn't think straight. Cris tried to talk to me and I couldn't take it. I couldn't stand the sound of his voice. But I do remember exactly what he said.

"You said it wasn't you," I answer. "What the fuck did that mean?"

Cris sighs and stares at the floor as he remembers the past, as it plays in his head, probably the way it plays in mine...like a nightmare.

"Emma told you that she and I got carried away one night, right?" Cris asks, his voice as heavy as lead. I nod. "She said that she and I were sharing a bottle of your dad's liquor in the old tree house while you and Duncan were in Chicago. Isn't that what she told you?"

I have to steel myself in order to nod. "You know that's what she said."

Cris nods. "She asked me if she could tell you that. But that's not what happened. Well, it *did* happen exactly that way. And all of it was true. Except for who she was with. The guy she was with that night, the guy who got her pregnant...it wasn't me."

The breath rushes from my body, out of my lips, and into the air around me as I struggle to comprehend what Cris just said.

Not him?

"You're lying," I spit. "Why would you carry the blame all of these years? That's ridiculous. Who in the world would be so important that you would sacrifice our friendship for? You were my best friend, man. You told me it was you."

"No," he argues. "I didn't. Emma told you it was me. I just let her."

"Then who the fuck was it?"

Cris stands still, his hands limp, his lips pressed together. "I don't know if this is the right thing to do after all," he finally says, like the coward he is. "Maybe it's best to let sleeping dogs lie."

"Fuck that," I snarl. "It's too late for that. Tell me."

Sin breaks in. "Just wait, Dom. Let's sort this out calmly. Take a breath and we'll—"

But I tune out my brother, because all I can see is Cris shaking his head... shaking his head like he's not going to tell me.

That's when I see red.

Red billows in once again from the corners of my eyes, and I attack him, raging like a bull, roaring like a wild animal as I leap onto him, pounding my fists into his face. My knuckles connect with his cheekbone in a satisfying crack.

"Who was it?" I demand from him, over and over.

But Cris doesn't fight back and he doesn't answer. He lets me hit him over and over. Everything is a blur of noise and emotion and colors and I don't even understand what anyone is saying to me.

Except for one thing. Horrible words break through my fury, slicing through the red clouds that are distorting my logic.

"It was me."

The voice is Sin's.

Chapter Twenty-Nine

Jacey

We all freeze when we hear those words.

It was me.

The world stops turning as Dom spins and looks at his brother with the most heartbreaking expression of betrayal and shock on his face.

"You?" He's incredulous. In utter shock. And so am I.

Sin nods. "But I didn't know that she got pregnant, Dom—"

Dominic interrupts him, spitting ugly words. "You. Fucking. Worthless. Piece. Of. Shit. You've always done anything you felt like doing... but this? This is fucking unforgivable."

Sin stands up, looking confused and still aghast.

"Dom, I... we... It was an accident. We were hanging out and we got drunk and it happened. We didn't tell you because we didn't want to hurt you. I didn't know she got pregnant. I didn't know that until today, until now. It meant nothing to us. It was... an accident. I thought that was all there was to it. I had no idea that... *this* came from it. We were just kids, Dominic."

"That's not an excuse," Dom says coldly as he walks over to him. "You weren't a kid. You were nineteen. A horny, worthless fuck who fucked his brother's girlfriend. Emma and I had a life planned, Sin. And you ruined it."

Sin holds up his hand. "Dom, calm down. It was a long time ago. I didn't mean to hurt you. I thought it would blow over and you'd go away to college and you'd never know. I'm sorry. She was sorry. She cried afterward."

Dom stares at him, an empty gaze filled with ice. "And that's supposed to make it better? What am I supposed to do with this?"

Sin's eyes are filled with guilt. "Dom, I swear to Christ that I didn't know that I had anything at all to do with her death. I honestly thought that she'd screwed around with Cris and that you couldn't forgive either of them. The dickhead in me was glad about that, that you could focus on that and never find out what *I* did. I put it out of my mind and tried to pretend that it didn't happen."

Dominic scowls. "But it *did* happen. *You fucked Emma.* I thought all along that my best friend fucked my girlfriend, that he got her pregnant, that I forced her into an abortion. I thought *I* caused her to commit suicide. But all along, it was you, Sin. It was you."

Everyone pauses, everyone stops. And while it doesn't really matter now what actually happened because both Emma and the baby are dead, it matters in a million different ways.

Dominic has blamed himself for so long, carried a guilt that might not have been his to carry. It makes this whole tragic situation a thousand times worse. I turn to him.

"Dom," I whisper. "It's going to be okay."

He looks at me, his dark eyes so filled with pain, then he looks at his brother.

"Is it? I'm pretty sure it's not. My fucking *brother*, Jacey."

I start to interrupt, but Dom looks at me. "I know that I'm the one who insisted that she get an abortion. I know that. But that's when I thought she cheated with Cris. I thought that I could forgive her. But if I'd known that it was Sin, I couldn't have gotten past it. If I'd known, I would've walked away. Because there's no way I could've forgiven that."

Cris stares at us, his face pale and bloody.

"You thought that Emma said my name at the end because there was something between us. But she was saying my name because she wanted me to tell you the truth. She couldn't do it herself and she wanted you to know. I've always loved you and Sin like brothers, Dom. I don't want to drive a wedge between you."

"You aren't the one who drove the wedge between us," Dominic spits angrily, turning his back on Cris. "My *brother* did that for himself."

He takes a step, then clocks Sin squarely on the mouth. Sin falls back, stumbling onto the floor from the force of the blow. Blood streams from his mouth as he looks up at his brother.

"Dominic. I love you. I never wanted to hurt you. It happened and it shouldn't have."

Dom looks down at his brother. "Yeah, you're right. It shouldn't have. But it did."

And then he walks away, leaving us all staring at each other.

I start to go after him, but Sin grabs my arm. "You might want to give him a little space right now. Trust me."

I stare at him. "Trust you? Trust the guy who couldn't keep his dick in his pants?"

Sin looks wounded, and I look away.

"I'm sorry. I know you were just a kid, too. This is all just so… tragic and terrible. I don't know how we're going to help Dominic. He was crushed by this before he knew the truth. I don't know how we'll reach him now. I really don't."

Sin hands me a bottle of whiskey and I take a long drink, relaxing when the warmth spreads to my belly.

"Tell me this," he asks, his eyes urgent. "Do you believe me that I didn't mean to do it? That I didn't mean to hurt Dominic?"

I stare at him, at the gorgeous rocker that the world adores, shaking as he stands in front of me, awaiting my judgment. *The world should see him now*, I think.

"I do believe that you didn't want to hurt him," I say quietly. "You were only a kid, too. What were you, nineteen? It was a mistake. Unfortunately, the situation is more tragic than it would've been because Emma died. Because everything is so fucked up, I don't know how you're going to fix it with Dom."

I hand the bottle back to Sin. "You're going to need this more than me. I need to go after Dom."

I don't know how I'm going to fix him or what I'll say to him to make it better; all I know is that I have to try.

"He's running," Sin says raggedly. "Give him some time to calm down and then meet him at his house. I know that's where he's going. You can take my jet."

❦

I stand in front of Dominic's door uncertainly. The flight to California had taken a few hours, and each of those hours was excruciating because I couldn't reach Dominic.

But I know he's here.

I know in my heart that he retreated here to his quiet hideaway. I know it because Sin called and asked the private hangar if Dom's jet had been used and where it was going. They had confirmed that he was flying home, just as Sin had suspected. Also, Dom's Porsche is sitting in front of the house and the hood is warm.

He's here.

But he's not answering the door. Fortunately, when I turn the handle, the door swings wide open. It's not locked.

"Dominic!" I call out as I walk in. My heels click on the tiled floors. There's no answer. I walk through, glancing outside to see if he's there, but he's not. I walk through the living room, through the dining room, through all of the rooms on the main floor.

When I approach the stairs, I hear something from upstairs.

Step by step, I get closer to the noise, to the talking.

It's a woman's voice.

The breath dies on my lips as I hear her words, over and over as Dom pauses the DVD, rewinds it, then replays it.

I love you, Dom. Don't hate me.

I love you, Dom. Don't hate me.

I love you, Dom. Don't hate me.

I step hesitantly into his bedroom to find him sitting on an ottoman in front of the TV, staring at the screen. The DVD player is on, and the envelope from Emma is open now, lying in torn pieces next to him.

Dominic's face is closed, drawn, cold.

He doesn't look up at me, but he knows I'm here.

"I did, you know. I hated her. For years, I've loved her and hated her. But since she was gone, I focused that hate on Cris. I never, in a million years, would have thought I should be focusing on Sin. I hate her, Jacey. She knew she was going to kill herself. She planned it out and recorded this fucking DVD as an apology. Then she left it for me in my car. I didn't find it until the day after she died. I've never opened the envelope because I didn't want to know what she had to say."

His voice is icy cold, as cold as he believes his heart to be. It breaks mine.

"Dom," I start out, rushing to him. I drop to my knees in front of him, grabbing his hands. He lets me hold them, but he doesn't grip mine. His are as cold as his voice.

"Dom, it's okay to hate her. I know that part of you does. But the other part loves her, and that's okay, too. This is a fucked-up situation. It really is. And it's a situation that you've carried on your back for years. There's no wonder that you feel so fucked up."

He stares at me, his eyes so dark. "Is this supposed to help?"

I ignore the icy tone. "I think part of what made it so terrible is that it was all a secret. You felt you couldn't talk about it. But now it's all out in the light where everyone can see. In order to get past something, you have to confront it. And it will be so much easier now that you can see what you're dealing with."

"I don't want to see it," Dominic says limply, turning off the TV. Emma's face disappears, a black screen remaining where she had been. "I want to forget that any of it ever happened. I don't even want to look at Sin. It'll be a long time before I can do that."

My heart hurts as I stare at him.

"I understand," I tell him. "The natural reaction would be to bury it and try not to think about it. But I don't know if that's the healthiest thing to do, or even if it'll be possible. And Dom. Just so you know, Sin is gutted over this. He was just a kid, like you, and he never realized the ramifications of his actions."

Dominic closes his eyes. "Please, just don't talk about Sin with me. I'm pissed at the entire world right now, Jacey. I'm not sure that you should be here with me. I should probably be alone. I'm not fit company."

"I would be surprised if you were," I tell him honestly. "But I'm not going anywhere. I'm not leaving you alone. I'll go downstairs and hang out by myself. And if you want to talk to someone—even if you want to vent and yell, come get me."

Dominic nods slowly. "I don't know what I did to deserve you."

"You exist," I tell him honestly. "You exist and I love you. All of you. All of the monsters and the hate and the ugliness. And the goodness and the honesty and the person that I know you are deep down."

Dominic closes his eyes and I slip from the room.

Chapter Thirty

Dominic

I sit for quite some time, but eventually the room closes in on me, dark and silent. The walls cave in and I swing at them, punching a hole into the drywall. But it's not enough. I glance into the mirror and hate how destroyed I look, so I pick up a heavy stone vase and throw it into the mirror. It all shatters onto the floor.

Within a minute, Jacey appears in the door, hesitant and beautiful. "Are you okay?" she asks as she stares at the broken glass.

I stare at her, hard.

"No."

She takes a step toward me, but I stop her.

"No," I tell her. "Don't come in. It's ugly in here, Jacey."

"I want to help," she says softly. "Tell me how to help, Dom."

I shake my head, staring at her. All of the feelings that I've suppressed so long—combined with the new ones that I have over Sin's betrayal—come bubbling to the surface, and I feel consumed by them. Consumed by the ugliness.

"You want to help?" I ask between my teeth, taking a step toward her. "Fine. Come help, Jacey."

I don't see her. Not really. I see her blond hair, her goodness, her innocence, and my pain. I see a lot of my pain. And my pain fuels my anger.

Jacey willingly steps into the room, right up to me.

"Go ahead," she says quietly, like she knows what I want to do. Like she knows what I need to do to get rid of this godforsaken pain.

I grab her arms, hard, shoving her onto the bed as I hover over her. "I've told you not to be with me," I snarl. "I told you. I warned you. You should've listened."

Jacey stares at me, unafraid, as I wrap my fist in the hair at her neck, pulling her to me to kiss her ferociously. There's nothing tender in my kiss. There's ugliness there. Roughness. Hatred and pain.

She kisses me back, angrily, her teeth scraping against mine.

"Fine. You need me to vent? Vent to me, Dom. Go ahead. Do it. Vent *in* me if you need to. I can take it."

Her dark eyes hold a challenge, and suddenly she's angry, too.

"You use this darkness, this roughness as a mask, Dom," she tells me, her brown eyes snapping. "For years, you've lingered on the edge of taboo, doing things that most people don't because that's what you think you deserve. You confused it for being something you actually like."

"Oh, I like it," I tell her firmly, pulling her to me roughly and nipping at her neck. There's a red mark where my teeth were. "Make no mistake about that. I like being rough. I like the pain, Jacey."

I pick her up and shove her against the wall, thrusting my hips into hers as I pin here there, staring into her eyes. "Trust me, I do it because I want to. Not because I'm confused."

I lift her thighs and slam her into the wall again, not too hard, but hard enough to prove my point. My dick is rock hard now, fueled by anger and the feeling of her pussy pressed against it.

"You like the pain because it takes your mind off of what really hurts, Dominic," Jacey says softly. "That's what you like."

But she kisses me, and her mouth is soft and sweet and it tightens my groin, against my better judgment, against any good that's left in me.

"You don't want to be with me right now," I warn her. "Trust me."

Jacey looks me in the eye.

"Don't tell me what I want to do," she commands softly. "If you can dish it, I can take it."

Fumbling with my jeans, I pull my dick out, shove her skirt up, and thrust into her hard, with no preamble, no foreplay. Her eyes widen, but she takes it without a whimper or a sigh.

Pinning her against the wall, I hold her wrists above her head with one hand, squeezing them hard.

"Still want to take it?" I growl into her mouth.

She nods, her eyes surprisingly glazed over…with lust. "Fuck me," she says breathlessly as I thrust into her over and over. "I can take it. I *want* to take it."

So I do.

I fuck her hard, I fuck her into the wall, grinding her back into it, an outlet for my ugliness. But as I open my eyes finally, hers are staring into mine.

And they're brown. Not blue.

She's Jacey, not Emma.

And all the rage that I'm feeling, it's not directed at her. The pain that I'm feeling…it's not because of her.

I freeze as the revelation occurs to me. As I realize that she was right. I like pain because it's an outlet for what I really feel. It's a *vent*. And I'm not venting into Jacey.

Sliding Jacey off the wall, I carry her to the bed.

"I'm sorry," I whisper to her urgently as I use my knee to open her legs. She lets them fall easily open, and I slide into her, gently this time. "I'm sorry, Jacey."

She closes her eyes and pulls me to her, letting my head rest in the crook of her shoulder. The energy of the room has changed from frenetic to soft, from rough to gentle.

I come softly, silently, straining into her, holding her to me.

I destroy everyone I touch.

I can't destroy her.

Chapter Thirty~One

Jacey

Dominic might not want to admit it, but I felt his heart break with every movement.

I'm quiet as I lie staring at him, and it's a long time before he opens his eyes. When he does, there's guilt in them.

"I'm sorry," he says simply. "I'm so sorry, Jacey. I was…angry. At the world, at Sin, at Emma, at you for being right. You were right. I get off on watching people have sex because I can do it without getting involved. I like sexual pain because it distracts me from what *really* causes me pain. And that's not you. You don't cause me pain. I have no right to hold you accountable for something you didn't do. I'm sorry."

My heart squeezes. "I know," I tell him softly. "I know."

And I do. I know what it's like to be so overwhelmed by emotion that you can't even think straight. I felt the same way the day Jared turned my world upside down.

I curl into Dominic's side and he holds me there, clutched to him.

"Where do you think she is?" he muses aloud after a while, staring out the window. "I worry about that sometimes."

I stroke his arm and I know he's talking about Emma.

"I don't know. I've wondered that about the people I love. I like to think that they're in a better place. That they're somewhere where tears and pain don't exist anymore."

"Then they're in a better place than we are," Dominic says tiredly.

"We can hope," I answer. "Death is going to come to us all, Dom. It's up to us how we handle it. It's hard, I know."

He remains silent, and I grab his hand. He lets me, but I can see his heart's not in it. His fingers are cold, his eyes are blank.

After a few more minutes I turn to him, desperate to make him understand that there's hope. After having such angry sex, I thought he might feel somewhat better, that it had been an outlet for his rage. And it had been.

But now he only seems hopeless.

"Dominic, I know you're pissed at the world. But we'll get past this. You'll see that you can trust the people you love. Sometimes they make bad decisions, but we all do. It's human nature. We'll get past this."

"Cris knew this the whole fucking time," Dom answers, with a black stare. "He could've told me years ago. Even though I didn't want to talk to him, he could've figured out a way."

I nod. "I know. He didn't handle it well. But he feels terrible, too. He didn't know what to do. And he handled it badly. Just like you did. He loved you and Sin both so much that he sacrificed his relationship with you to save your relationship with Sin. I think that says a lot. And if it makes you feel any better, he and Fiona broke up. She was pissed that he didn't tell someone."

Dominic nods, turning to face the window, turning away from me. I have a feeling that the emotions of the day are just too overwhelming for him to take right now.

I understand how that feels. I feel the same way.

I wrap my arms around him and press my face to his back, letting my weary eyes close as the weight of the world seems to rest on my eyelids.

The silence grows and grows, until eventually Dominic falls asleep. I stay with him for the longest time, holding him tightly. If anyone deserves the oblivion that sleeps brings, he does.

He only wakes once, after I have Chinese delivered. He stays awake long enough to eat with me and then he suggests that I sleep in the guest room so that I can get some rest.

"I'll be tossing and turning," he says wryly. "You've already been patient enough with me today. You deserve a break."

I don't want a break, but I don't argue.

Dominic slips back into the darkened master suite and I close the door to the guest room. If he wants to be alone, I'll let him be alone.

Whatever it takes for him to process this.

Chapter Thirty-Two

Dominic

I try to sleep alone.

But strangely, after years of seeking out solitude, it's the last thing I want now.

And I don't just want anyone...I want Jacey.

I look at the clock. Two seventeen A.M. I squeeze my tired eyes closed, then open them again, throwing the covers back as I get out of bed. I pad down to Jacey's room.

She's sleeping peacefully, her hand curled under her chin. Her eyelids flutter when I climb in beside her, and she turns into me when I wrap my arms around her.

Her warmth envelops me, soaking into the cold that has surrounded me for so long.

"Thank you for being so good to me," I whisper to her. For the life of me, I can't figure out why she would be. I haven't done anything to deserve it.

She sighs sleepily, not answering. Her hands flutter across my chest and down to my waist. It's answer enough, and just like that, because of the brush of her fingertips, I want her.

She lifts her hips and I pull off her underwear. Her mouth meets mine sleepily, hotly. And I slip into her.

Her warmth surrounds me and I groan, throwing my head back and losing myself in the sensations . . . in her.

I feel her hands on my back, her fingernails. I hear her moans, her breath. I feel the world exploding, then I fall limply onto her, rolling over so I don't hurt her.

Then we sleep.

When I wake, sunshine is pouring into the bedroom, and I blearily look around, trying to see what woke me. My phone buzzes again.

My phone.

I pick it up and focus on it, finding a text from Sin.

You're my brother and there's nothing more important than that. I love you. I'll love you forever. I'm sorry I fucked up.

I put the phone back down and close my eyes.

Chapter Thirty-Three

Jacey

I get off the phone with Joe, smiling as I think about how badass he always tries to act, but how soft his heart actually is.

I'd explained the situation, in very vague terms, and said that we wouldn't be back to work until Monday. He was perfectly fine with that. We won't be in trouble. That's a relief, because that's the last thing we need on top of everything else.

I tiptoe back into the bedroom and stare at Dom.

In sleep, he's peaceful. Nothing can hurt him when he sleeps, and that's the reason I've let him sleep for two straight days. It's almost as if his body needed it to absorb the emotional shock that it's undergone the last few days.

At night, I climb into bed and he wraps his arms around me, holding me close. During the day I get up, but I check in on him from time to time. He's woken up a couple of times for water, but nothing else.

As I stand over him, I feel the intense need to protect him from anything else that might hurt him.

That's why when Sin shows up on the doorstep a couple hours later, I'm hesitant to let him in.

"I know you're sorry," I tell him hesitantly. "I know. But he's messed up, Sin. He's been sleeping for two days. I don't think he's in a place where he's ready to talk to you."

Sin stares at me with his doleful rocker stare. "You know, I was right when I told you that you were good for Dominic. Wasn't I?"

I swallow. "Yeah. And if it were up to me, I'd invite you in and you could talk to Dom. But..."

"It's all right." Dominic's voice comes from behind me. "Let him in."

I turn around to find Dom sitting on the bottom step, staring at his brother. His hair is mussed, but other than that, you'd never guess he'd just slept for two days.

"Are you okay?" I ask softly. He glances at me, and there's something so potent in his eyes...something powerful and shining.

He loves me. He hasn't said it, but I know it's true. I swallow as he nods.

"Yeah, I'm fine, babe." He glances at his brother. "I ignored your texts for a reason, Sin. I didn't want to talk to you."

Sin swallows, then nods. "I figured. But I take no for an answer as well as you do. Dom, this shit happened six years ago. Think of everything that happened over the past six years. Now think of who has been with you that whole time. *Me.* I swear on my life that I will never fuck up like that again."

Dom sighs, rubbing his face, then looking up at his brother. "I know. I know, Sin."

I exhale the breath I'd been holding, and Sin stares at him.

"You know?"

Dom nods. "Yeah. I know. I'm still pissed at you, but I know."

Sin stares at him hesitantly. "When you say you *know*, what do you mean?"

Dominic sighs. "I know that it was one night. You were both drunk and she wasn't thinking clearly. You were nineteen and you were thinking with your cock. You didn't know she got pregnant. You didn't know that I made her get an abortion. You didn't know any of it. It was a huge, fucked-up mess, but I can't dwell on it any longer. I'll get over it. I'm not over it *yet*, but I'll get over it."

"You will?" Sin sounds hopeful, yet nervous. Dom nods.

"Yeah. Eventually. I can't believe you fucking did it, but I'll try to get over it. We're brothers, and I know you'd never do it now. Right?"

Sin immediately shakes his head. "Fuck no. I've grown up, Dom. I would never try to take what's yours. I didn't try to take what was yours *then*, I was just too young and stupid to rein in my hormones. I won't make that same mistake twice."

Sin lifts Dom to his feet and pulls him into a hug. He practically clings to Dom as he murmurs into Dom's hair.

"I didn't know, dude. I swear to Christ I didn't know that I was to blame for fucking you up. I swear to Christ. If I knew, I would've told you long ago."

Dom doesn't respond for a minute, but then wraps his arms around his brother, hugging him back. He's reluctant, but it's still a hug. It's something.

"I'm sorry, man," Sin tells him again, and I can honestly hear the sadness in his voice. "You know I loved Emma…but not like that. That night was just a mistake. Neither of us meant it."

"I know." Dominic nods. "I know."

I can see from his face that he means it. He does know. And that's a far cry from the Dominic that I saw two days ago. As we wind our way out to the veranda, I turn to him.

"That must've been some sleep you had."

He smiles ever so slightly. "I don't think I've slept a full night since Emma died. So, yeah. It was pretty good. I'm thinking more clearly now."

Sin stops and turns to Dom, his dark blue eyes unsure. "Dom. I didn't come alone. Cris is in the car. He's in a bad way. Can you talk to him?"

I freeze, watching Dom. He knows that Cris was trying to protect his relationship with Sin, but knowing it and *knowing* it are two different things, because he also knows that Cris could've spoken up years ago.

"Fine." Dom sighs. "I'm going to have to someday. It might as well be now."

I breathe a sigh of relief as Sin and I watch him duck around the side of the house and head out to the car. In a minute, we see them through the windows of the house, sitting at the kitchen table and talking earnestly.

"Do you think they're okay?" I ask Sin nervously. He eyes them, glancing at the way they're angled toward each other, still talking.

"Well, there's no blood yet, so that's a good sign."

I roll my eyes. "Oh, that's helpful."

They're in there for what seems like forever, and when they come out, they're both quiet.

"We have to do something," Dom says to me, his voice serious and dark. "We *all* have to do something so that we get closure. But to do it, we need to go home."

We're on the jet within an hour.

Chapter Thirty~Four

Dominic

The faces staring back at me from around my parents' dining room table are covered in a myriad of emotions. Sadness, anger, confusion, grief, guilt.

My parents, Fiona, Duncan, Cris, Emma's parents, and, of course, Sin and Jacey are all here so we can discuss what happened to Emma. What I did, what Emma did, what Emma and Sin did. It's not an easy conversation, but it's one that needs to be had.

What Jacey said once about Emma's parents' needing closure was true. While they hated to hear what happened with Sin, with me, with their daughter getting an abortion, at least they know now.

They have a reason for the suicide, something that makes sense.

"So you can blame me," I finally tell them quietly. "Emma and Sin slipped up, but they were kids. I'm the one who pushed her to get an abortion. The blame rests on my shoulders."

Mr. Brandt grips his own hands tightly, so tight that his fingers turn white. But he doesn't say anything. He just stares at the table.

Mrs. Brandt looks at me with Emma's bright blue eyes, and they're filled with tears. I fight the urge to look away, but I don't. I expect to see hate in them, but I don't.

"Dominic, it's not your fault. It's a tragedy and you just have to let it go. You do."

A lump forms in my throat for the millionth time this month, and I swallow hard against it. "We just thought you should know," I tell her quietly. "The truth is always necessary for real closure. A smart person told me that once."

I squeeze Jacey's hand under the table.

Everyone talks to each other quietly, and while it's uncomfortable, a part of me is relieved. Jacey was right. Getting things into the light makes it easier to deal with them. I tune out everyone's low voices and stare out the window.

Down by the pond the tree house hangs, faded and old. My heart constricts just looking at it, thinking of all the time Emma and I spent in it. And of what she and Sin had done in it. I swallow hard and glance up to find my father looking at me.

"Dom, come with me for a minute. I want to show you something."

I follow him out of the house, out to the barn, and stare at him in confusion as he hands me a large mallet.

"You want to show me a mallet?" I raise an eyebrow.

"Did you say that Sin and Emma... that they were together in the old tree house?" my dad asks quietly. I nod.

"It's all well and good that Sin apologized. And you and I both know that he never meant to hurt you like he did. That's well and good, too. But as long as it's standing, it's gonna remind you of what happened. It's gonna remind you of all kinds of ugliness. Go tear it down, son. Tear it all down and you'll never have to look at it again."

He hands me the mallet. I stare at him, the heavy mallet in my hands, and I know he's right. Tearing that old thing down is going to feel good.

I head down to the pond and climb the old rickety ladder on the side of the tree. With my first swing, I smash a hole in the roof. After three more swings, the roof caves completely in. The walls follow. Then the floor.

By this time, my shoulders are on fire, my biceps ache. But I don't stop swinging. Because my dad was right. I'm not just tearing down a tree house. I'm tearing a memory down. I don't stop until it's splintered into a million pieces and I've even torn the ladder off the tree trunk.

When I'm done, it's all gone.

Every board, every bad memory is lying in a splintered pile in front of me. I'll never have to look at it again.

I don't know how it makes me feel better, but it does. With the tree house gone, the memory can start to fade, too. I won't pretend that it didn't happen, but at least it won't be so potent, so vivid. It won't have the same power over me.

I turn to head back to the house and find Jacey sitting on the edge of the pond, her legs tucked under her. She's watching me, concerned.

"Are you okay?" she asks when I draw nearer. I nod.

"Yeah. For the first time in a long time, I can say that I am...after I do one more thing." I pull her up and drag her with me to the barn.

The old Nova is in the back corner, covered with a tarp. I pull off the tarp and stare at it. It's got a few more scratches now than it used to, and there's a crack in the windshield, but just looking at it brings back a thousand memories.

"I lost my virginity in this car," I tell Jacey. "And Emma and I had our first kiss in it. Is that too much information?"

Jacey looks slightly pained, but shakes her head.

"She and I went on a million dates in this thing. It's what I rode to her house in that night... that last night. My dad had to replace the floor mats because my shoes tracked so much blood into it. To be honest, I can't look at it anymore. Come with me?"

Jacey doesn't even ask where, she just nods and climbs into the dusty passenger seat.

I turn the key, and miraculously the battery is charged enough to start. "Brown Eyed Girl" floats from the speakers, the familiar words filling my ears.

"I must've heard this song a million times," I tell Jacey as I steer the old car down to the pond. "To tell you the truth, I'm sick of it."

When we reach the edge of the water, I pull Emma's pendant from my pocket, the stone cool between my fingers.

Closing my eyes, I picture her wearing it, how it used to lay just right on her chest. How it was the exact shade of her eyes.

I open my eyes and hang it on the rearview mirror.

And then I shift the car into neutral.

"Can you help me push?" I look at Jacey and her eyes widen in surprise, but she nods.

Together we push the old car filled with my memories into the lake.

It seems fitting. We stand and watch as the car sinks, bubbles erupting around it until it's no longer visible. In my head, I imagine it sinking to the very bottom, where it will stay forever.

Jacey looks at me. "Will your dad be mad? That was a classic."

I smile, just a little. "Nah. I'll buy him another one. One that has a working tape deck."

Even though the old car is gone, sunken in the water, I swear I can still hear that song. *Do you remember when, we used to sing... sha-la-la-la-la-la-la-la-la-la-la-te-da...*

Glancing over my shoulder, the pond seems quietly eerie, the last of the bubbles forming in the middle, the only evidence that it is the watery grave for my memories.

"Good-bye, Emma," I murmur.

Jacey squeezes my hand and we walk for the house. As we wind along the old path, I pause, staring into Jacey's brown eyes, eyes that contain such warmth and goodness.

"I love you," I murmur to her, finally able to say the words. "I think I've known that for a while. I'm sorry that it's taken so long for me to say it. I love you so fucking much."

She smiles, a radiant white smile.

"All that matters is that you're saying it now," she says gently. "I love you, too. I love you to the moon and back. You know that, right?"

I do.

"I want you to know that even though Emma was such a big part of my past, *you* are my future. *You* are my present. You're everything, Jacey. I need you to know that. I love you more than anything, more than life itself."

"I know," she whispers softly, and I can see from her gentle expression that she does.

I pull her to me and kiss her, thorough and sweet and with just a hint of wild. It's the way she deserves to be kissed ... it's everything she is. Sweet, with just a hint of wild.

There's no ugliness here.

Chapter Thirty~Five

Jacey

One Month Later

My brother's excited voice echoes into my ear loudly, and I hold the phone just a little bit away from my head.

"Elijah Gabriel Vincent. He's eight pounds and three ounces and he's beautiful, Jacey. He's so fucking beautiful."

I smile and congratulate my big brother, so happy to hear him so happy. There was a time when I didn't think I'd see the day. But here it is. And he so deserves it.

"Brand just happened to be here for a meeting when Maddy's water broke. You should've seen his face," Gabe crows. "Oh my god. It was priceless. I thought he might pass out."

I laugh. "I can imagine. Please tell him hello for me. I miss him. I haven't seen him in a few weeks."

Gabe sobers up. "You can tell him yourself. He's right here."

Before I can say anything, I hear Brand's sigh.

"Hey, Jacey."

My heart squeezes. I hurt him. I hurt the most amazingly gentle badass on the planet.

"Hey, Brand," I say brightly, forcing enthusiasm. "How are you?"

"Well, I've now seen amniotic fluid on the floor. I can cross that off my bucket list. And after hearing Maddy scream during labor, I don't know how you women do it."

I can practically see him shudder and I smile, imagining that he sat right outside of her delivery room, waiting to hear that everything was all right.

"Um. I'm sorry, Brand. For everything," I say tentatively. Sorry is all I can think of to say. It's what I feel . . . I just don't know how to express it to him enough.

He sighs again.

"It's okay. Don't think anything else about it. This is my issue, not yours. I'll get past it and things will be like they were, okay?"

He sounds tired and sad and I hate it. But I know him and I know he doesn't want to dwell on it. So I nod into the phone.

"Okay. I want you to know that I love you. Not like you want me to love you, but I still love you."

"I know. I'll talk to you later, Jace."

I hear the muffled sounds as he hands the phone back to my brother, leaving my heart clenched in my chest.

"He's going to be okay, Jacey," my brother tells me quietly. "Just so you know. So don't worry about him. I think he always knew that you and he weren't meant to be."

I nod. "I know. But it still hurts me that I hurt him."

"He's fine," Gabe insists. "Maddy's gonna work on setting him up with some of her friends. Trust me, he'll be fine."

"I'm sure he will be," I agree. "He's strong. He's survived far worse things than me."

"You got that right, kiddo. When are you coming to see your

nephew? How's the new job? What are they calling their new restaurant chain?"

I think back to the day a couple of weeks ago when Dom, Duncan, and Sin argued over a name for the new restaurant chain that they're launching together. They'd bickered for hours until I chimed into the conversation.

How about The Dirty Dog? Because that's what you three are. Dirty fucking dogs. Perverted as hell.

They'd stared at me in shock, then had a toast to the name, because they knew that it fit them like a glove. And then Sin had asked me to come work for them on their business development team, since I have "restaurant experience."

Since I'll have my business degree finished up in a couple of weeks, it made sense, so I accepted.

"It's The Dirty Dog. We're going to sell seafood and craft beer. I've actually already started part-time, since I quit Saffron, but I'll be starting full-time in a couple of weeks when I officially finish my business degree."

"I'm so proud of you, Jacey," Gabriel tells me happily. "You've really pulled your shit together."

"I know," I answer. "I'm just sorry that I gave you so much trouble along the way."

"It's all right," he replies with a chuckle. "Like Brand, I've been through far worse than you."

I laugh. "Okay. I've gotta go. I'll try to get up there in a couple of weeks. Give that baby a kiss for me and send me pics, okay? And tell Maddy that I love her."

Gabriel agrees and we hang up.

"You ready, babe?"

I turn to find Dominic lounging in the doorway. Like always, he takes my breath away. He's just that sexy. He's wearing dark slacks and a dark shirt today, dressed up to go to the ribbon-cutting of the newly renovated Joe's Gladiators.

"Yeah. I'm ready."

He leads me through my little house to his car, where he opens the door for me. When he gets in, I glance at my home.

"I'm going to miss this little place, Dom. Are you sure you want to buy a fancy condo for when we're here in Chicago? We could just stay here. It wouldn't be a big deal."

Dom glances at it. "Um. There's no garage for my car."

I roll my eyes. "Whatever. Fine. We can get a fancy condo. You're spoiled, though."

He throws his head back and laughs. "Really? Coming from the woman who just bought four new sets of sheets for absolutely no reason?"

"Don't judge. Good sheets are essential." I stick my nose in the air and he leans over to kiss me.

"That's all right, babe," he adds. "I want to spoil you."

We pull up to Joe's a few minutes later, and I barely recognize the place. The building has been completely renovated, inside and out. A state-of-the-art gym with all new equipment and offices, an after-school meal program, and even a running track out back.

They've been waiting on us to arrive, so when we approach they hand Dominic the giant scissors to snip the red velvet ribbon across the door.

"On behalf of the Emma Brandt Foundation, we are pleased to present you with the reopening of Joe's Gladiators!" Dominic announces. Flashbulbs pop, and for once Dom isn't bothered by his picture being taken.

He shakes Joe's hand, and Joe looks pleased as he can be by the big turnout. I know that in large part, the press showed up because of Dominic, but regardless. They're here, and any attention we can get for the underprivileged kids is worth it.

"Why did your foundation choose this particular project, Dominic?" one of the reporters calls out.

Dominic smiles. Jake waves to the cameras off to the side and everyone laughs.

"We chose this project because there was a need. There are good kids here, and all they need is a chance. Sometimes, bad things happen, unfair things…and all we can do is handle it the best we can. Most of the time, with a little help, we come through it just fine. A smart person once told me, 'Before we fall, we fly.' We just wanted to help these kids fly."

Everyone applauds, and I'm so proud of Dominic I could burst.

We head into the reception where we chat with the boys, eat, and drink punch. I'm utterly filled with happiness when we finally walk out to our car.

"Are you sure you don't mind that we named the foundation after Emma?" Dom asks as we climb inside. I stare at him.

"You know me better than that. I think it was the only thing to do. She never had a chance to live her dream. We've got to give other kids the chance to live theirs."

Dominic fires the engine up, then turns to me. "You know what I love? How you always say *we*. You never say *I*. Or *you*. It's always *we*."

I shrug. "That's how I think. In my head, we're a team. We're always going to be *we*, Dom. Get used to it."

He kisses me, long and thoroughly. When he pulls away, I'm breathless.

"I have a surprise for you," he announces. "You're going to love it. I hope."

"Oh, I love surprises," I tell him, even though he knows that already. "Don't give me any hints. I want to be really surprised."

I have to admit, I'm completely stumped as we drive toward the country, out of the city. But then we approach Palos Park, his childhood home.

"We're going to Castle Kinkaide?" I ask in confusion. He smirks, but doesn't answer.

When we pull up to his parents' house, there's a red, yellow, and black hot air balloon set up on their lawn. It's huge and majestic as it billows against the sky.

"Your chariot, my lady." Dom bows low.

I roll my eyes. "Lord. Is this what I've got to look forward to all during filming? I know you like to get into character, but you realize that you're not really a knight, right?"

Dom's been rehearsing for a sixteenth-century period movie, and it's made life interesting, to say the least. I fully intend to see him in a suit of armor around the house soon.

He shakes his head. "Can you just go with it?"

I giggle. "Fine. Yes, my squire. I'd love a ride in your fine chariot."

"Squire?" Dom's the one rolling his eyes now. "Try *sir*. I'm a knight, Jace."

But he takes my hand and helps me into the balloon, introducing me to the pilot. Within minutes, we're floating up and above Palos Park, above Chicago. The city is amazing from up here, with the evening sun reflecting off all of the glass.

"It's breathtaking." I breathe, looking down. "Thank you, Dom. But what's the occasion?"

Dominic turns to me, his dark gaze serious. It's a gaze that causes butterflies to flutter in my chest.

"Jacey, before I met you, I thought all I deserved was the darkness in life. The dark corners, the taboo, the unspeakable. But you've given me a new start. A fresh life. A new outlook. I don't know what I did to deserve you, but I'll be forever grateful that you saw potential in me. That you saw what no one else did. You looked past the asshole, past the actor, past the name. You saw *me*. I love you for that. I love you for always grounding me, always reminding me of what's important. I love you for always being my breath of fresh air, the challenge to my question."

He pauses and my heart pounds in my chest.

Is he...? Is this...?

And then Dominic bends down, on one knee.

It is.

OHMYGOD.

"My lady," he begins in an exaggerated English accent, the one he's been working on for a week. "I have but one question to ask of you. One favor that I wish for you to bestow, if but only you desire."

I stare at him, laughter in my eyes and the utmost of happiness in my heart.

"Yes, good knight. Anything you wish to ask."

Dom looks at me, his eyes smoldering, and he drops the accent.

"Will you marry me? Yes or no?"

He holds out a ring, a gorgeous princess cut diamond, and I feel like swooning. It's the most gorgeous thing I've ever seen, held by the sexiest man in the world.

I look up at him, losing myself in his dark, dark eyes.

"Yes."

He breathes in sharply. "Yes? You're sure you want me? You know all of my monsters, Jace. You want me anyway?"

I nod, choking up. "I want you because of your monsters," I tell him. "They've made you who you are, and I can't imagine loving you any more than I do. I'll want you every day of my life. That's a promise."

Dominic smiles a gentle smile as he slips the ring onto my finger and pulls me into his side. He kisses me slowly and gently before he wraps his arm around my shoulders, and we watch the city passing beneath us.

As we watch it, I think of everything that's happened...to both of us. We're both messed up in our own ways, but we're both overcoming it. It's a process, but we're doing it. Everything that's happened has made us stronger, individually and together.

Looking up at Dominic, I brush my fingers along his cheek.

"Are you happy? Yes or no?"

Dominic looks down at me and I see a million promises in his eyes, a million forevers.

"Hell, yes."

I smile.

That's all I needed to hear.

Epilogue

Jacey

I race through the tropical flowers, through the plants, and over the twisted path that leads to our little rented cottage off of the most beautiful beach in Hawaii. It's the perfect place for a honeymoon, a true garden of Eden.

"Are you coming?" I call over my shoulder to my husband.

My husband.

The words ring through my head, and even though they sound foreign, they don't feel that way. Dominic and Jacey Kinkaide. Bound together forever. *By love and by lust and by everything in between.* That's what Duncan announced earlier at our ceremony on the beach. He'd gotten his license to perform marriages specifically for this occasion.

Dominic catches up to me and scoops me into his arms.

"You thought you'd walk over the threshold yourself?" he asks impishly. "Not gonna happen."

"But this isn't our house," I start to say. But then I drop it. If the man wants to carry me, he can carry me. He scoops me up into his arms and carries me to the bed, a four-poster-covered-in-filmy-gauze bed.

Sitting me down, he peels me out of my dress, kissing every inch of me as he does. When he's done, by the time I stand in front of him naked, I'm dying for him.

"I need you," I tell him simply. "Fill me up, Dominic. Make me yours."

He smiles, the smile I love, the private one...the one just for me. "You've always been mine," he whispers. "You just didn't know it."

He pushes me back onto the bed and kisses me again, his tongue so hot and wet and perfect against mine.

"And I've always been yours," he adds. "*I* just didn't know it. But I know it now, and that's the important thing."

He straddles me, bending over me, owning me.

He knows just what to do to make my body sing, to crest me toward the precipice of orgasm as he slides his fingers in all the right places.

Emotion wells up in me, overwhelming and hot. *Love, lust, and everything in between.*

I grip Dom's shoulders, pulling him into me, closer and closer. I wrap my leg around his hip, pulling him deeper inside.

He groans, then drags his tongue along my nipples. He circles them, then sucks, driving me to the brink of madness.

I arch upward, pressing against his strong chest, and he groans again as he thrusts, the muscles in his back flexing. I call out and scratch into him, breathing in the smell of his skin as I bury my face in his shoulder.

"I love you, Mrs. Kinkaide," he breathes as he slides in and out of me, slower now, gentle. "Always."

I want to roll my eyes and tell him that he's so dramatic, that this isn't a movie script. But I don't. Because like always, scripted or not, his words are perfect.

I arch into him and come, the waves of my orgasm carrying me up and away, far from here. And then he throws his head back and follows me. It's a few minutes before I return to the present, before I can once again think logical thought.

"I love you, too," I answer finally, when I can catch my breath. "Always."

I fall asleep in his arms.

I'm awakened by a sound. The world is dark outside the cottage and the gauzy curtains flutter in the breeze. I sit up and look around, only to be startled by a woman sitting in the chair next to the bed.

She's humming "Brown Eyed Girl" ever so softly.

Her aquamarine eyes meet mine, and I know who she is. Oddly enough, I'm not afraid.

"Emma," I whisper. She nods, her face young and beautiful in the night. "Am I dreaming?"

She smiles. "Are you?"

I don't know. I must be.

"I needed you to know something," she tells me softly, and her voice is like a song, gentle and melodic. She looks down at Dominic, her gaze full of love. "I chose you for him," she says quietly.

I stare at her in confusion. "What?"

"You don't remember me? I met you. Years ago on Goose Beach. I was there with my mom, you were there with your grandma. You got my ice cream money back from a horrible little girl."

The hazy memory comes back, but I struggle to put the pieces together. "Heather Edel. She was the meanest girl in the sixth grade. You were wearing a red swimsuit."

Emma nods.

"She terrified me, but you stood up to her like it was nothing and got my money back."

"You gave me a seashell," I say slowly, remembering how the little girl had handed it to me and then ran off with her mom. "A white one."

Emma smiles. "I used to collect them."

A memory of the tiny shells in Dominic's black velvet box comes to mind and the shell on her pendant...I stare at her soundlessly, my breath lingering on my lips.

"I was so in awe of you," she continues. "Of how you were so brave and stood up for someone you didn't even know. It seemed like you weren't afraid of anything. You swam out to the buoy line a hundred times that day, while I was afraid to go past the sandbar. After I went home, I never saw you again. But when Dominic needed saving, I knew it had to be you. He needed someone brave and strong, so I brought you to him."

I stare at her, transfixed. "This is a strange dream."

Emma laughs, a tinkling sound in the night.

"It's okay to think that," she assures me. "There are some things that can't be explained, so you probably shouldn't try."

"But how did you 'bring me to Dominic'?" I ask doubtfully. "Surely that can be explained."

She smiles patiently. "Wasn't it strange how drugs ended up in Dominic's car...when you both swore they weren't yours? It's almost as if they just appeared there."

My eyes widen.

"You." I breathe. "Why?" She smiles and the room seems to glow with it.

"Because love eclipses death, Jacey. It's forever. And because I love him, I want him to be happy. I knew you could make him happy, so I brought you together the only way I knew how. I'm at peace now. Tell him that. Tell him I'm glad that he's moving on, that he's forgetting me. Tell him good-bye."

"He's not forgetting you," I protest. "He'll never forget you. You're a healthy memory now, instead of a painful one. That's all. And that's *good*."

She smiles and nods. "I know. That's all I ever wanted. Thank you, Jacey. Thank you for saving him. I knew you would."

She trails her fingers along his leg as she walks to the door. Once she gets there, she looks back, her face luminescent in the night.

"Oh, and Jacey? Take care of him."

I nod, transfixed and in awe. "I will."

She walks away, humming.

Do you remember when, we used to sing... sha-la-la-la-la-la-la-la-la-la-la-te-da... You're my... brown eyed girl.

I try to wake up, but then realize that I'm not sleeping. I have no conscious recollection of waking up. Or if I was ever actually asleep. Everything's a haze. A blur. Except for the memory of Emma's striking blue eyes staring at me from two feet away.

I sit up in bed, trying to wrap my mind around it.

It couldn't have... it didn't... it didn't happen.

I turn to Dominic to wake him up, to share the crazy dream with him, when something catches my eye on the bedside table. Something that glistens pearly white in the light of the moon.

A seashell.

While the curtains rustle with the breeze and the ocean crashes against the beach, my heart pounds. And as the soft wind blows my hair away from my face, I hear it.

Sha-la-la-la-la-la-la-la-la-la-la-te-da...

The faint strain of "Brown Eyed Girl," floating in from the water.

A Note from the Author

"The world breaks everyone, and afterward, some are strong at the broken places."

That's my favorite quote from Ernest Hemingway, and it perfectly sums up why I'm writing this series.

The older I get, the more it seems that everyone in the world is broken in some way, whether it is from divorce, death, drugs, etc. I wanted to write stories that people could relate to, stories where my characters were far from perfect, but had readers rooting for them to succeed, to overcome their personal demons.

While my characters' problems are sometimes more exaggerated than real-life problems for the sake of fictional entertainment, the roots of their issues are firmly planted in real life.

The fact of the matter is, real life can be a bitch sometimes. It can slap you, shove you around, and then kick you while you're down.

But the important thing to remember is always this:

Life is hard sometimes, but it can only break you if you let it.

No matter what, you have to always stick your chin out and keep going. You have to keep going through the motions even if you don't feel like it. Flip your problems the bird and keep fighting to make your life how you want it.

Your life is your own. If you don't like it, if it makes you sad, if it makes you discouraged on a daily basis, change it. Change everything about it until you're in love with your life and it's exactly how you want it.

If Dominic, Jacey, Madison, Gabriel, Pax, and Mila have shown you anything, I hope it is that. That you can be dealt a really crappy hand in life, but the power to change everything rests within you. You hold the key to your own happiness.

We've each got one life. Live the heck out of yours.

If You Stay

The Beautifully Broken Series: Book 1

Courtney Cole

Twenty-four-year-old Pax Tate is not always a nice guy. He's a tattooed, rock-hard bad boy with a bad attitude to match. But he's got his reasons. His mother died when Pax was seven, leaving a hole in his heart filled with guilt. As Pax grew up, he tried to be the perfect golden boy but his dad couldn't overcome his grief long enough to notice. Pax couldn't keep up the impossible perfect façade, so he slipped far, far from it. Now, he uses drugs and women to cope with the ugly, black void in his heart. Until he meets sweet, beautiful Mila Hill. Mila is a carefree smile to his hardened frown, the beauty to his beast.

When memories of his mother's death resurface, Mila is there to help him mend his broken heart . . . but only if he can stop being a jerk long enough to allow it. Pax says he's working on it. But is that enough to make her stay?

HODDER

Read on for a taster . . .

Chapter One

"Pax."

I can't be sure that the girl said my name. Her voice is muffled and unintelligible and hard to understand, mostly because my dick is in her mouth.

Slumping against the black leather seat of my car, I push the girl's head down farther, wordlessly urging her to bury more of me in her throat.

"Don't talk," I tell her. "Just suck."

I close my eyes and listen. I can hear the spit pooling in her mouth and sliding out the corners. Her cheek makes a soft sound as it grazes my open zipper. She moans periodically, although I don't understand it. She's not getting anything out of this. My hand is on her head, pushing, pushing. Guiding her movements and her speed. I grip the hair at the base of her neck, winding it in my fingers; pulling it, releasing it, then pulling it again.

She moans again.

I still don't know why.

I still don't care.

I'm high as fuck.

And I don't know her name.

Everything is a fog, except this moment. I tune out the crashing sounds of Lake Michigan to our right, and the sounds of the cars on the highway a few miles away. I block out the glowing lights from town. I tune out the roaring quiet and the occasional thought that someone might happen by and see us. No one is out here on the beach, not at eleven P.M. Not that I would care anyway.

Right now, all I'm focused on is this blow job.

I already know that I'm not ready to come, but I don't tell her because I don't want her to stop yet, either. I let her go for a few minutes more before I push her away.

"Take a break," I tell her as I settle back into my seat.

I don't bother to put myself away. I just sigh loud and long as I relax in the breeze. The girl turns her attention to the visor mirror, trying to straighten her mess of a face.

"Wait," I instruct. "Hold on for a minute."

She looks at me in confusion, her lipstick smeared. I smile.

"I know you want some of this," I tell her, grabbing a little bottle from my jacket pocket. I dump a few coke pebbles onto a little mirror on my console and crush them with a razor, dragging the powder into two straight lines.

I offer her the little straw and now she's the one smiling with her distorted clown mouth.

She snorts at her line, coughs, then snorts it again.

Settling back into her seat, she tilts her face to the car roof as she lets the drug take effect. Her eyes are empty as she thrusts the straw at me and I hesitate for only a second.

I've hit it hard today and I've done more than I usually do.

Of everything.

But for some reason, the need to disappear into the black is strong today, stronger than usual. And it's on days like this that I hit the hard stuff. I grab the straw and do my line, breathing in the powder that never fails to take me away. Even when I can count on nothing else, I can always count on this.

The familiar burn immediately numbs my throat. The emptiness spreads throughout the rest of my body, dulling my senses, speeding up my heart. I can feel the blood pulsing through it, hard and pounding, carrying oxygen to my numb fingers.

I fucking love this shit.

I love the way it dulls everything but my attention. I love how it heightens my awareness while still turning everything else black and numb.

This is where I am comfortable. Drifting here into this nothingness, this obscurity.

Coke makes it easy to exist in the emptiness.

I run my fingers through the traces of the remaining powder and slide it along the skin of my erection before grabbing the girl by the back of the neck. I shove her head back down and she opens her mouth willingly. This is most definitely not against her will. She wants to be here.

Especially now that I have fed her habit.

Especially now that she can lick her habit from my dick. If she moans now I'll believe it because she's getting something out of it, too.

"Finish," I tell her. I stroke her back while she moves and I can't feel my fingers.

Her head bobs for a few more minutes and then without warning, I come in her mouth. Her eyes widen and she starts to pull away as my ejaculate seeps from the edges of her lips, but I hold her fast by the back of the neck until my dick stops throbbing.

"Swallow," I tell her politely.

Her blank eyes widen, but she swallows obediently.

I smile.

She gags, but she doesn't heave.

"Thank you," I say, still polite. And then I lean past her and shove open the passenger-side door. It creaks as it swings wide, evidence that cars were still made from iron back in 1968. I pull out my wallet and hand her a dog-eared twenty.

"Get yourself something to eat," I tell her. "You're too skinny."

She's got the look that girls on nose candy get. The way-too-thin look. That's one downfall of the stuff. It's good for drifting away into oblivion, but it's hell on your appetite. If you don't make yourself eat, you'll waste away and start looking like shit.

This girl doesn't look like shit. Yet. She's not ugly. But she's not pretty, either. She mostly looks hardened. Mousy brown hair, pale blue eyes. Bland, stick-thin body. I can take her or leave her.

And I'm leaving her.

She glares at me as she wipes her mouth.

"My car is in town. Aren't you at least going to take me back to it?"

I look at her and note how there are three of her that blur into one, then back into three, before I shake the blurriness from my head and try to focus again.

Nope. Still three of her.

"Can't," I tell her, dropping my head heavily against the headrest. "I'm too fucked up to drive. It's not that far, anyway. It's not my fault that you wore five-inch stripper shoes. Just take them off. It'll make it easier to walk."

"You're a fucking asshole, Pax Tate," she spits angrily. "You know that?"

She grabs her purse from the floor and slams my car door as hard as she can. My car, Danger, shakes from her efforts.

Yes, I named my car. A 1968 Dodge Charger in pristine condition deserves a name.

And no, I don't care that this coked-up little bitch thinks I'm an asshole. I *am* an asshole. I'm not going to deny it.

As if to prove that point, I can't even think of her name right now even though it only took me one second to recall the name of my car. I might remember the girl's in the morning or I might not. That doesn't matter to me at this point. She'll come back. She always does.

I've got what she wants.

I strip off my jacket and lay it on the passenger seat, zipping my pants back up as I watch her stomp away. Then I open my own door, dangling one black boot over the doorsill, letting the cool breeze rustle over my flushed, overheated body.

The landscape up and down the coast is jagged and rolling and wild. It is so vast that it makes me feel small. The night is inky black and there are barely any stars. It's the kind of night where a guy can just disappear into the dark. My kind of night.

I rest my head against the seat and allow the car to spin around me. It feels as though the seat is the anchor that is holding me to the ground. Without it, I might drift off into space and no one will ever see me again.

It's not a bad notion.

But the car is spinning too fast. Even in this state, I know it's too fast. I'm not going to worry about it, though. I simply pull out my vial and take something to slow things down. My vial is like a magician's hat. It's got a little bit of everything in it. Everything I need, fast or slow, white or blue, capsule, pill, or rock. I've got it.

I wash the pill down with a gulp of whiskey. I don't even feel the burn as it slides down my throat. I consider it for a minute, the speed that things are turning and blurring around me. I decide I should take another pill, maybe even two. I put them in my mouth and take another slug of Jack before I toss the bottle onto the passenger-side floor. I realize that I don't know if I put the cap back on or not.

Then I realize that I don't care.

The drug-induced fog blurs my vision and all of the blacks and grays swirl together and I close my eyes against it. I still feel like I'm moving, like the car is spinning round and round.

The night swallows me and I am propelled into the darkness, far above the clouds and into the night sky, sailing through the stars, past the moon. Reaching out, I touch it with a finger.

I laugh.

Or I think I laugh.

It's hard to say at this point. I don't know what's real or not real. And that's just the way I like it.

If You Leave

The Beautifully Broken Series: Book 2

Courtney Cole

Ex-army soldier Gabriel Vincent is a badass hero. Or he used to be. Home from Afghanistan, Gabe can't stop thinking about that one horrible night on the battlefield, a night that changed his life for ever. He knows he's messed up, but with the help of a little beer and a lot more women, he's keeping it together. Until he meets Madison Hill.

Madison is happily single – or so she thinks. After the tragic death of her parents, she took on the responsibility of running the family restaurant, and that's all she has time to worry about. Until she meets Gabriel.

Though they don't know realise it at first, Gabe and Maddy will soon develop a weakness: each other. They need to be together to be whole, but can they find a way to heal the past . . . before they lose each other?

HODDER

Find your next delicious read at

THE Book BAKERY

The place to come for cherry-picked monthly reading recommendations, competitions, reading group guides, author interviews and more.

Visit our website to see which great books we're serving up this month.

www.TheBookBakery.co.uk

BookBakeryUK
TheBookBakeryUK